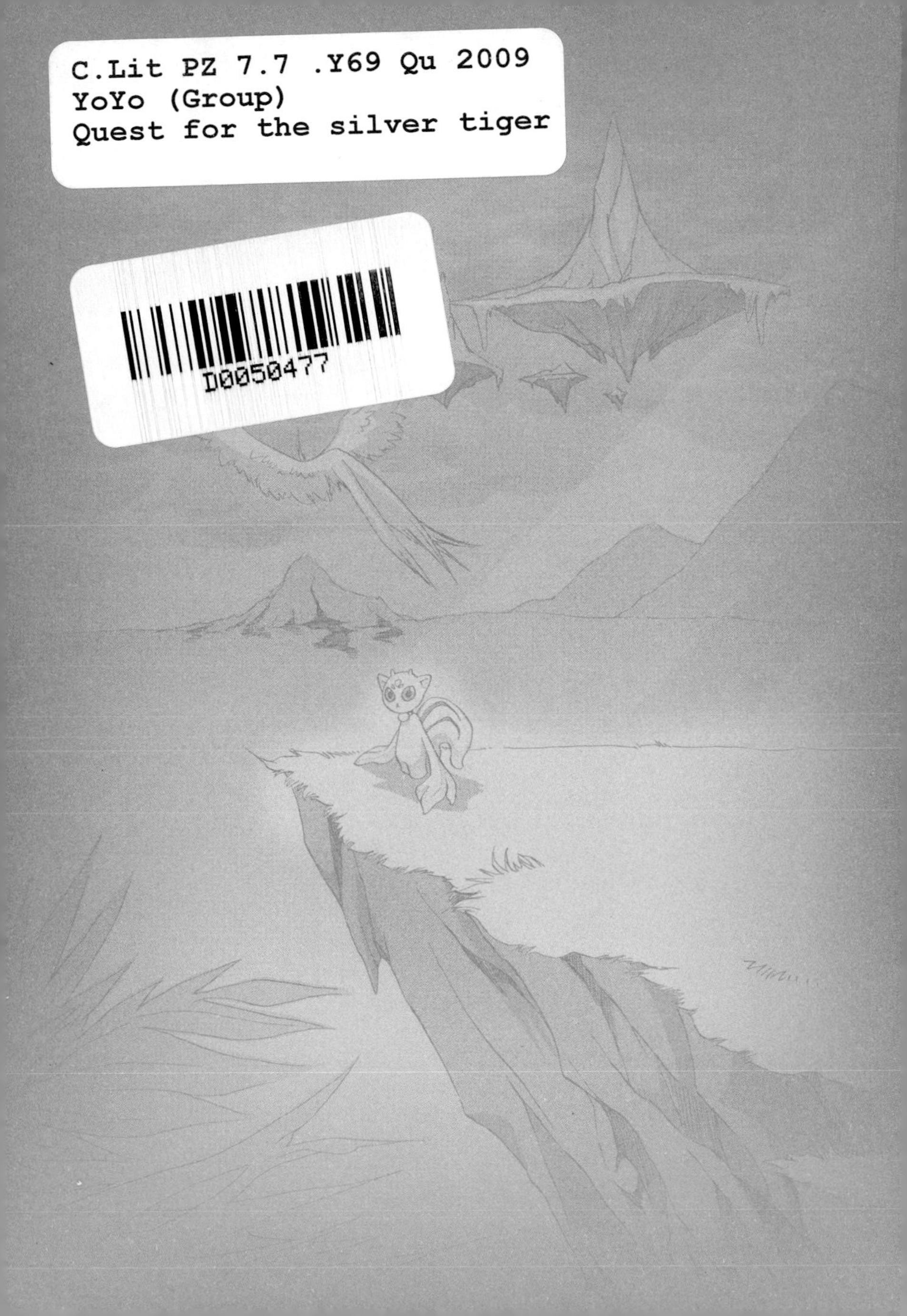

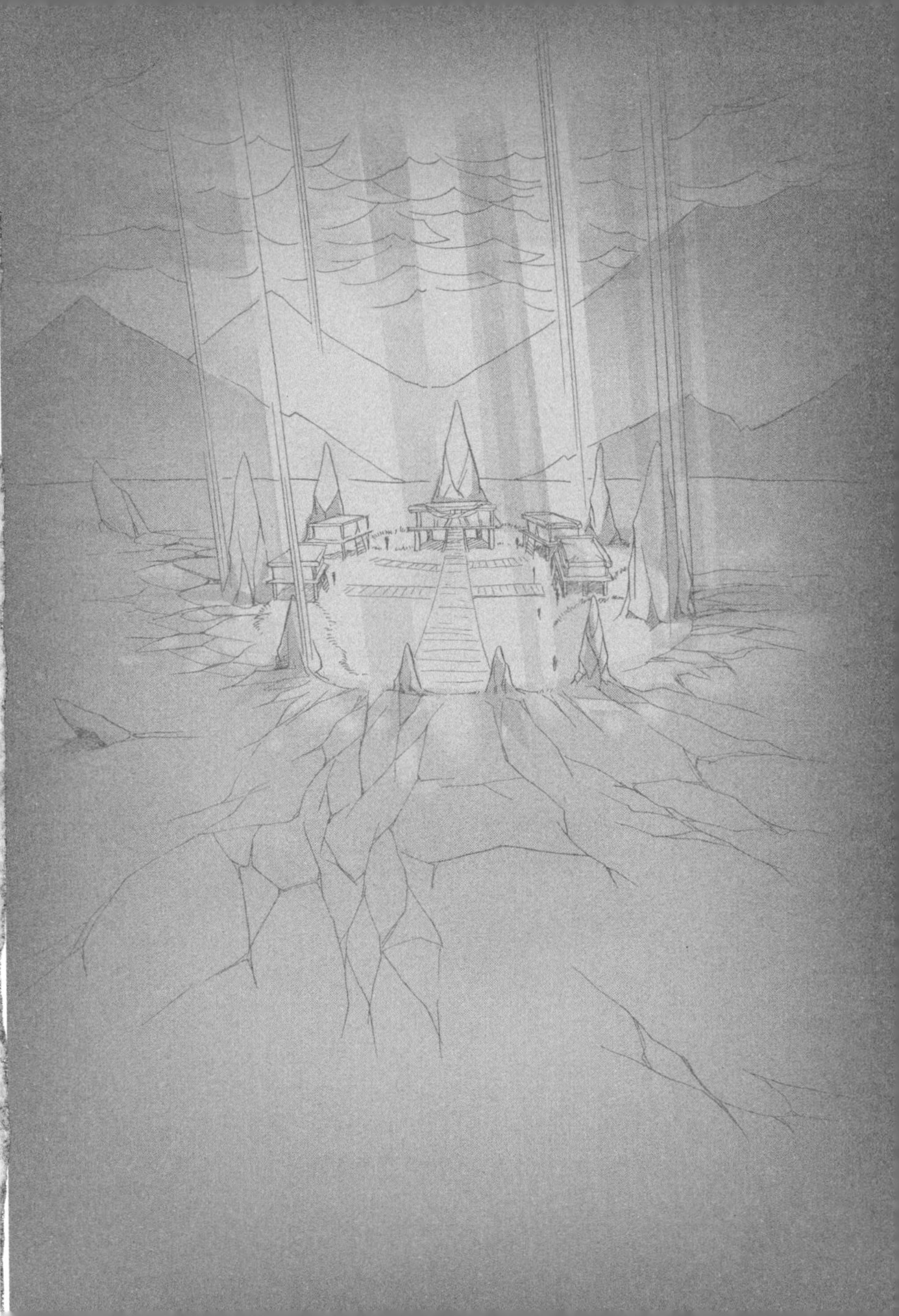

At the center of the universe, at the beginning and end of all creation, sits the planet of Vermonia, ruled by Queen Frasinella.

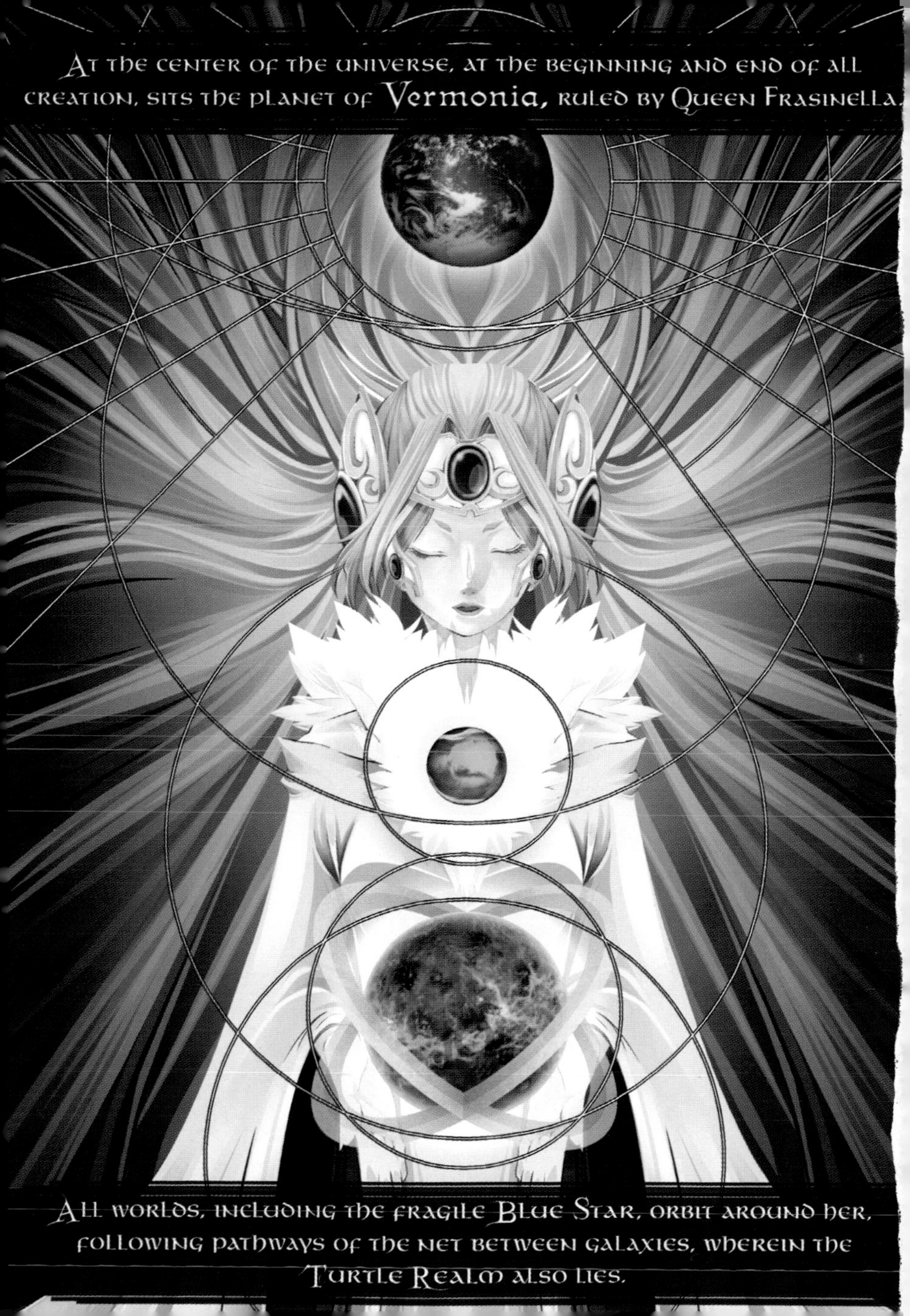

All worlds, including the fragile Blue Star, orbit around her, following pathways of the net between galaxies, wherein the Turtle Realm also lies.

Queen Frasinella's reign of harmony is ending in civil war due to the betrayal of the commander of her army, General Uro. Hungry for personal power, he seeks the queen's sacred Bolirium, fighting his own twin brother, the loyal Lord Boros, to obtain it.

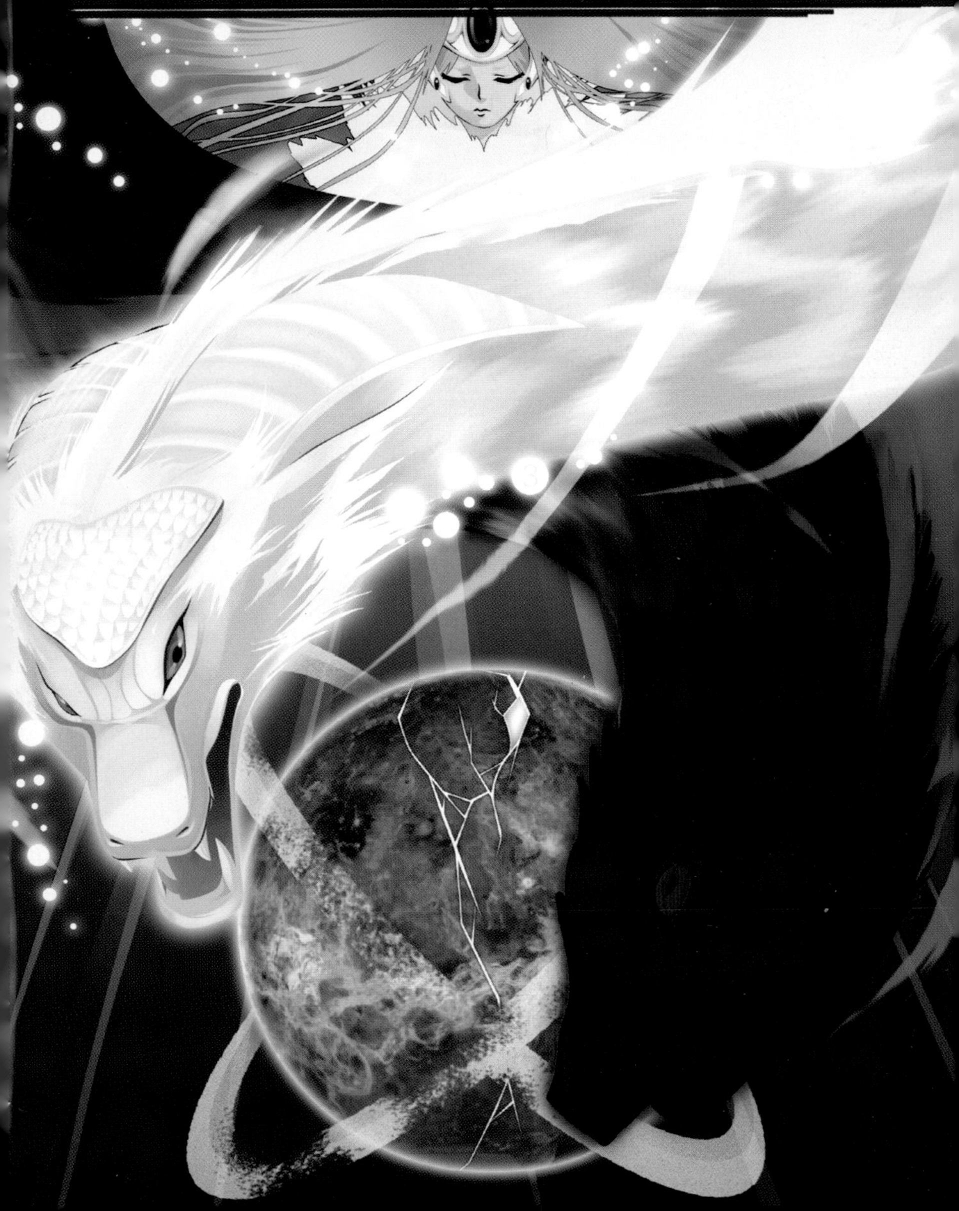

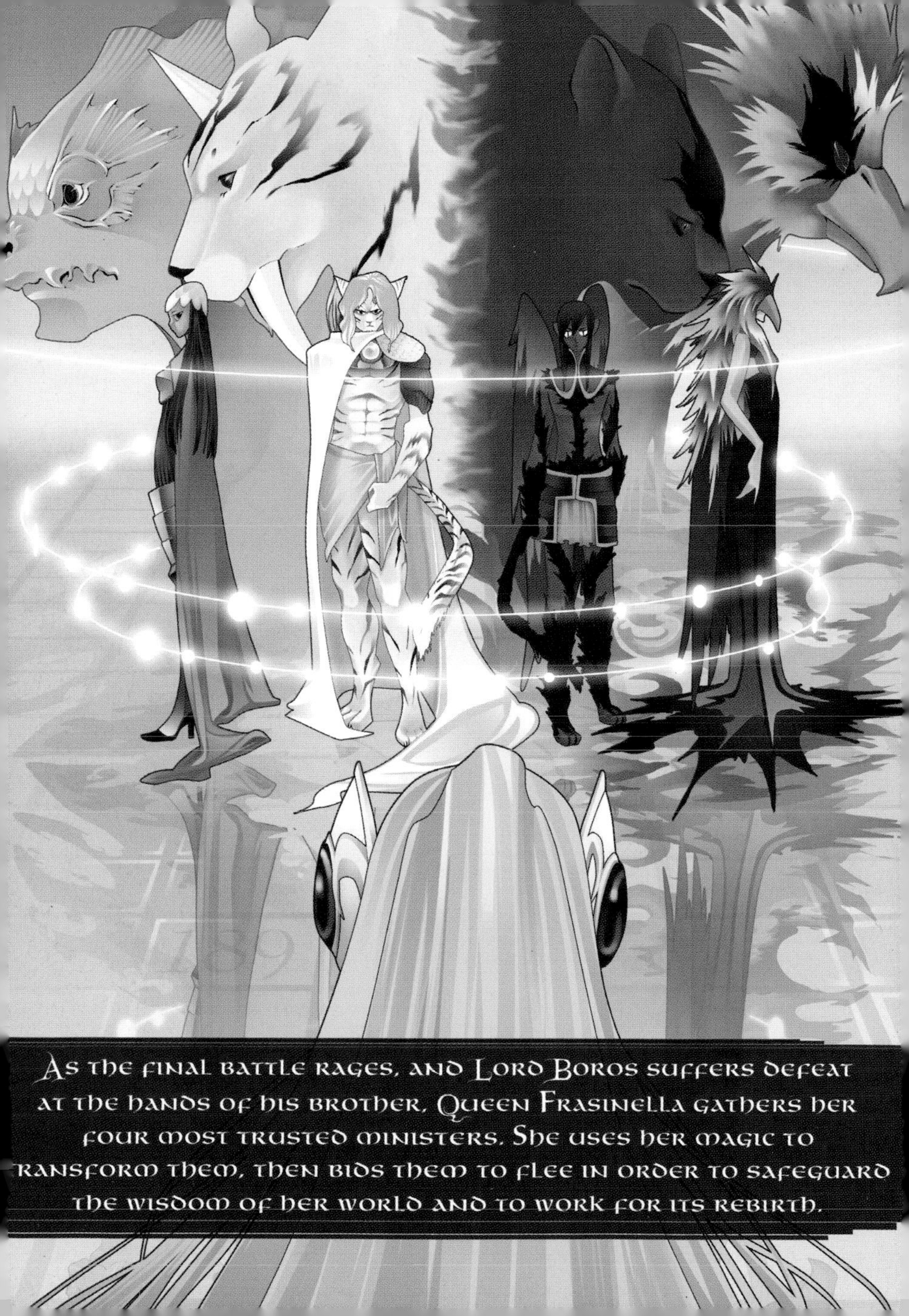
As the final battle rages, and Lord Boros suffers defeat
at the hands of his brother, Queen Frasinella gathers her
four most trusted ministers. She uses her magic to
ransform them, then bids them to flee in order to safeguard
the wisdom of her world and to work for its rebirth.

COPYRIGHT © 2009 BY RAITETSU MEDIA LLC AND RAY PRODUCTIONS

FIRST U.S. EDITION 2009

LIBRARY OF CONGRESS CATALOGING-IN-PUBLICATION DATA

YOYO.
QUEST FOR THE SILVER TIGER / YOYO. —1ST ED.
P. CM. —(VERMONIA)
SUMMARY: FOUR TWELVE-YEAR-OLD SKATEBOARDING FRIENDS FULFILL AN ANCIENT PROPHESY AS THEY DISCOVER THEIR TRUE WARRIOR SPIRITS IN AN EPIC BATTLE TO SAVE THE PLANET OF VERMONIA. THE READER IS INVITED TO LEARN MORE ABOUT THE CHARACTERS BY PLAYING AN ONLINE GAME AFTER FINDING HIDDEN CLUES IN THE ILLUSTRATIONS.
ISBN 978-0-7636-4554-0
1. GRAPHIC NOVELS. [1. GRAPHIC NOVELS. 2. FANTASY. 3. PROPHECIES—FICTION. 4. ADVENTURE AND ADVENTURERS—FICTION.] I. TITLE. II. SERIES.
PZ7.7.Y69QU 2009
741.5'973—DC22
2009008684

2 4 6 8 10 9 7 5 3 1

PRINTED IN CHINA

THIS BOOK WAS TYPESET IN CCLADRONN ITALIC.

CANDLEWICK PRESS
99 DOVER STREET
SOMERVILLE, MASSACHUSETTS 02144

VISIT US AT WWW.CANDLEWICK.COM

WWW.VERMONIA.COM

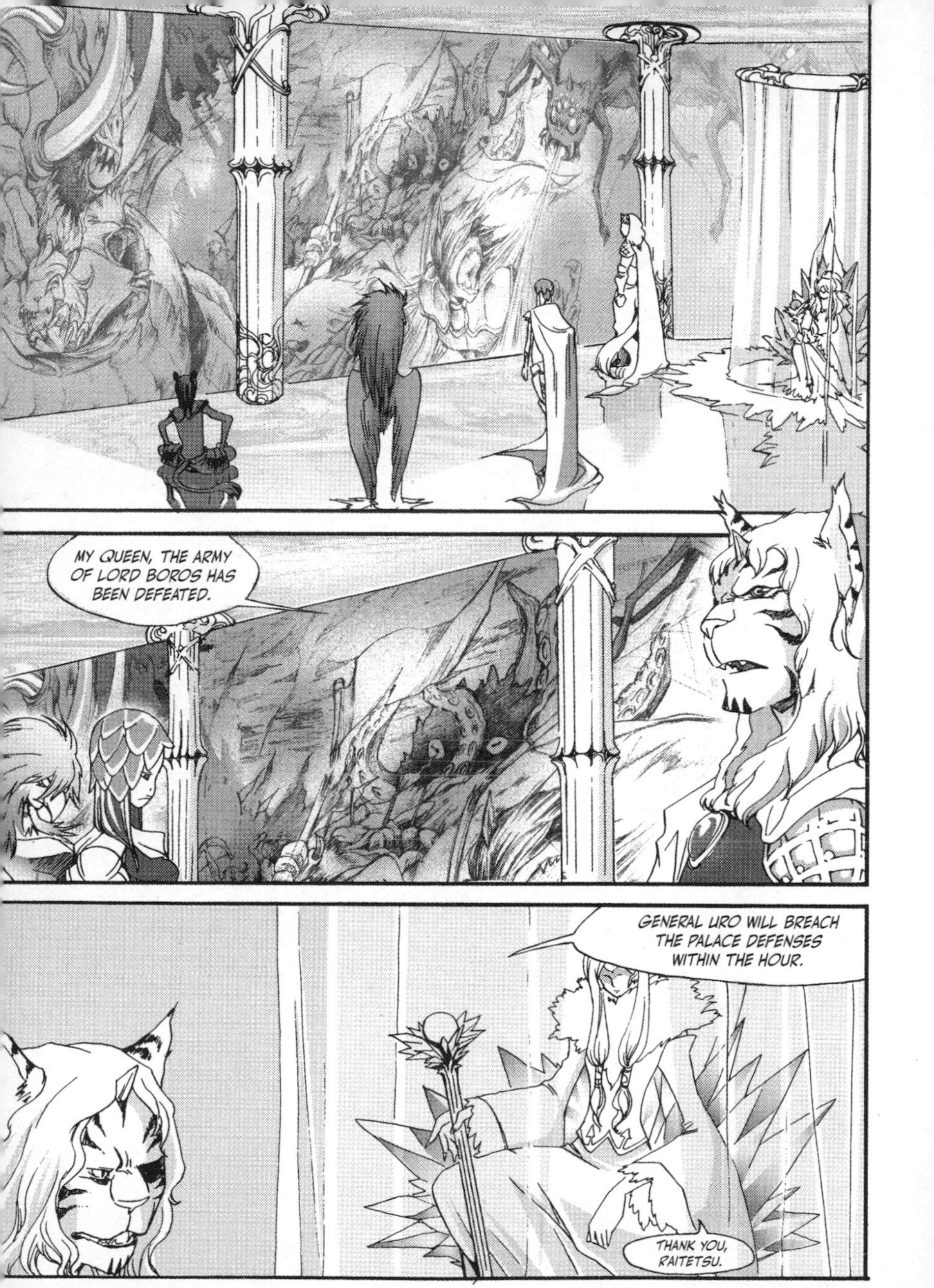
MY QUEEN, THE ARMY OF LORD BOROS HAS BEEN DEFEATED.
GENERAL URO WILL BREACH THE PALACE DEFENSES WITHIN THE HOUR.
THANK YOU, RAITETSU.

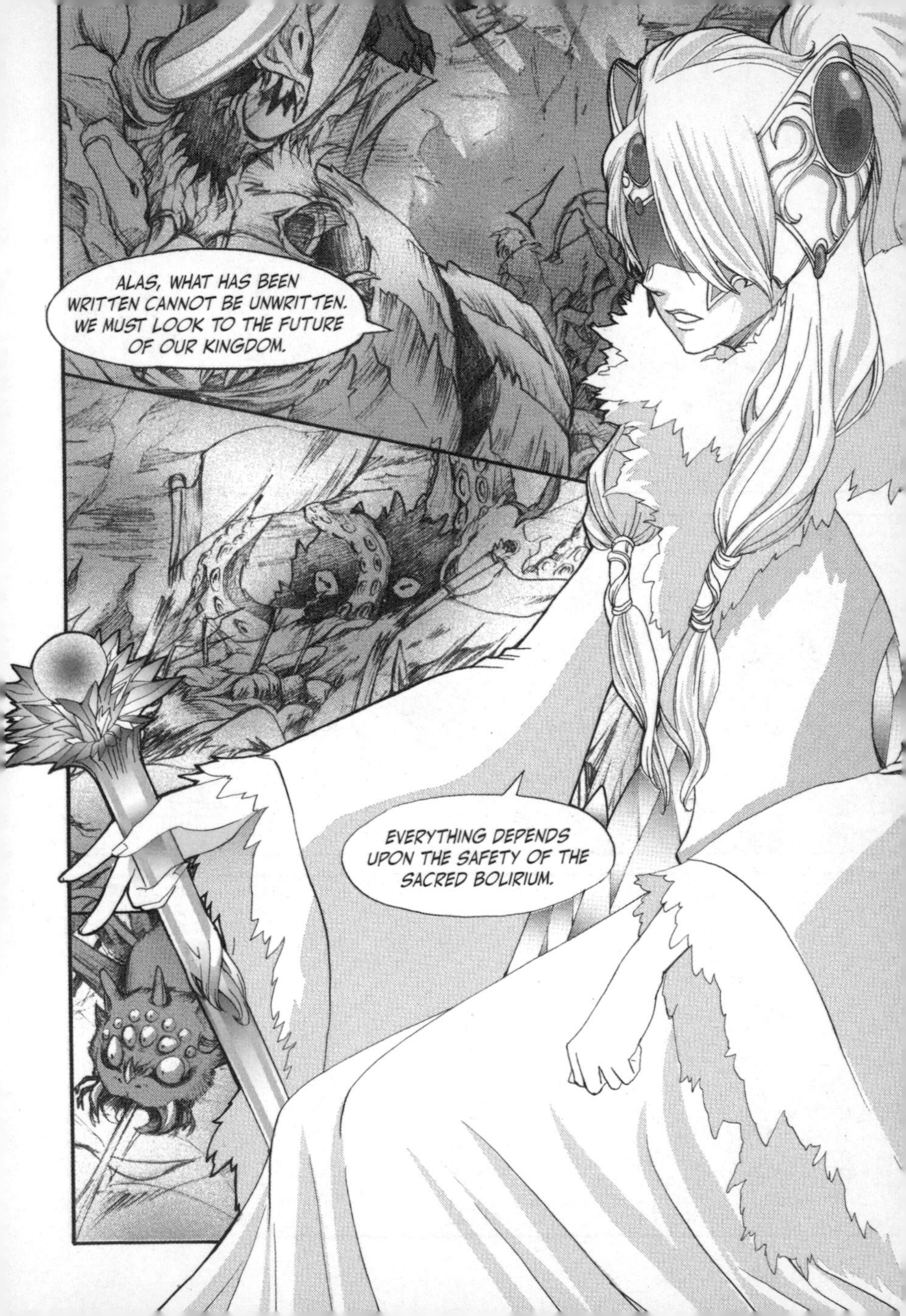
ALAS, WHAT HAS BEEN WRITTEN CANNOT BE UNWRITTEN. WE MUST LOOK TO THE FUTURE OF OUR KINGDOM.
EVERYTHING DEPENDS UPON THE SAFETY OF THE SACRED BOLIRIUM.

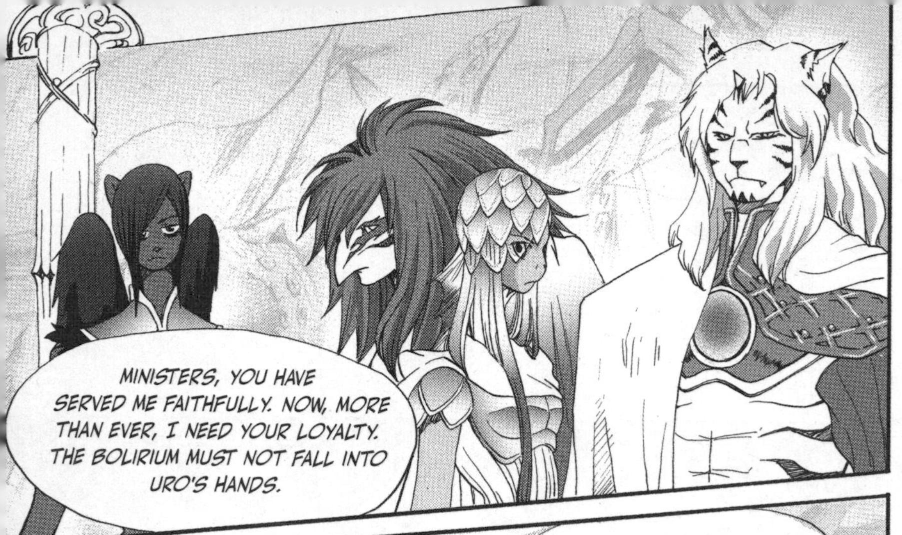
MINISTERS, YOU HAVE SERVED ME FAITHFULLY. NOW, MORE THAN EVER, I NEED YOUR LOYALTY. THE BOLIRIUM MUST NOT FALL INTO URO'S HANDS.

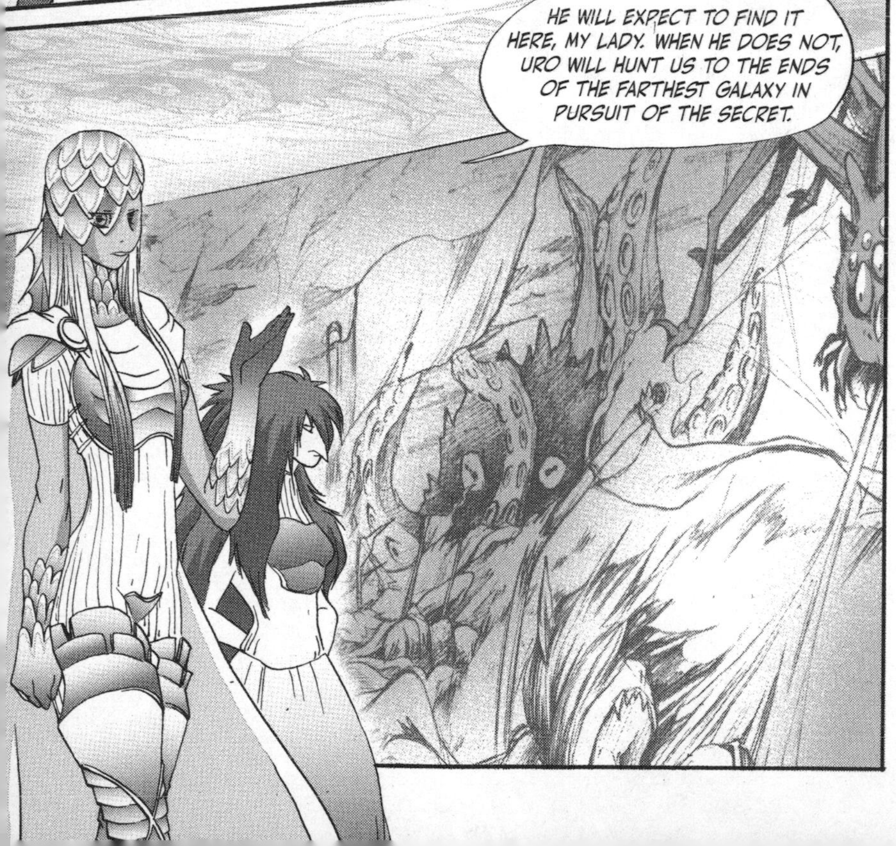
HE WILL EXPECT TO FIND IT HERE, MY LADY. WHEN HE DOES NOT, URO WILL HUNT US TO THE ENDS OF THE FARTHEST GALAXY IN PURSUIT OF THE SECRET.

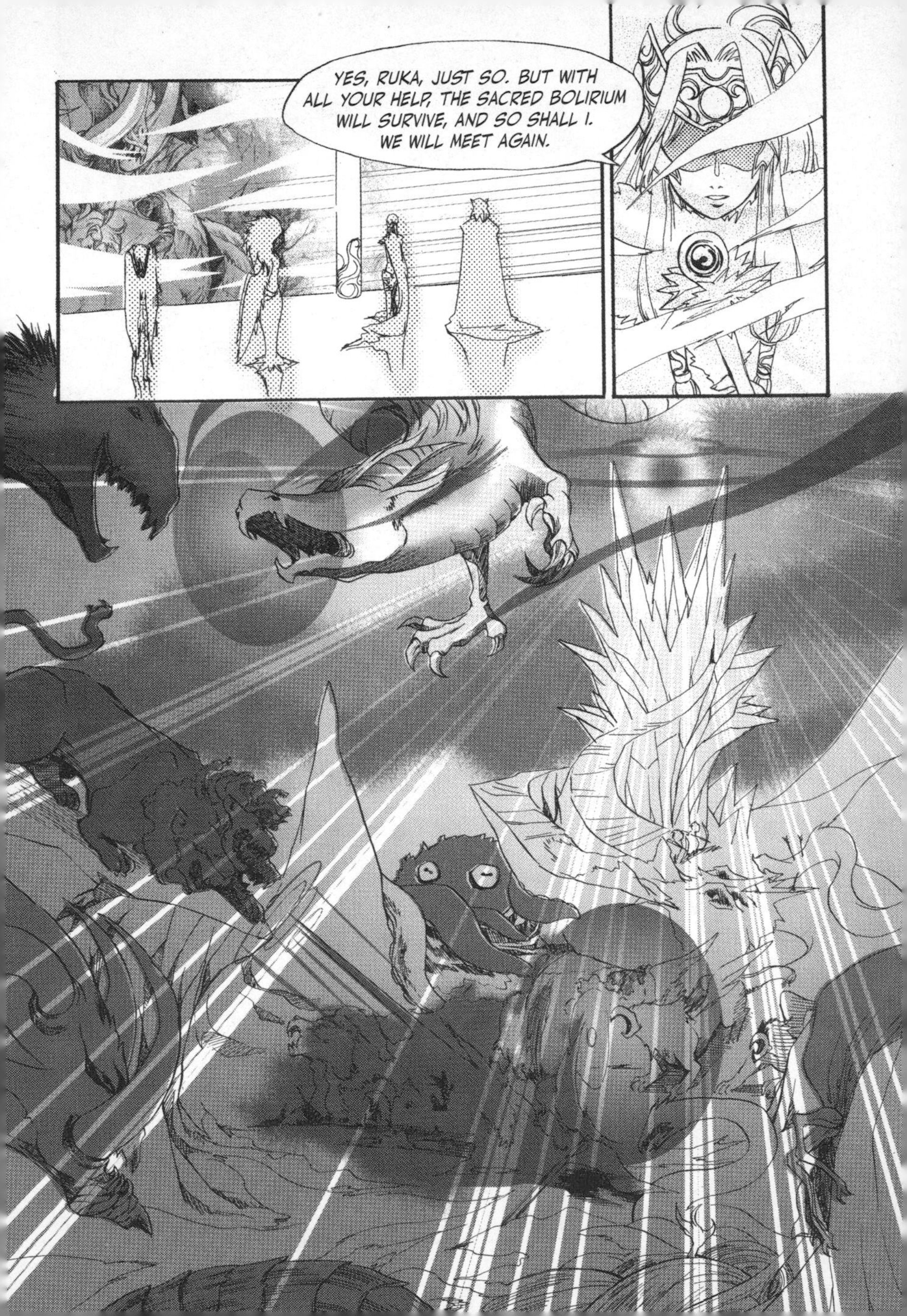
YES, RUKA, JUST SO. BUT WITH ALL YOUR HELP, THE SACRED BOLIRIUM WILL SURVIVE, AND SO SHALL I. WE WILL MEET AGAIN.

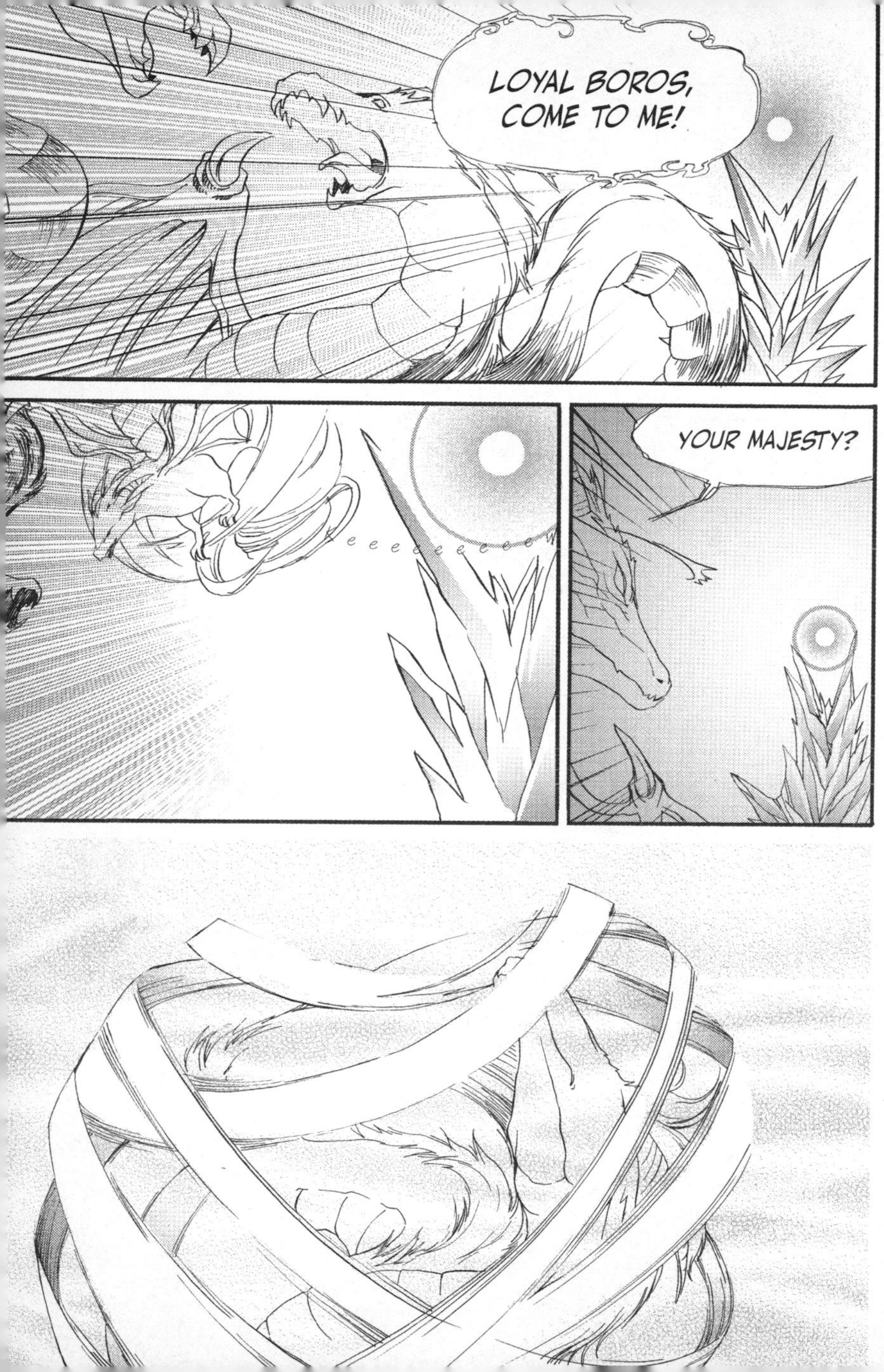
LOYAL BOROS, COME TO ME!
YOUR MAJESTY?

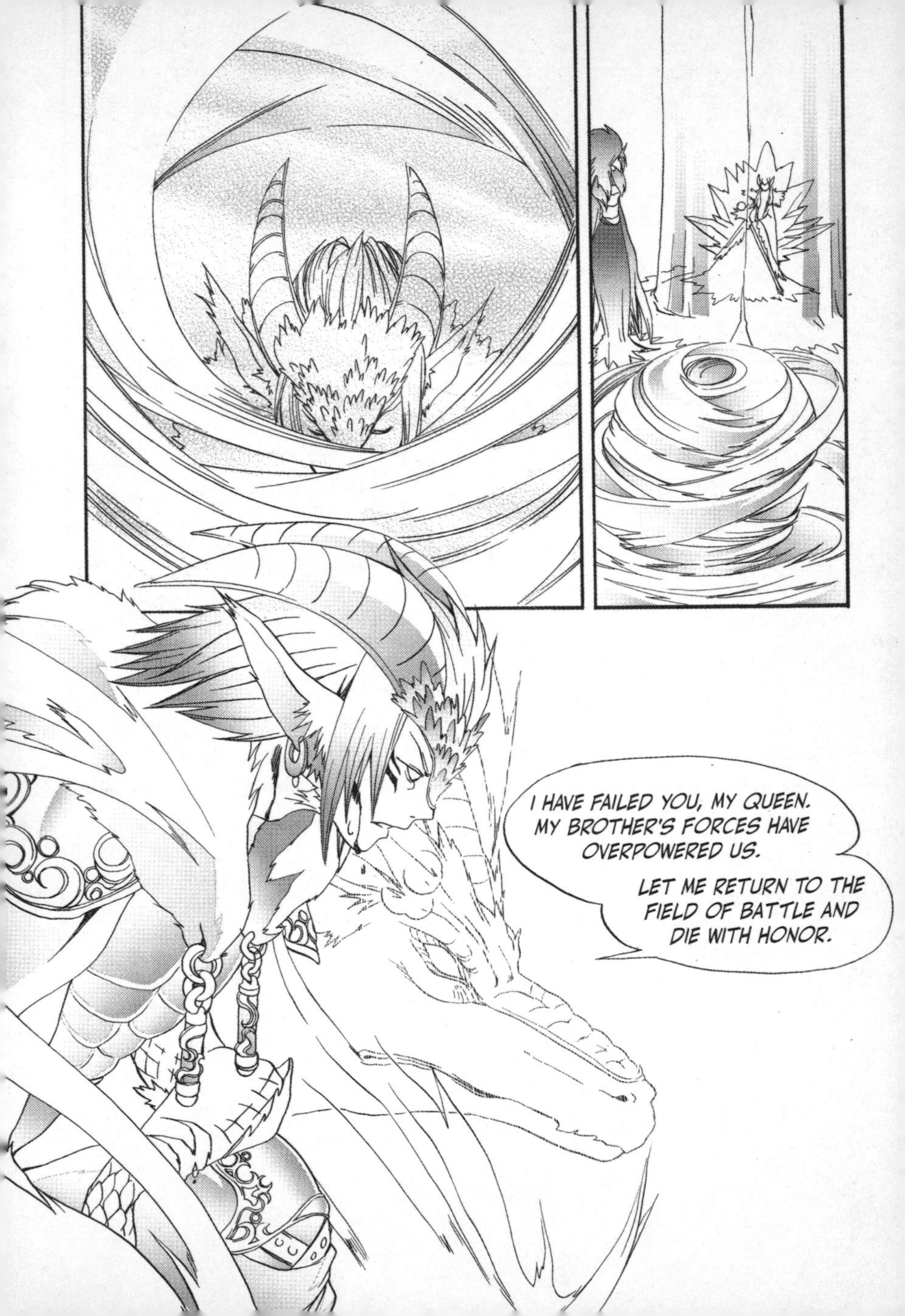
I HAVE FAILED YOU, MY QUEEN. MY BROTHER'S FORCES HAVE OVERPOWERED US.
LET ME RETURN TO THE FIELD OF BATTLE AND DIE WITH HONOR.

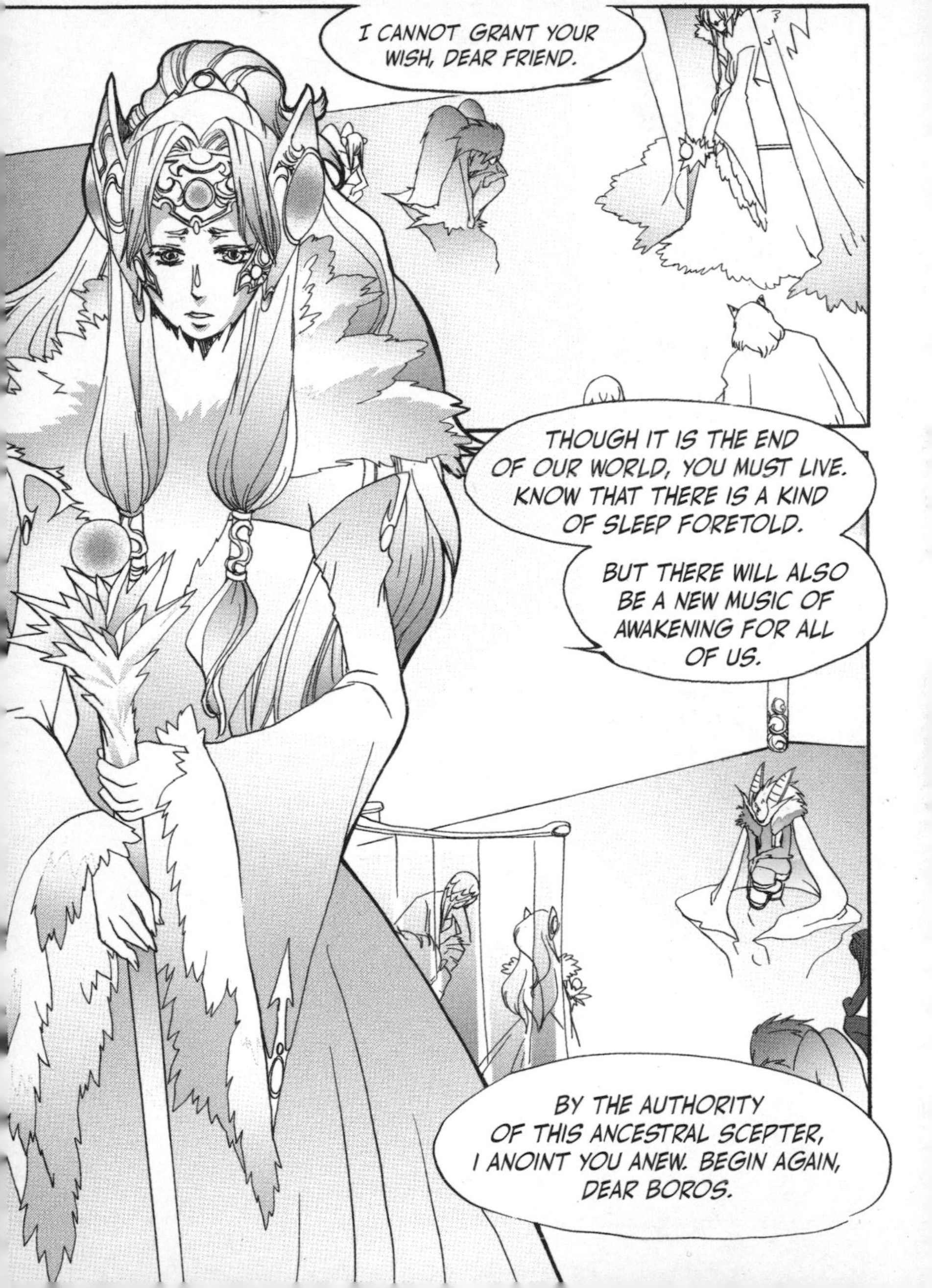
I CANNOT GRANT YOUR WISH, DEAR FRIEND.
THOUGH IT IS THE END OF OUR WORLD, YOU MUST LIVE. KNOW THAT THERE IS A KIND OF SLEEP FORETOLD.
BUT THERE WILL ALSO BE A NEW MUSIC OF AWAKENING FOR ALL OF US.
BY THE AUTHORITY OF THIS ANCESTRAL SCEPTER, I ANOINT YOU ANEW. BEGIN AGAIN, DEAR BOROS.

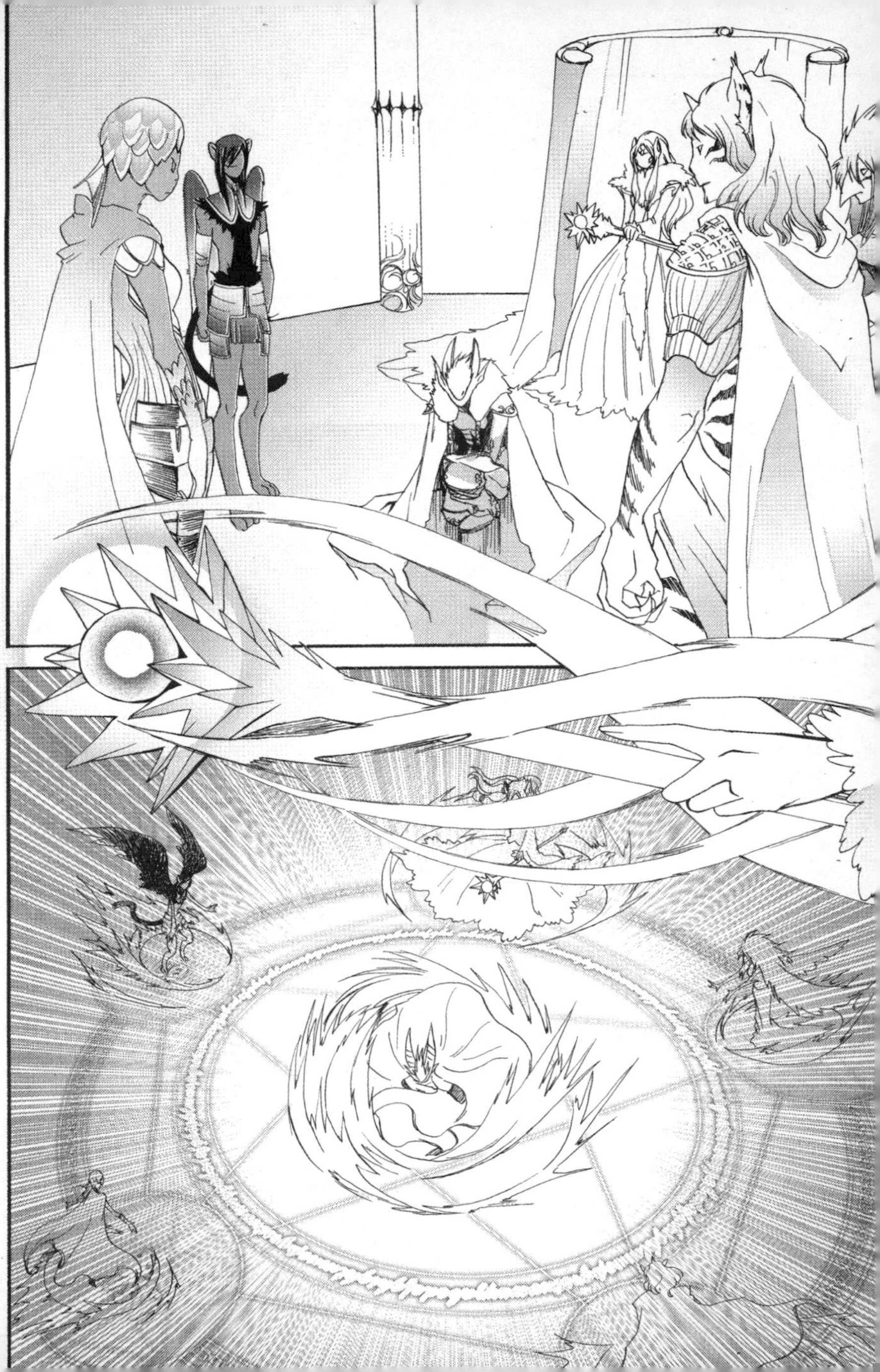

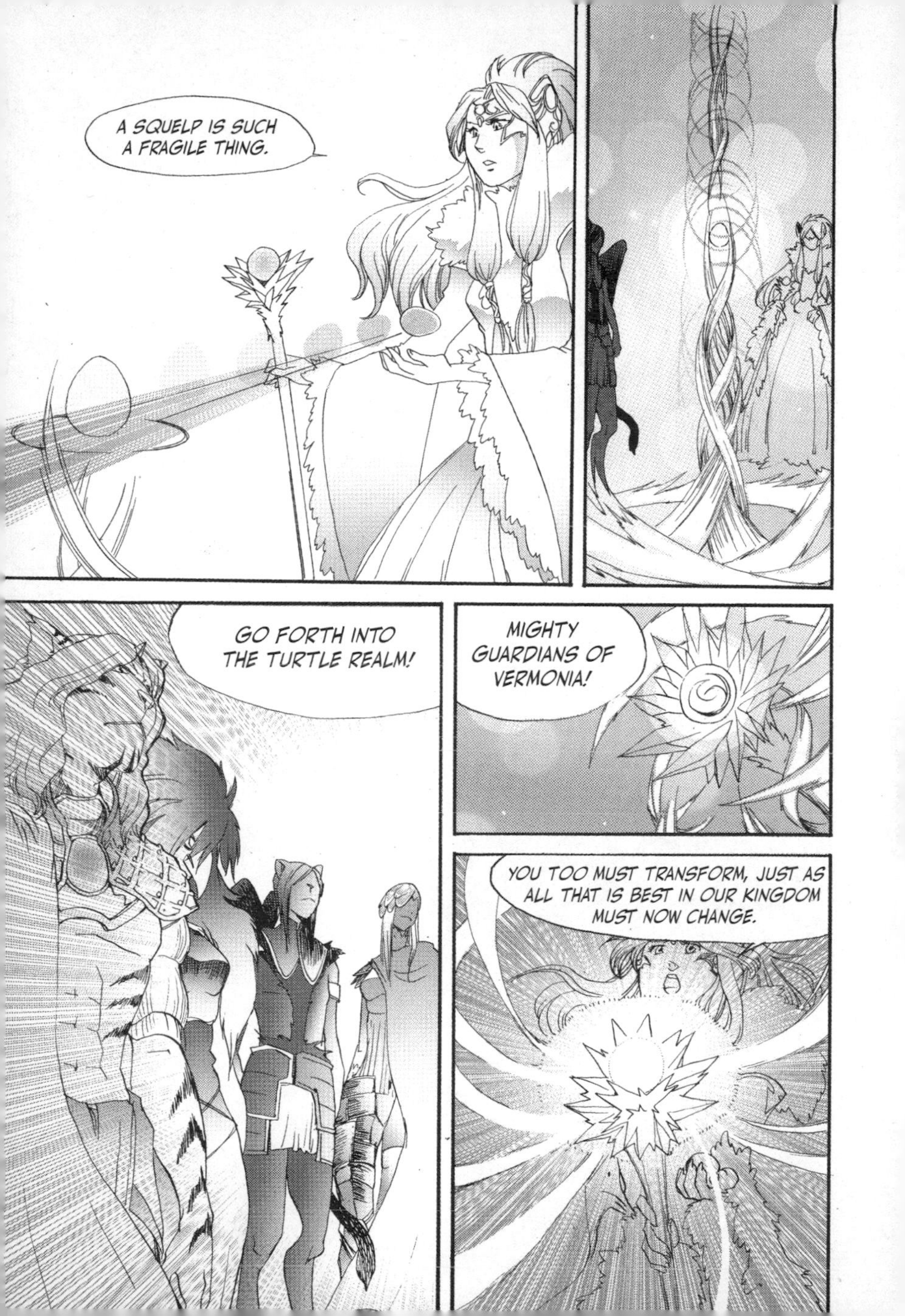
A SQUELP IS SUCH A FRAGILE THING.
GO FORTH INTO THE TURTLE REALM!
MIGHTY GUARDIANS OF VERMONIA!
YOU TOO MUST TRANSFORM, JUST AS ALL THAT IS BEST IN OUR KINGDOM MUST NOW CHANGE.

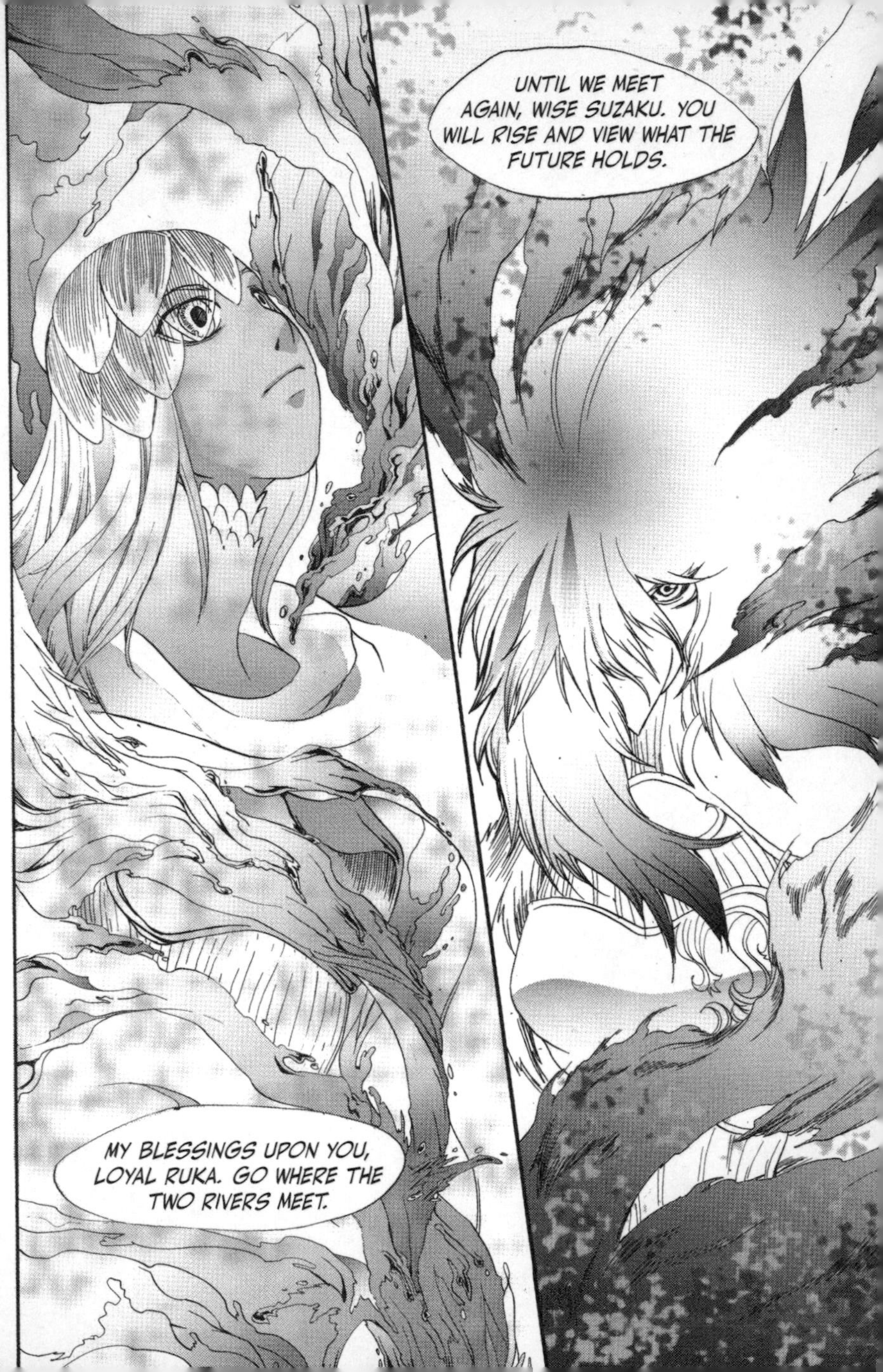
UNTIL WE MEET AGAIN, WISE SUZAKU. YOU WILL RISE AND VIEW WHAT THE FUTURE HOLDS.
MY BLESSINGS UPON YOU, LOYAL RUKA. GO WHERE THE TWO RIVERS MEET.

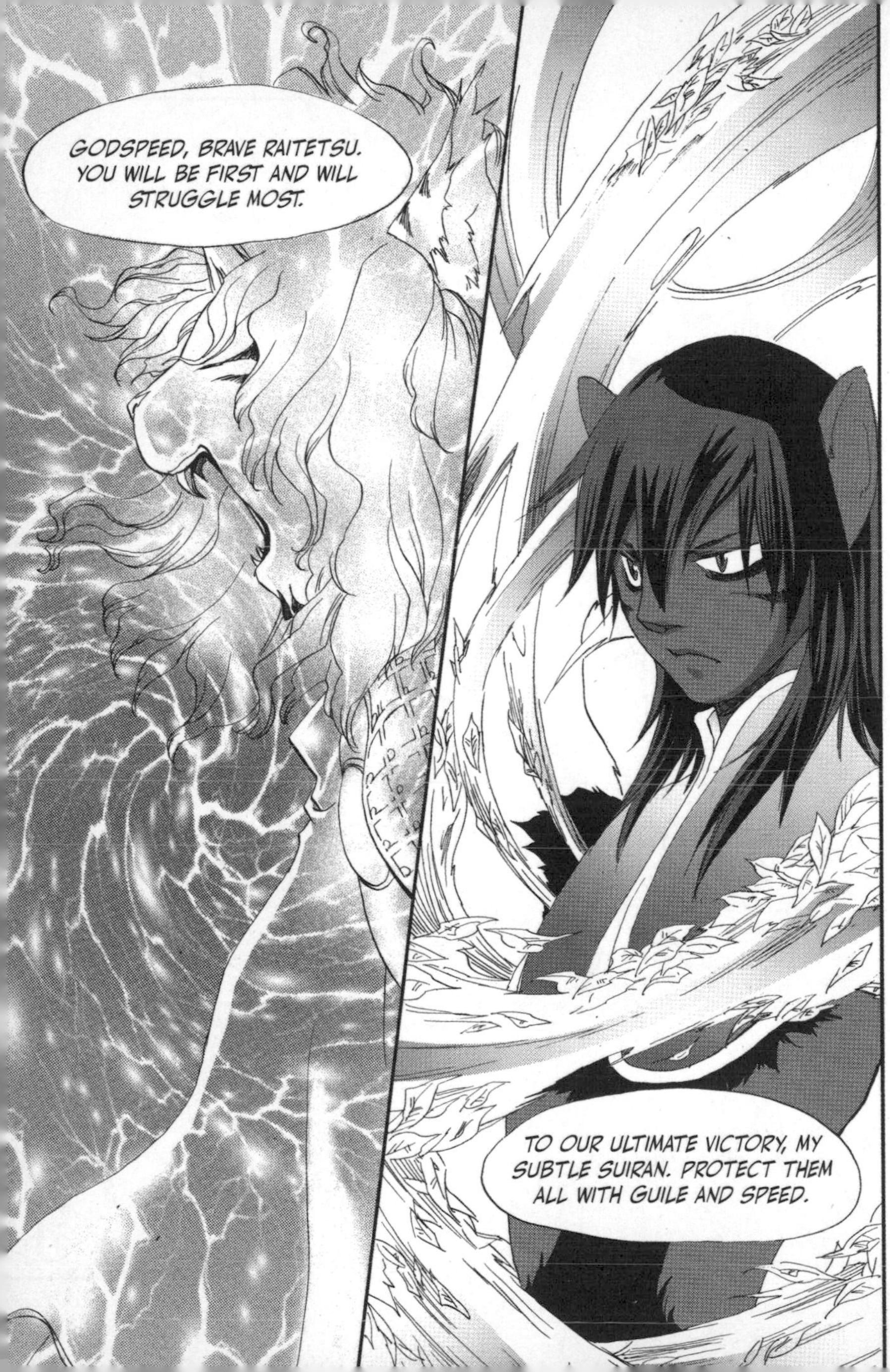
GODSPEED, BRAVE RAITETSU. YOU WILL BE FIRST AND WILL STRUGGLE MOST.
TO OUR ULTIMATE VICTORY, MY SUBTLE SUIRAN. PROTECT THEM ALL WITH GUILE AND SPEED.

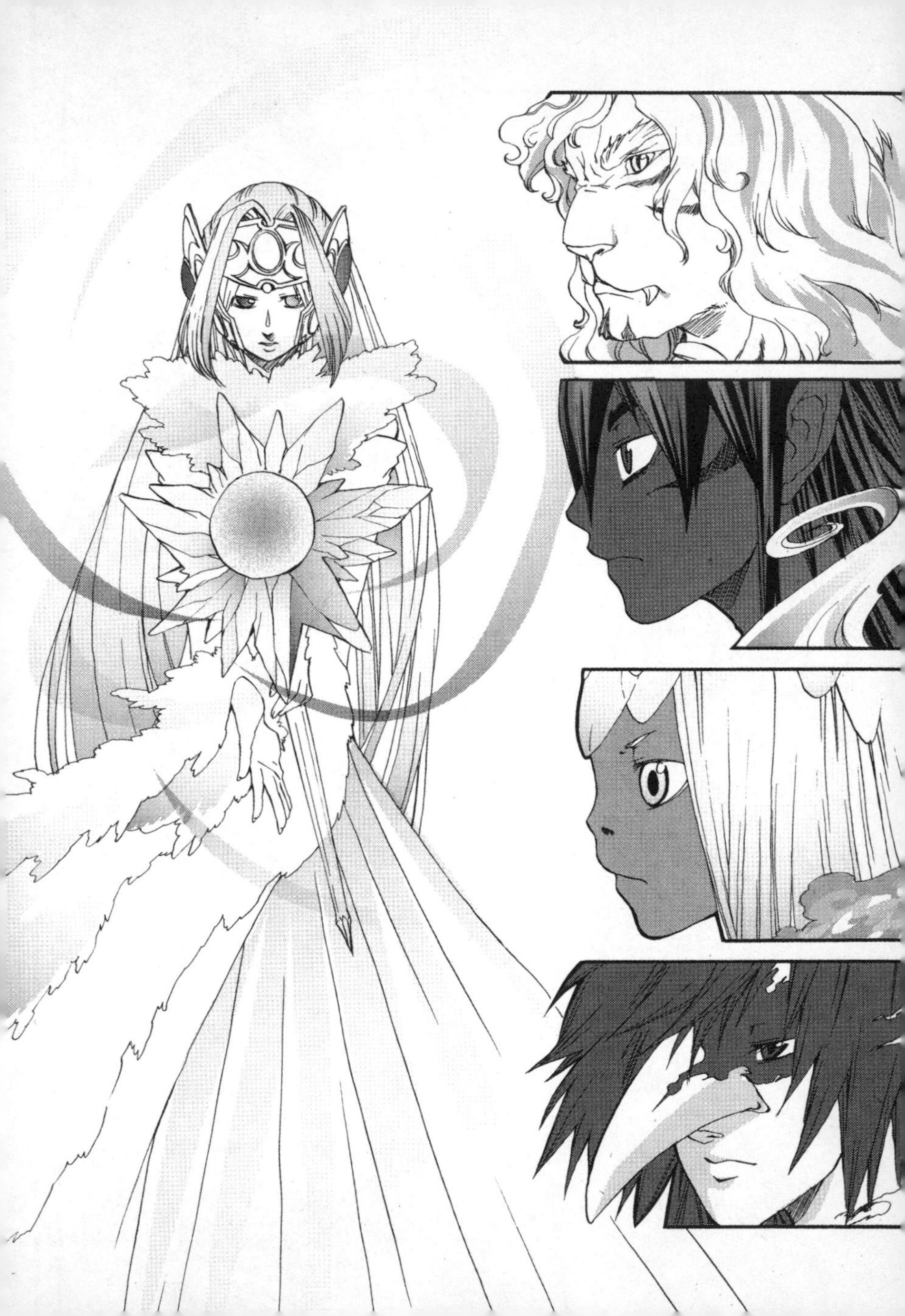

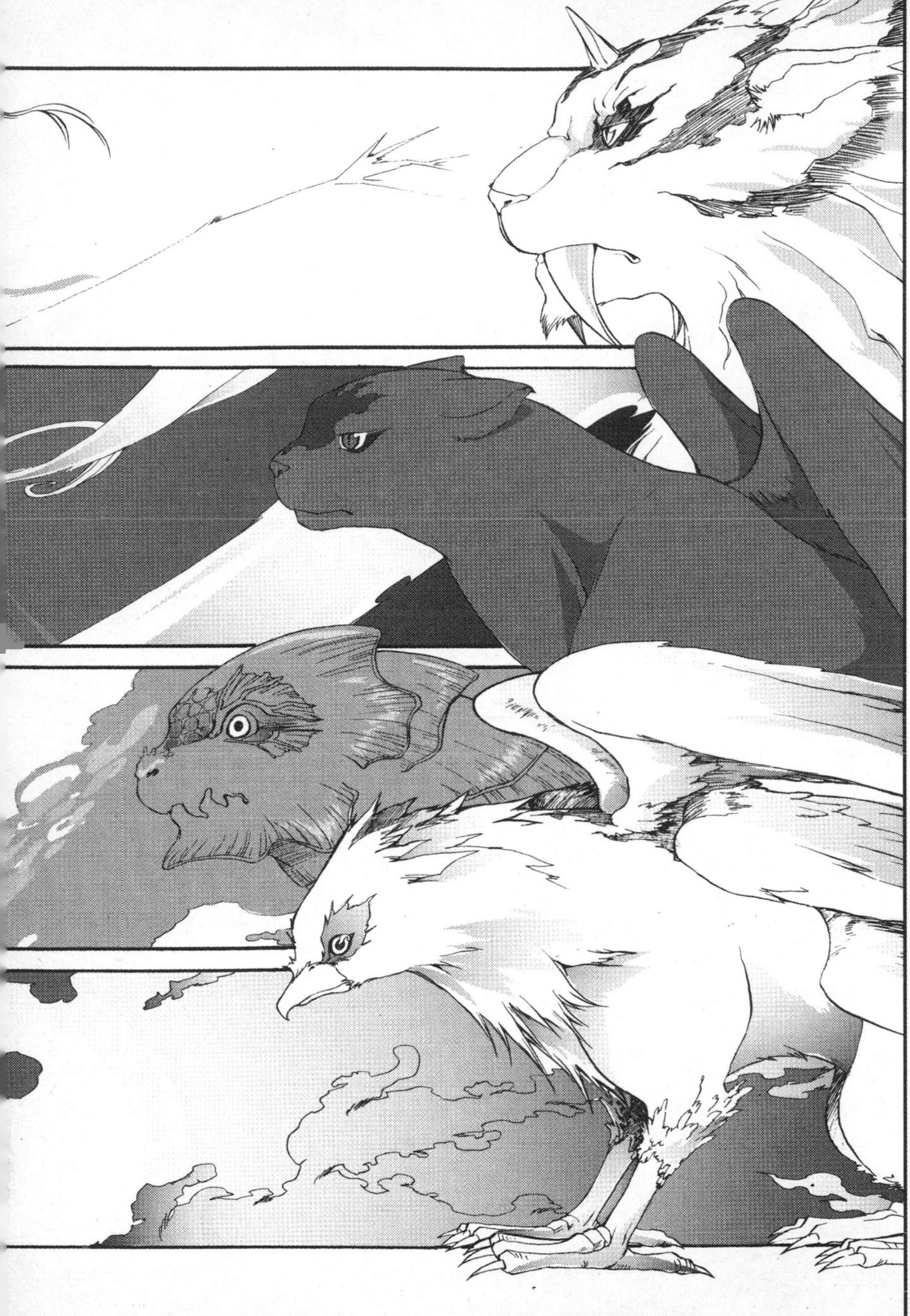

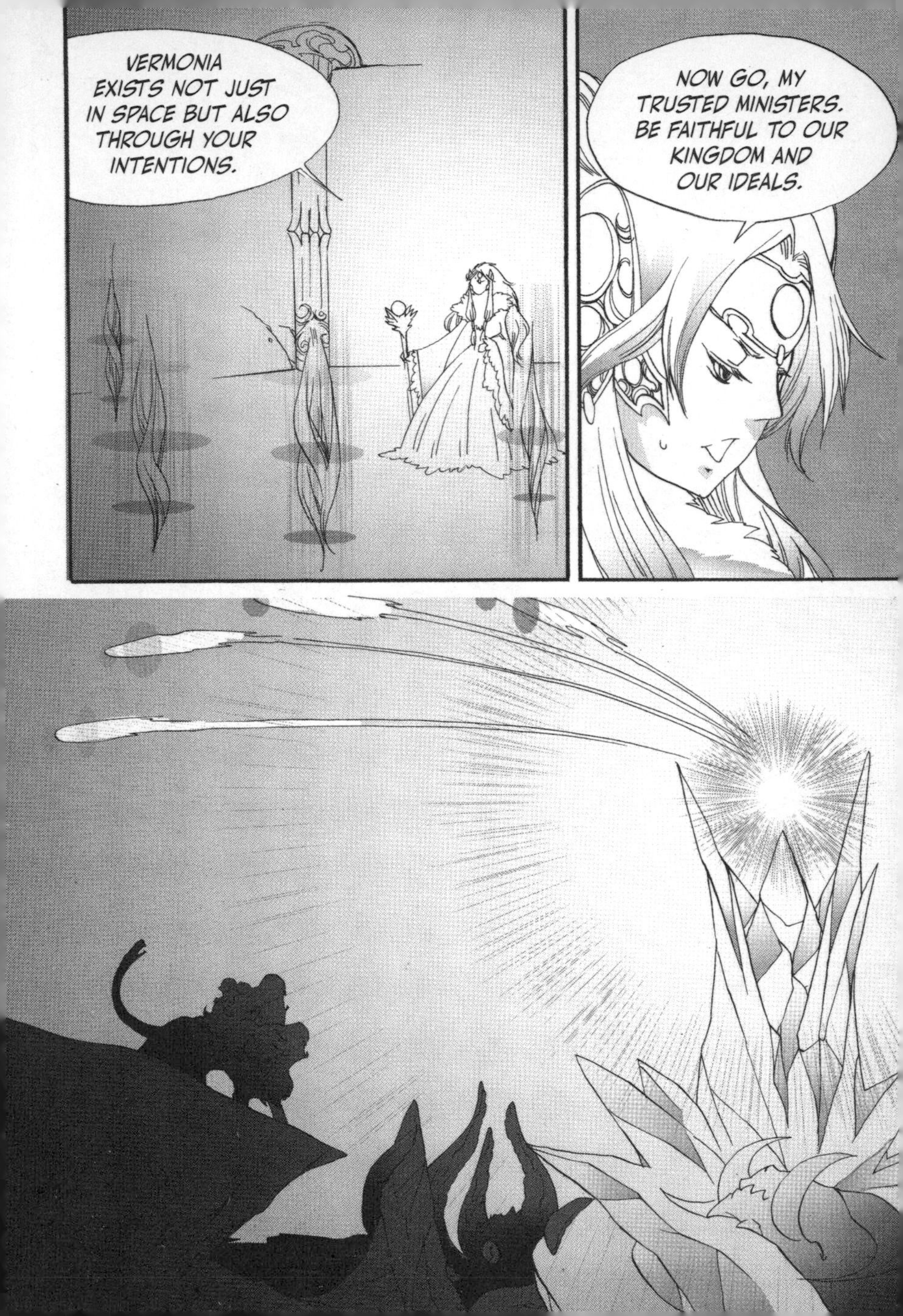
VERMONIA EXISTS NOT JUST IN SPACE BUT ALSO THROUGH YOUR INTENTIONS.
NOW GO, MY TRUSTED MINISTERS. BE FAITHFUL TO OUR KINGDOM AND OUR IDEALS.

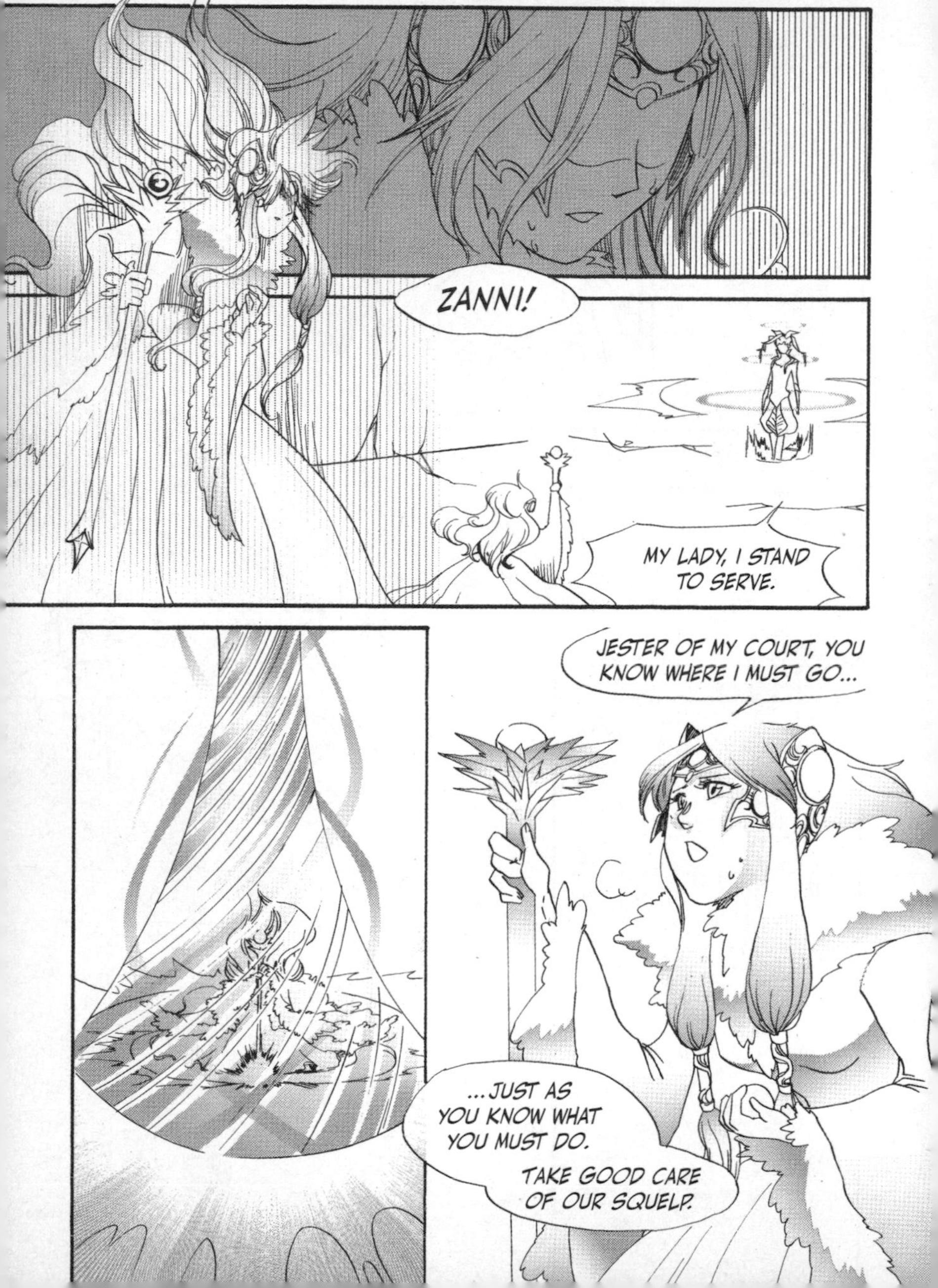
ZANNI!
MY LADY, I STAND TO SERVE.
JESTER OF MY COURT, YOU KNOW WHERE I MUST GO...
...JUST AS YOU KNOW WHAT YOU MUST DO.
TAKE GOOD CARE OF OUR SQUELP.

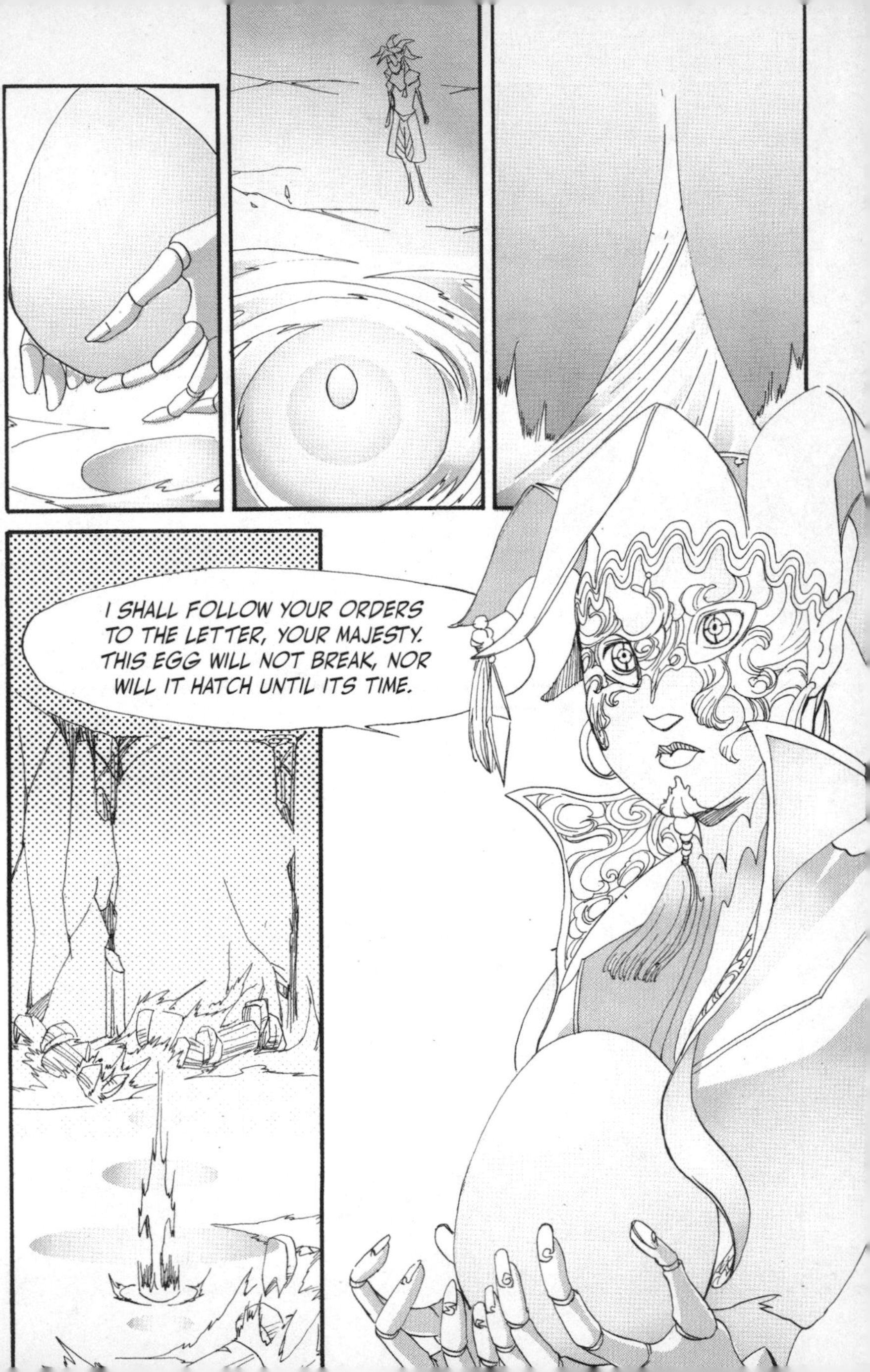
I SHALL FOLLOW YOUR ORDERS TO THE LETTER, YOUR MAJESTY. THIS EGG WILL NOT BREAK, NOR WILL IT HATCH UNTIL ITS TIME.

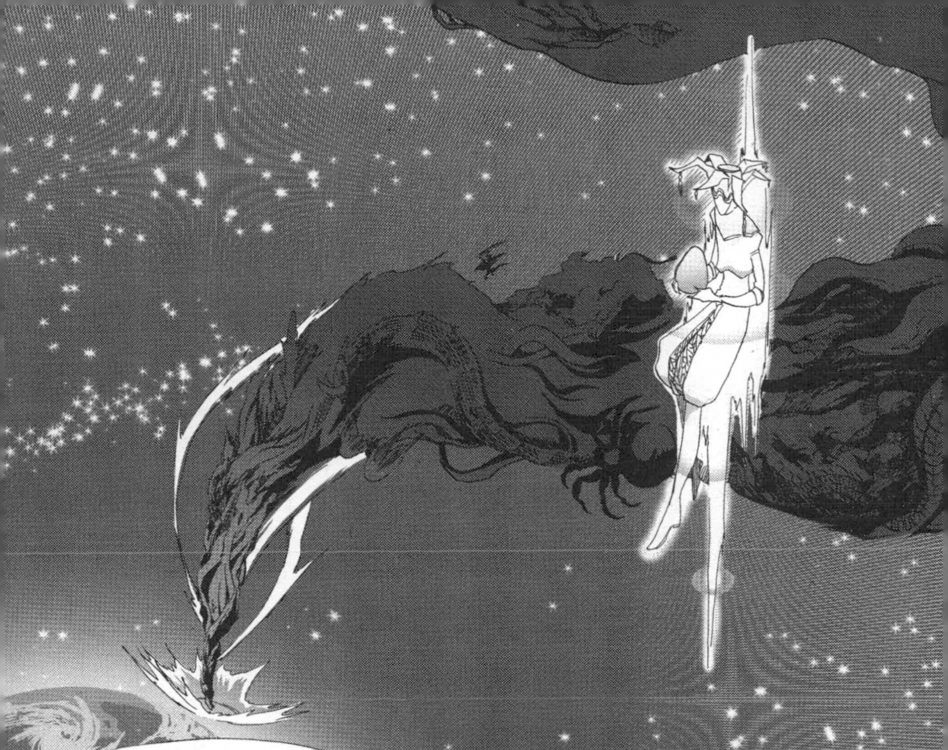
I MUST HURRY. URO'S SOLDIERS ARE ALREADY IN PURSUIT OF THE FOUR MINISTERS.
I MUST GO TO BLUE STAR.

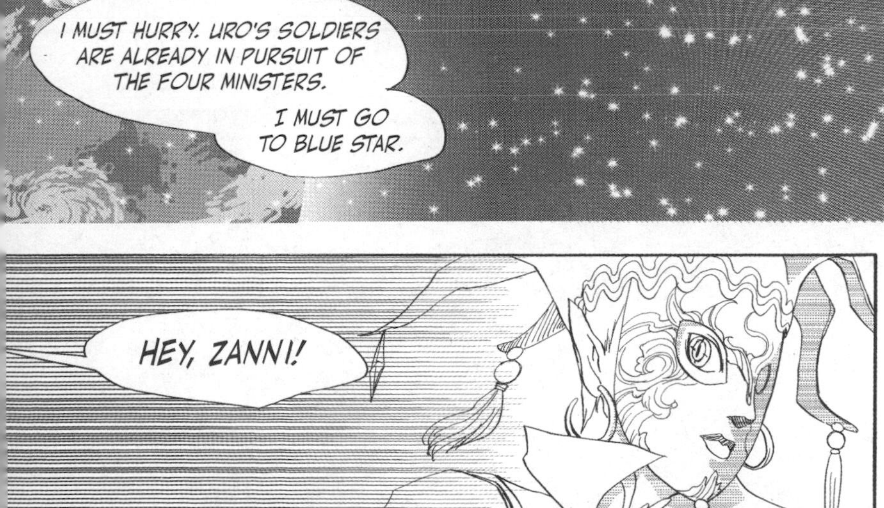
HEY, ZANNI!

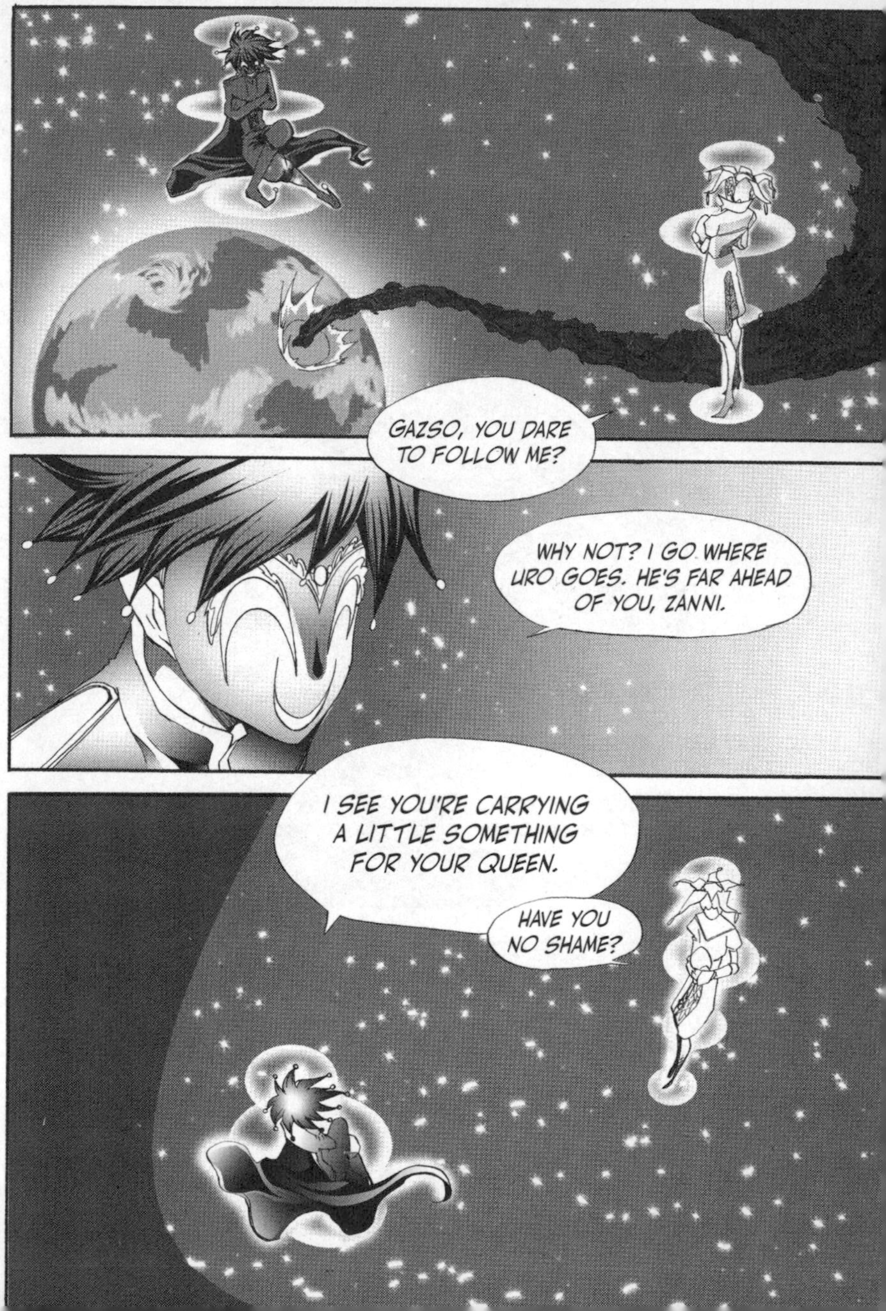
GAZSO, YOU DARE TO FOLLOW ME?
WHY NOT? I GO WHERE URO GOES. HE'S FAR AHEAD OF YOU, ZANNI.
I SEE YOU'RE CARRYING A LITTLE SOMETHING FOR YOUR QUEEN.
HAVE YOU NO SHAME?

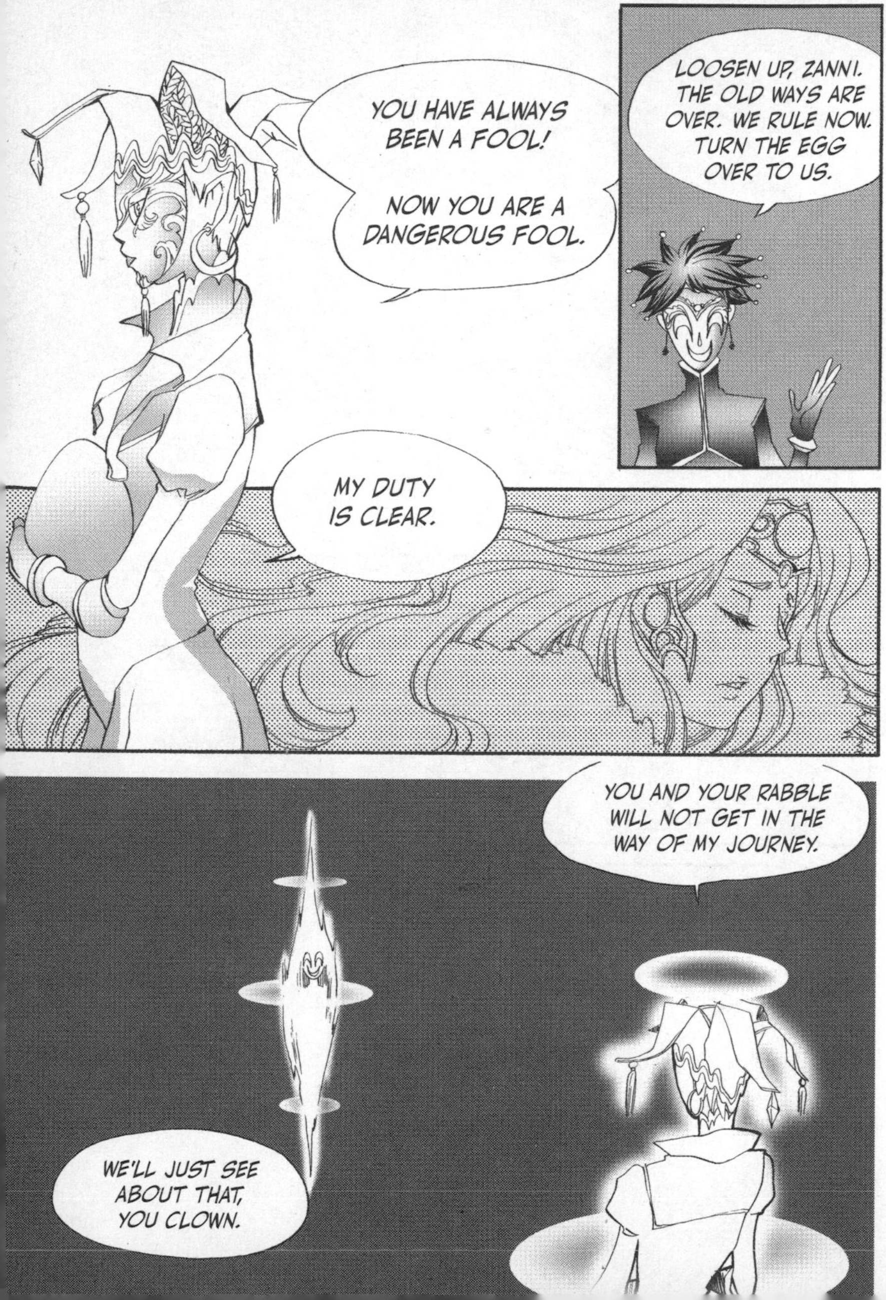
YOU HAVE ALWAYS BEEN A FOOL!
NOW YOU ARE A DANGEROUS FOOL.
LOOSEN UP, ZANNI. THE OLD WAYS ARE OVER. WE RULE NOW. TURN THE EGG OVER TO US.
MY DUTY IS CLEAR.
YOU AND YOUR RABBLE WILL NOT GET IN THE WAY OF MY JOURNEY.
WE'LL JUST SEE ABOUT THAT, YOU CLOWN.

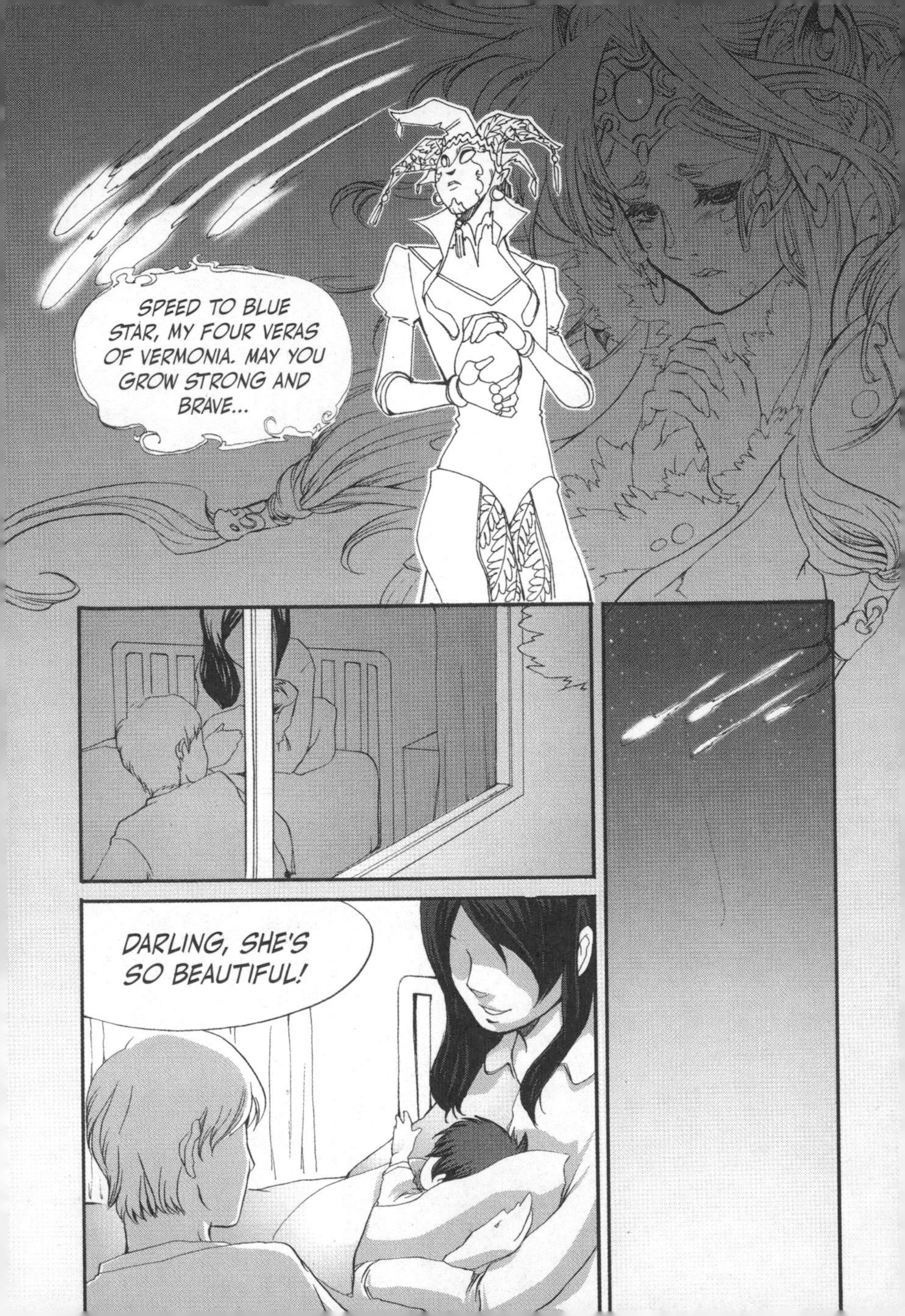
SPEED TO BLUE STAR, MY FOUR VERAS OF VERMONIA. MAY YOU GROW STRONG AND BRAVE...
DARLING, SHE'S SO BEAUTIFUL!

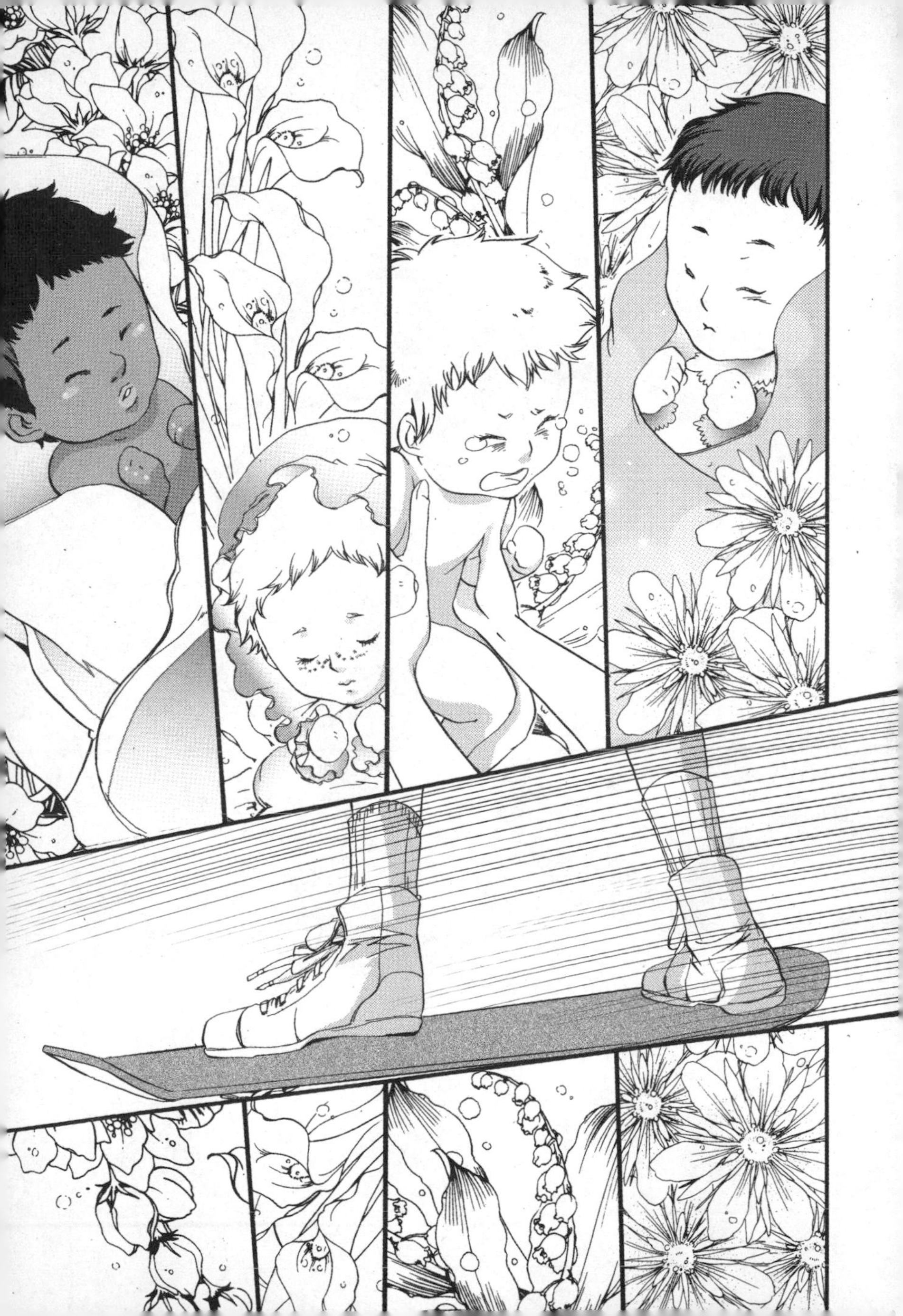

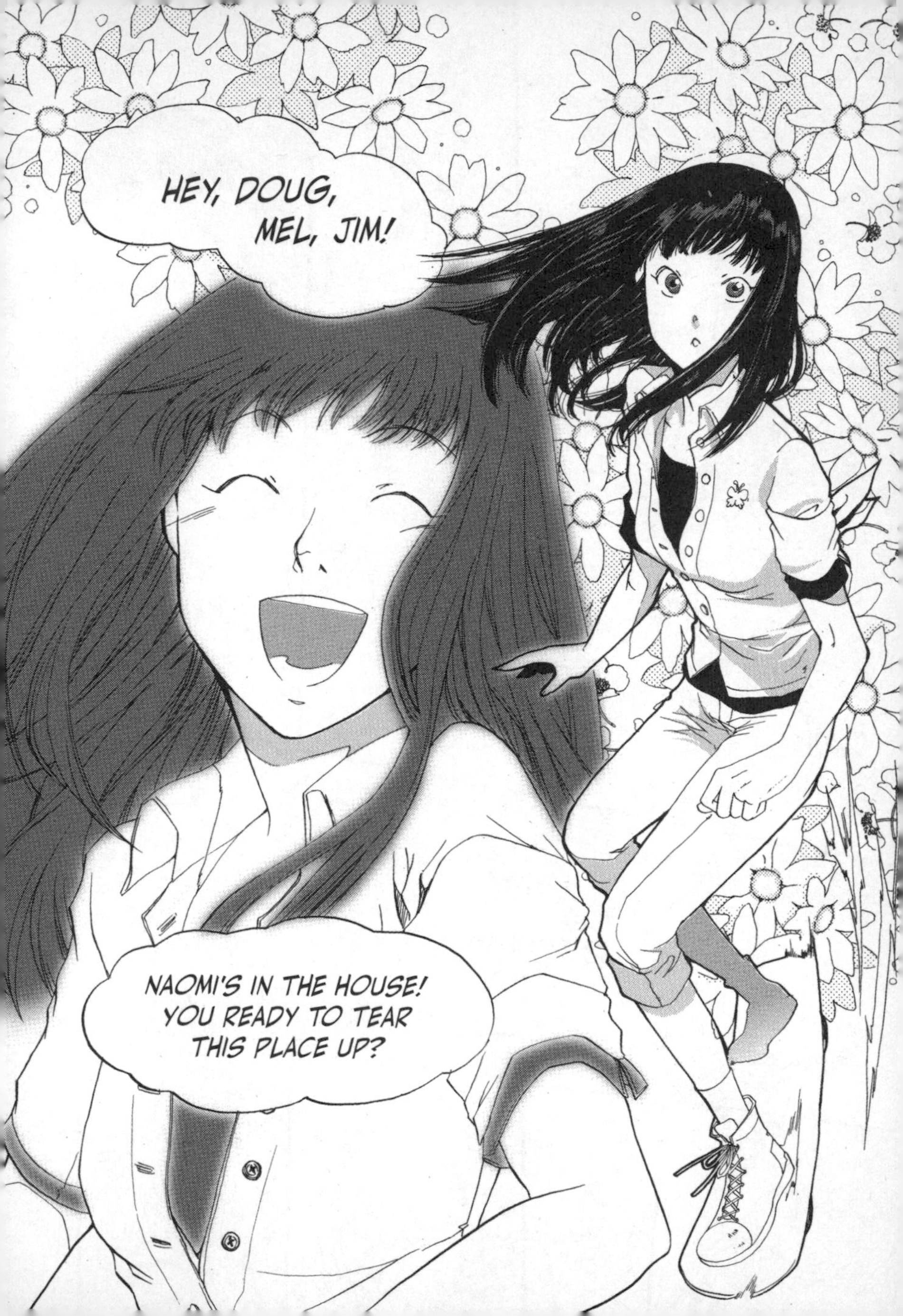
HEY, DOUG, MEL, JIM!
NAOMI'S IN THE HOUSE! YOU READY TO TEAR THIS PLACE UP?

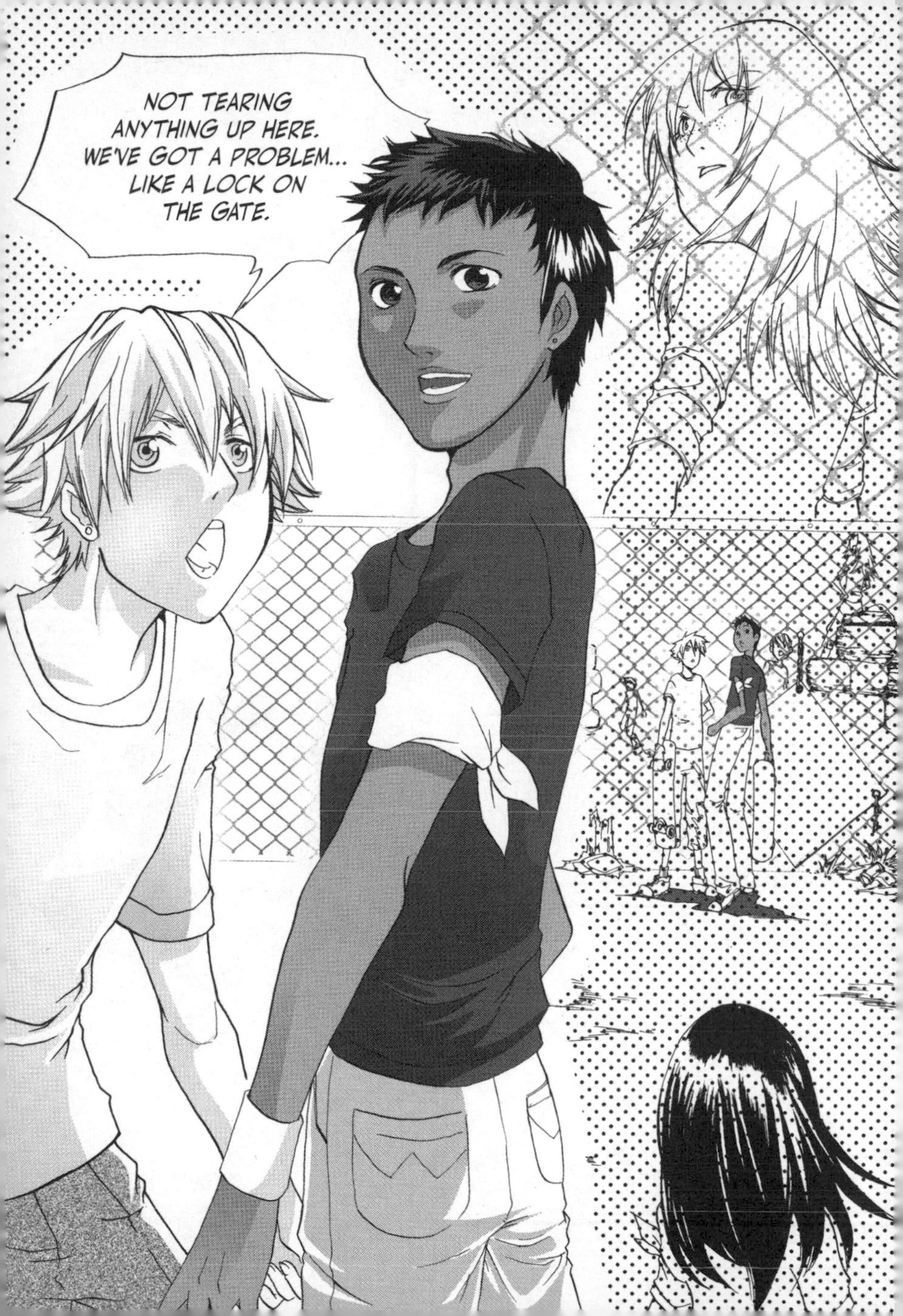
NOT TEARING ANYTHING UP HERE. WE'VE GOT A PROBLEM... LIKE A LOCK ON THE GATE.

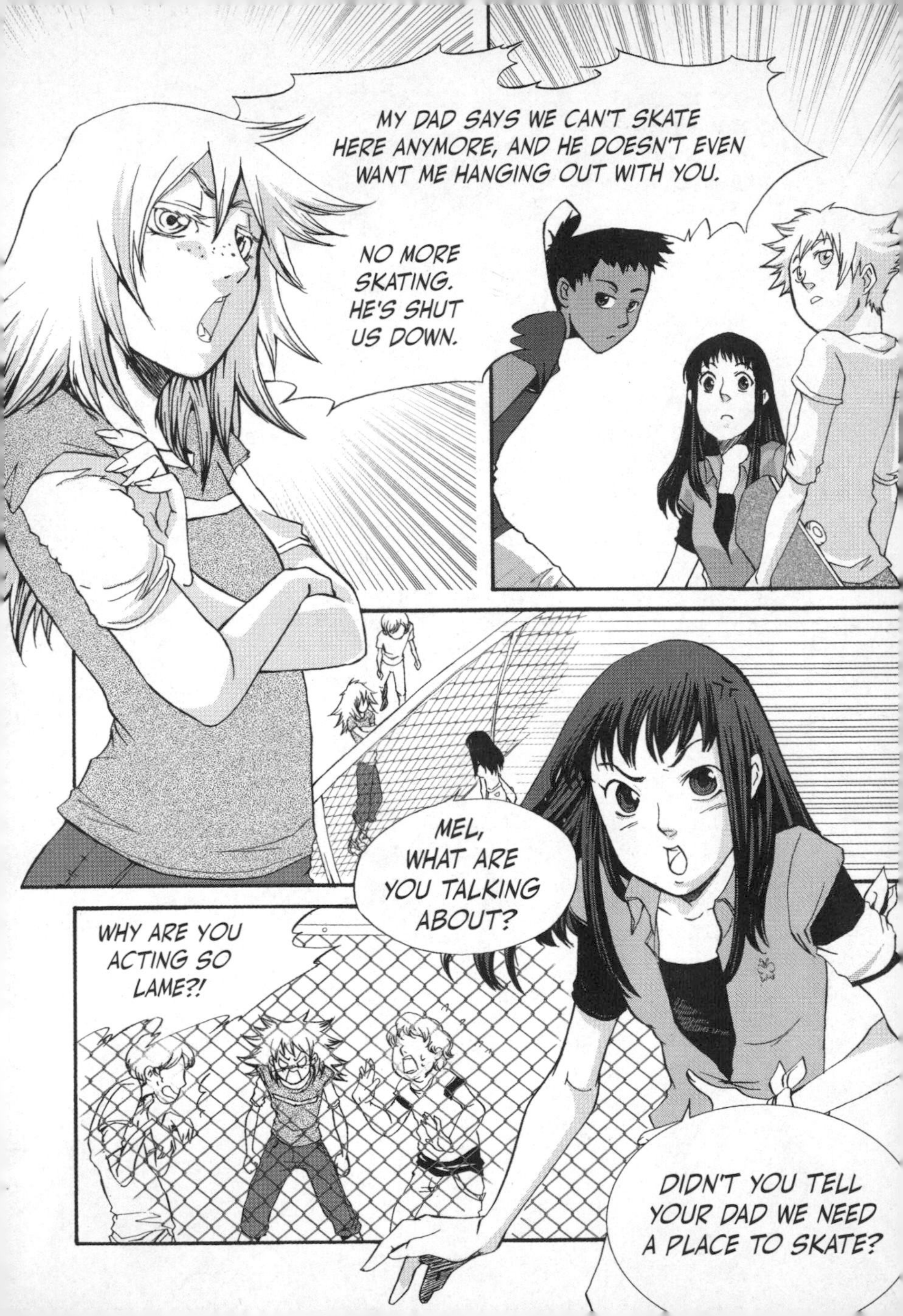
MY DAD SAYS WE CAN'T SKATE HERE ANYMORE, AND HE DOESN'T EVEN WANT ME HANGING OUT WITH YOU.
NO MORE SKATING. HE'S SHUT US DOWN.
MEL, WHAT ARE YOU TALKING ABOUT?
WHY ARE YOU ACTING SO LAME?!
DIDN'T YOU TELL YOUR DAD WE NEED A PLACE TO SKATE?

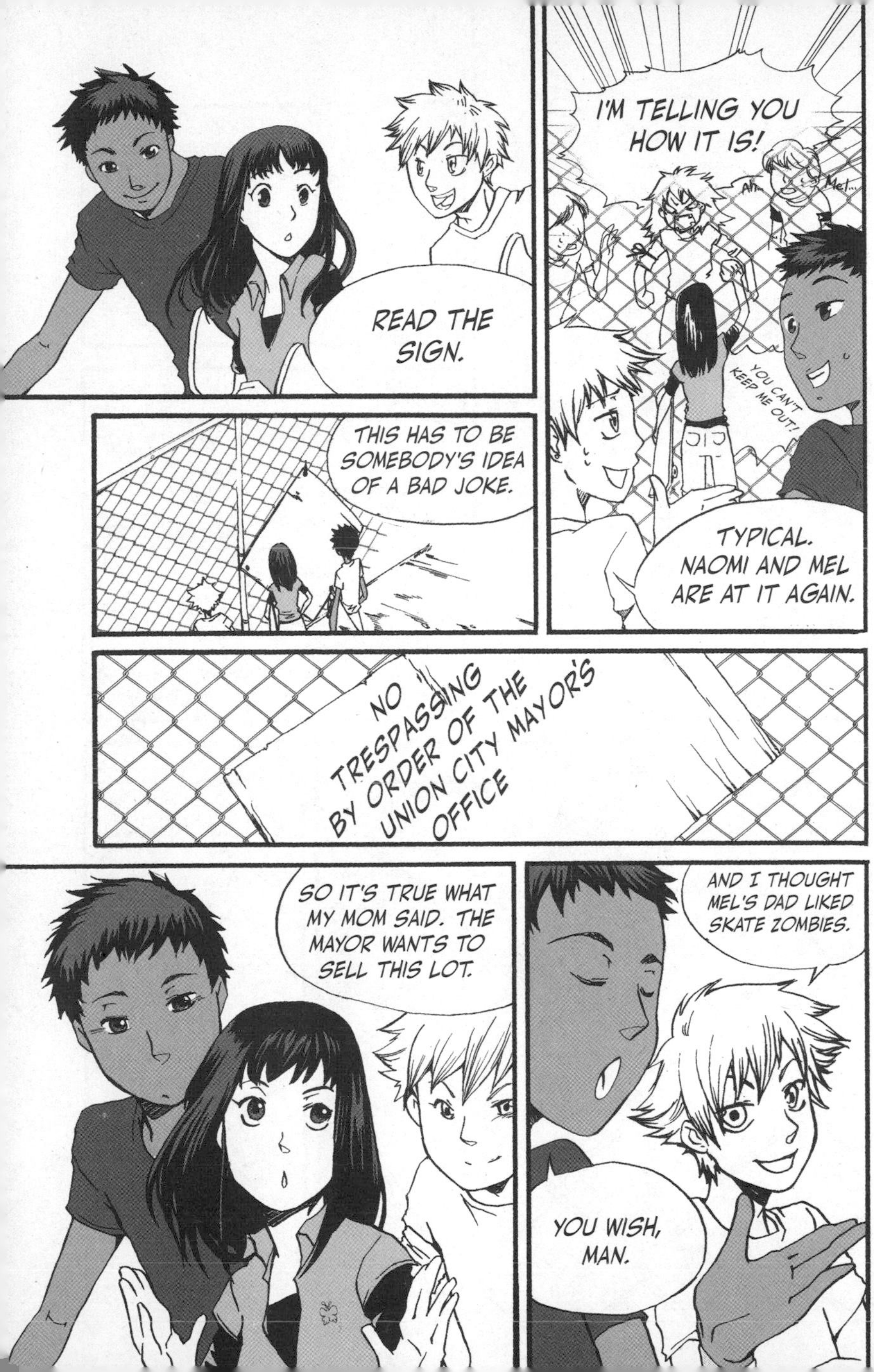
READ THE SIGN.
I'M TELLING YOU HOW IT IS!
Ah...
Mel...
YOU CAN'T KEEP ME OUT!
THIS HAS TO BE SOMEBODY'S IDEA OF A BAD JOKE.
TYPICAL. NAOMI AND MEL ARE AT IT AGAIN.
NO TRESPASSING BY ORDER OF THE UNION CITY MAYOR'S OFFICE
SO IT'S TRUE WHAT MY MOM SAID. THE MAYOR WANTS TO SELL THIS LOT.
AND I THOUGHT MEL'S DAD LIKED SKATE ZOMBIES.
YOU WISH, MAN.

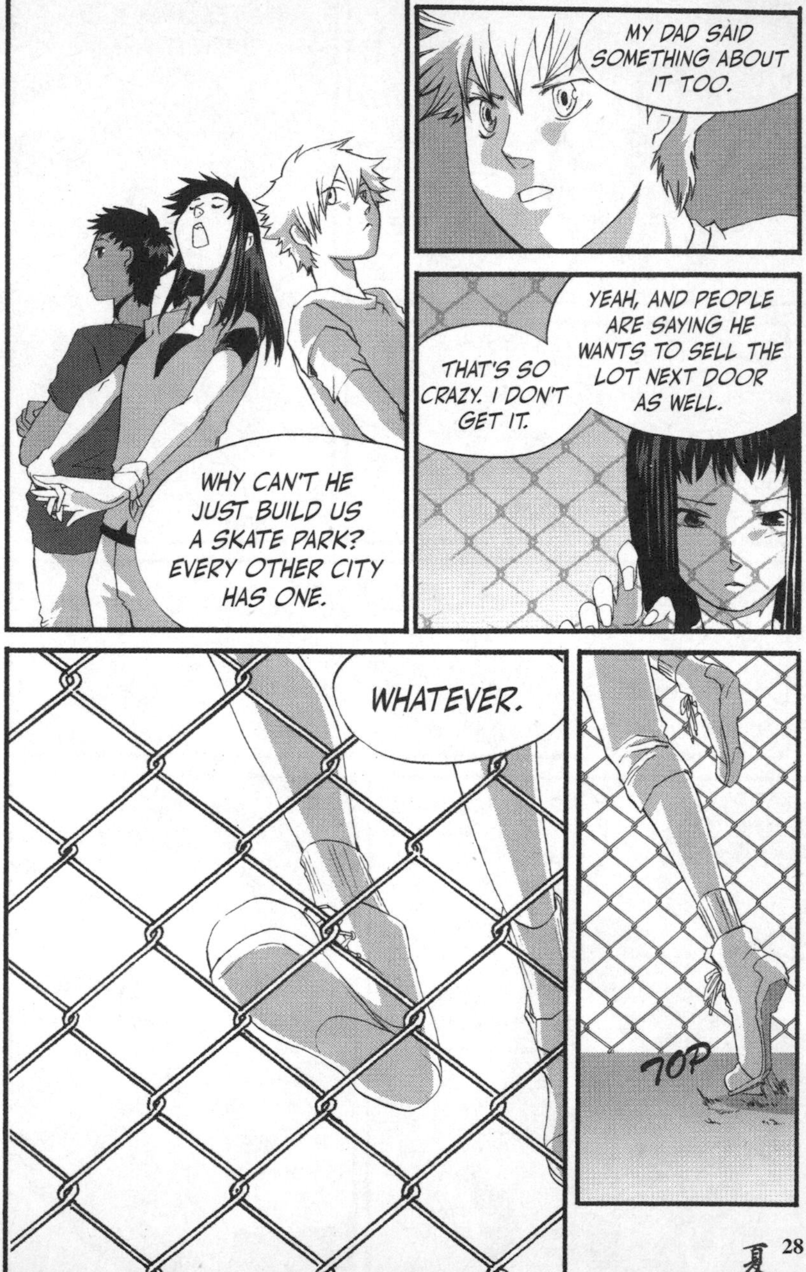

WHY CAN'T HE JUST BUILD US A SKATE PARK? EVERY OTHER CITY HAS ONE.
MY DAD SAID SOMETHING ABOUT IT TOO.
YEAH, AND PEOPLE ARE SAYING HE WANTS TO SELL THE LOT NEXT DOOR AS WELL.
THAT'S SO CRAZY. I DON'T GET IT.
WHATEVER.
TOP

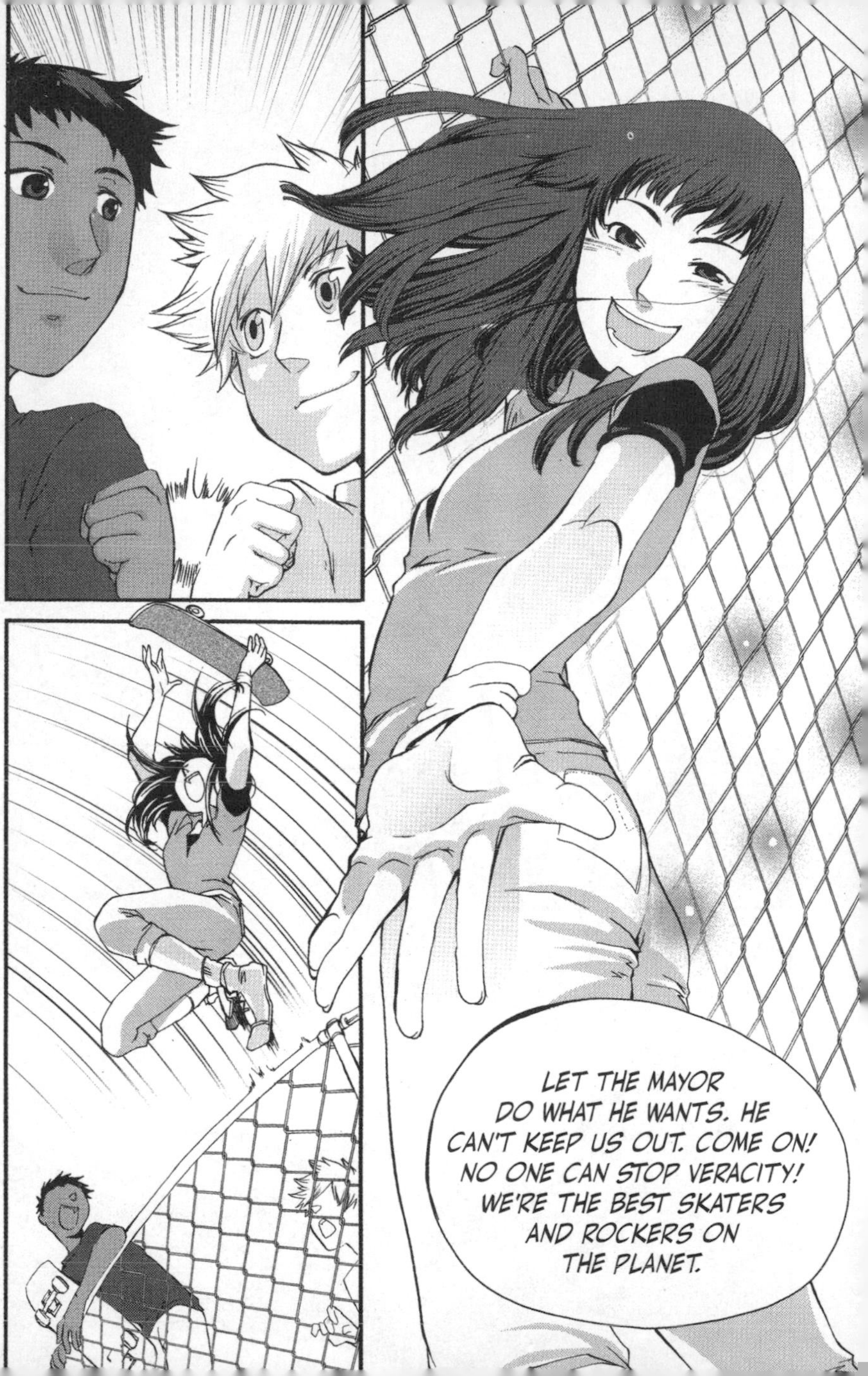
LET THE MAYOR DO WHAT HE WANTS. HE CAN'T KEEP US OUT. COME ON! NO ONE CAN STOP VERACITY! WE'RE THE BEST SKATERS AND ROCKERS ON THE PLANET.

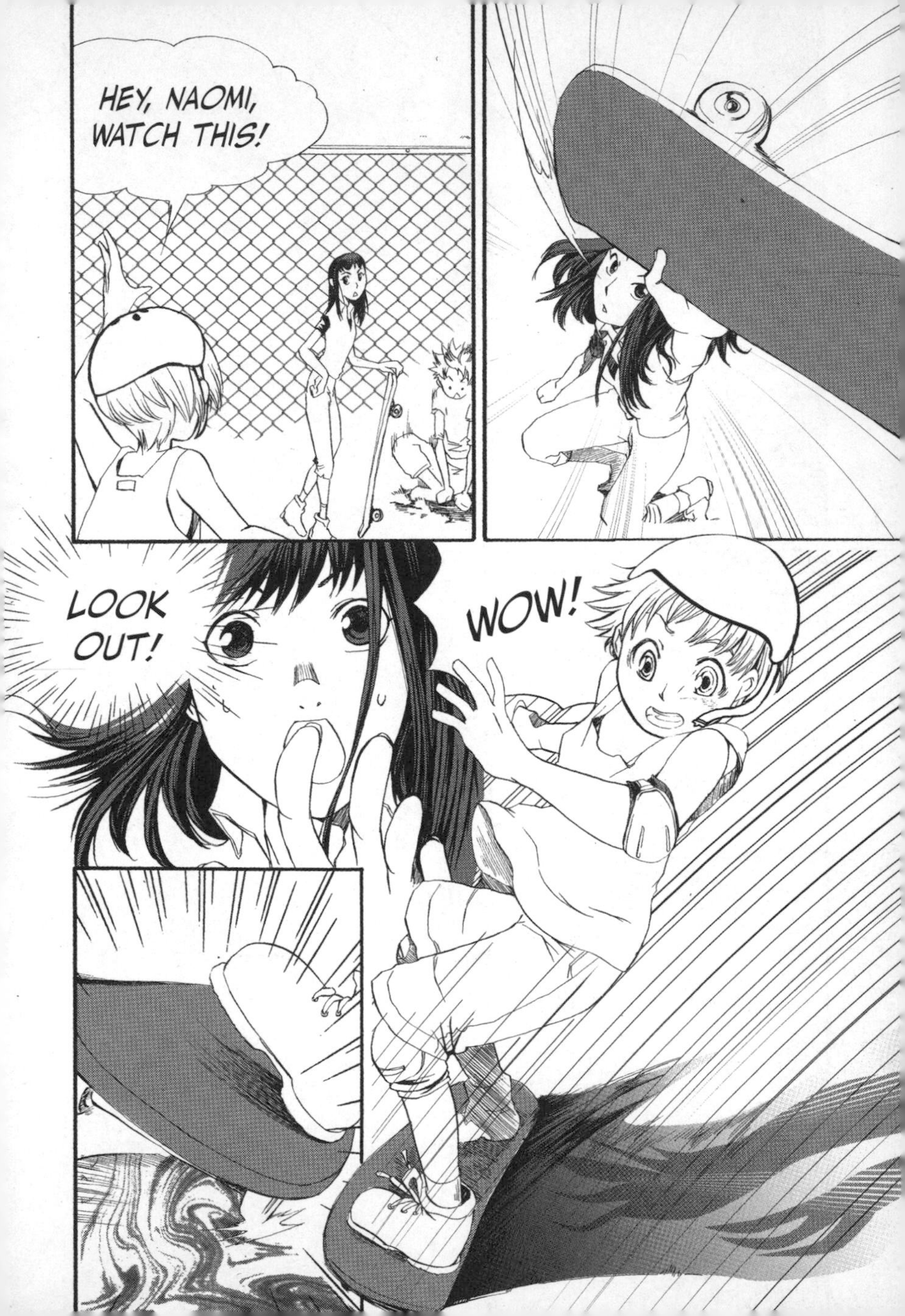
HEY, NAOMI, WATCH THIS!
LOOK OUT!
WOW!

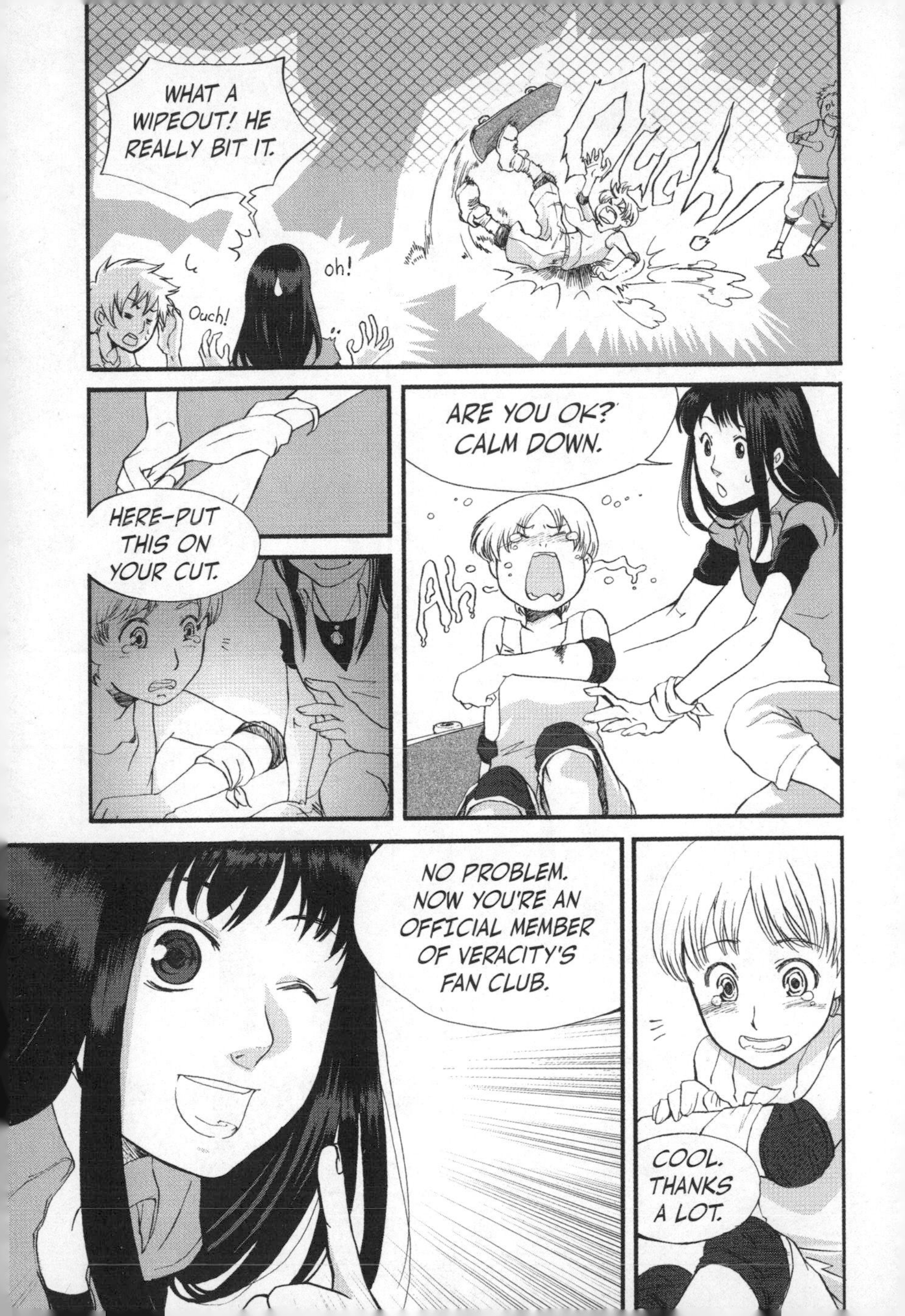
WHAT A WIPEOUT! HE REALLY BIT IT.
Ouch!
oh!
Ouch!
ARE YOU OK? CALM DOWN.
Ah
HERE-PUT THIS ON YOUR CUT.
NO PROBLEM. NOW YOU'RE AN OFFICIAL MEMBER OF VERACITY'S FAN CLUB.
COOL. THANKS A LOT.

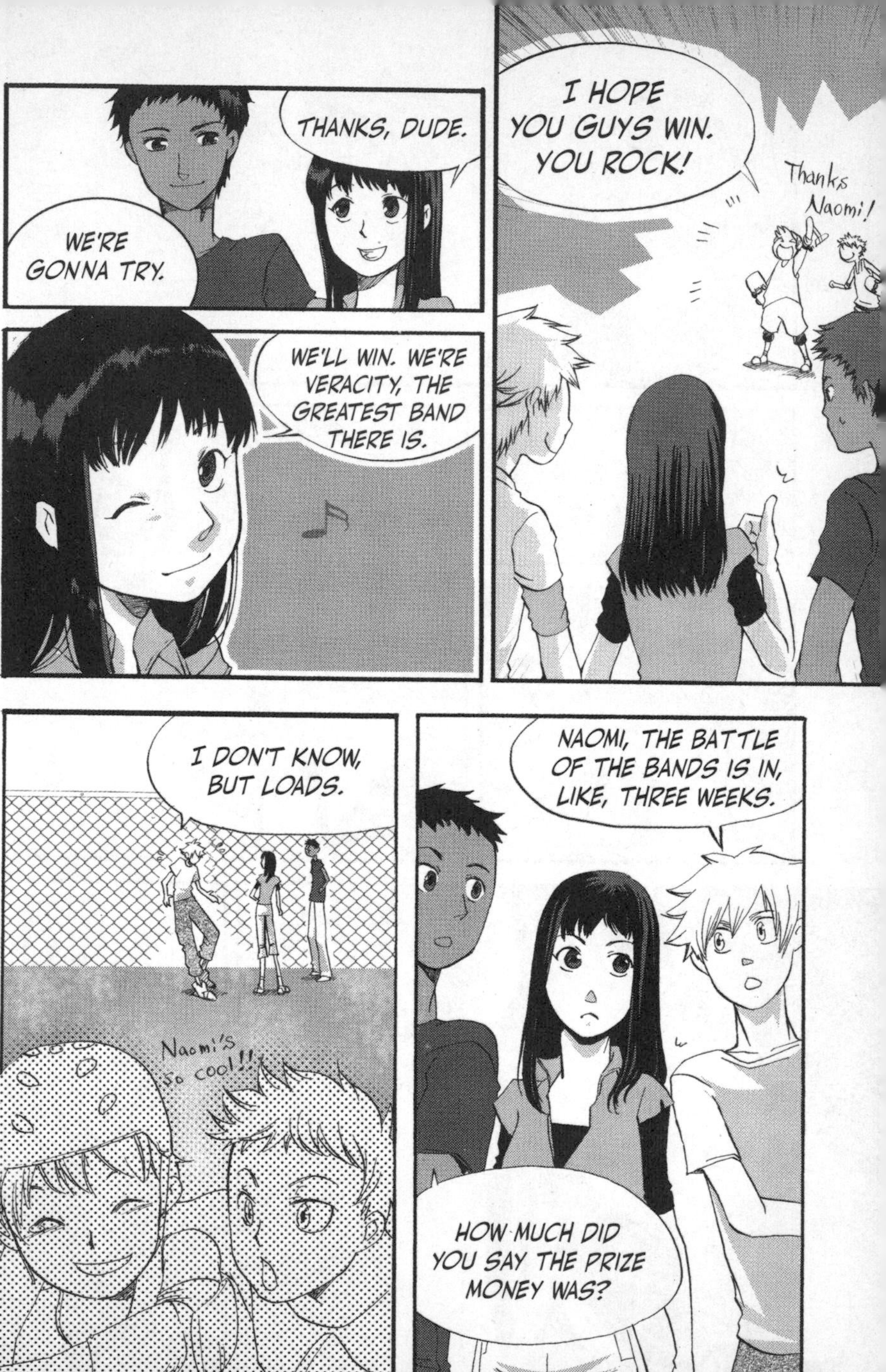
THANKS, DUDE.
WE'RE GONNA TRY.
I HOPE YOU GUYS WIN. YOU ROCK!
Thanks Naomi!
WE'LL WIN. WE'RE VERACITY, THE GREATEST BAND THERE IS.
I DON'T KNOW, BUT LOADS.
Naomi's so cool!!
NAOMI, THE BATTLE OF THE BANDS IS IN, LIKE, THREE WEEKS.
HOW MUCH DID YOU SAY THE PRIZE MONEY WAS?

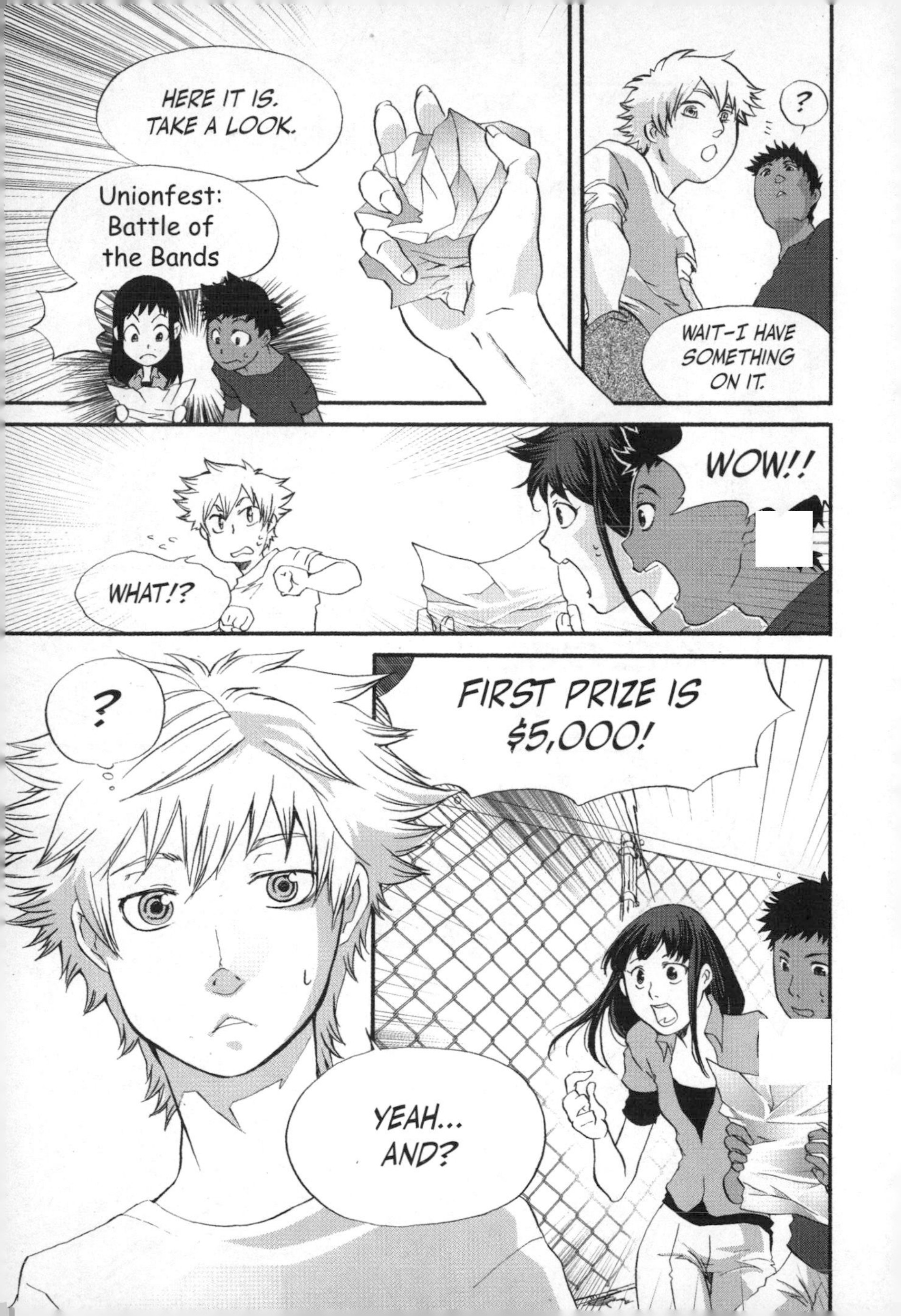

HERE IT IS.
TAKE A LOOK.
Unionfest: Battle of the Bands
?
WAIT—I HAVE SOMETHING ON IT.
WOW!!
WHAT!?
FIRST PRIZE IS $5,000!
?
YEAH... AND?

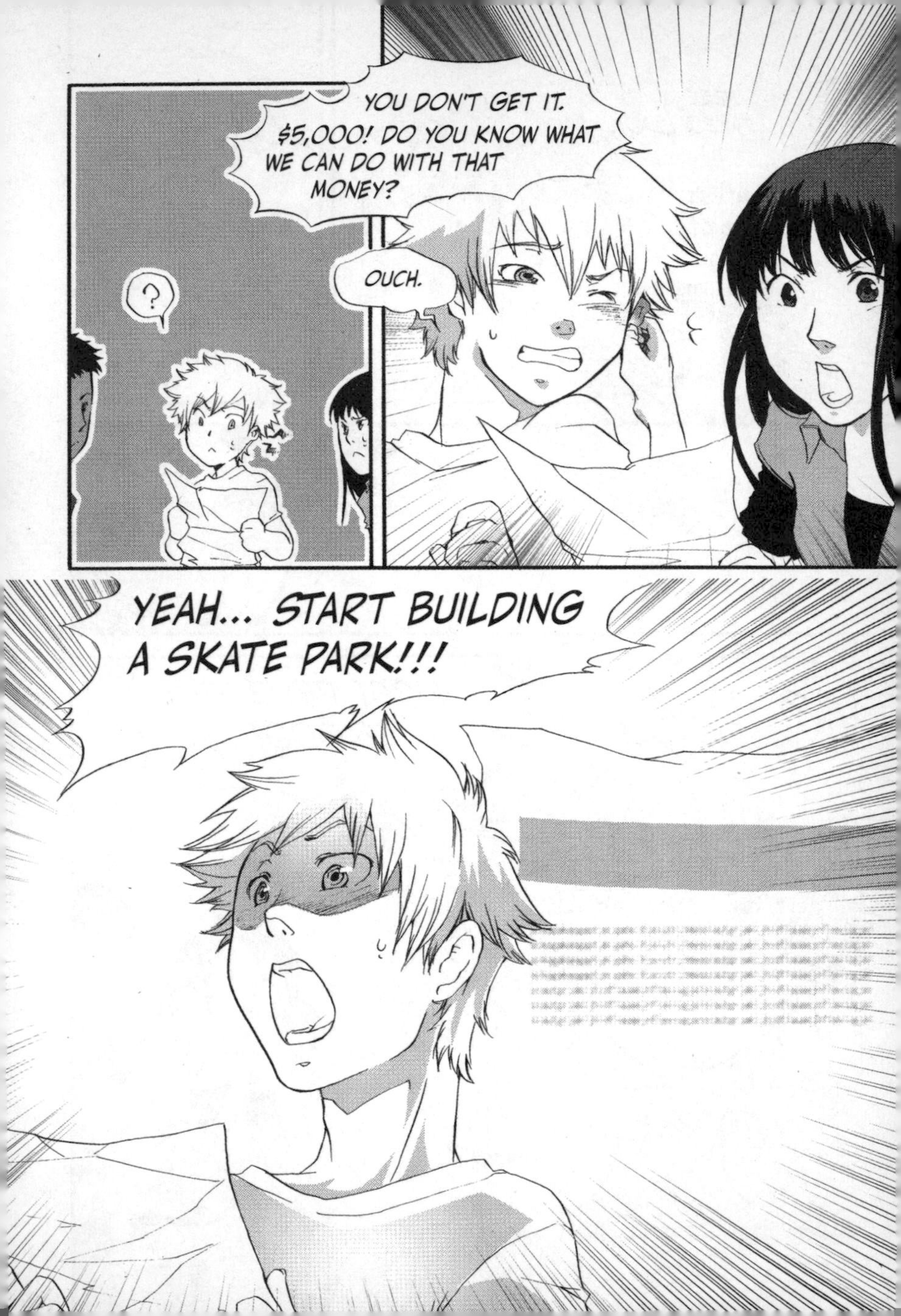
YOU DON'T GET IT. $5,000! DO YOU KNOW WHAT WE CAN DO WITH THAT MONEY?
OUCH.
?
YEAH... START BUILDING A SKATE PARK!!!

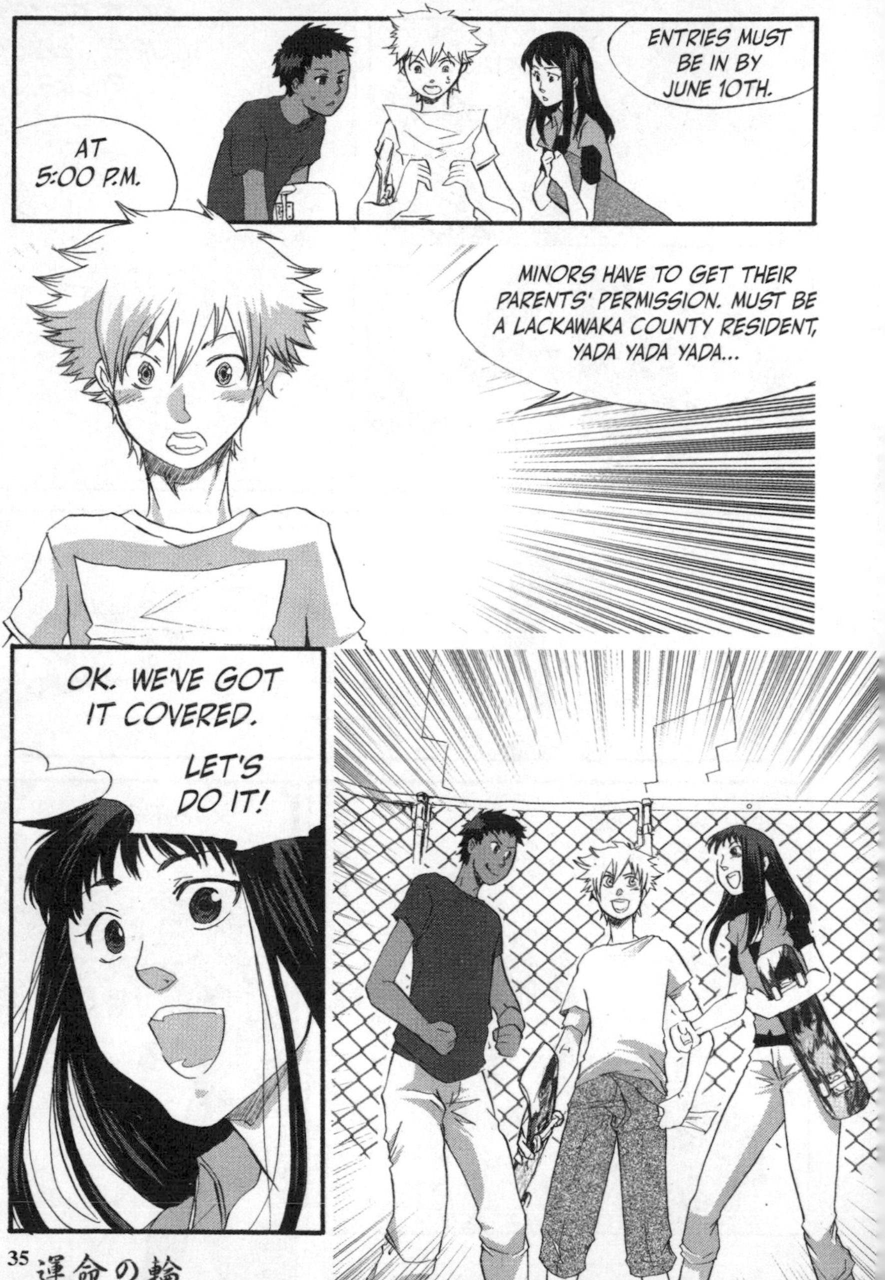
ENTRIES MUST BE IN BY JUNE 10TH.
AT 5:00 P.M.
MINORS HAVE TO GET THEIR PARENTS' PERMISSION. MUST BE A LACKAWAKA COUNTY RESIDENT, YADA YADA YADA...
OK. WE'VE GOT IT COVERED.
LET'S DO IT!

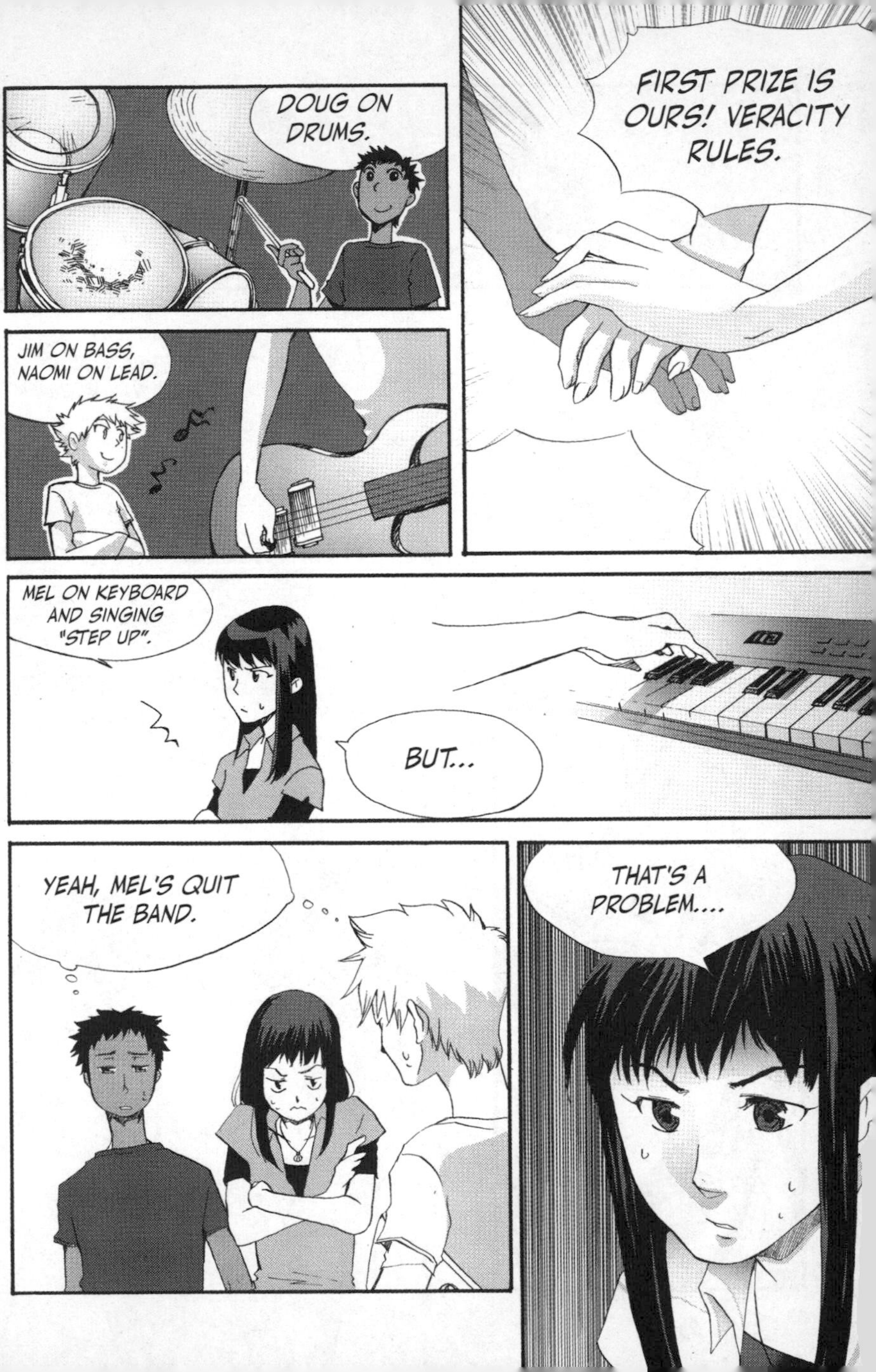
DOUG ON DRUMS.
JIM ON BASS, NAOMI ON LEAD.
FIRST PRIZE IS OURS! VERACITY RULES.
MEL ON KEYBOARD AND SINGING "STEP UP".
BUT...
YEAH, MEL'S QUIT THE BAND.
THAT'S A PROBLEM....

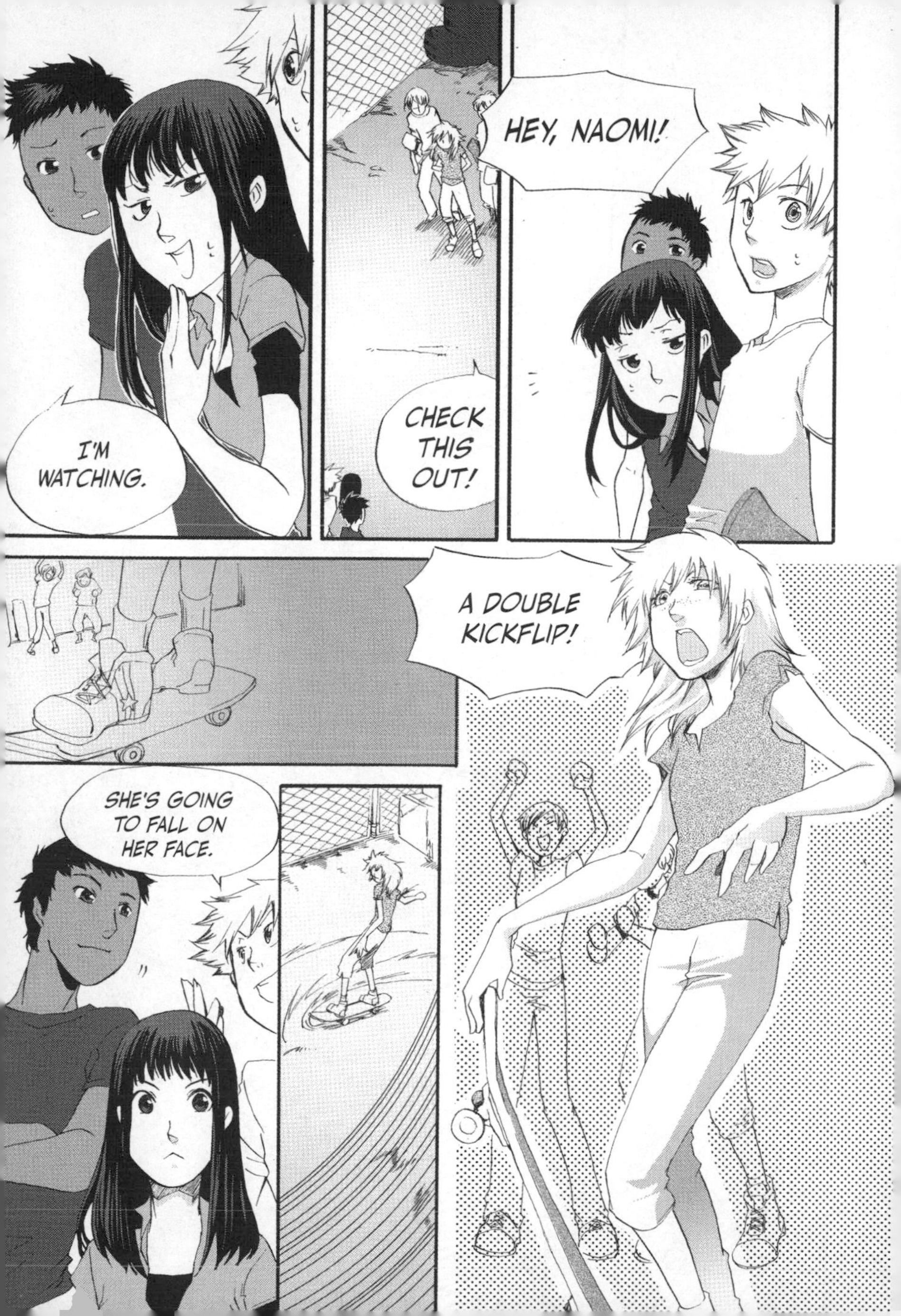
I'M WATCHING.
CHECK THIS OUT!
HEY, NAOMI!
A DOUBLE KICKFLIP!
SHE'S GOING TO FALL ON HER FACE.

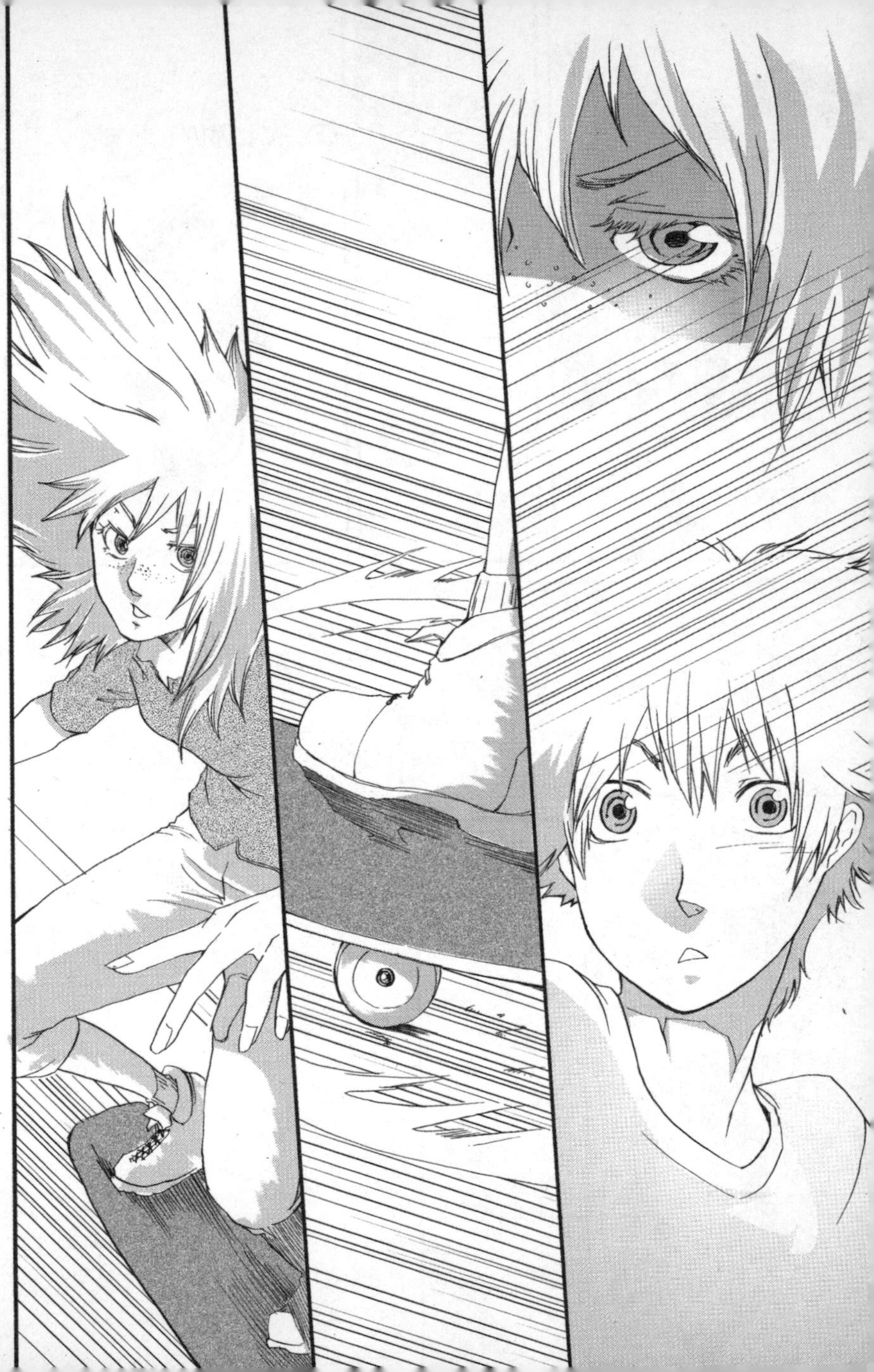

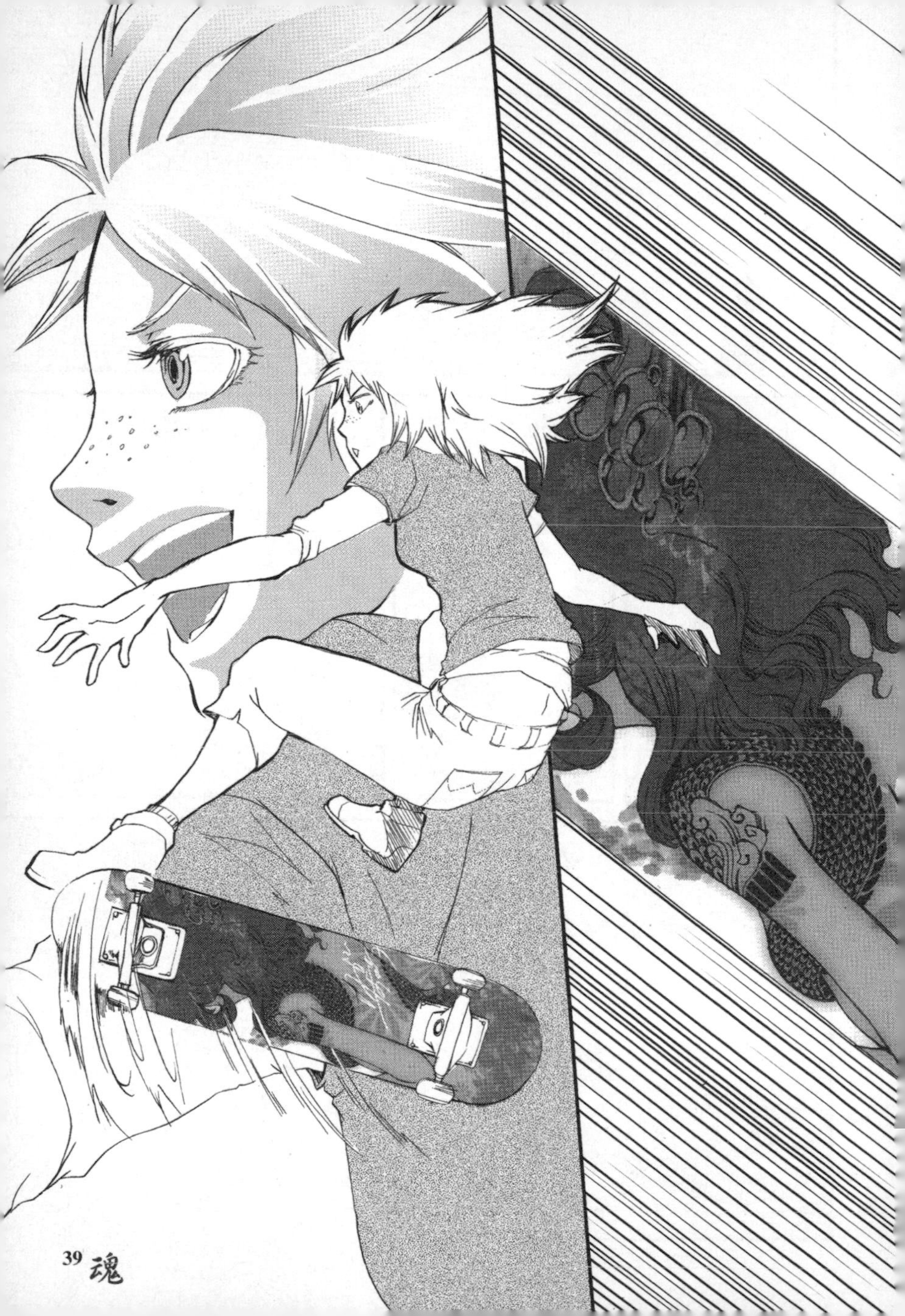

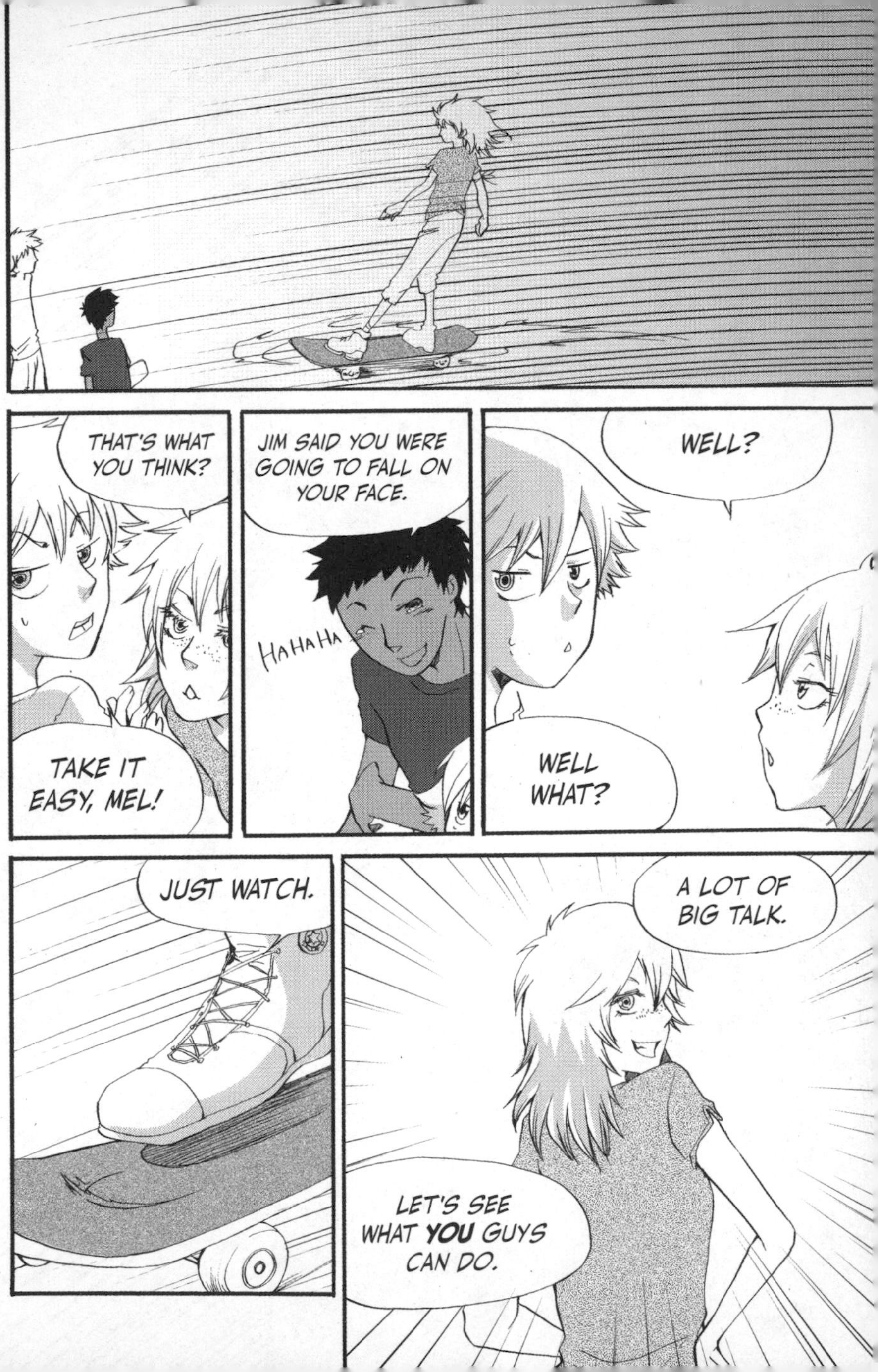
THAT'S WHAT YOU THINK?
TAKE IT EASY, MEL!
JIM SAID YOU WERE GOING TO FALL ON YOUR FACE.
HAHAHA
WELL?
WELL WHAT?
JUST WATCH.
A LOT OF BIG TALK.
LET'S SEE WHAT **YOU** GUYS CAN DO.

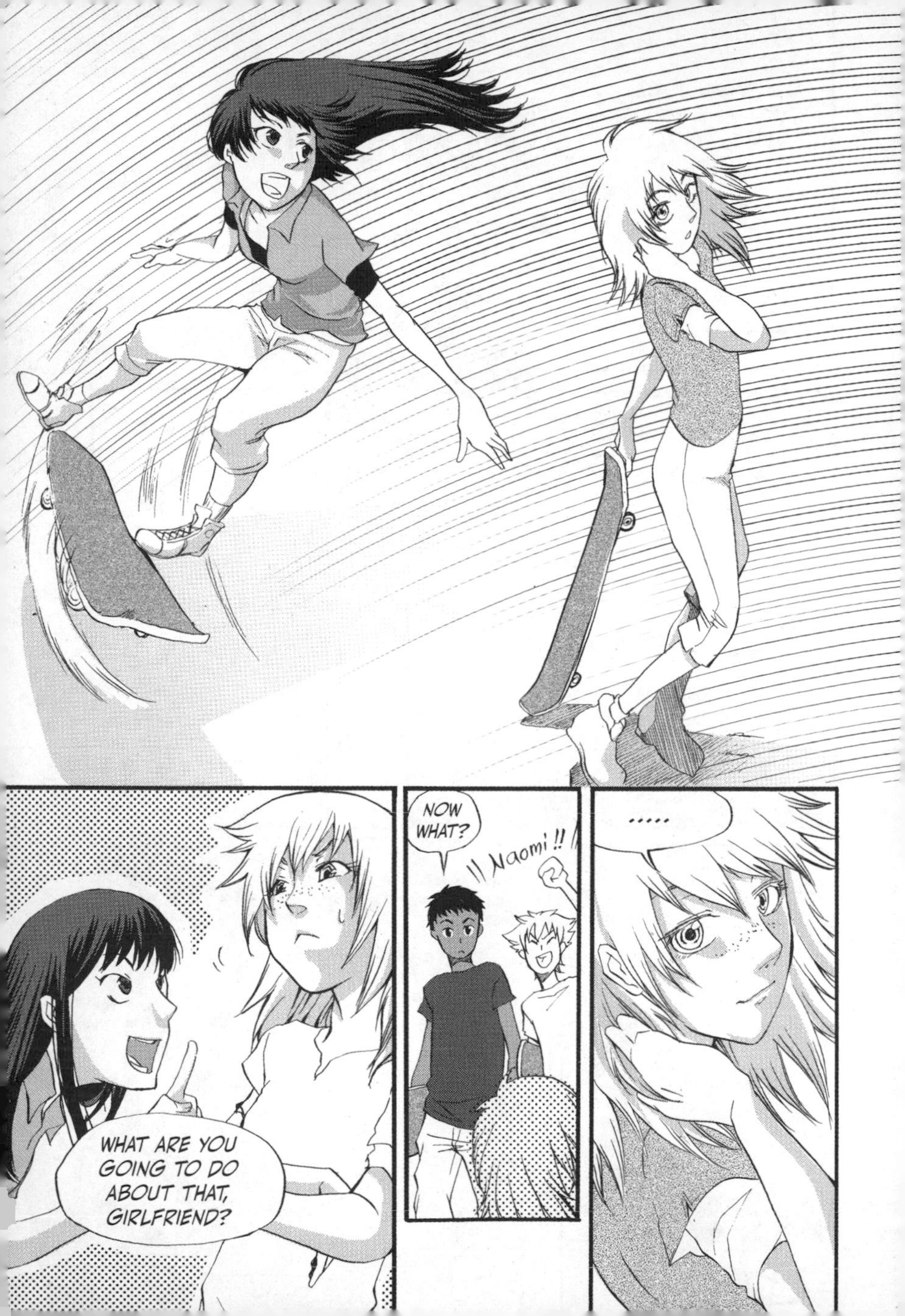
NOW WHAT?
Naomi!!
.....
WHAT ARE YOU GOING TO DO ABOUT THAT, GIRLFRIEND?

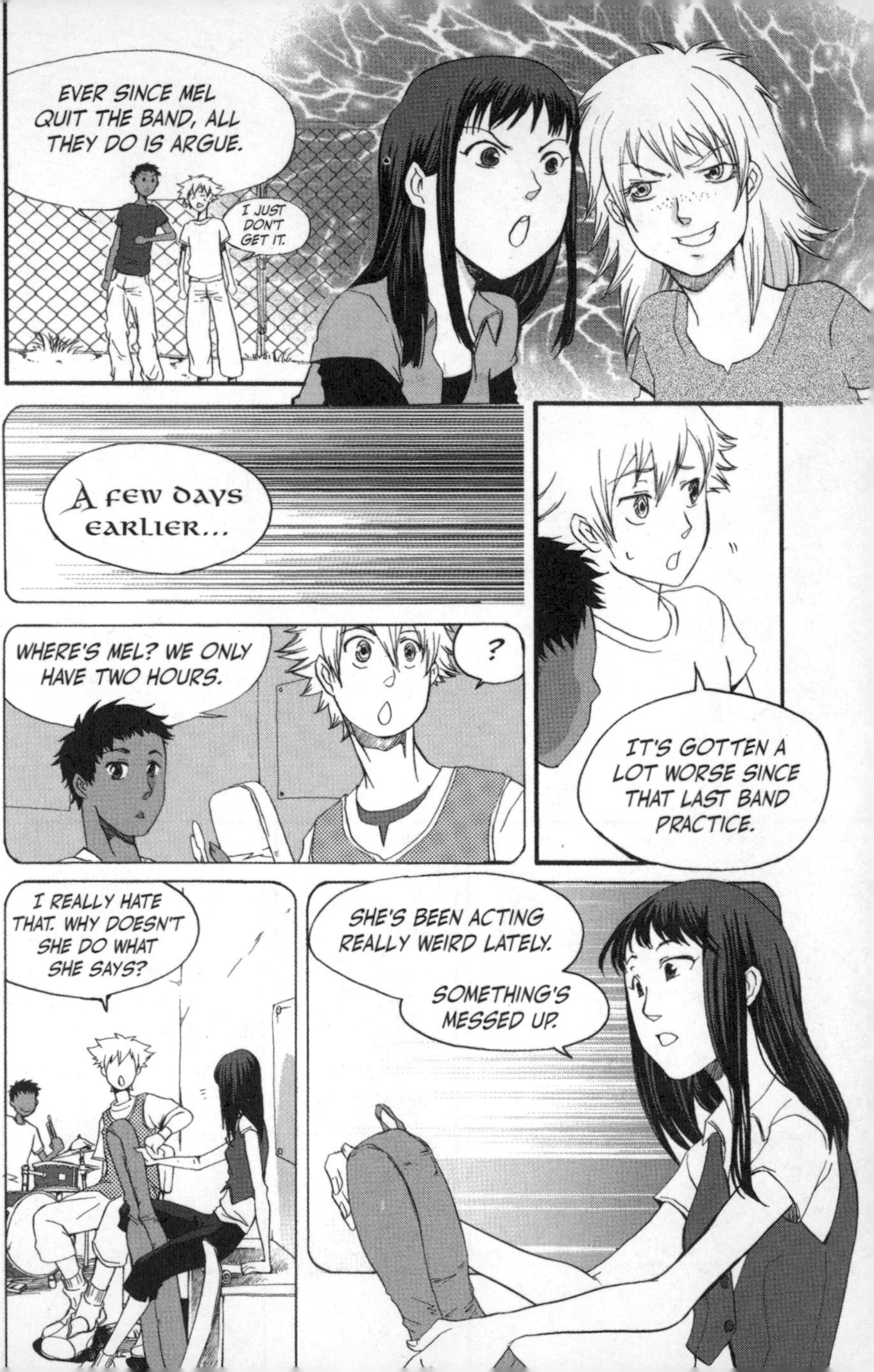
EVER SINCE MEL QUIT THE BAND, ALL THEY DO IS ARGUE.
I JUST DON'T GET IT.
A FEW DAYS EARLIER...
WHERE'S MEL? WE ONLY HAVE TWO HOURS.
?
IT'S GOTTEN A LOT WORSE SINCE THAT LAST BAND PRACTICE.
I REALLY HATE THAT. WHY DOESN'T SHE DO WHAT SHE SAYS?
SHE'S BEEN ACTING REALLY WEIRD LATELY.
SOMETHING'S MESSED UP.

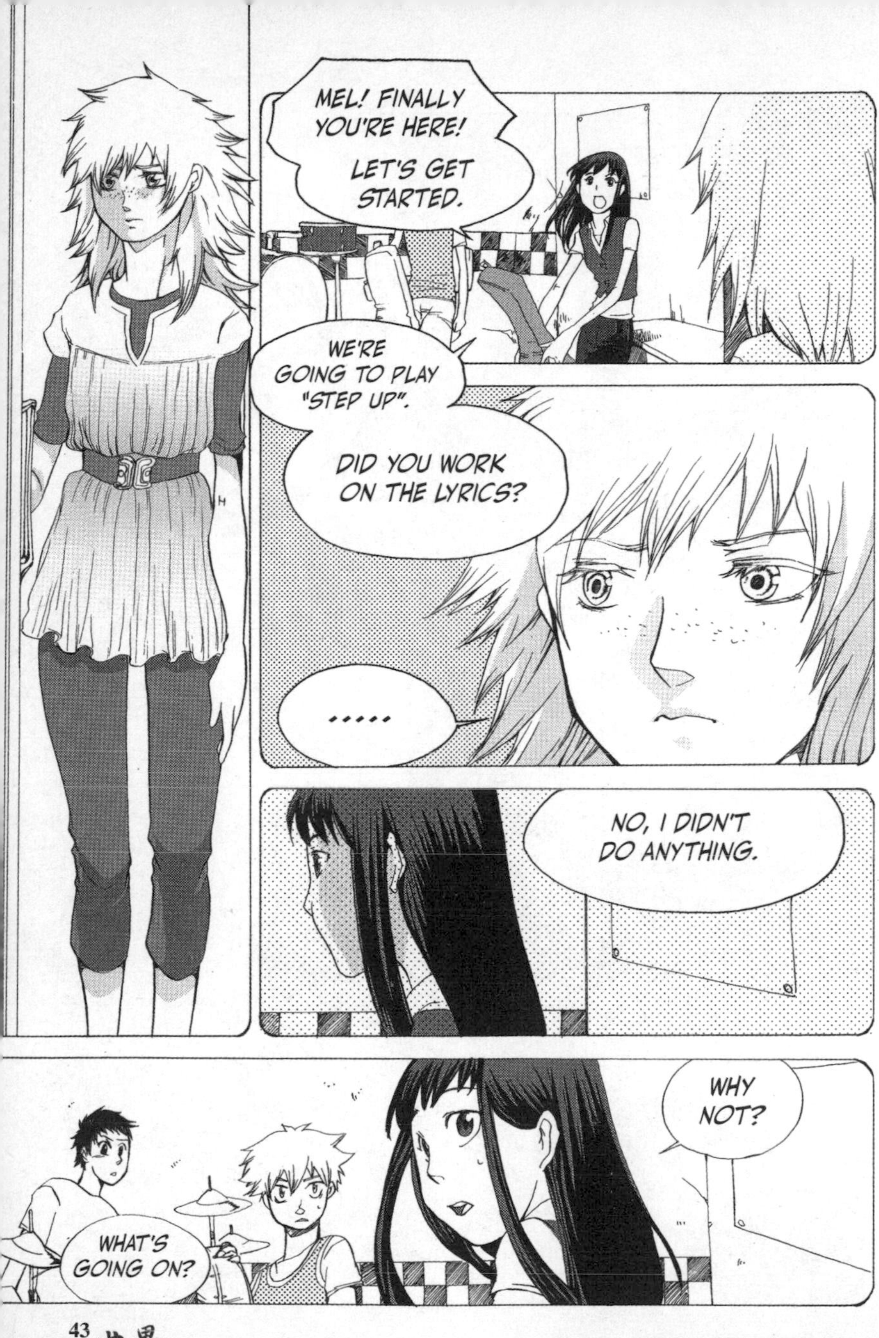
MEL! FINALLY YOU'RE HERE!
LET'S GET STARTED.
WE'RE GOING TO PLAY "STEP UP".
DID YOU WORK ON THE LYRICS?
.....
NO, I DIDN'T DO ANYTHING.
WHY NOT?
WHAT'S GOING ON?

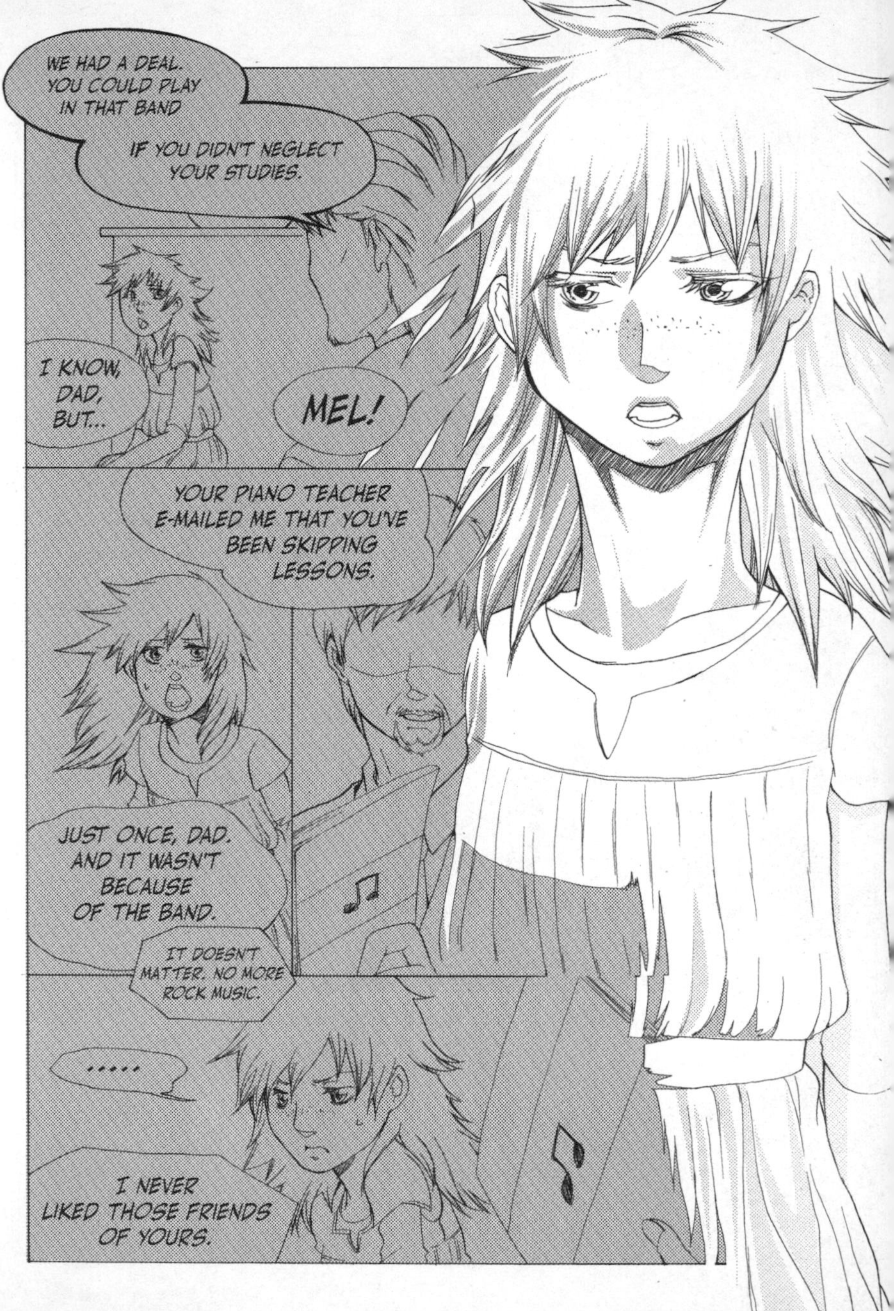

WE HAD A DEAL. YOU COULD PLAY IN THAT BAND
IF YOU DIDN'T NEGLECT YOUR STUDIES.
I KNOW, DAD, BUT...
MEL!
YOUR PIANO TEACHER E-MAILED ME THAT YOU'VE BEEN SKIPPING LESSONS.
JUST ONCE, DAD. AND IT WASN'T BECAUSE OF THE BAND.
IT DOESN'T MATTER. NO MORE ROCK MUSIC.
.....
I NEVER LIKED THOSE FRIENDS OF YOURS.

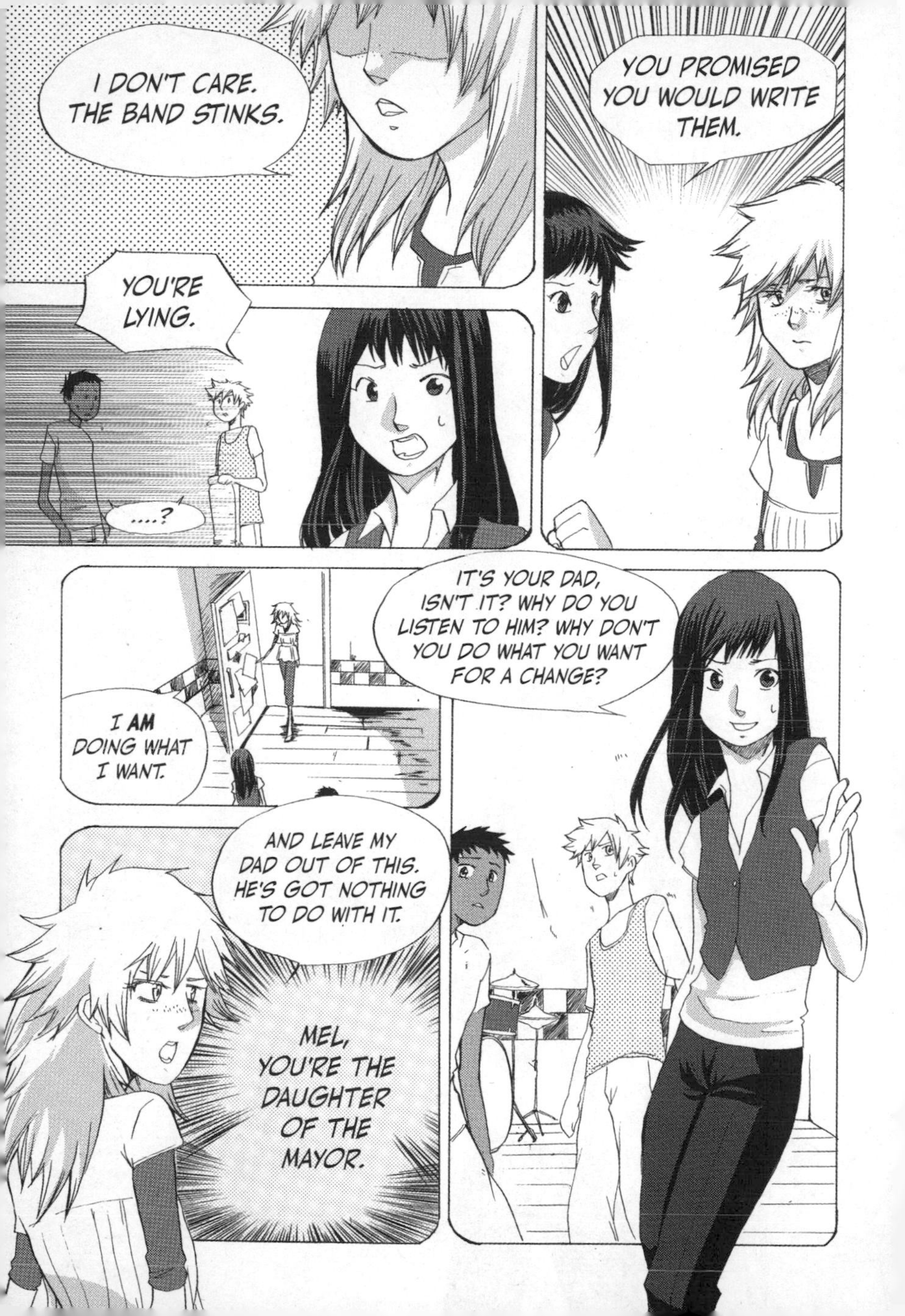
I DON'T CARE. THE BAND STINKS.
YOU PROMISED YOU WOULD WRITE THEM.
YOU'RE LYING.
....?
IT'S YOUR DAD, ISN'T IT? WHY DO YOU LISTEN TO HIM? WHY DON'T YOU DO WHAT YOU WANT FOR A CHANGE?
I **AM** DOING WHAT I WANT.
AND LEAVE MY DAD OUT OF THIS. HE'S GOT NOTHING TO DO WITH IT.
MEL, YOU'RE THE DAUGHTER OF THE MAYOR.

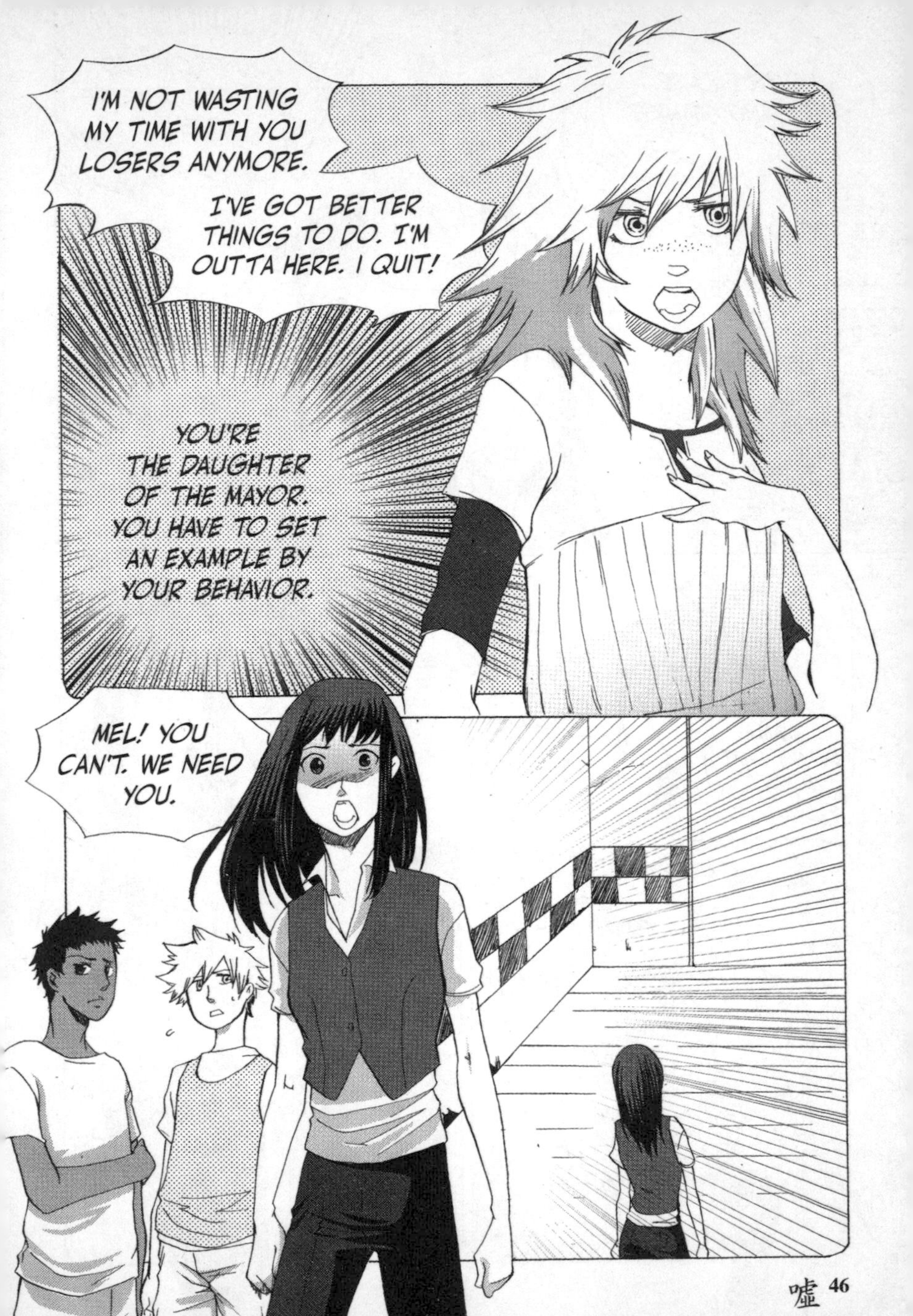
I'M NOT WASTING MY TIME WITH YOU LOSERS ANYMORE.
I'VE GOT BETTER THINGS TO DO. I'M OUTTA HERE. I QUIT!
YOU'RE THE DAUGHTER OF THE MAYOR. YOU HAVE TO SET AN EXAMPLE BY YOUR BEHAVIOR.
MEL! YOU CAN'T. WE NEED YOU.

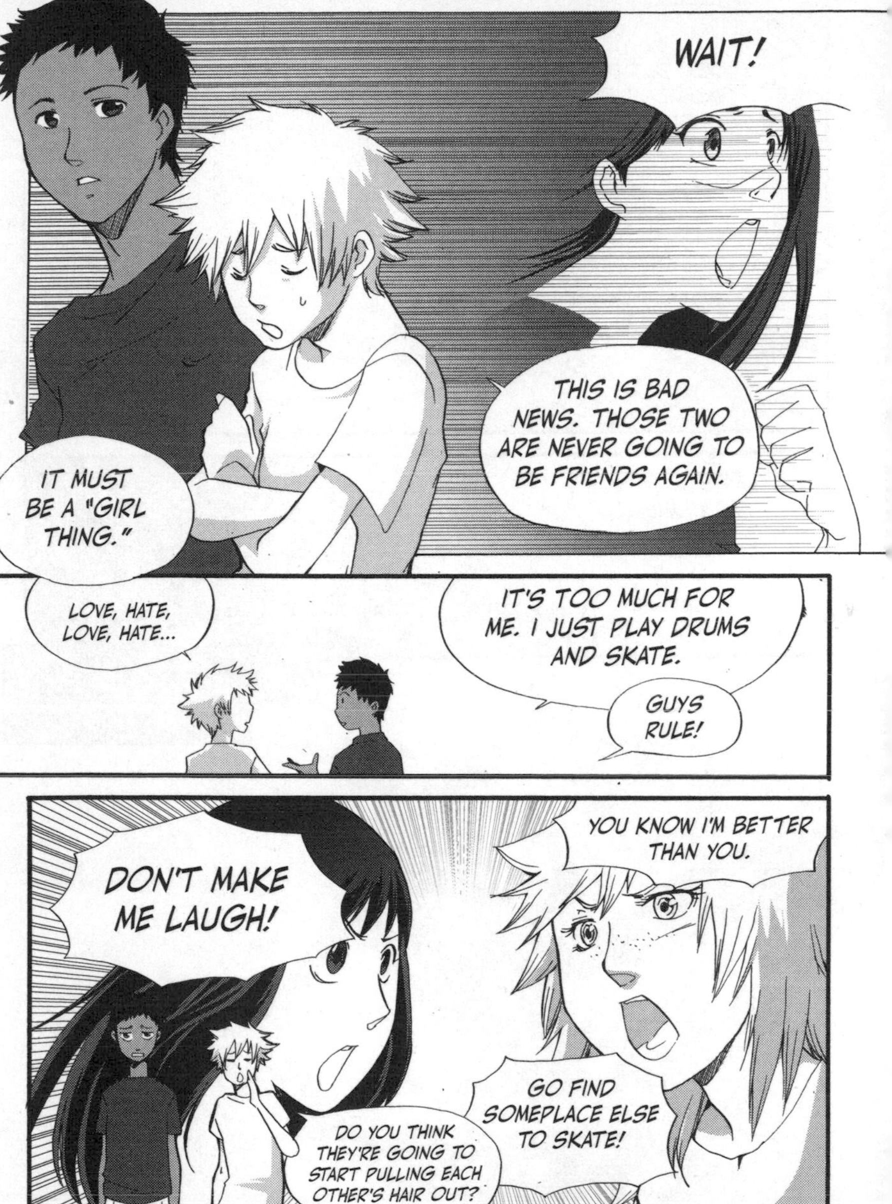
WAIT!
IT MUST BE A "GIRL THING."
THIS IS BAD NEWS. THOSE TWO ARE NEVER GOING TO BE FRIENDS AGAIN.
LOVE, HATE, LOVE, HATE...
IT'S TOO MUCH FOR ME. I JUST PLAY DRUMS AND SKATE.
GUYS RULE!
YOU KNOW I'M BETTER THAN YOU.
DON'T MAKE ME LAUGH!
GO FIND SOMEPLACE ELSE TO SKATE!
DO YOU THINK THEY'RE GOING TO START PULLING EACH OTHER'S HAIR OUT?

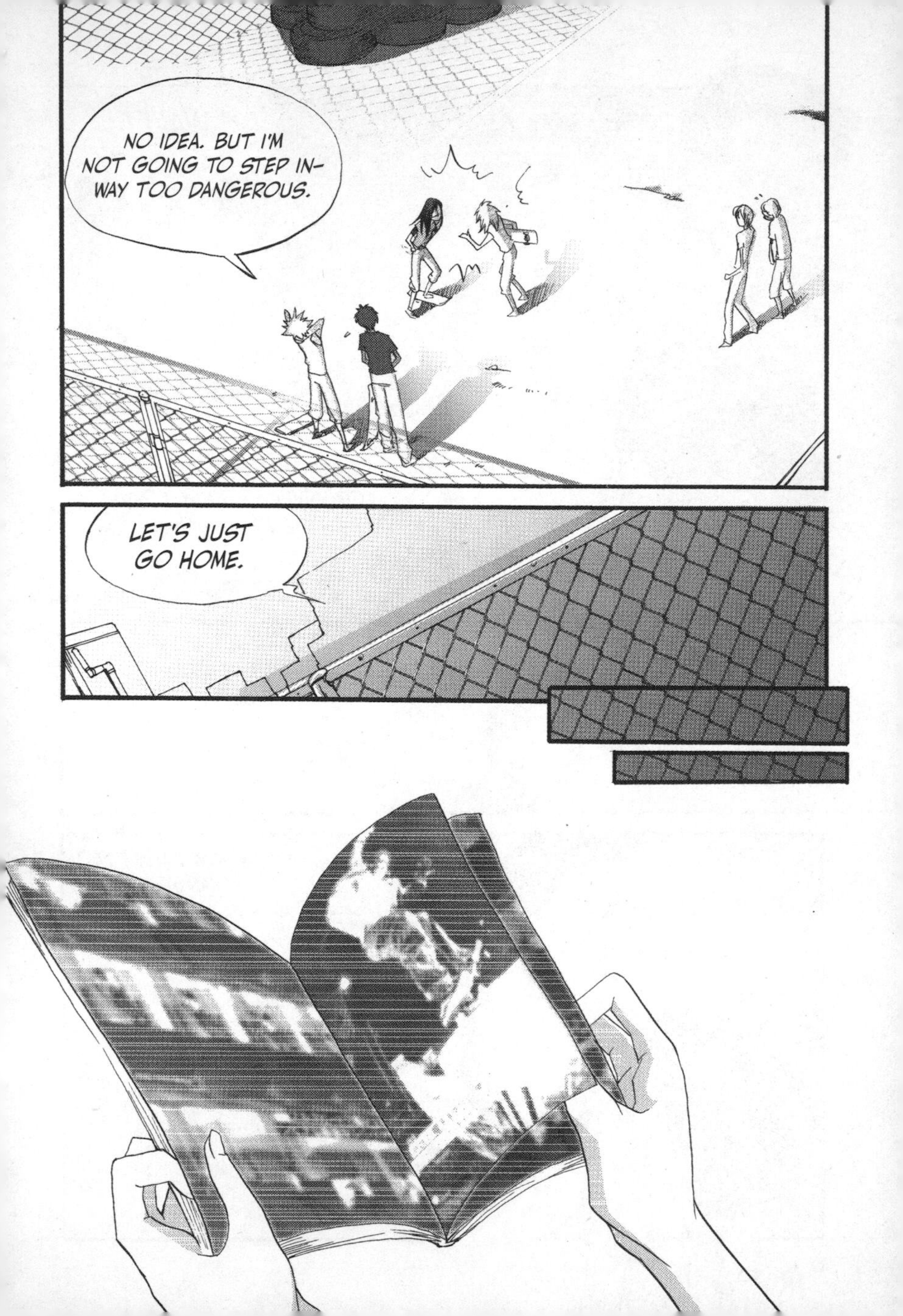
NO IDEA. BUT I'M NOT GOING TO STEP IN— WAY TOO DANGEROUS.
LET'S JUST GO HOME.

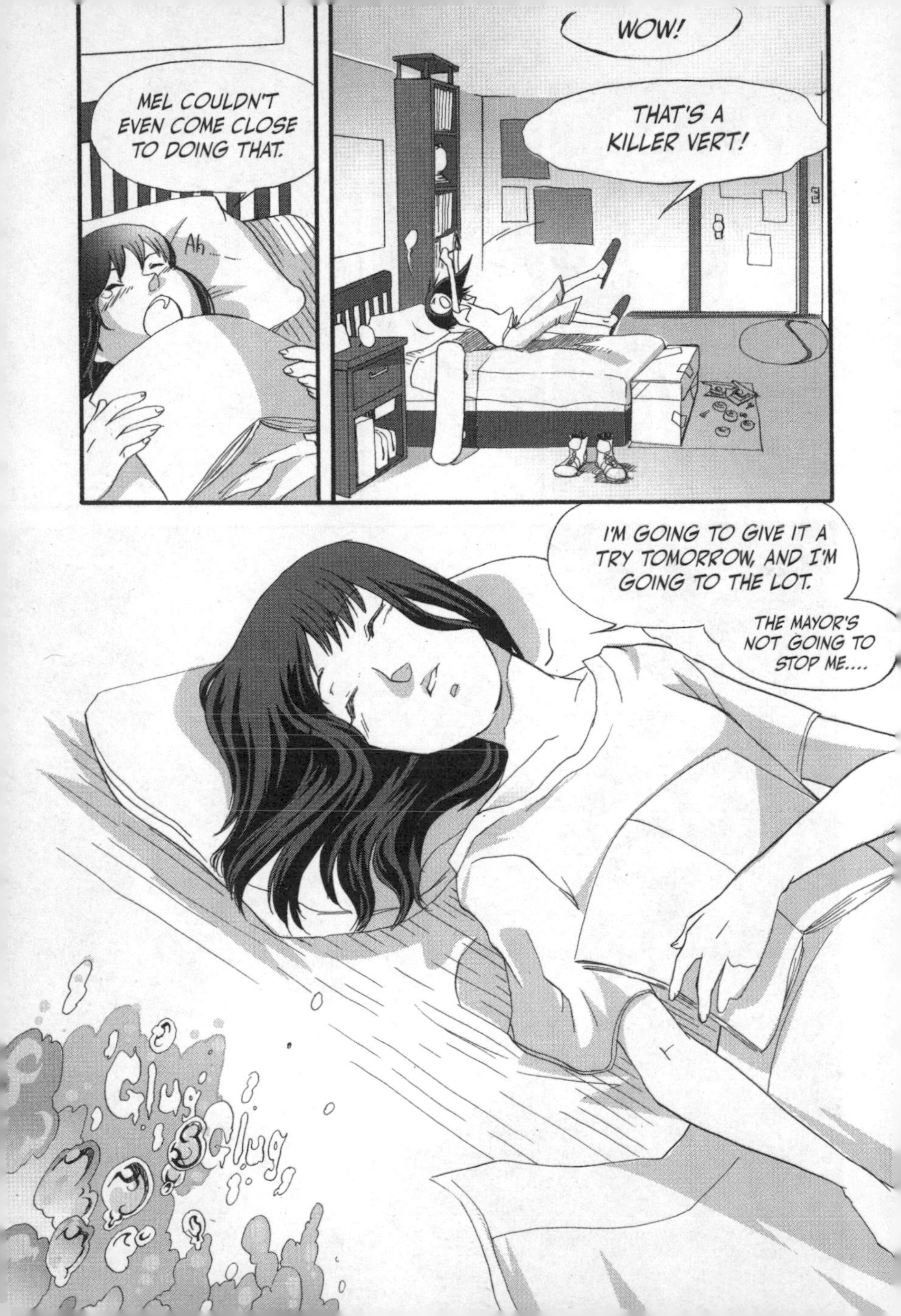
MEL COULDN'T EVEN COME CLOSE TO DOING THAT.
Ah...
WOW!
THAT'S A KILLER VERT!
I'M GOING TO GIVE IT A TRY TOMORROW, AND I'M GOING TO THE LOT.
THE MAYOR'S NOT GOING TO STOP ME....
Glug Glug

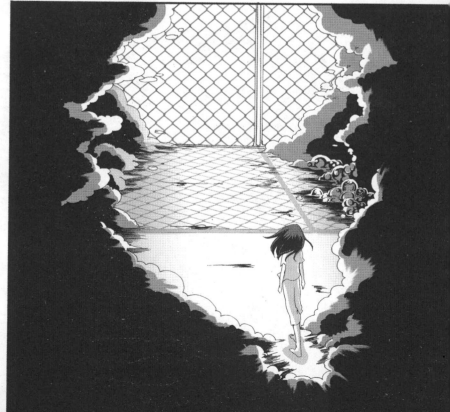

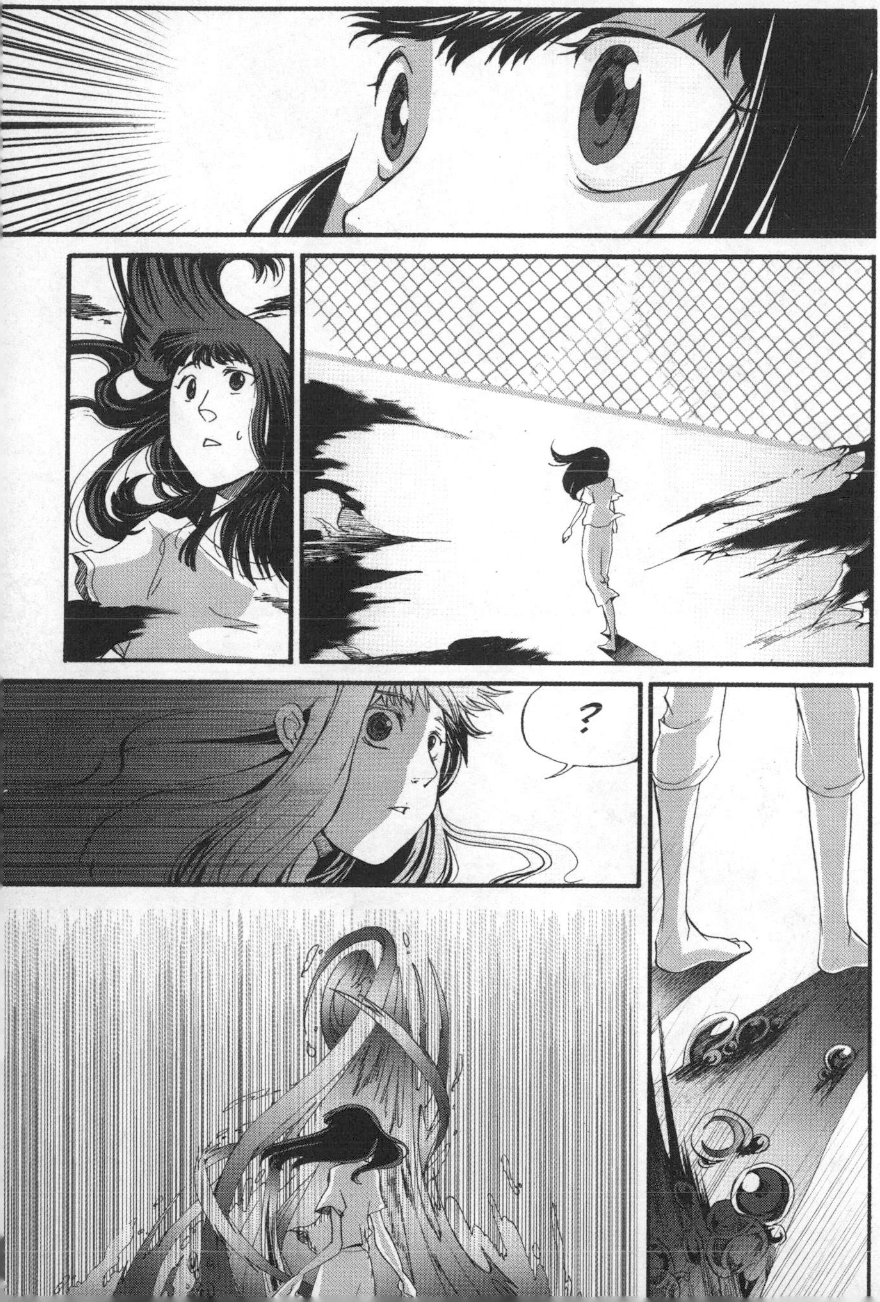
?

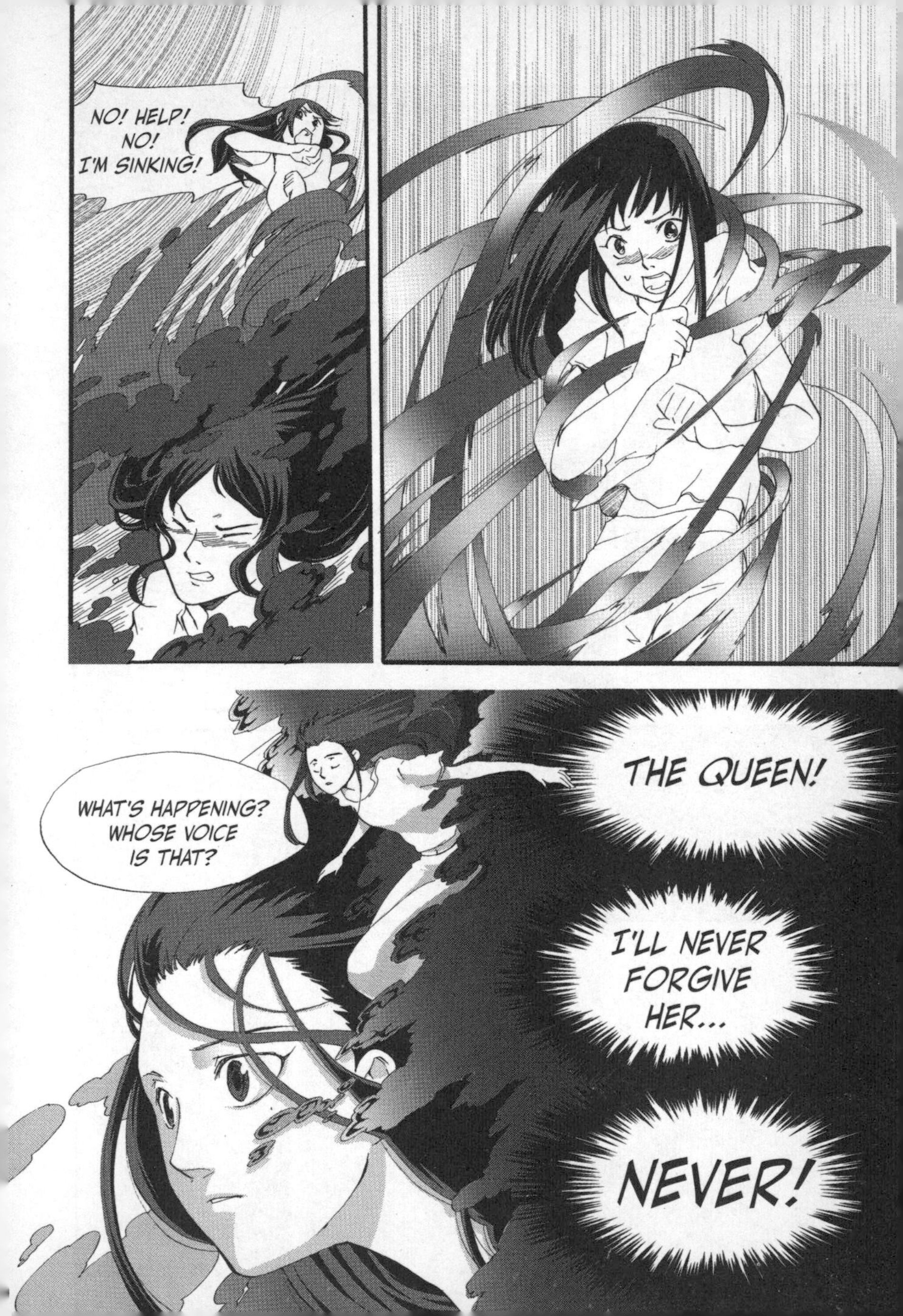
NO! HELP! NO! I'M SINKING!
WHAT'S HAPPENING? WHOSE VOICE IS THAT?
THE QUEEN!
I'LL NEVER FORGIVE HER...
NEVER!

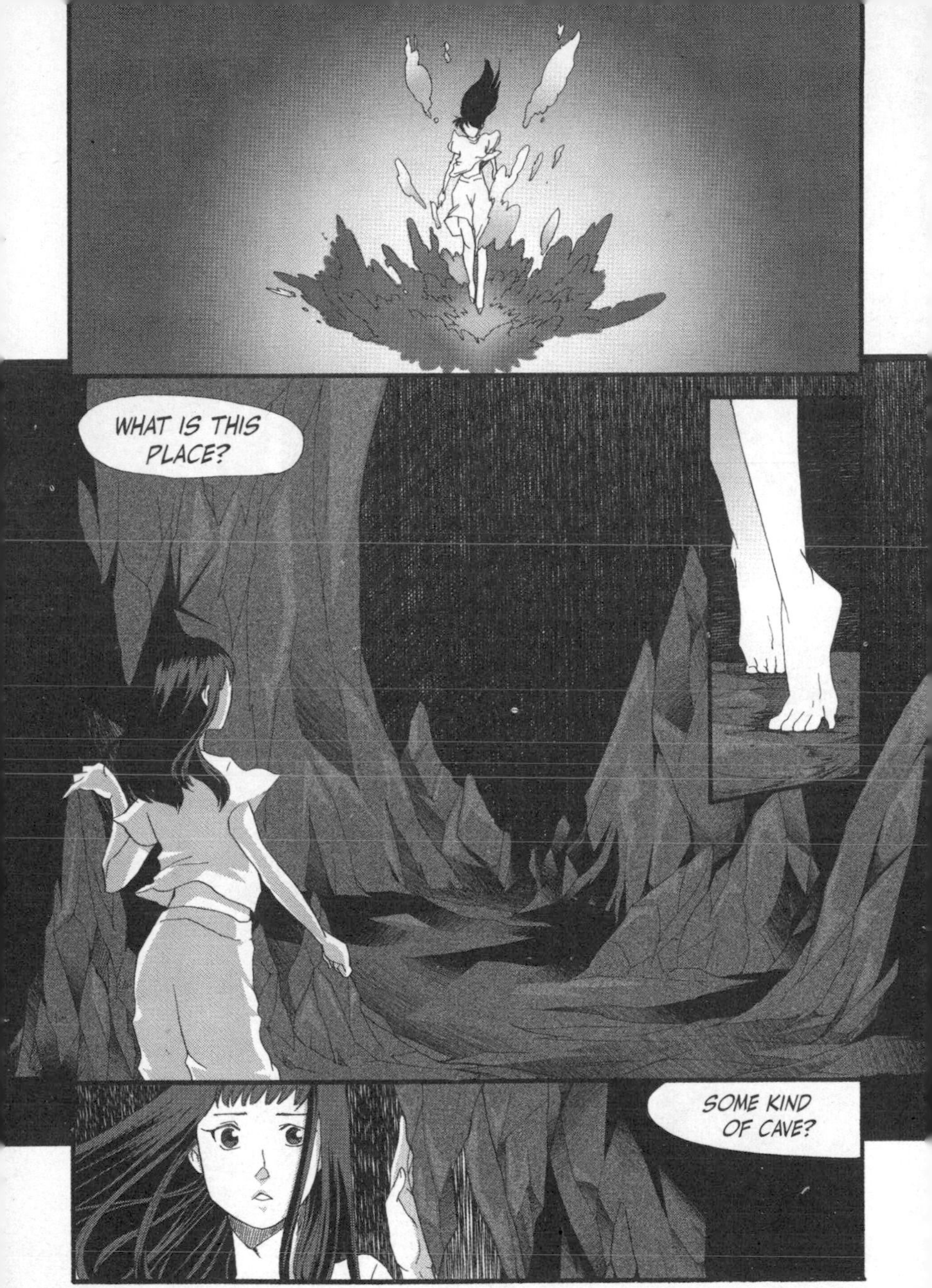
WHAT IS THIS PLACE?
SOME KIND OF CAVE?

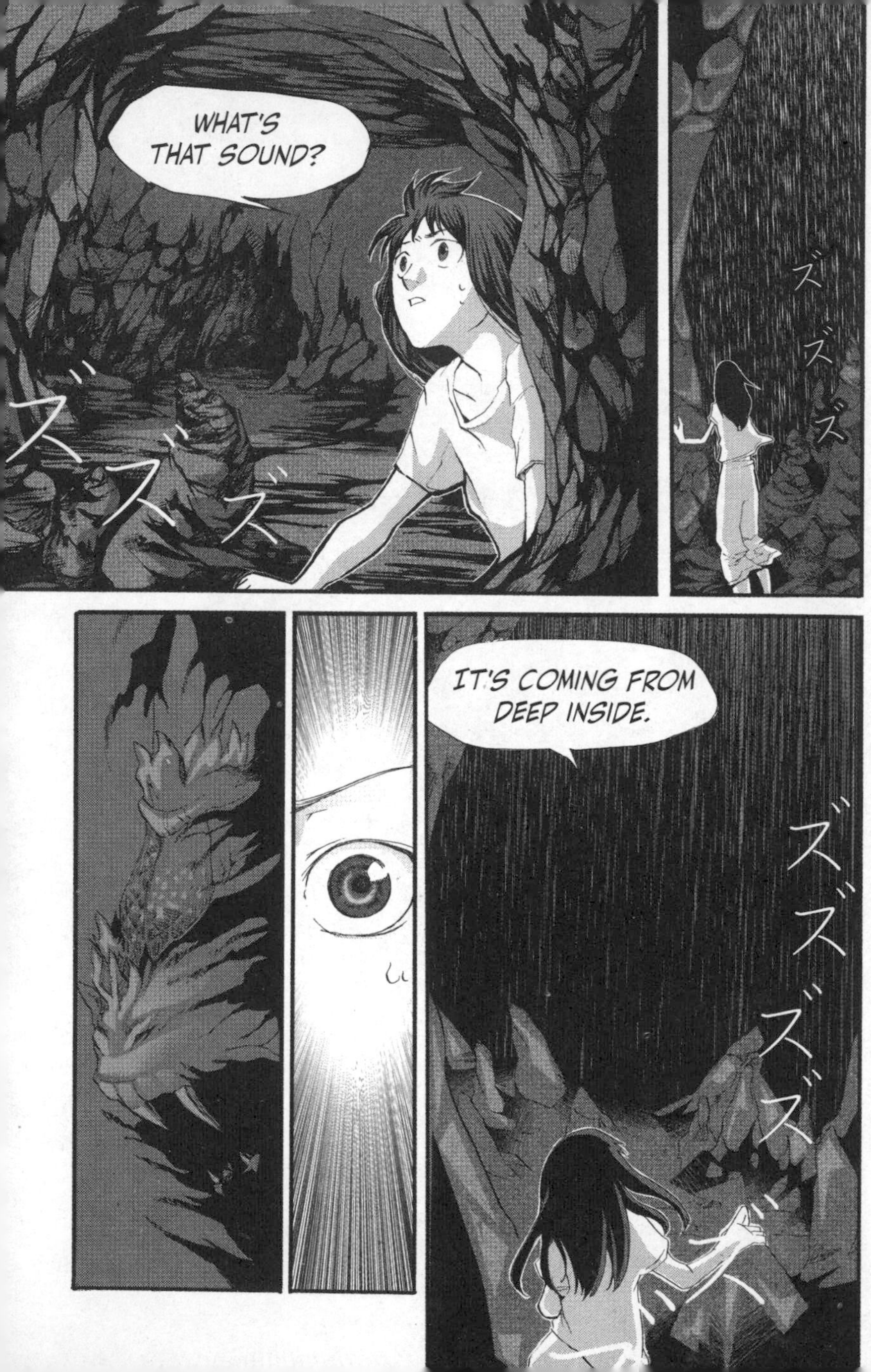

ズズズ
WHAT'S THAT SOUND?
ズズズ
ズズズズズ
IT'S COMING FROM DEEP INSIDE.

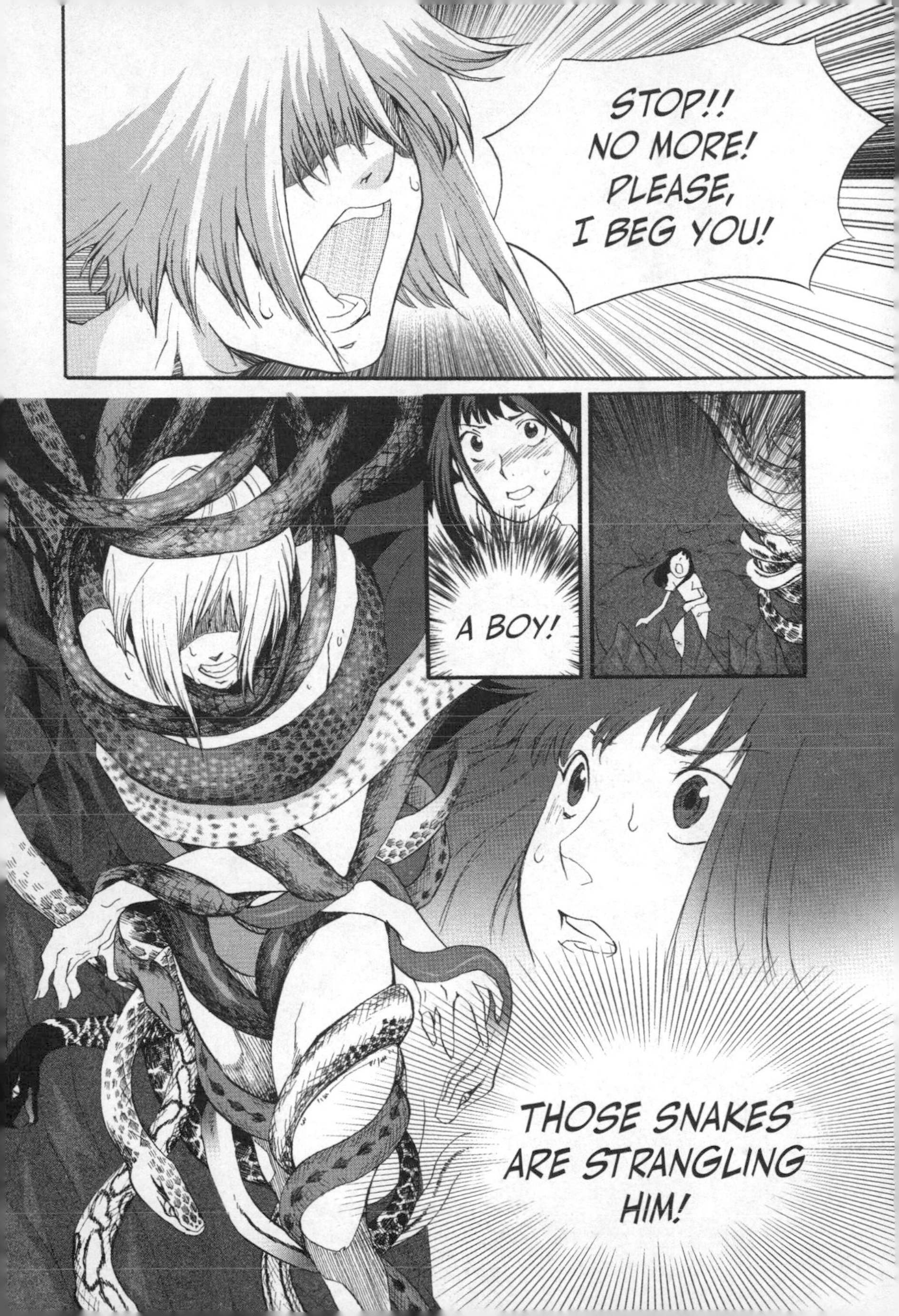
STOP!! NO MORE! PLEASE, I BEG YOU!
A BOY!
THOSE SNAKES ARE STRANGLING HIM!

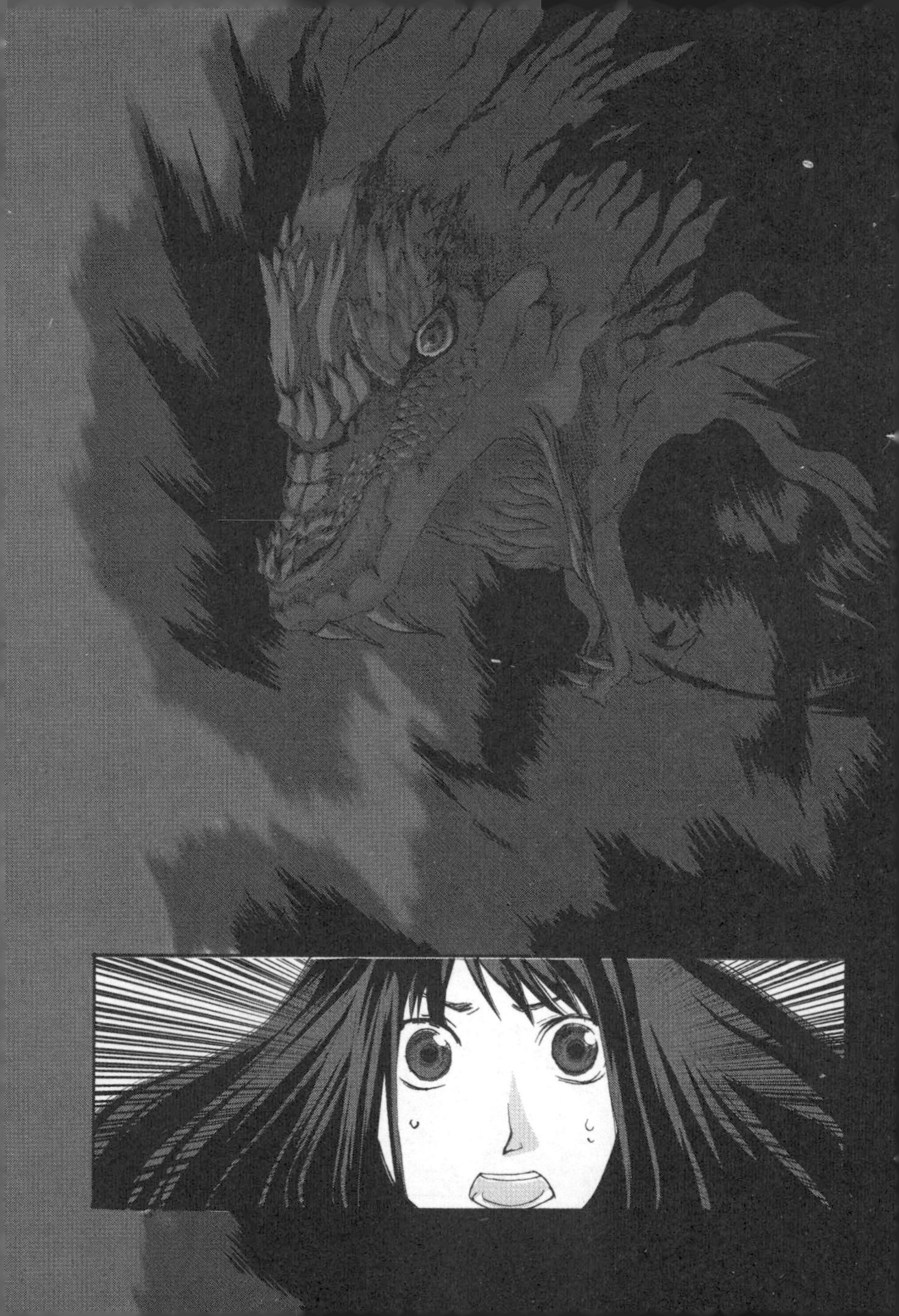

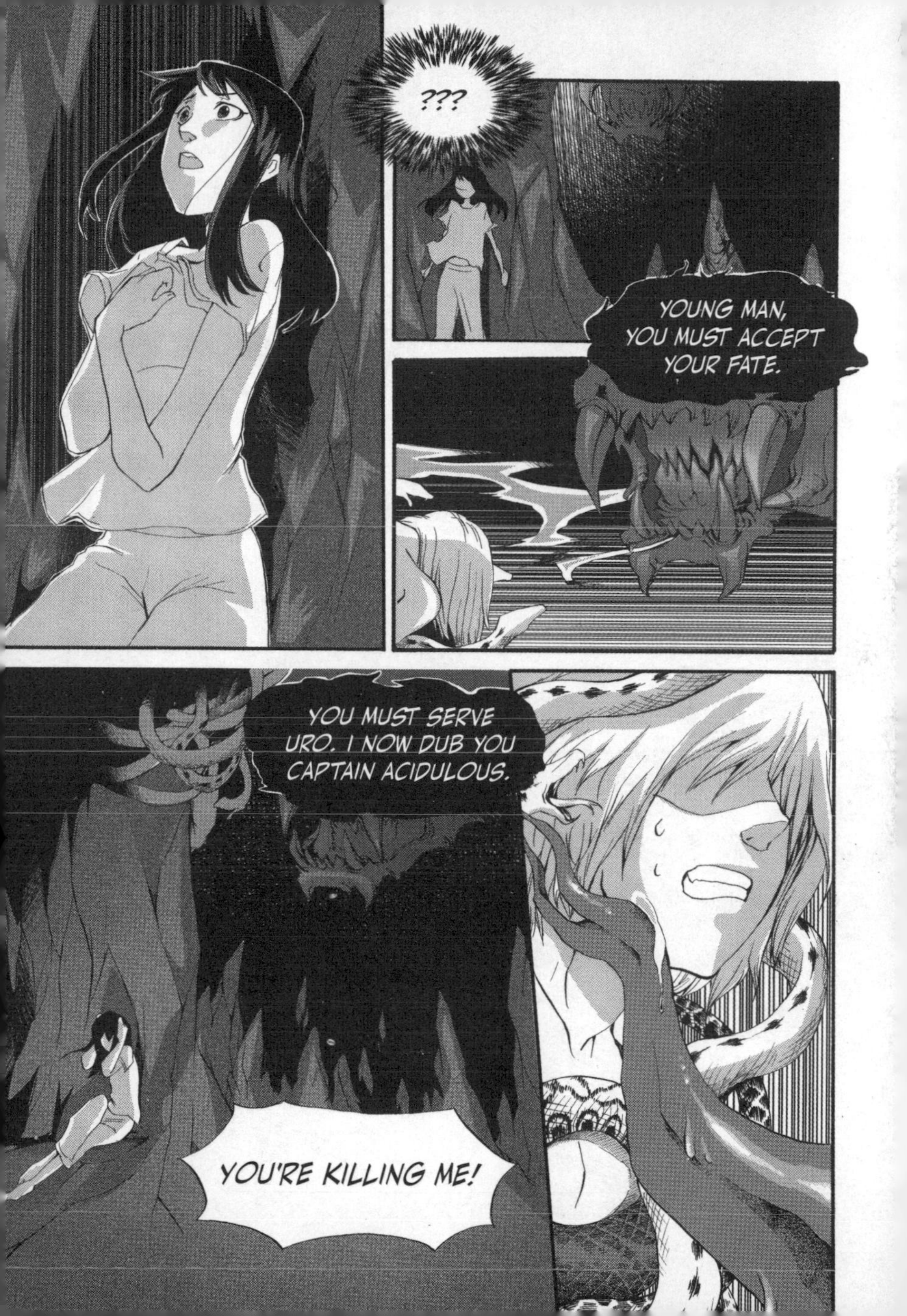
???
YOUNG MAN, YOU MUST ACCEPT YOUR FATE.
YOU MUST SERVE URO. I NOW DUB YOU CAPTAIN ACIDULOUS.
YOU'RE KILLING ME!

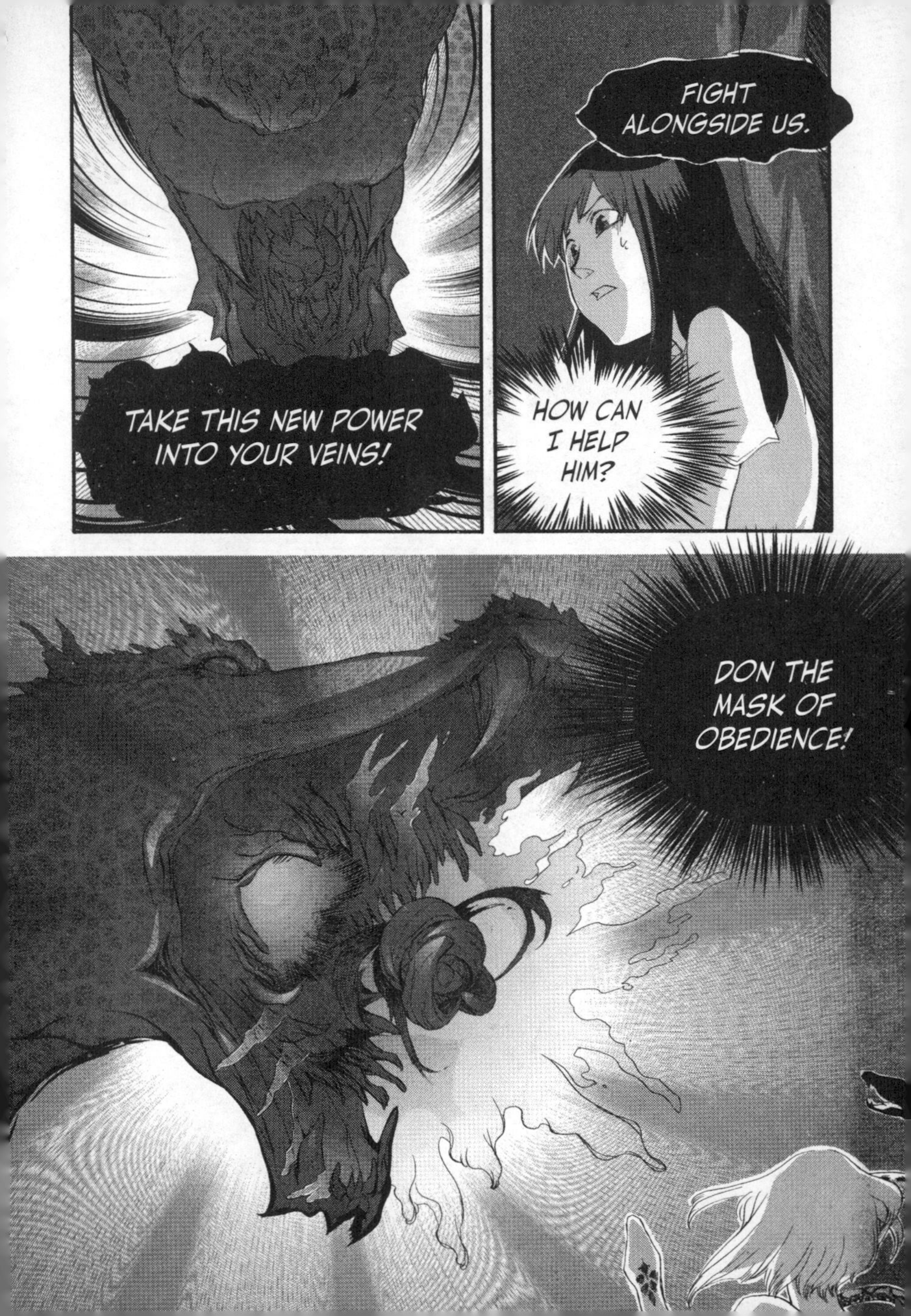
FIGHT ALONGSIDE US.
TAKE THIS NEW POWER INTO YOUR VEINS!
HOW CAN I HELP HIM?
DON THE MASK OF OBEDIENCE!

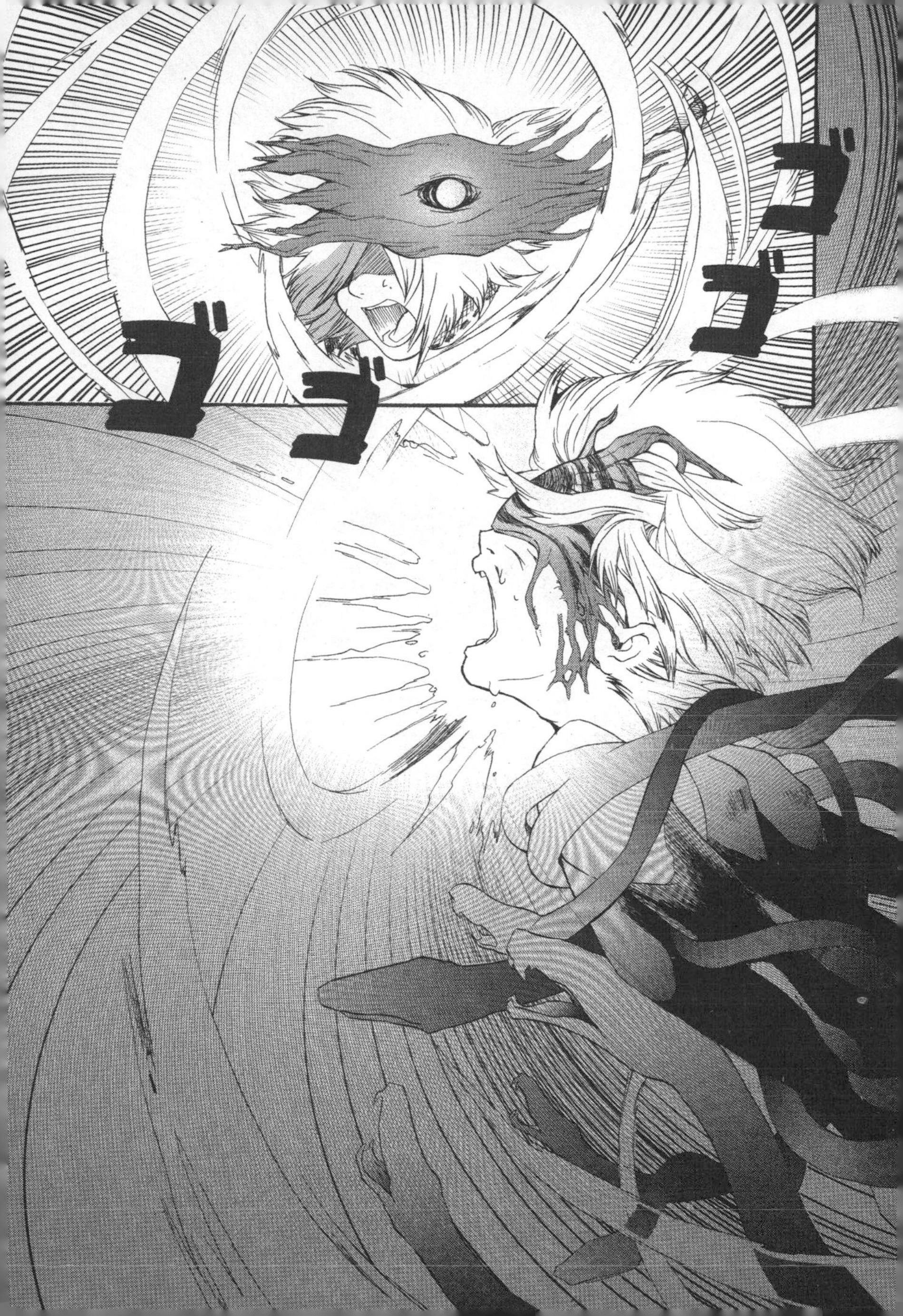
ゴゴゴ
ゴゴゴ

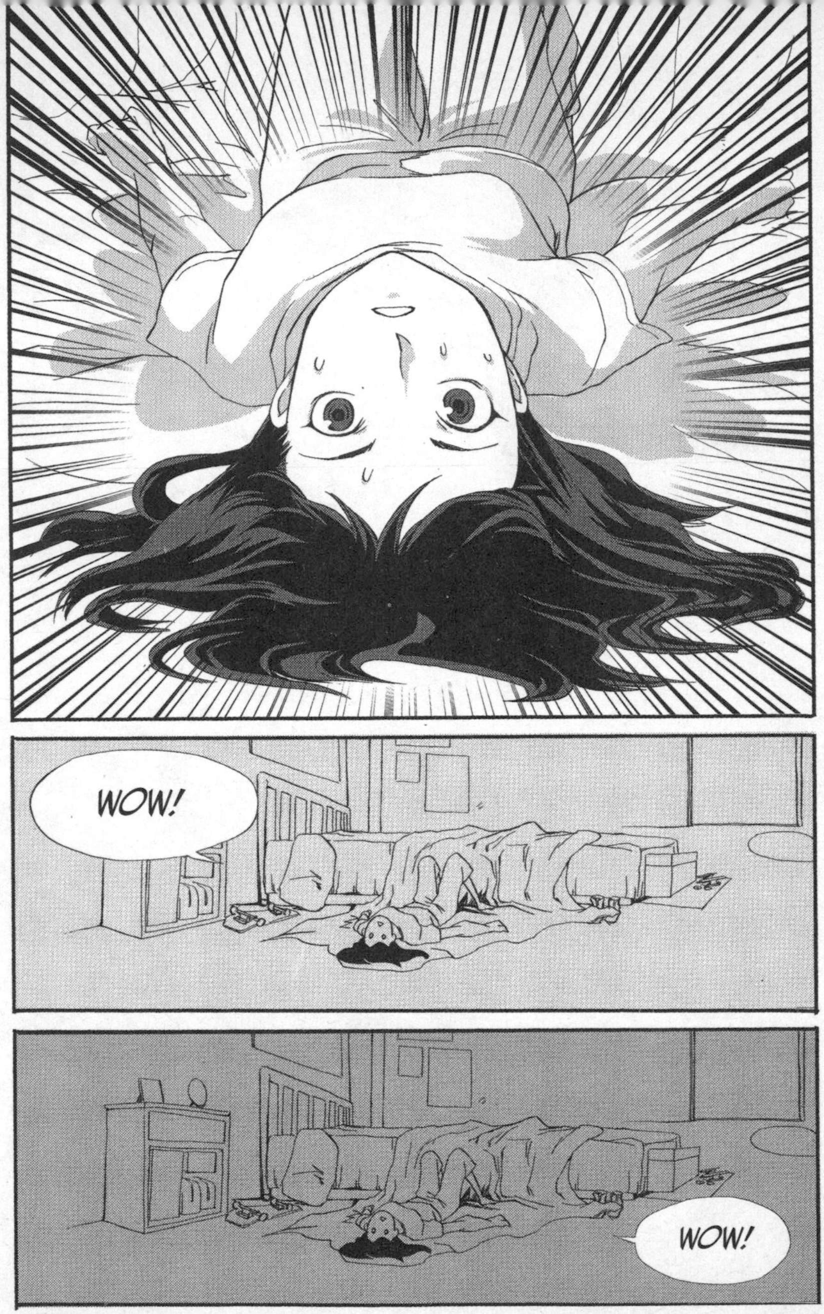
WOW!
WOW!

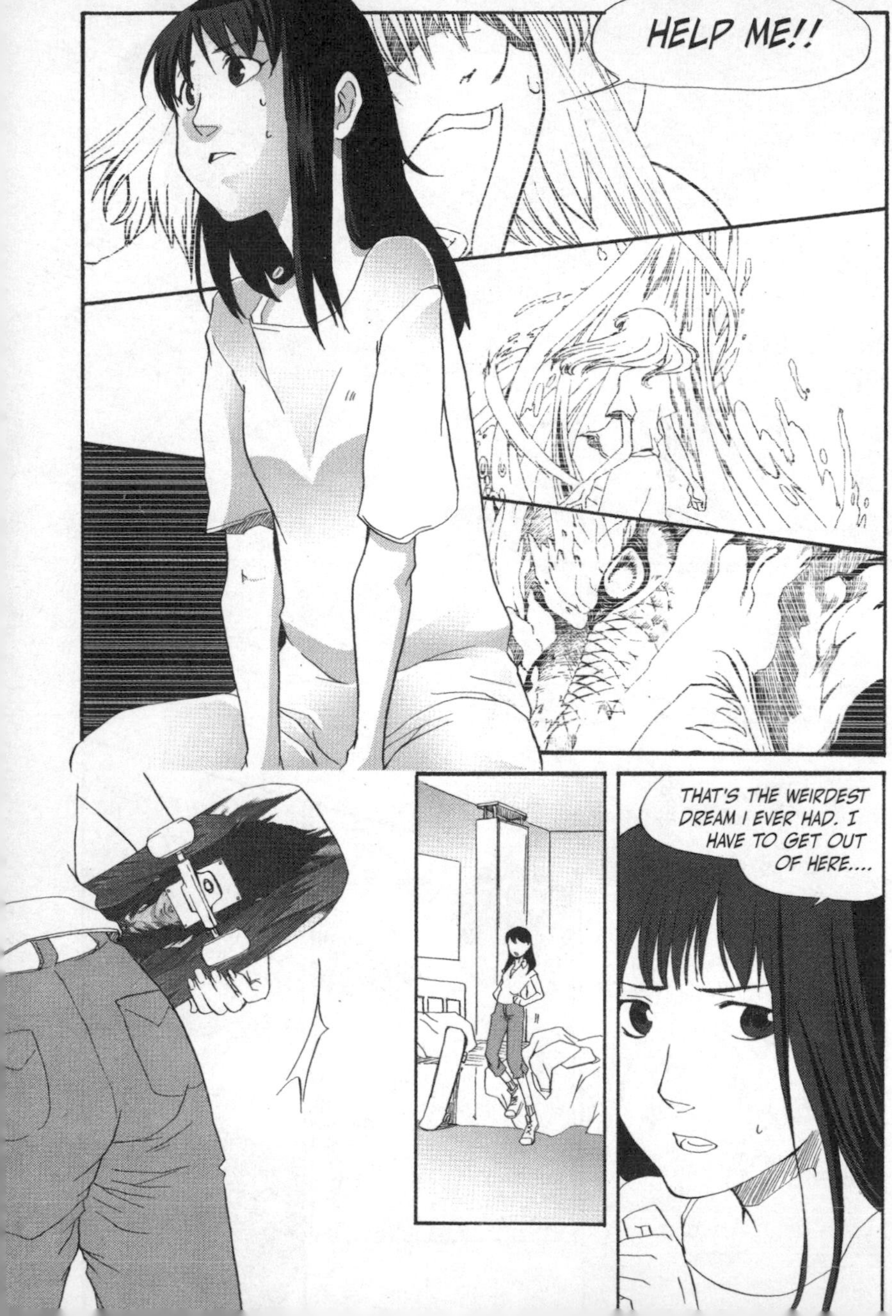
HELP ME!!
THAT'S THE WEIRDEST DREAM I EVER HAD. I HAVE TO GET OUT OF HERE....

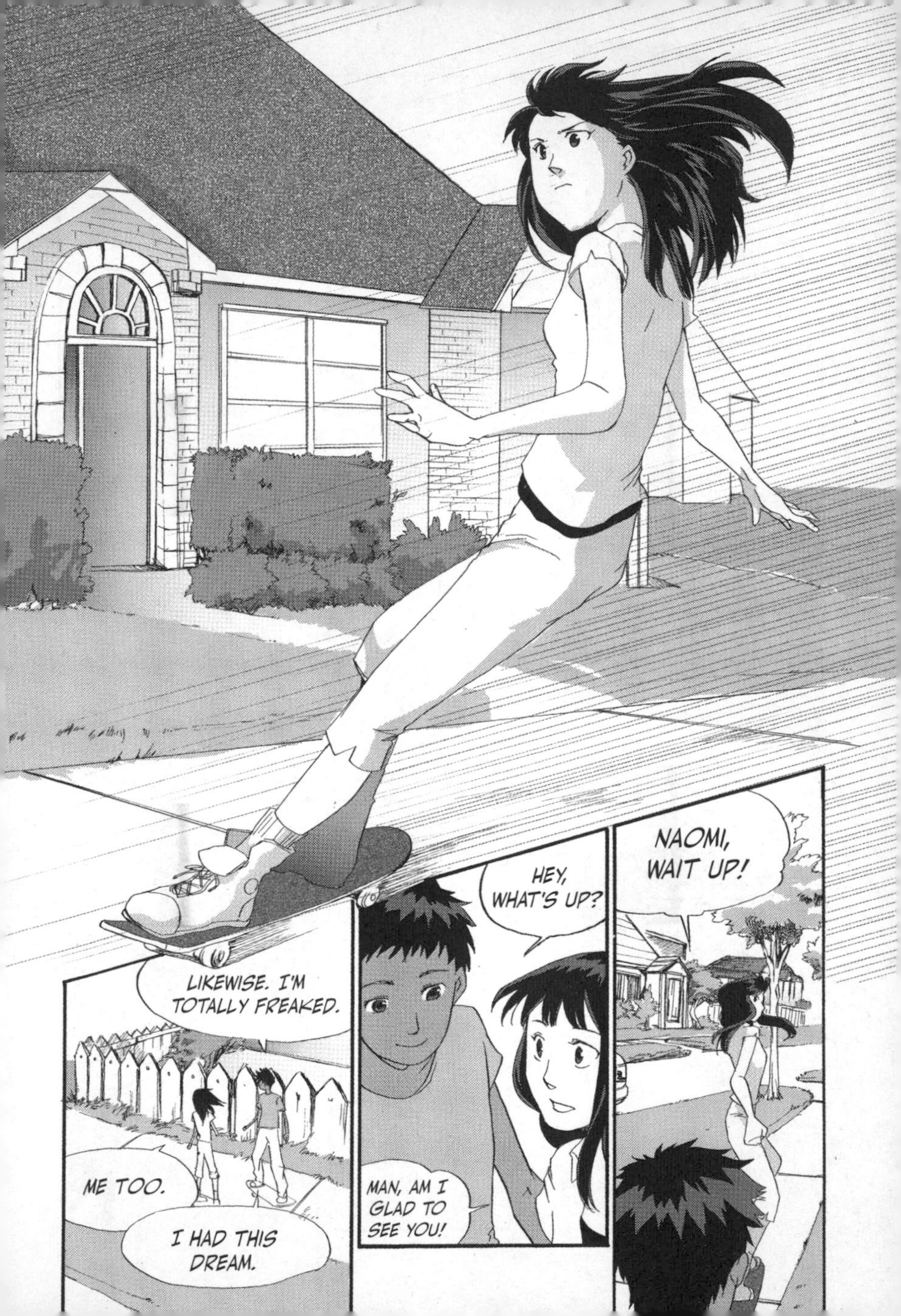
NAOMI, WAIT UP!
HEY, WHAT'S UP?
MAN, AM I GLAD TO SEE YOU!
LIKEWISE. I'M TOTALLY FREAKED.
ME TOO.
I HAD THIS DREAM.

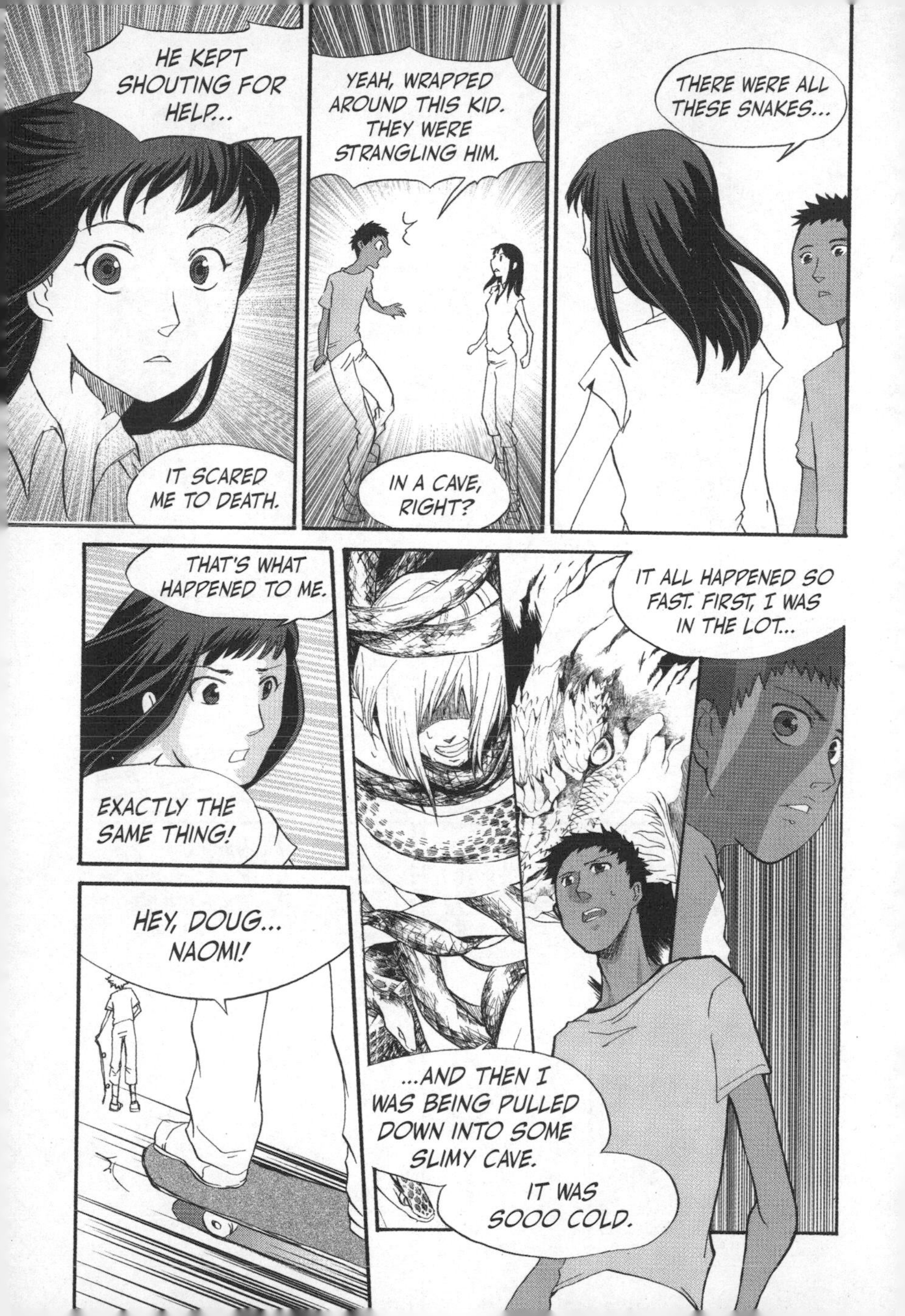
HE KEPT SHOUTING FOR HELP...
IT SCARED ME TO DEATH.
YEAH, WRAPPED AROUND THIS KID. THEY WERE STRANGLING HIM.
IN A CAVE, RIGHT?
THERE WERE ALL THESE SNAKES...
THAT'S WHAT HAPPENED TO ME.
EXACTLY THE SAME THING!
IT ALL HAPPENED SO FAST. FIRST, I WAS IN THE LOT...
...AND THEN I WAS BEING PULLED DOWN INTO SOME SLIMY CAVE.
IT WAS SOOO COLD.
HEY, DOUG... NAOMI!

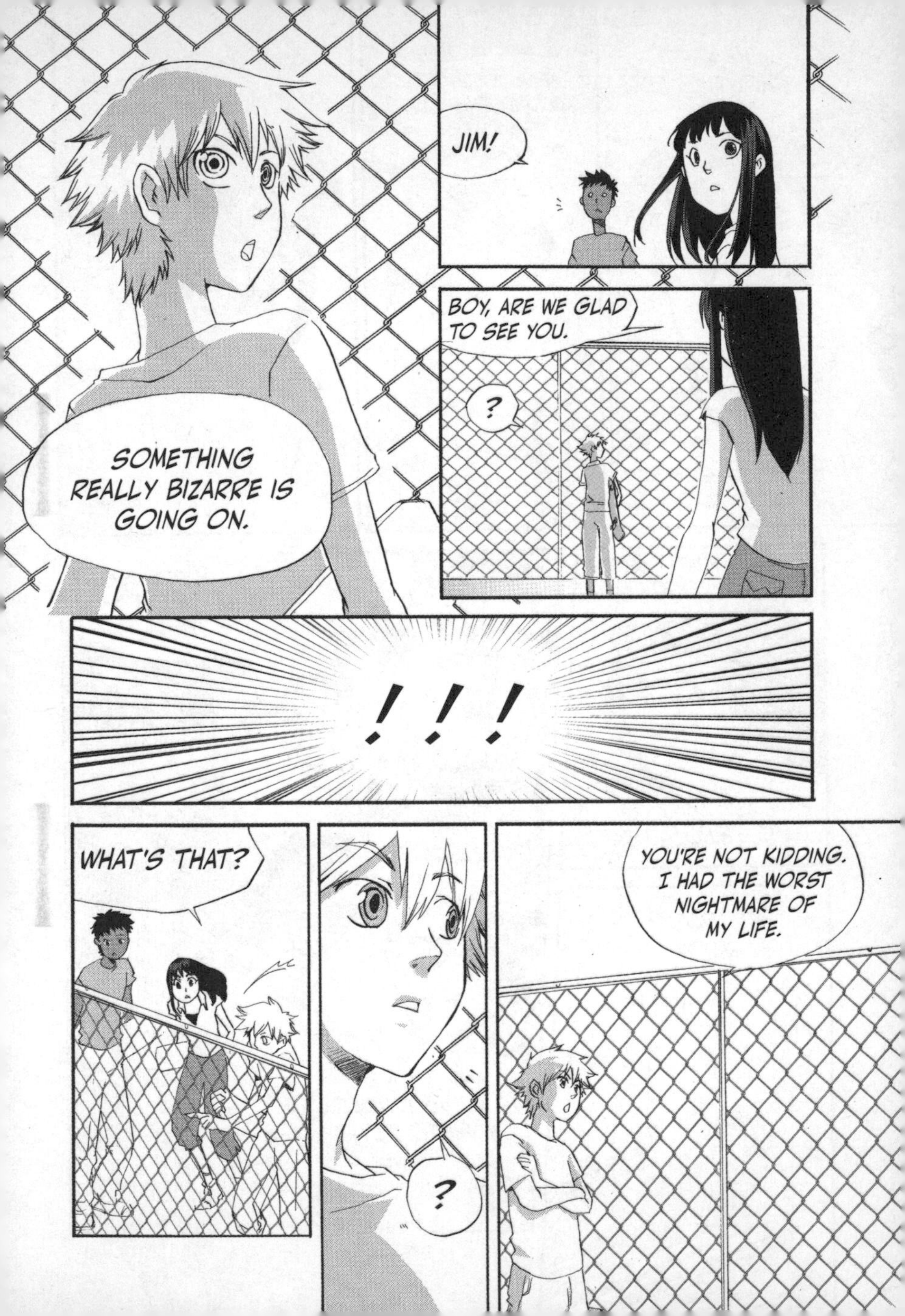
JIM!
SOMETHING REALLY BIZARRE IS GOING ON.
BOY, ARE WE GLAD TO SEE YOU.
?
!!!
WHAT'S THAT?
?
YOU'RE NOT KIDDING. I HAD THE WORST NIGHTMARE OF MY LIFE.

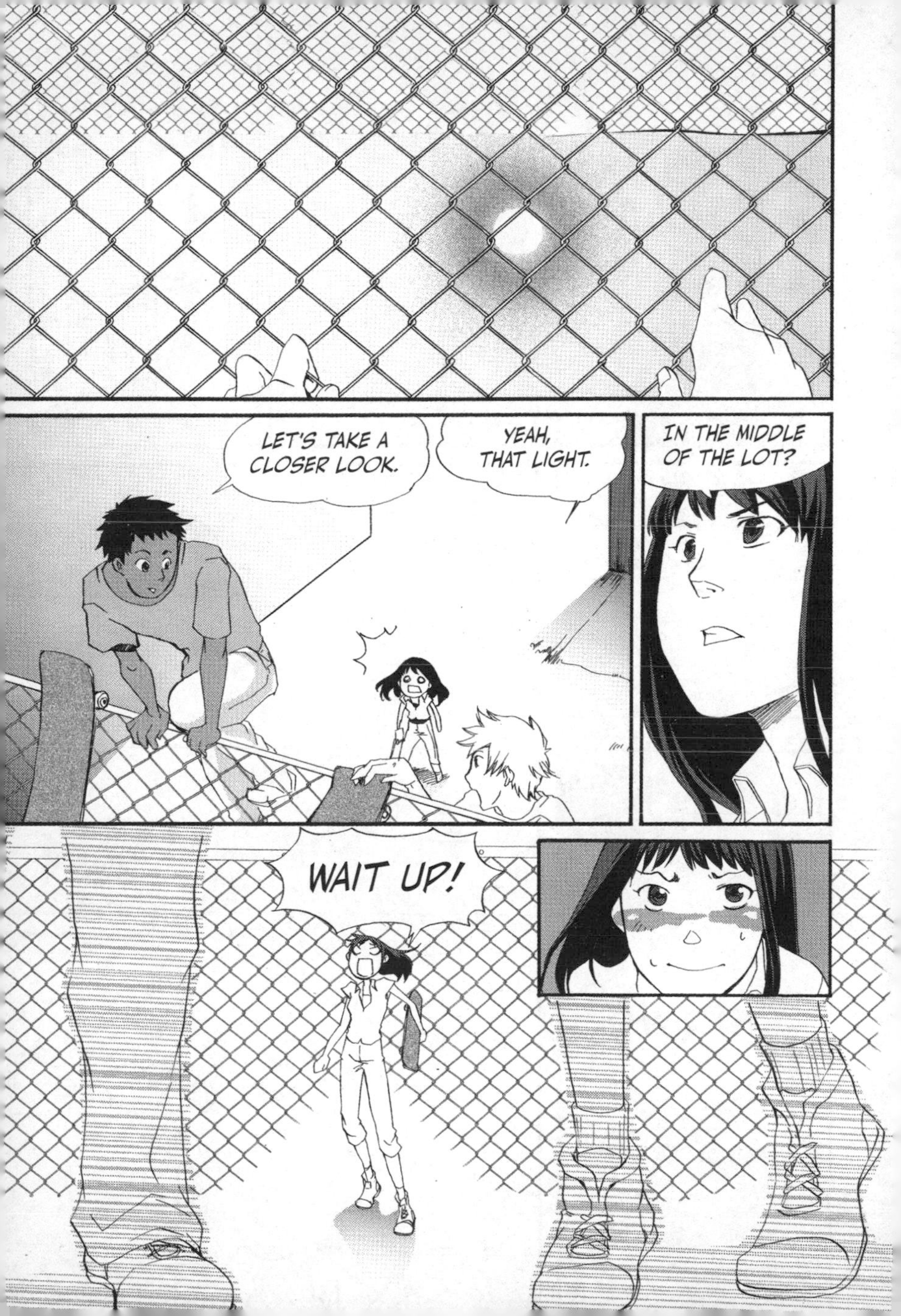

LET'S TAKE A CLOSER LOOK.
YEAH, THAT LIGHT.
IN THE MIDDLE OF THE LOT?
WAIT UP!

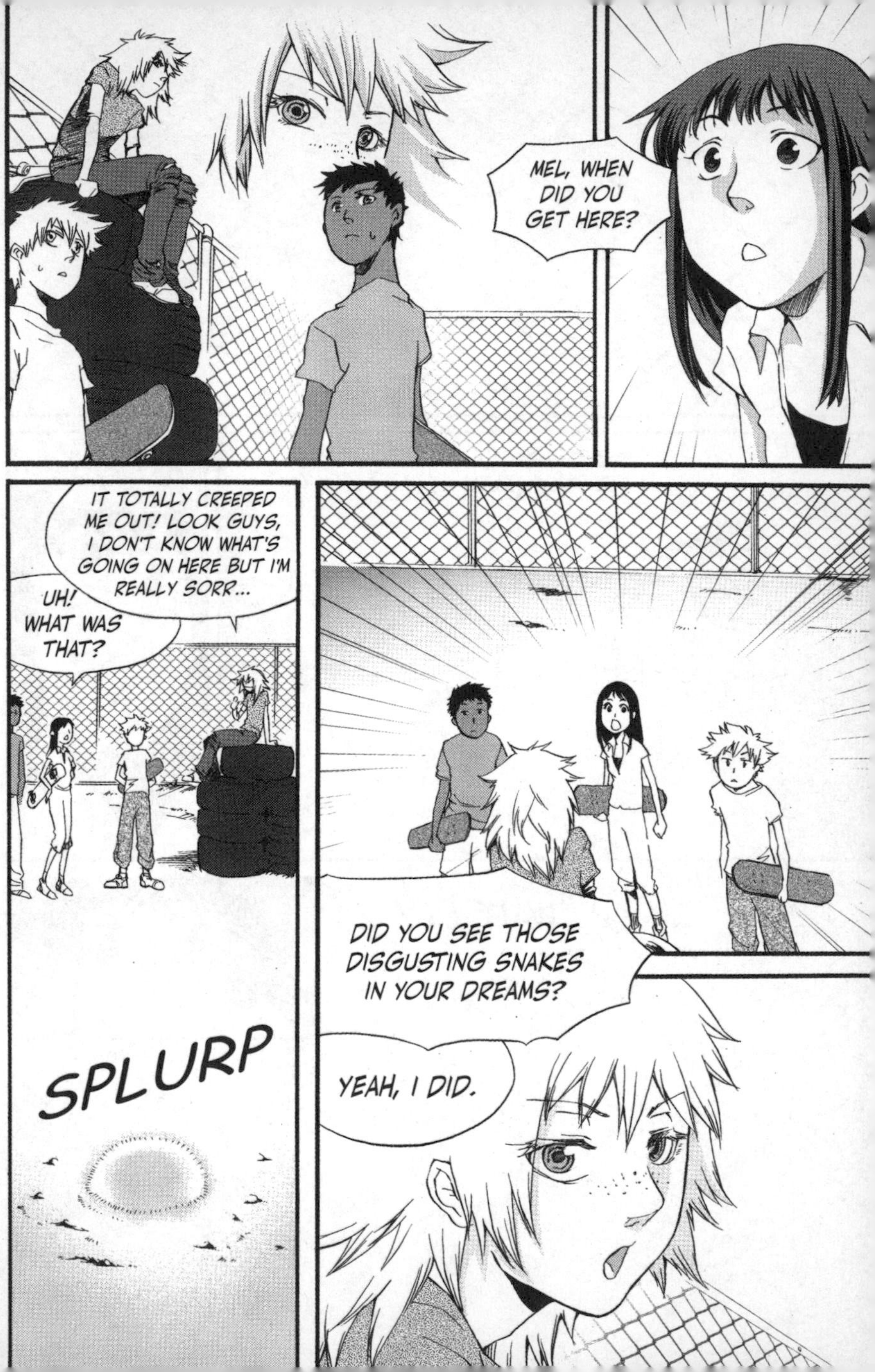

MEL, WHEN DID YOU GET HERE?
IT TOTALLY CREEPED ME OUT! LOOK GUYS, I DON'T KNOW WHAT'S GOING ON HERE BUT I'M REALLY SORR...
UH! WHAT WAS THAT?
SPLURP
DID YOU SEE THOSE DISGUSTING SNAKES IN YOUR DREAMS?
YEAH, I DID.

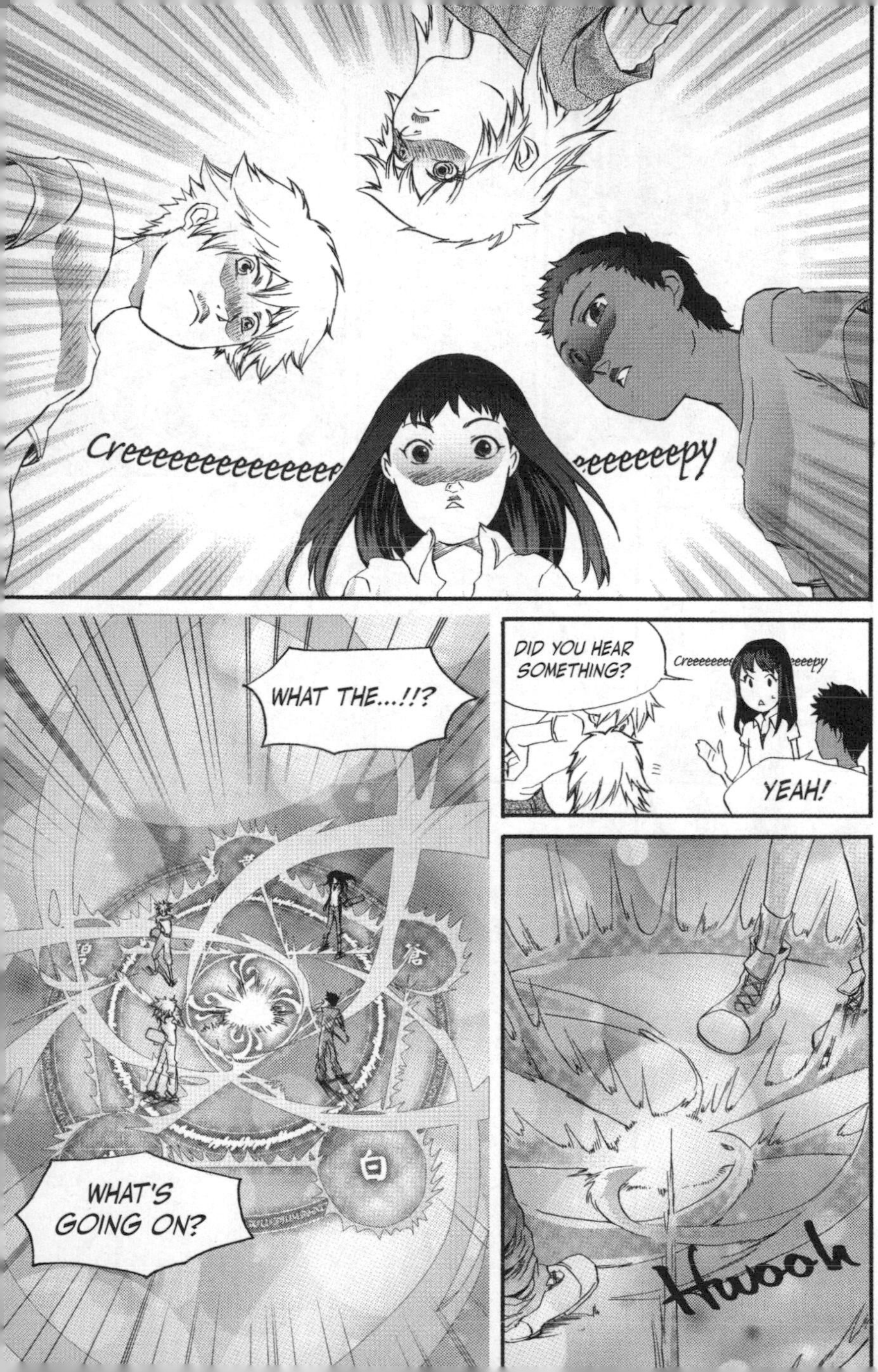

Creeeeeeeeeeeeeee
eeeeeeepy
WHAT THE...!!?
WHAT'S GOING ON?
DID YOU HEAR SOMETHING?
Creeeeeee
eeeepy
YEAH!
白
Hwooh

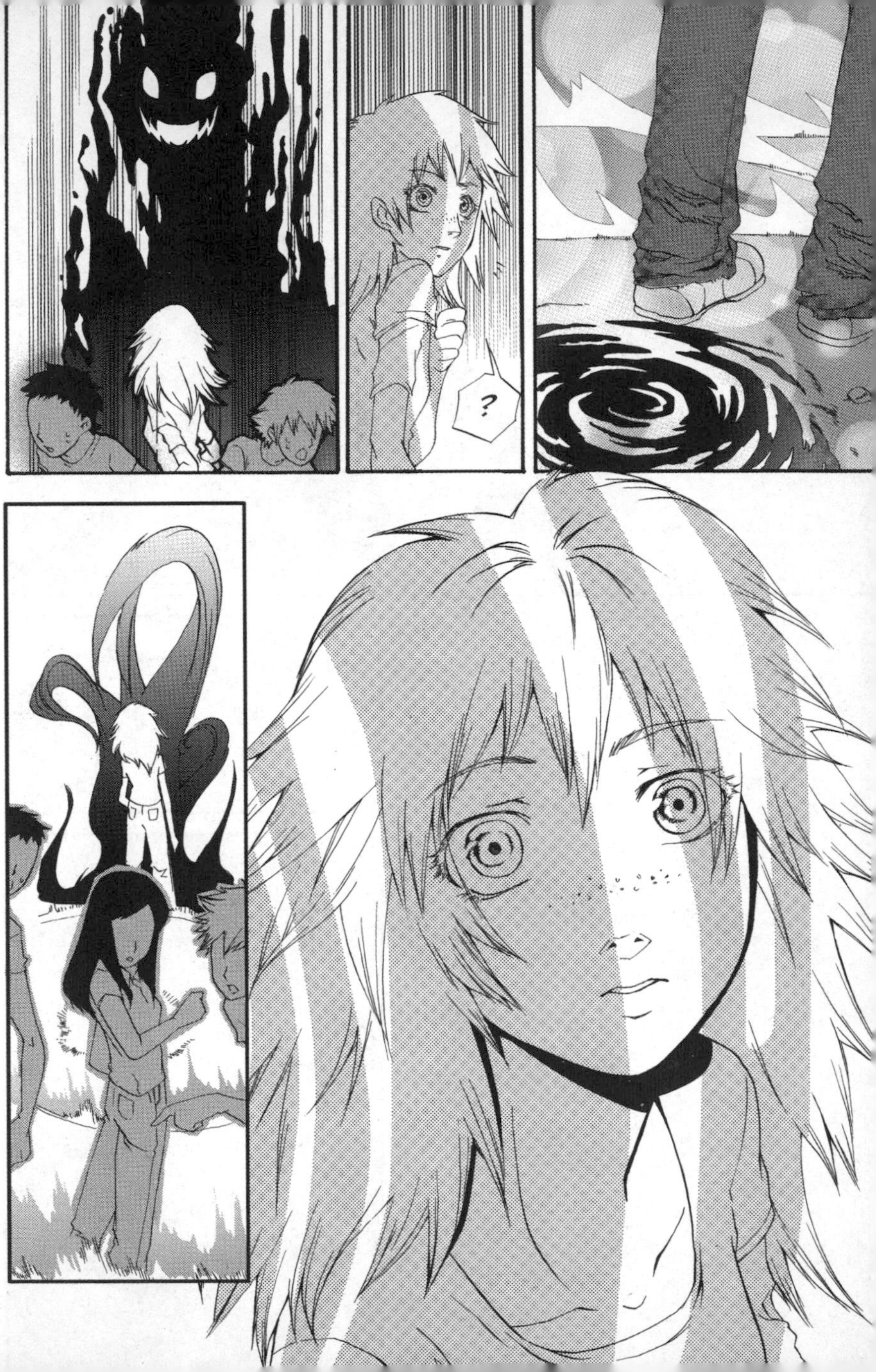
?

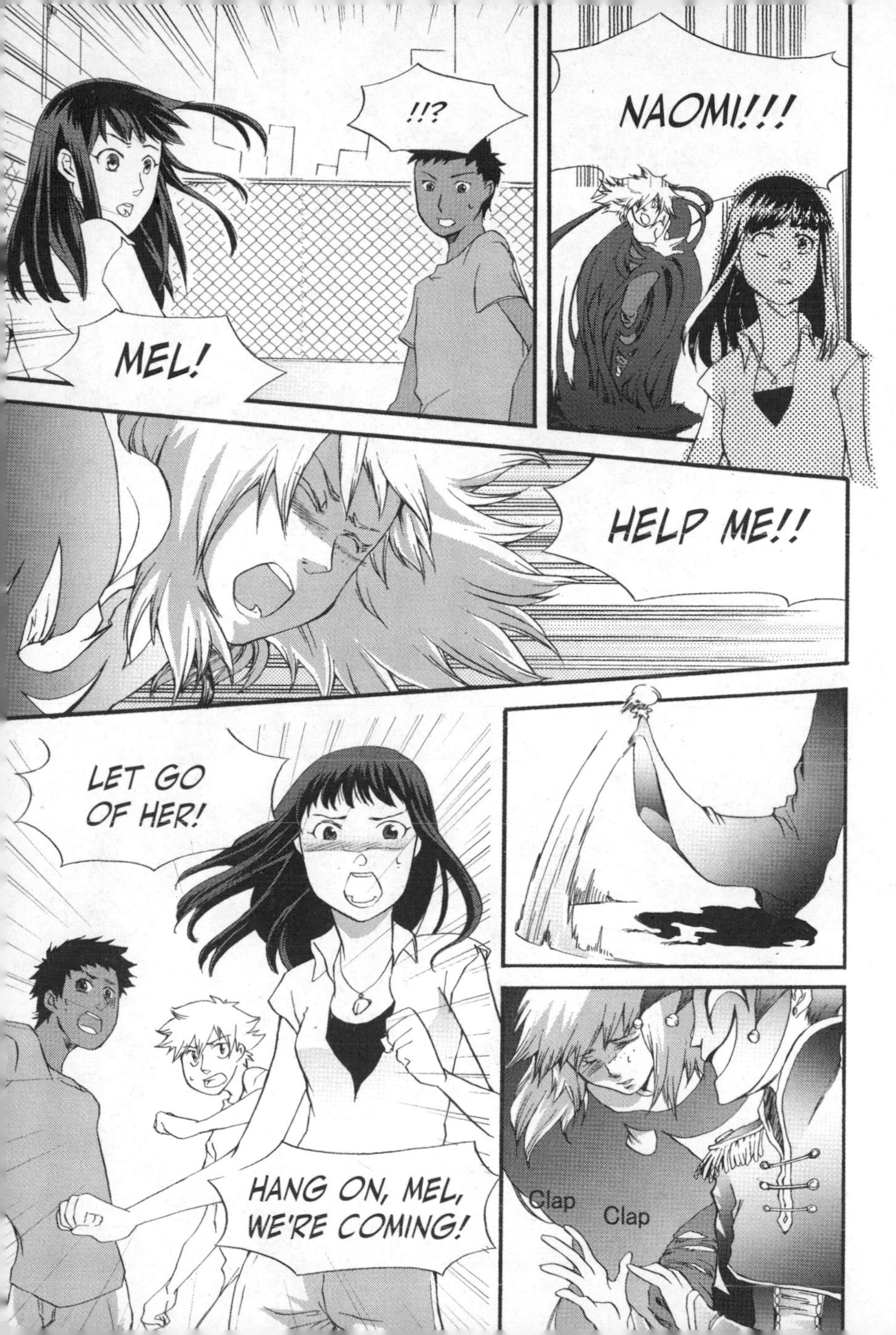
!!?
MEL!
NAOMI!!!
HELP ME!!
LET GO OF HER!
HANG ON, MEL, WE'RE COMING!
Clap
Clap

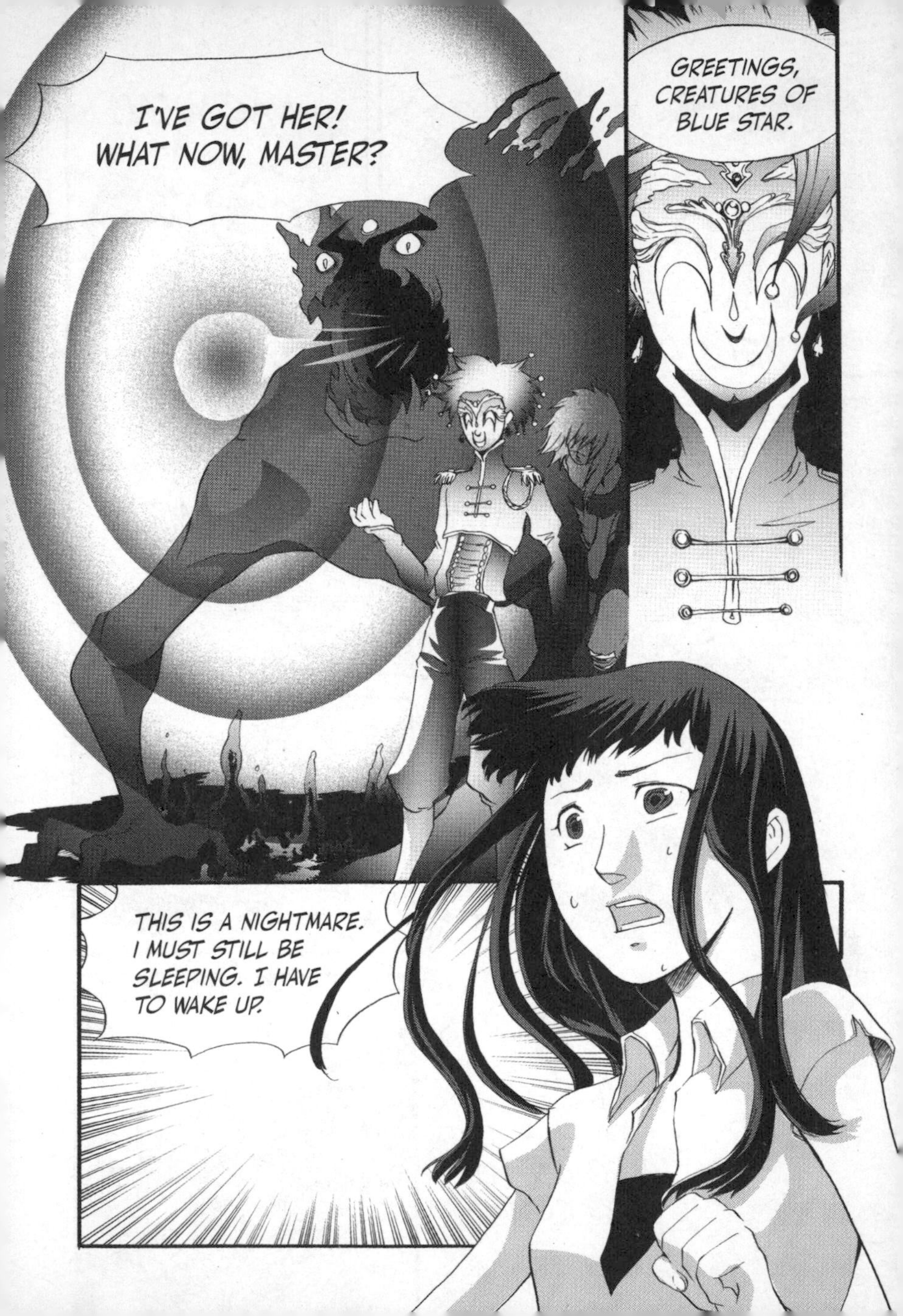
GREETINGS, CREATURES OF BLUE STAR.
I'VE GOT HER! WHAT NOW, MASTER?
THIS IS A NIGHTMARE. I MUST STILL BE SLEEPING. I HAVE TO WAKE UP.

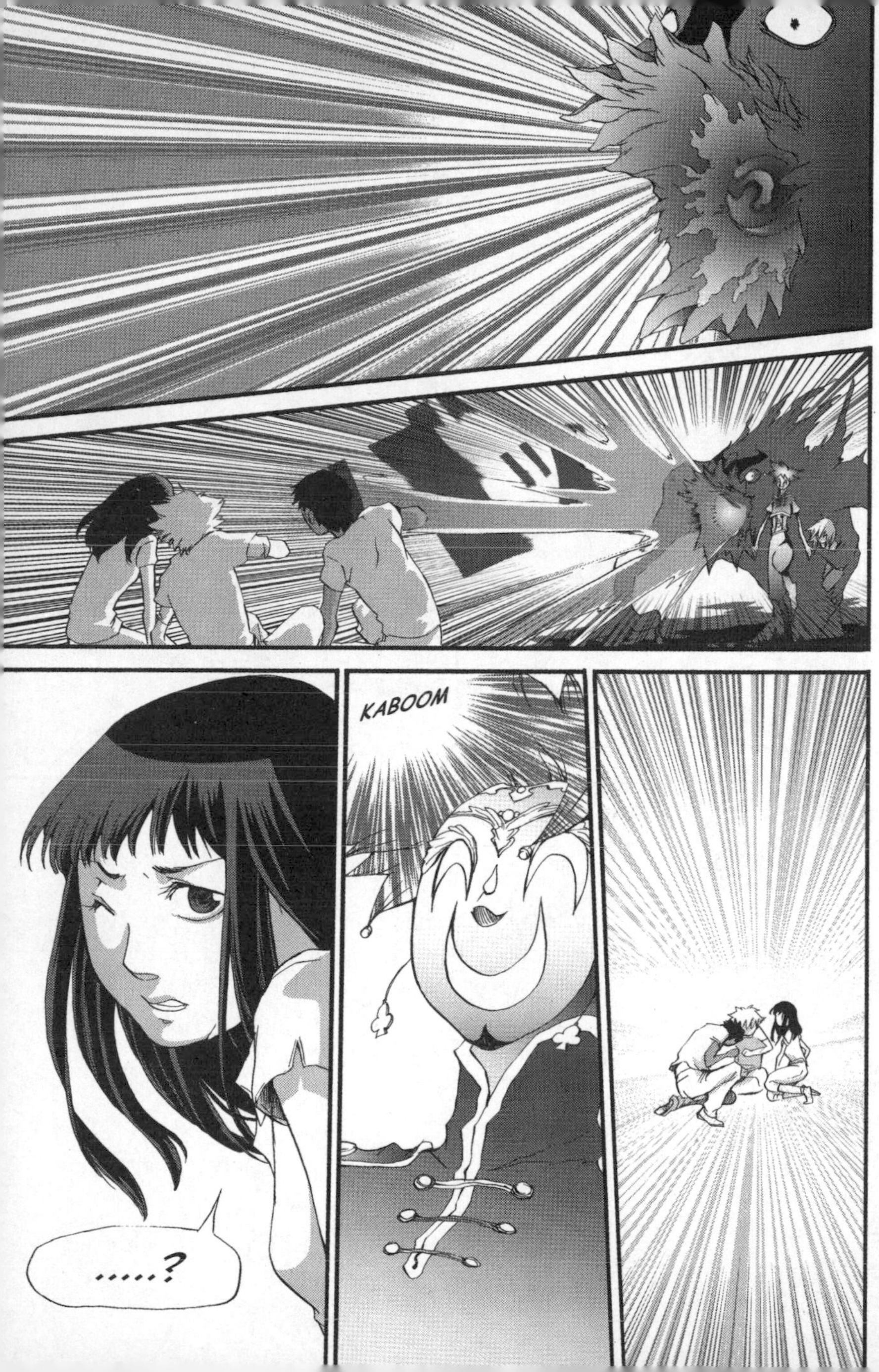
KABOOM
.....?

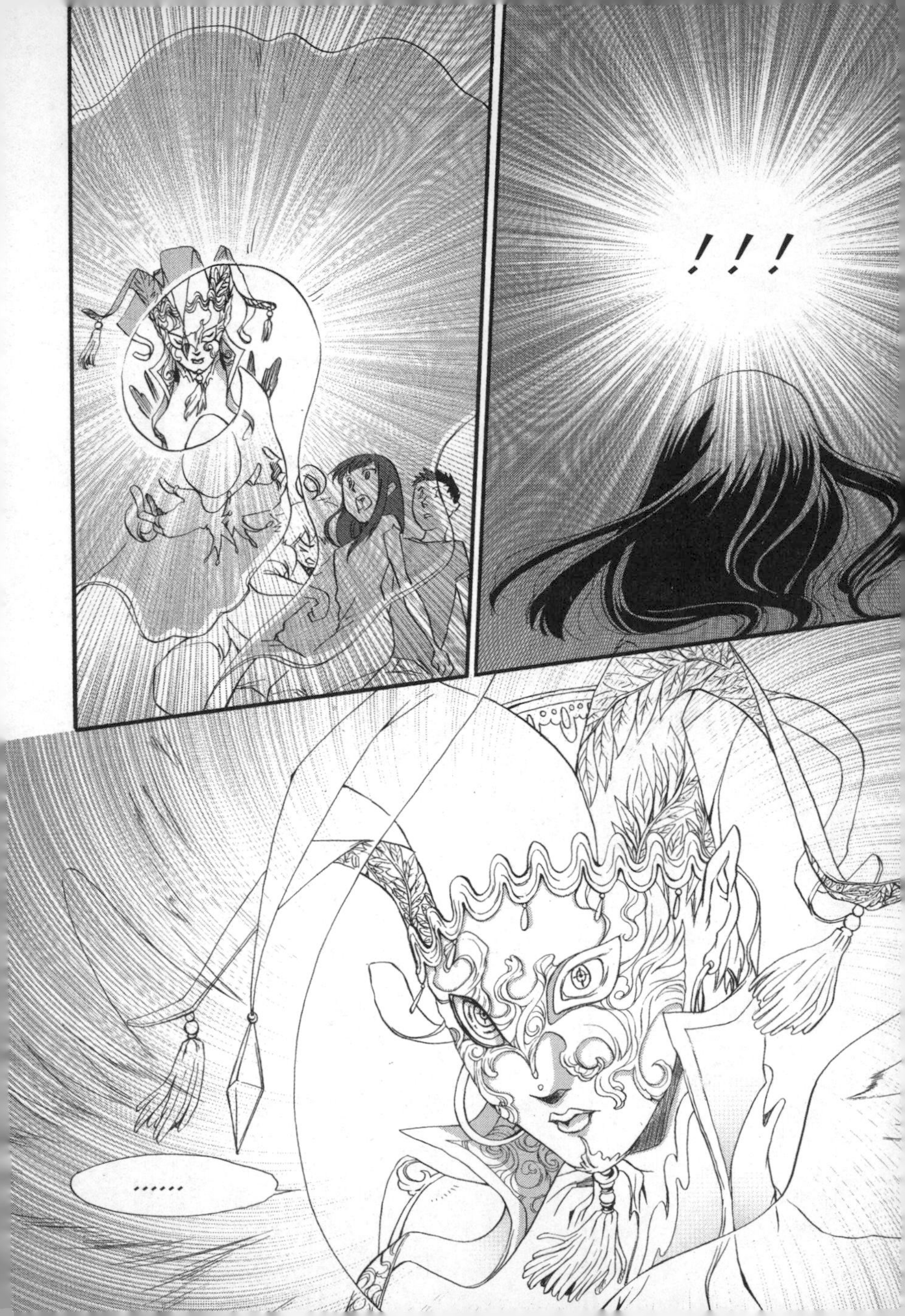
!!!
......

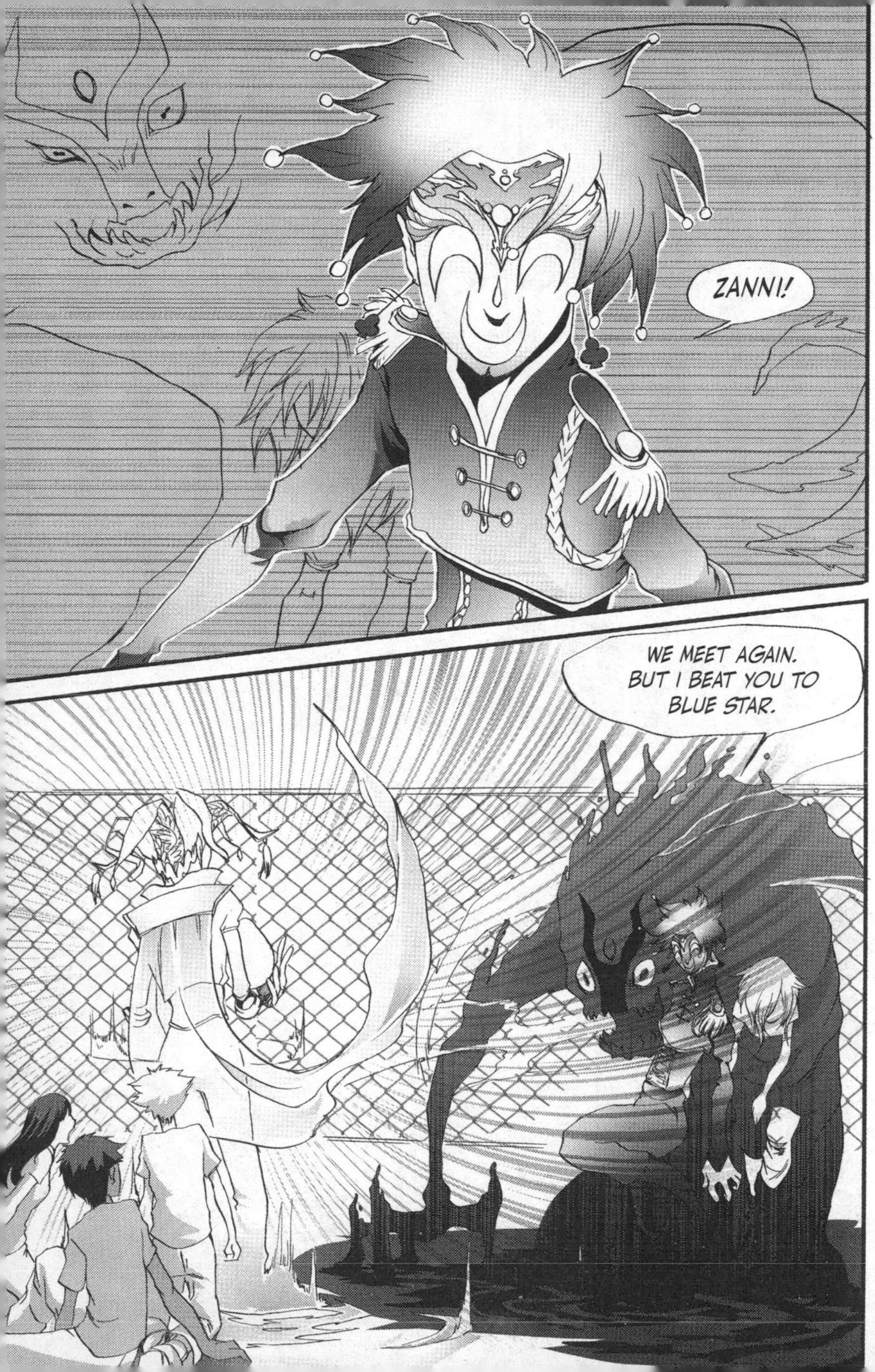
ZANNI!
WE MEET AGAIN. BUT I BEAT YOU TO BLUE STAR.

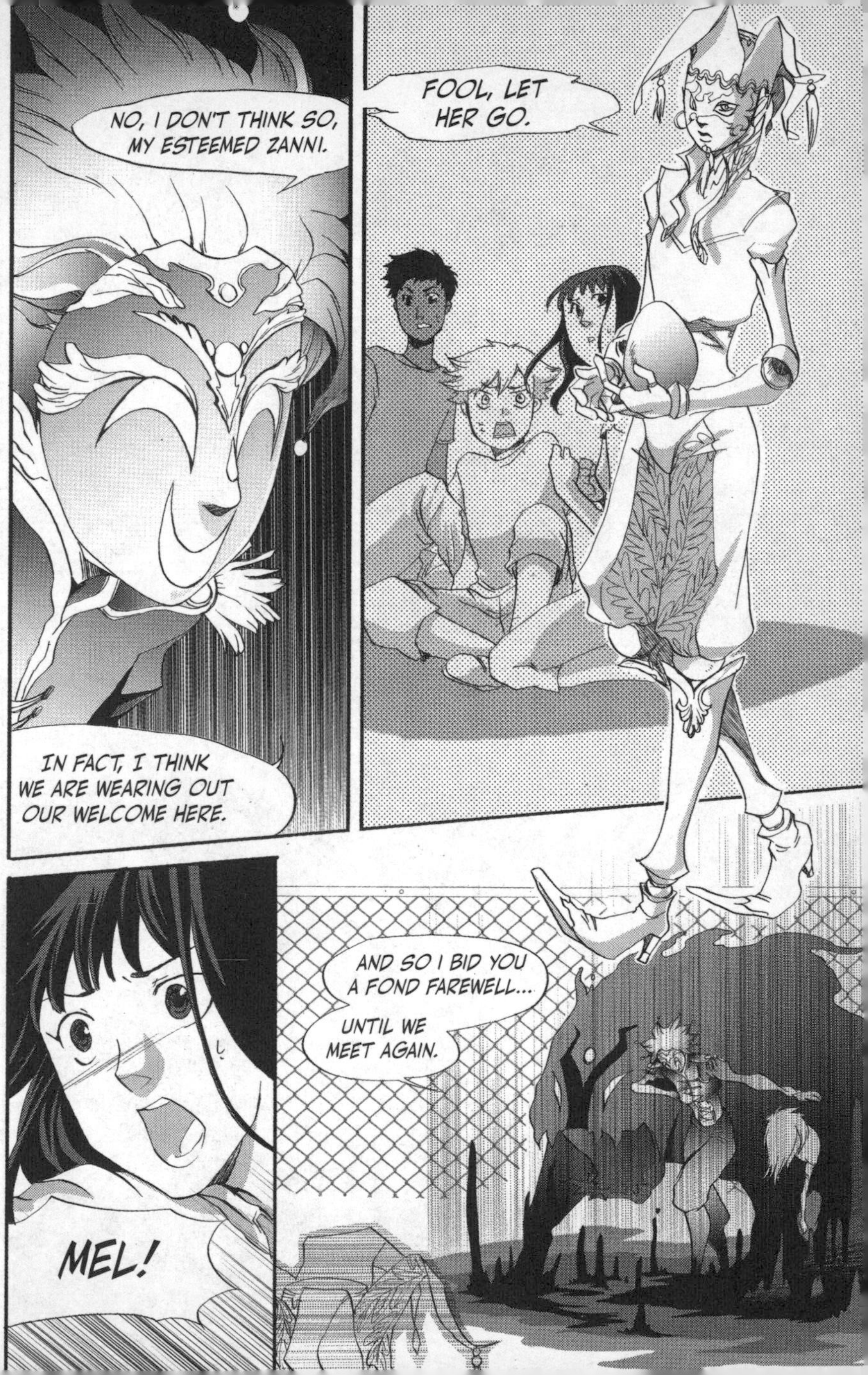
NO, I DON'T THINK SO, MY ESTEEMED ZANNI.
FOOL, LET HER GO.
IN FACT, I THINK WE ARE WEARING OUT OUR WELCOME HERE.
MEL!
AND SO I BID YOU A FOND FAREWELL...
UNTIL WE MEET AGAIN.

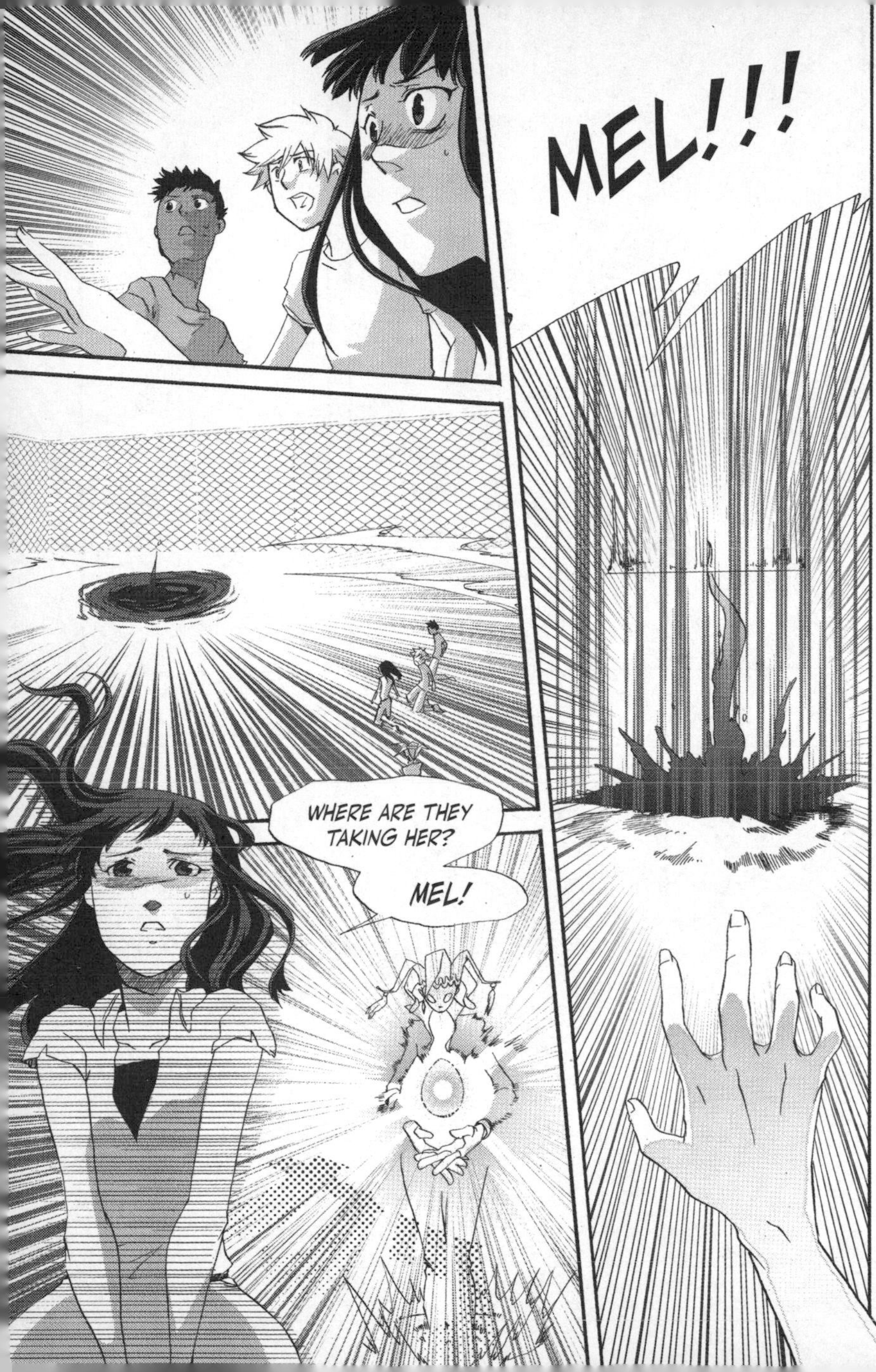
MEL!!!
WHERE ARE THEY TAKING HER?
MEL!

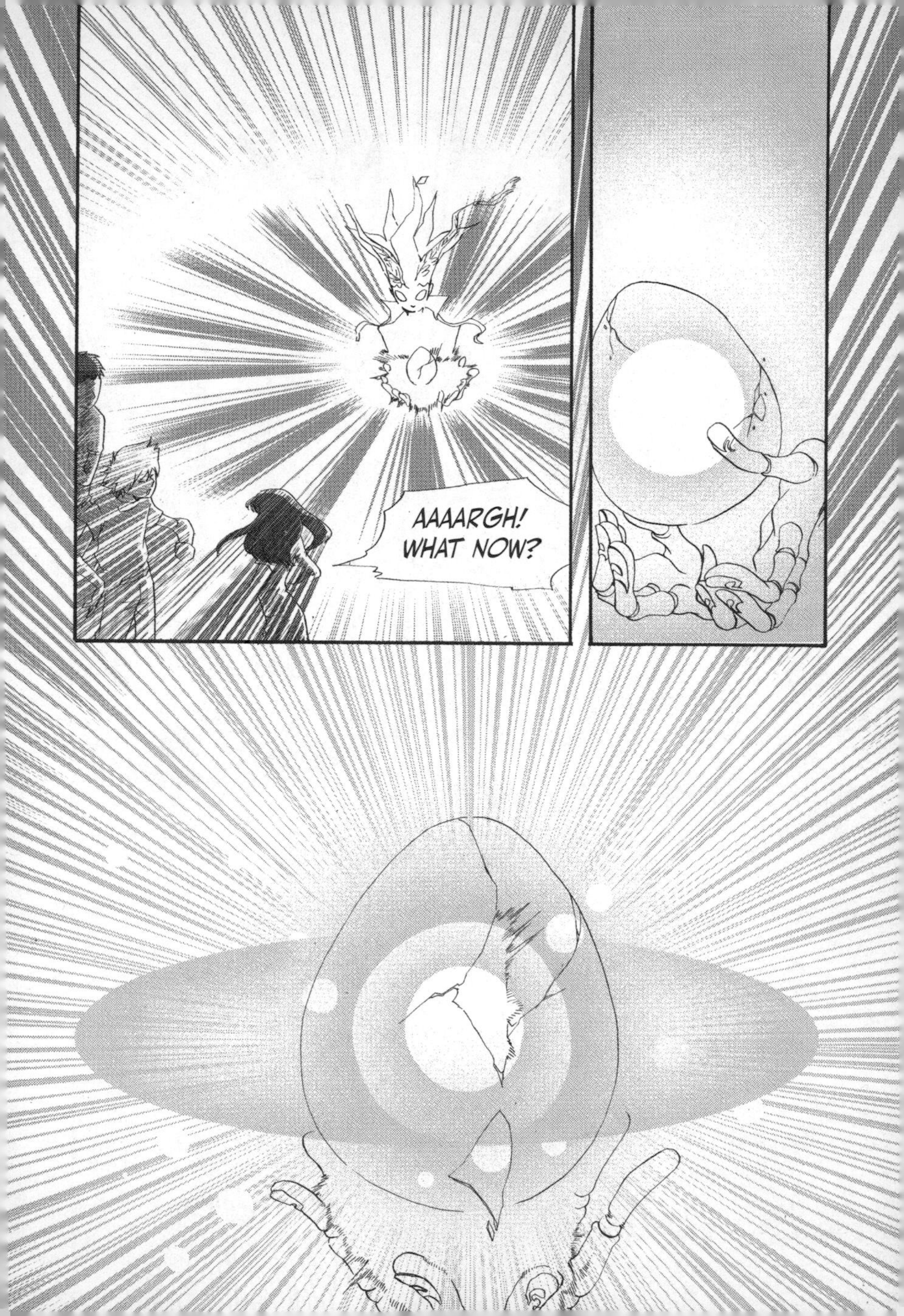
AAAARGH! WHAT NOW?

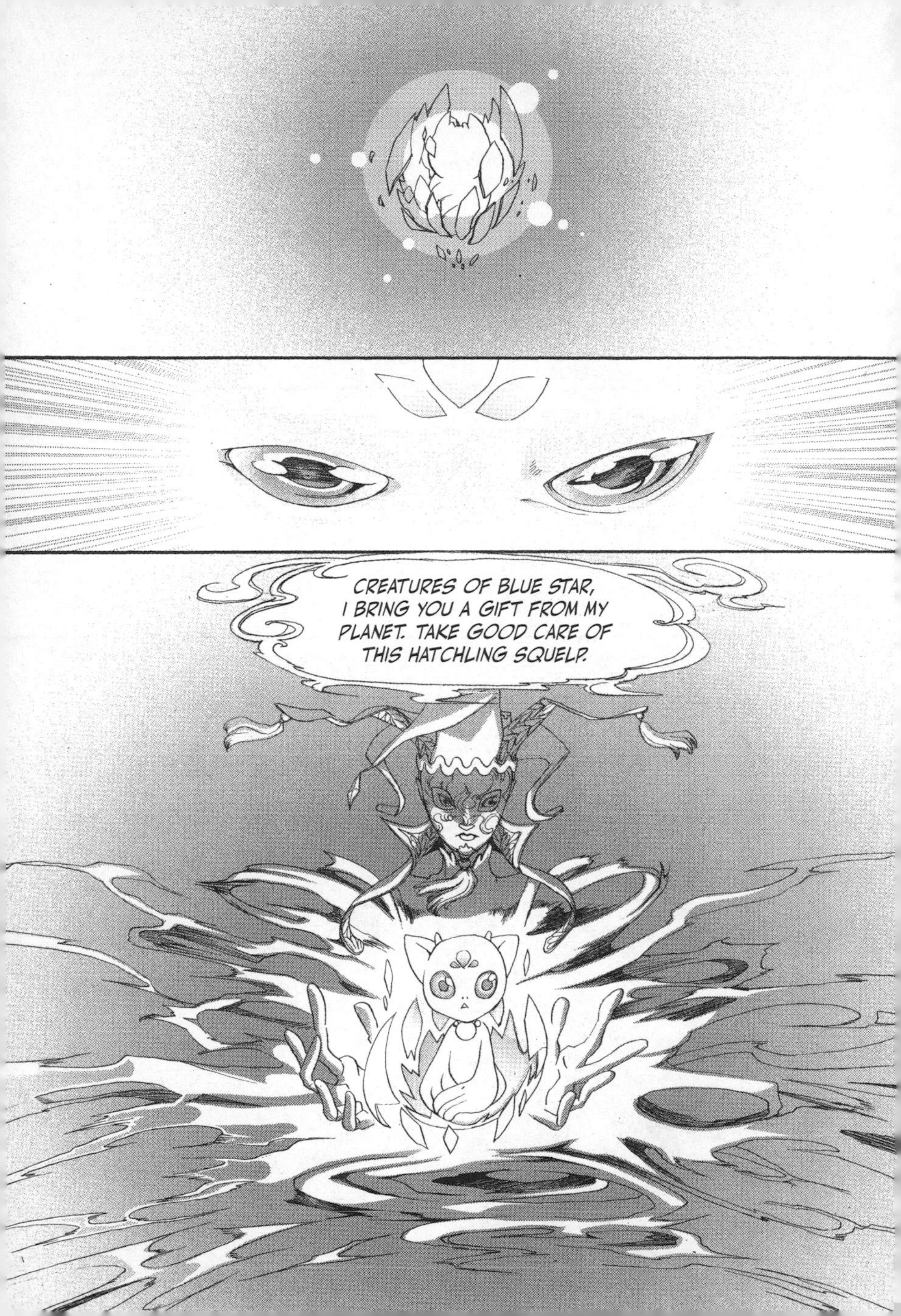
CREATURES OF BLUE STAR, I BRING YOU A GIFT FROM MY PLANET. TAKE GOOD CARE OF THIS HATCHLING SQUELP.

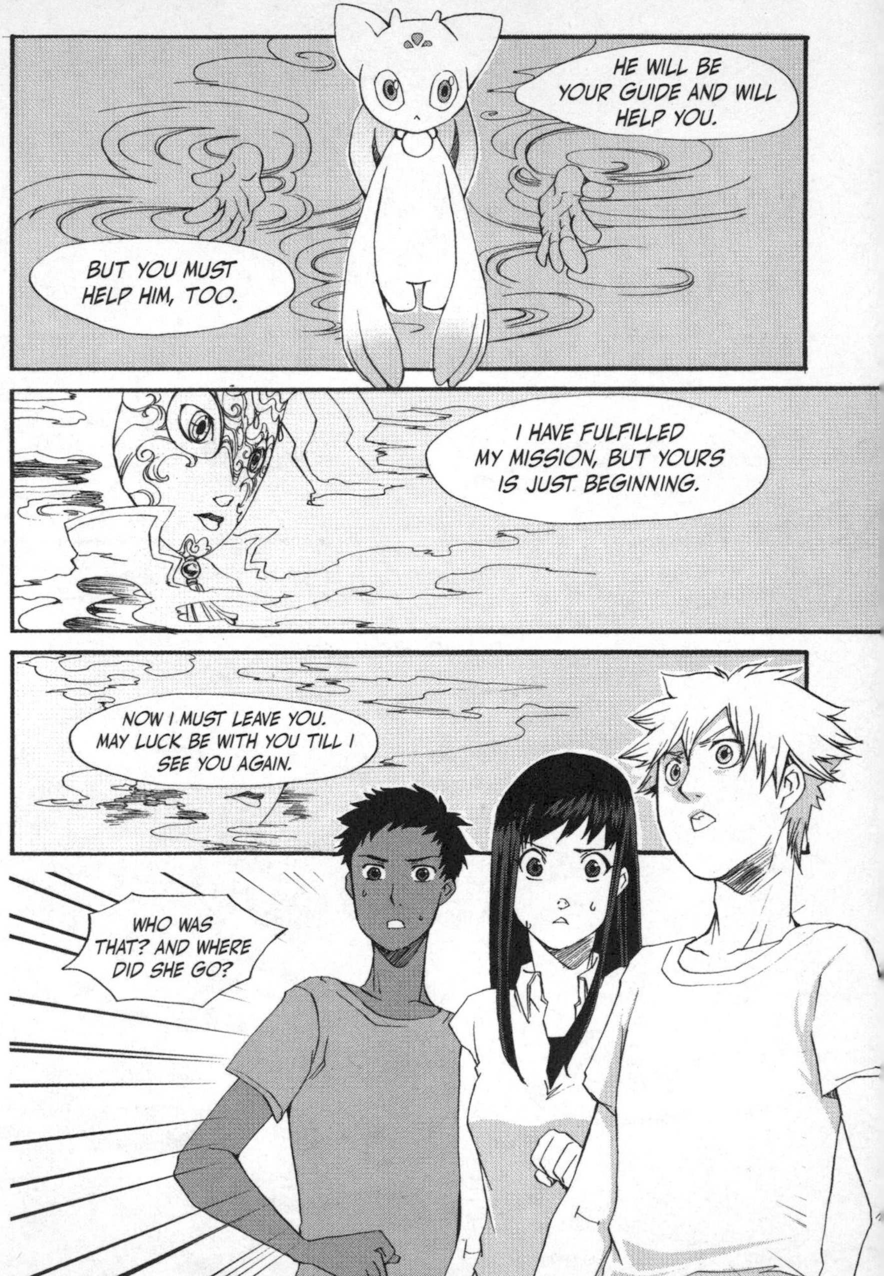
HE WILL BE YOUR GUIDE AND WILL HELP YOU.
BUT YOU MUST HELP HIM, TOO.
I HAVE FULFILLED MY MISSION, BUT YOURS IS JUST BEGINNING.
NOW I MUST LEAVE YOU. MAY LUCK BE WITH YOU TILL I SEE YOU AGAIN.
WHO WAS THAT? AND WHERE DID SHE GO?

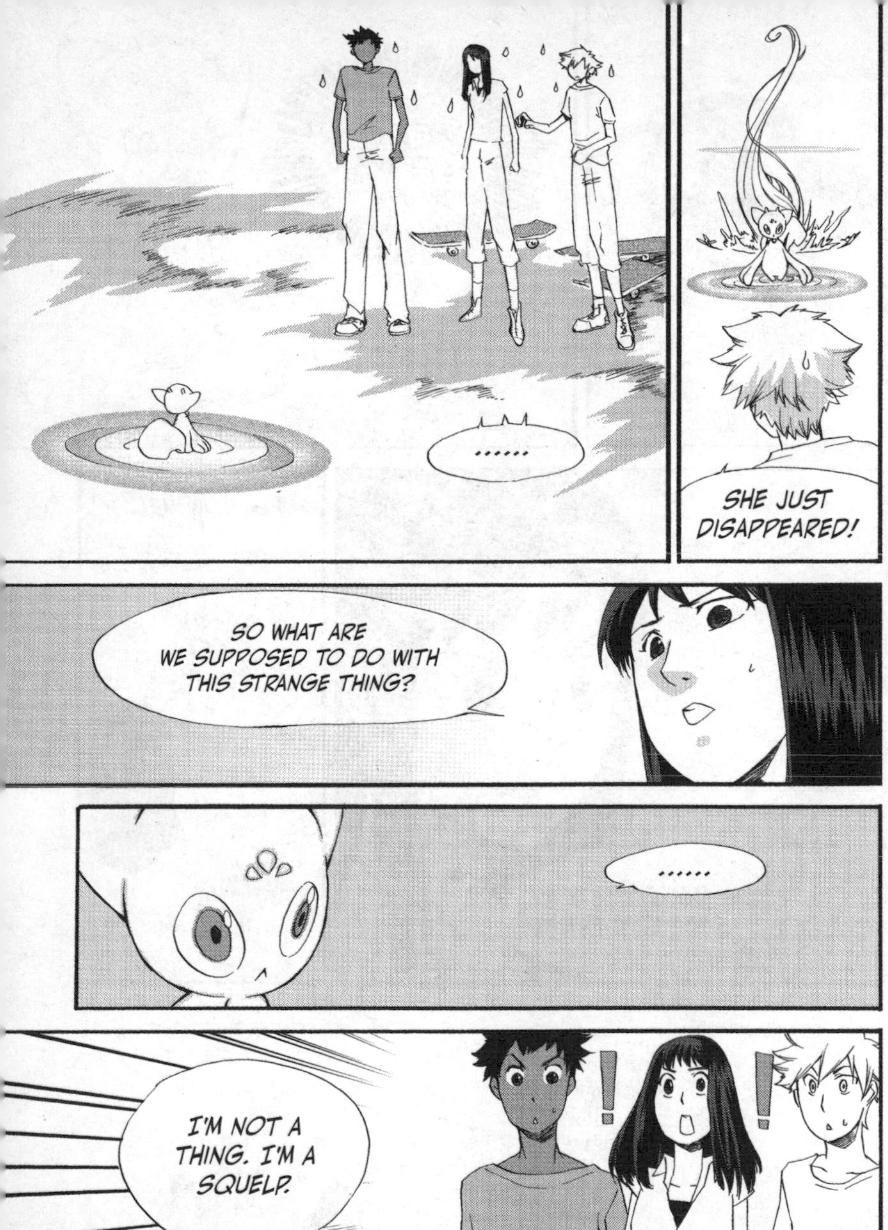
......
SHE JUST DISAPPEARED!
SO WHAT ARE WE SUPPOSED TO DO WITH THIS STRANGE THING?
......
I'M NOT A THING. I'M A SQUELP.

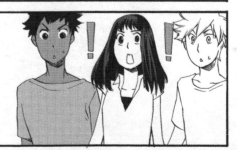

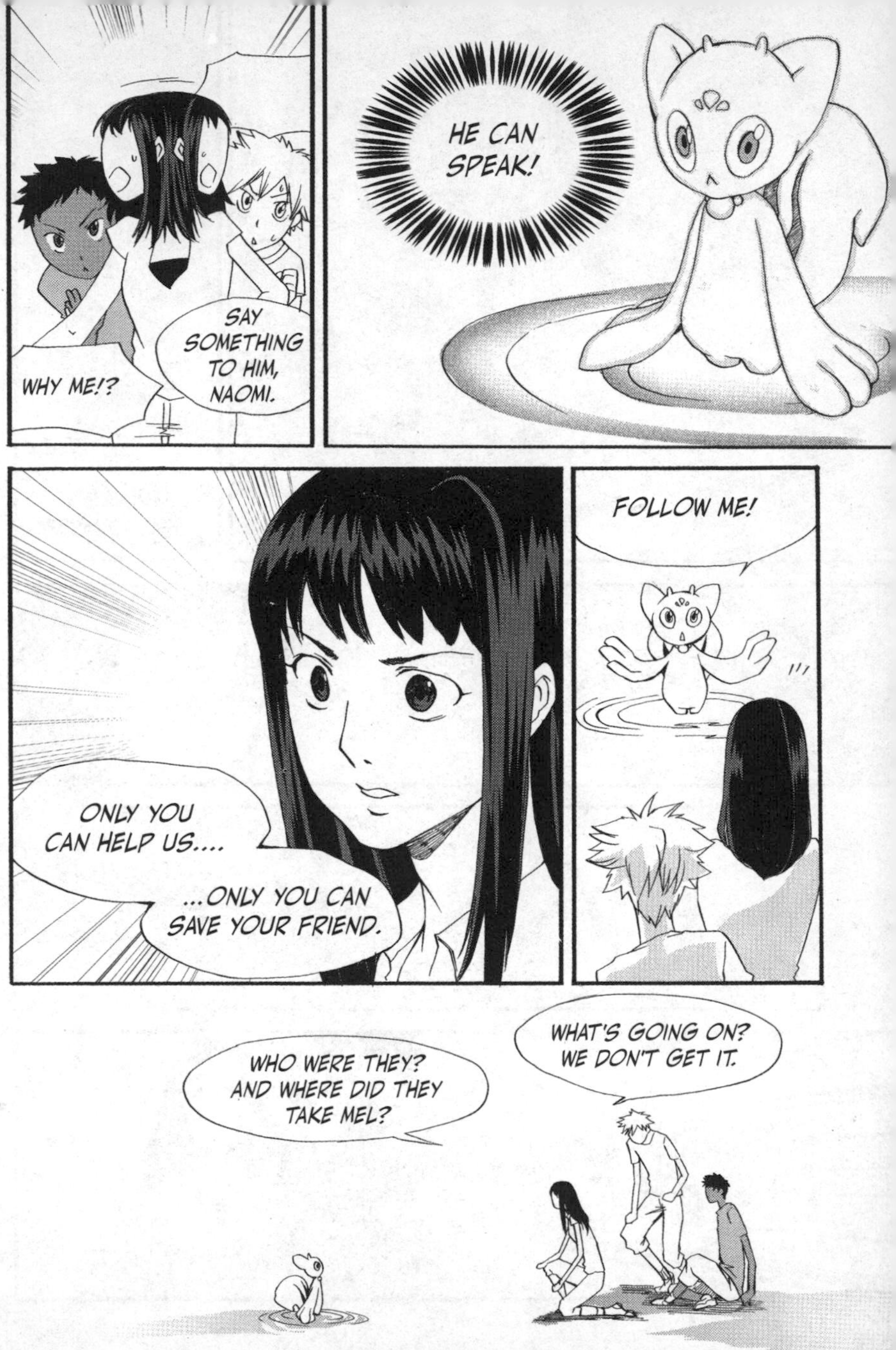
SAY SOMETHING TO HIM, NAOMI.
WHY ME!?
HE CAN SPEAK!
ONLY YOU CAN HELP US....
...ONLY YOU CAN SAVE YOUR FRIEND.
FOLLOW ME!
WHAT'S GOING ON? WE DON'T GET IT.
WHO WERE THEY? AND WHERE DID THEY TAKE MEL?

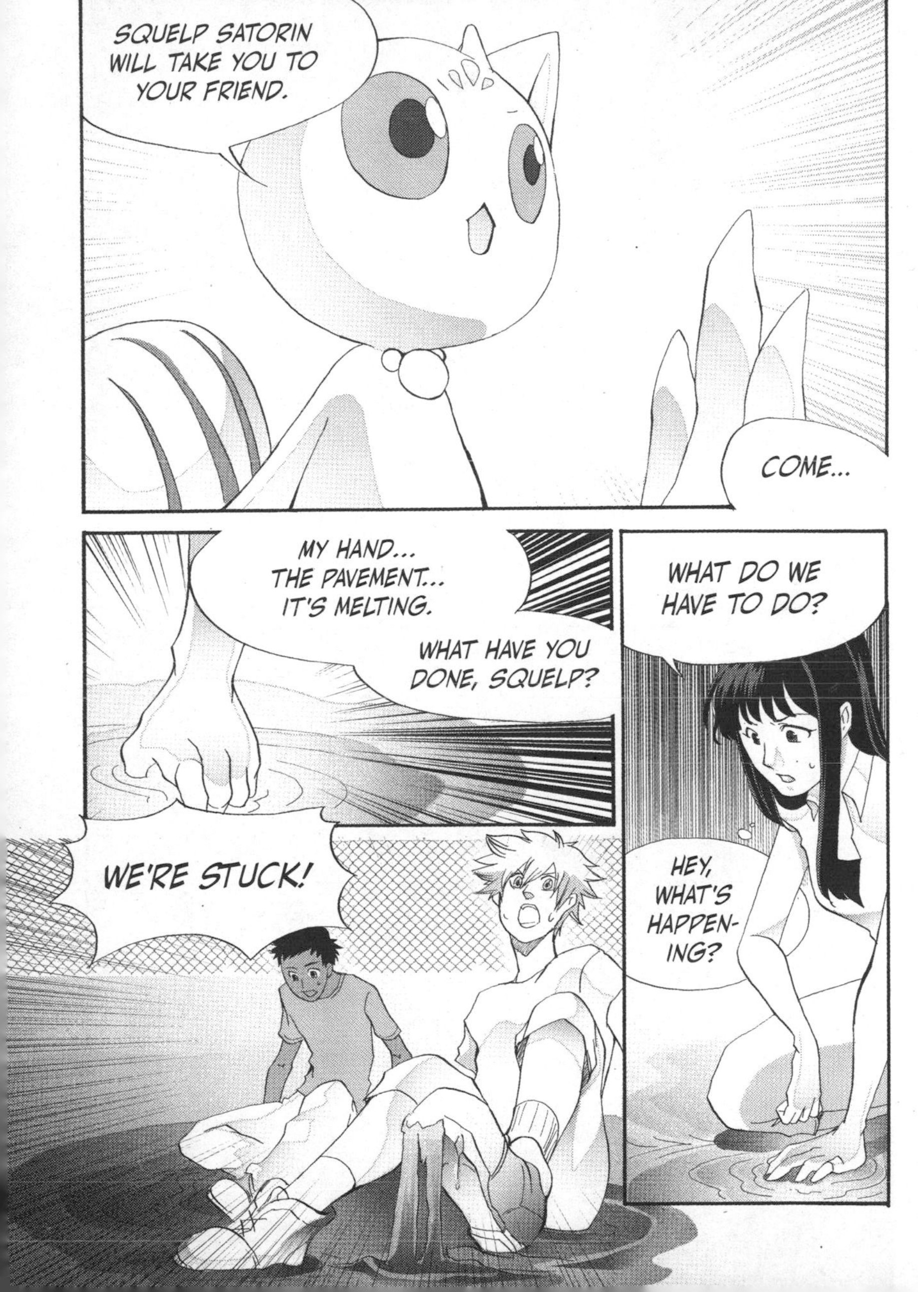
SQUELP SATORIN WILL TAKE YOU TO YOUR FRIEND.
COME...
MY HAND... THE PAVEMENT... IT'S MELTING.
WHAT HAVE YOU DONE, SQUELP?
WHAT DO WE HAVE TO DO?
WE'RE STUCK!
HEY, WHAT'S HAPPEN-ING?

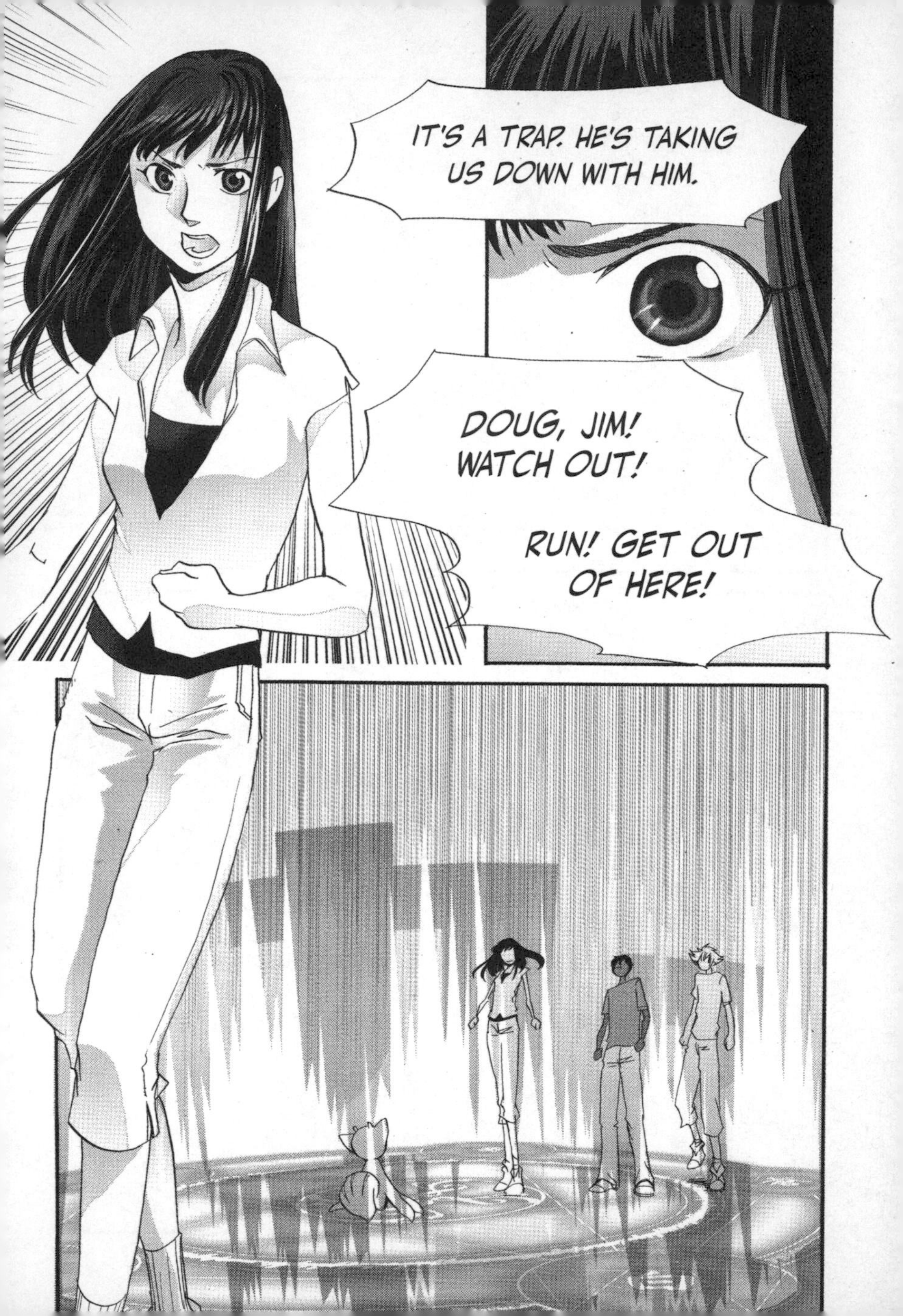
IT'S A TRAP. HE'S TAKING US DOWN WITH HIM.
DOUG, JIM! WATCH OUT!
RUN! GET OUT OF HERE!

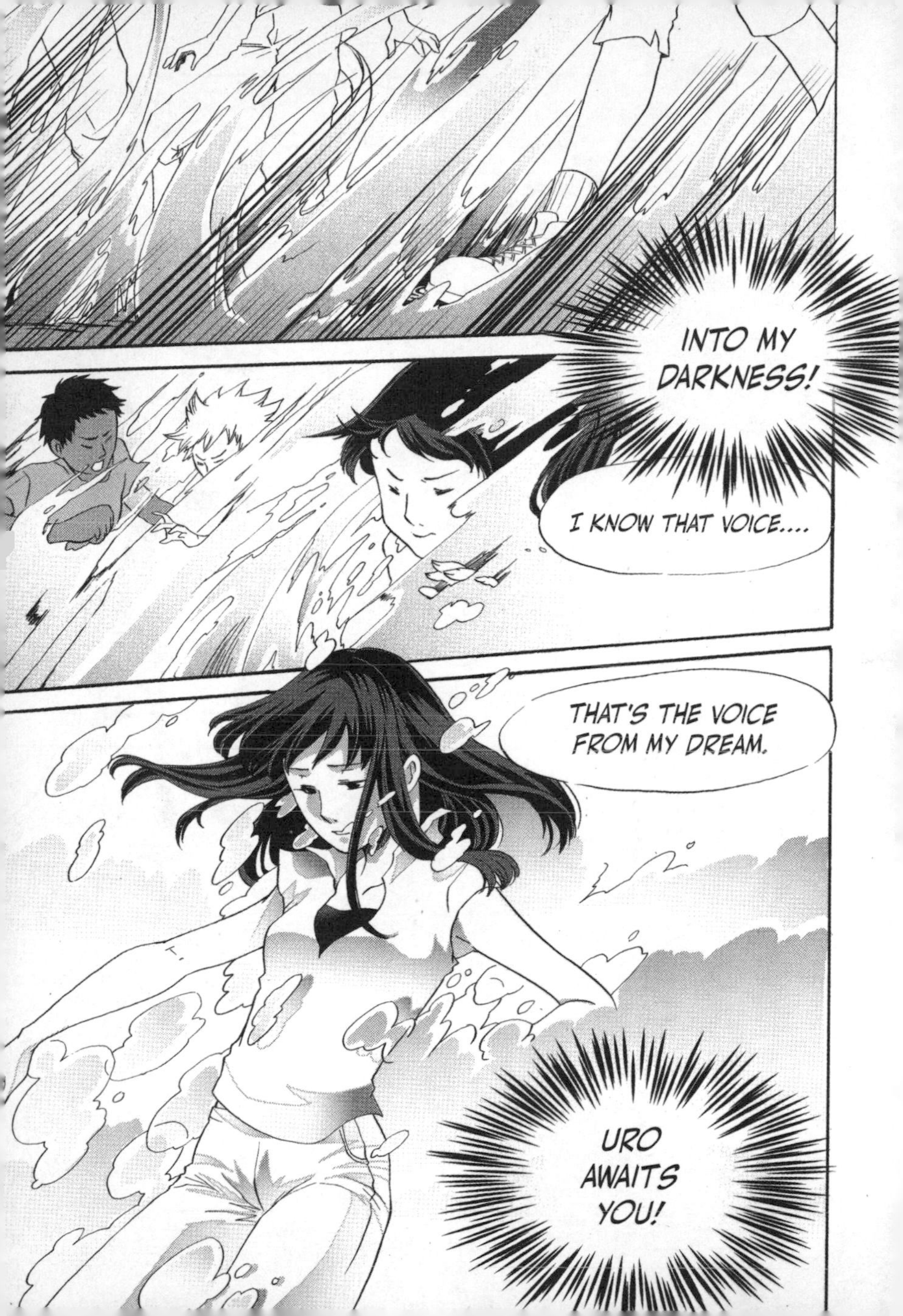
INTO MY DARKNESS!
I KNOW THAT VOICE....
THAT'S THE VOICE FROM MY DREAM.
URO AWAITS YOU!

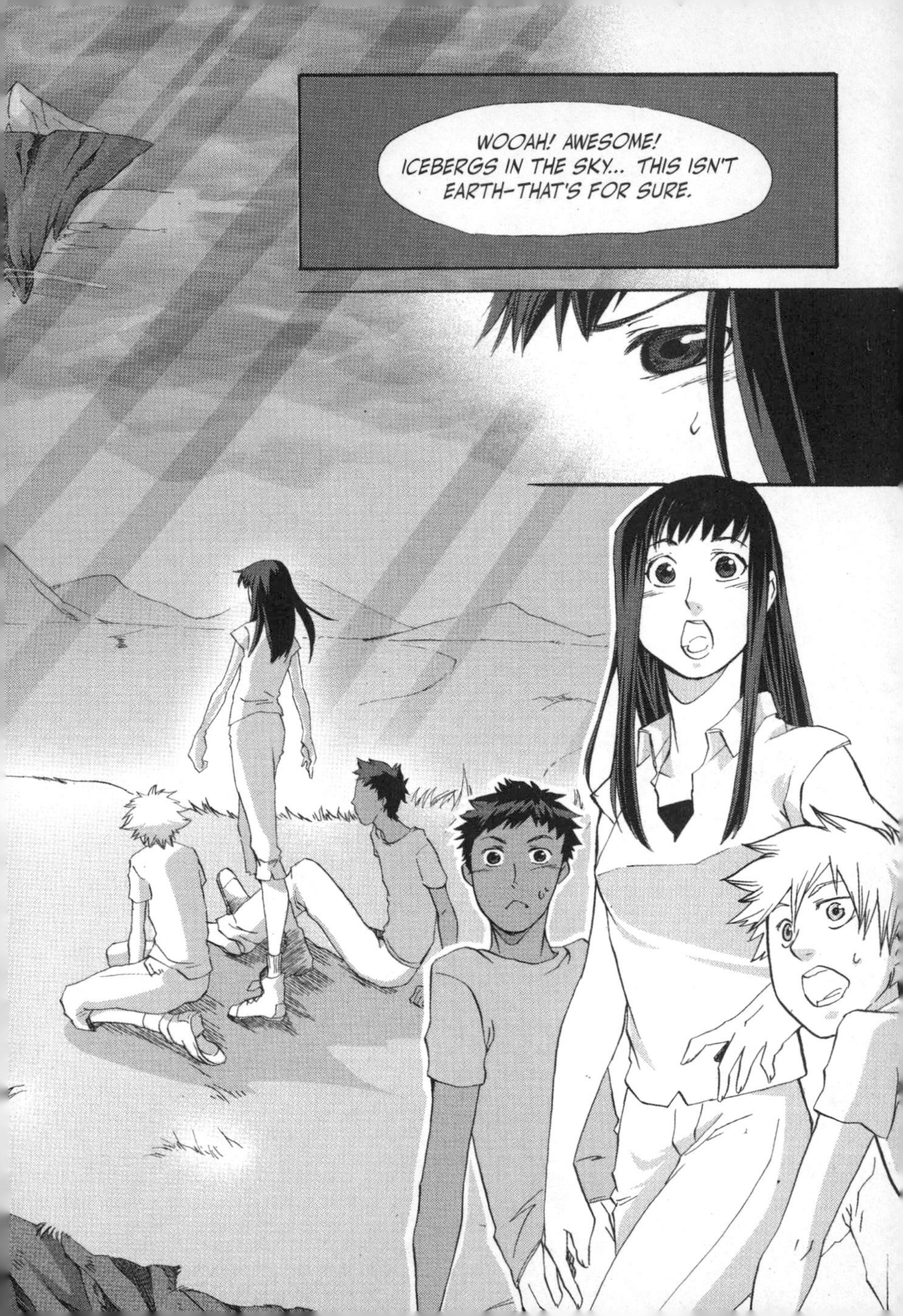
WOOAH! AWESOME! ICEBERGS IN THE SKY... THIS ISN'T EARTH–THAT'S FOR SURE.

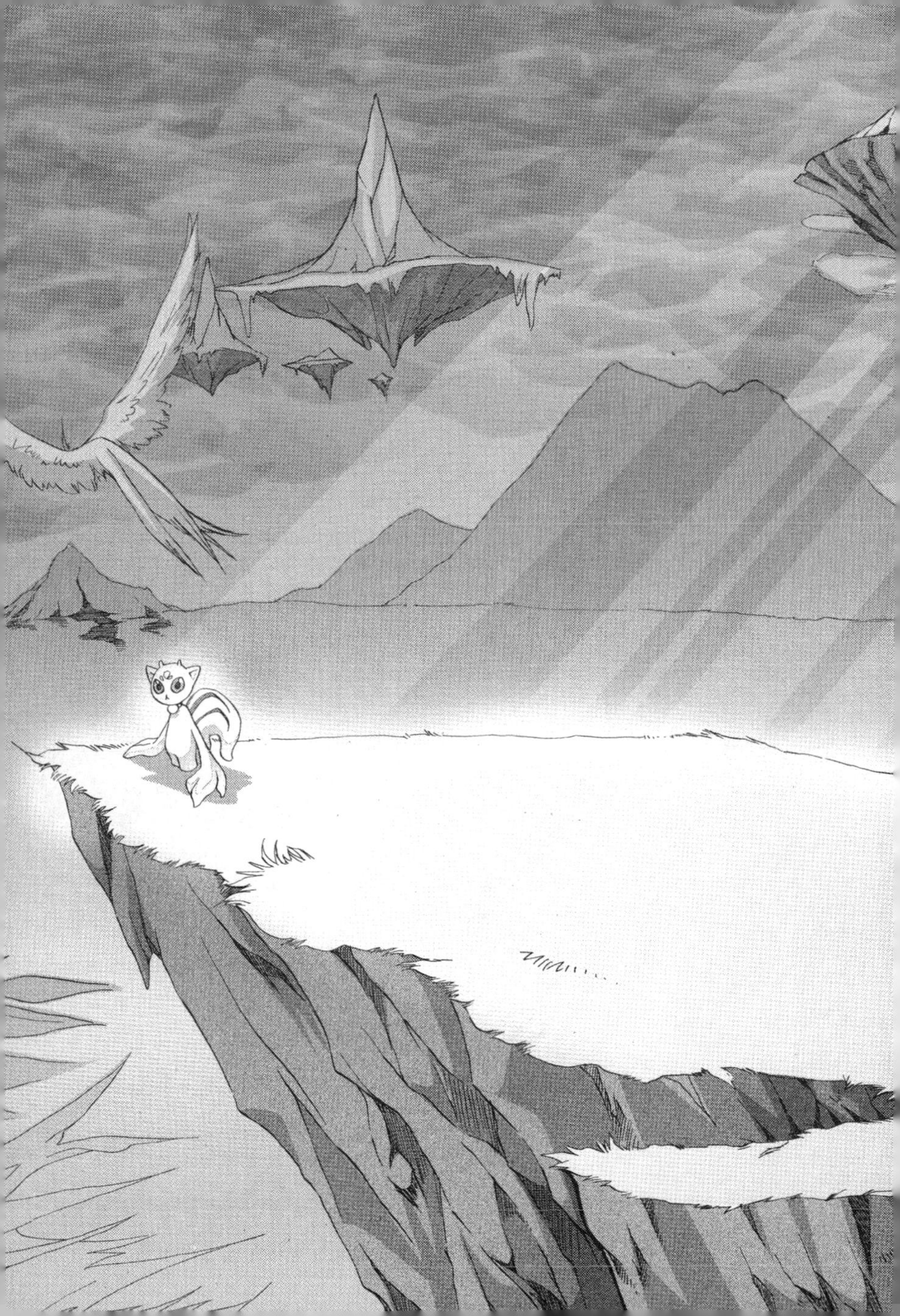

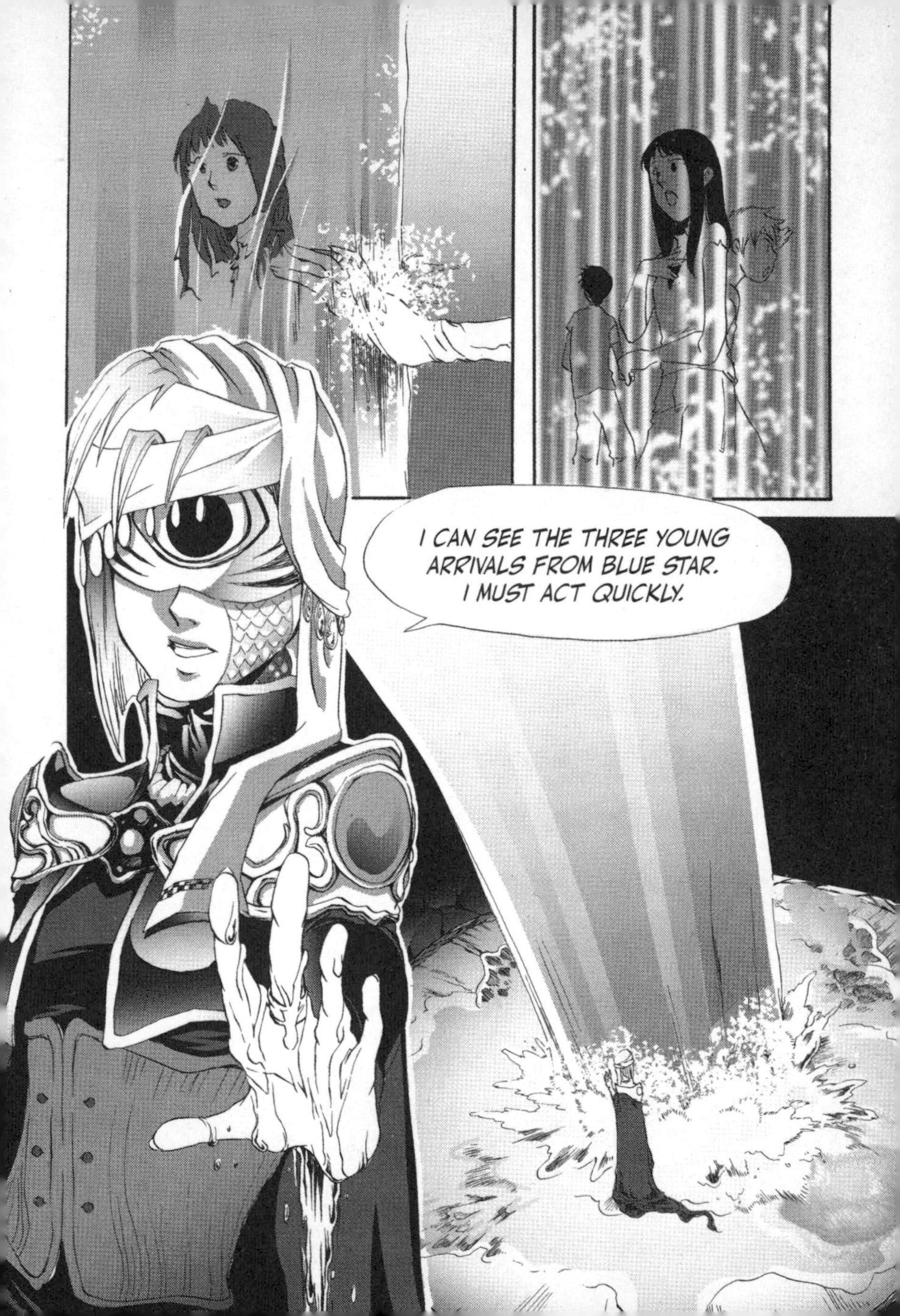
I CAN SEE THE THREE YOUNG ARRIVALS FROM BLUE STAR. I MUST ACT QUICKLY.

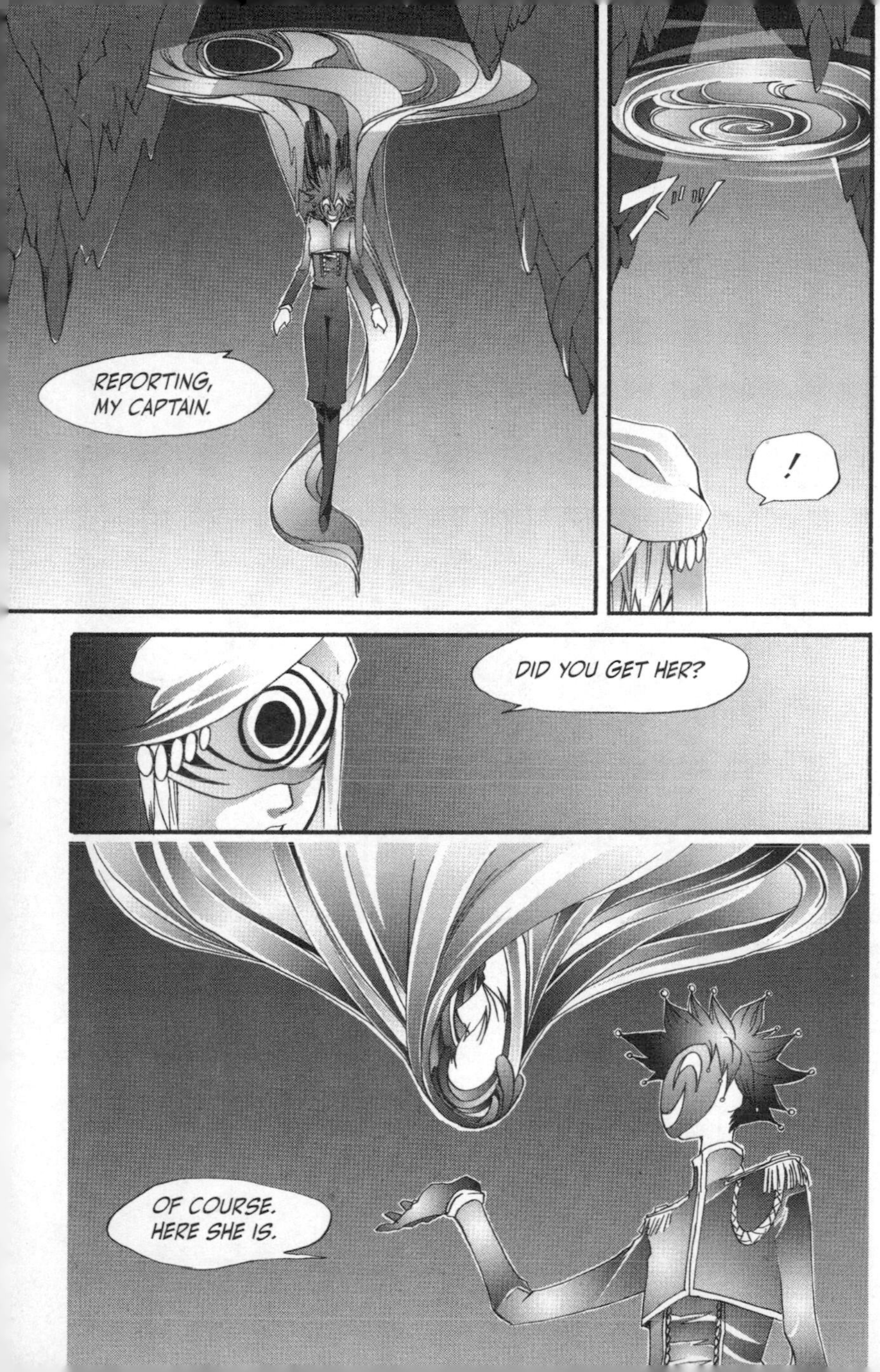
REPORTING, MY CAPTAIN.
!
DID YOU GET HER?
OF COURSE. HERE SHE IS.

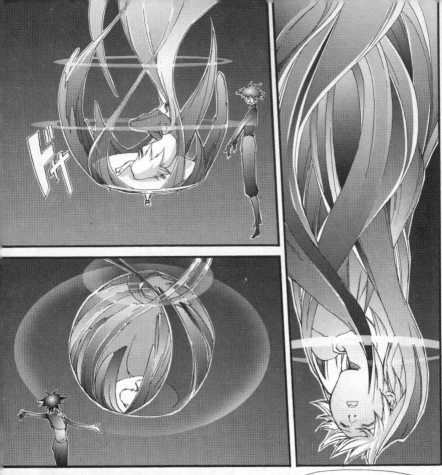

SHE CANNOT ESCAPE FROM THIS BUBBLE.

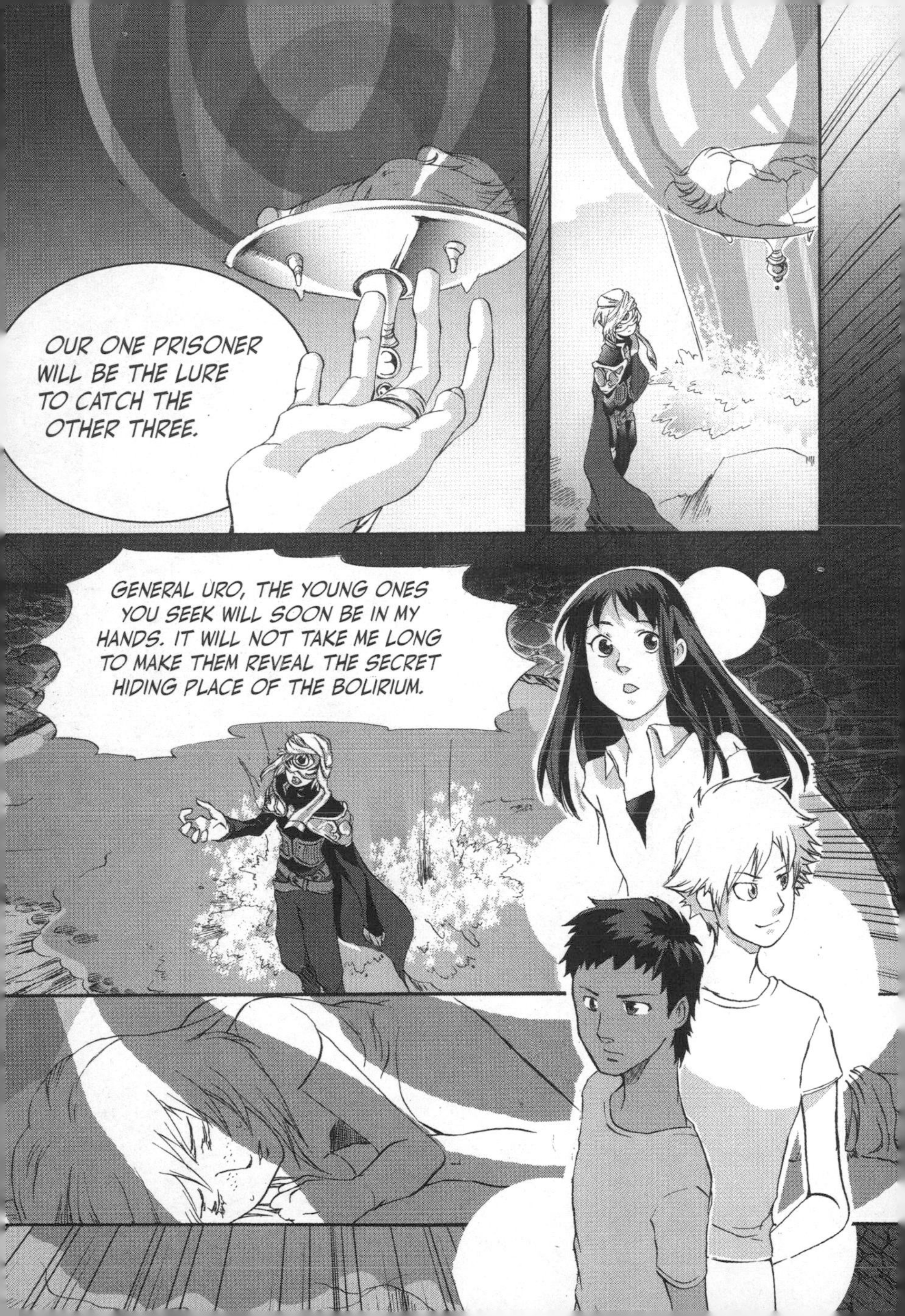
OUR ONE PRISONER WILL BE THE LURE TO CATCH THE OTHER THREE.
GENERAL URO, THE YOUNG ONES YOU SEEK WILL SOON BE IN MY HANDS. IT WILL NOT TAKE ME LONG TO MAKE THEM REVEAL THE SECRET HIDING PLACE OF THE BOLIRIUM.

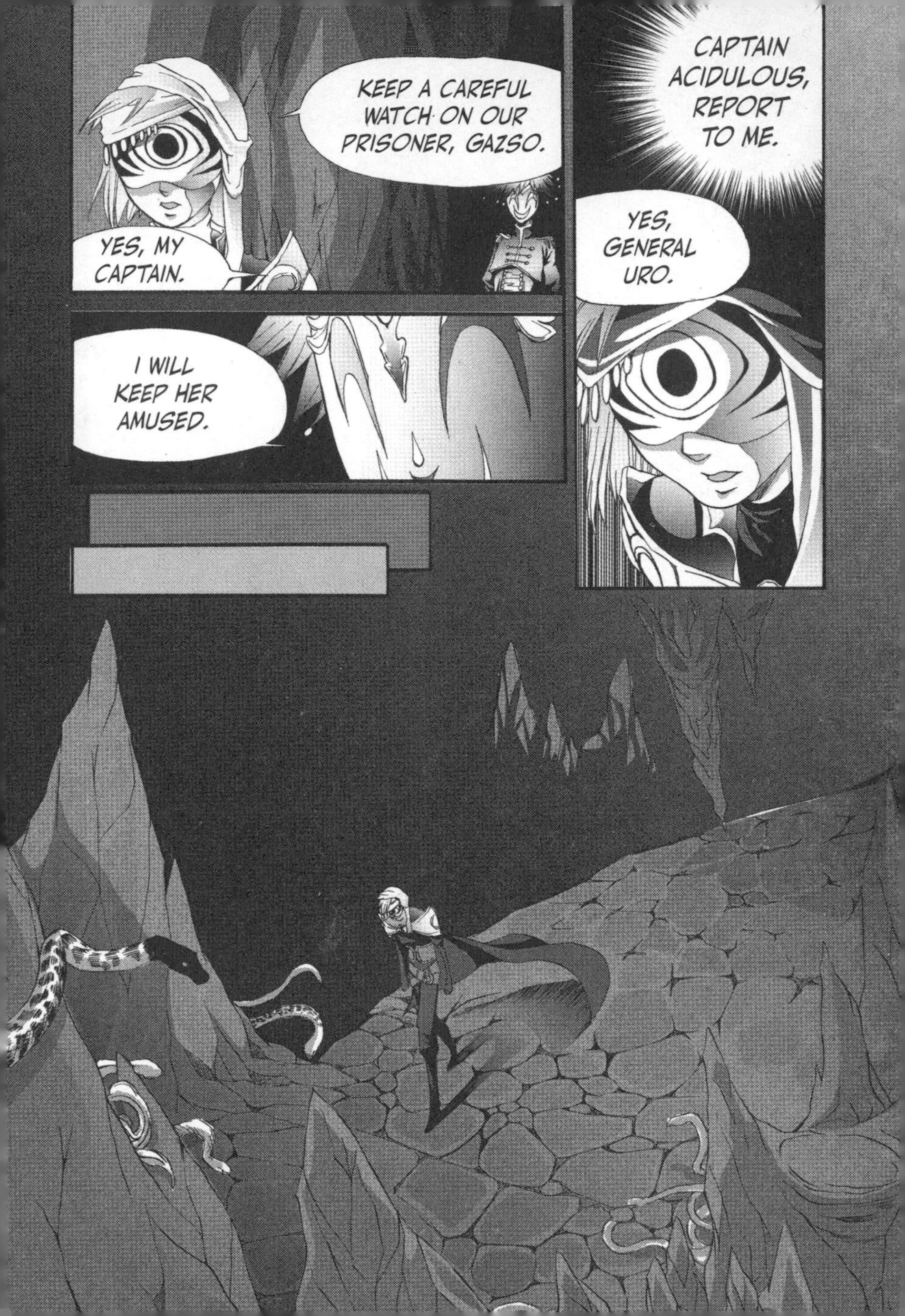
KEEP A CAREFUL WATCH ON OUR PRISONER, GAZSO.
YES, MY CAPTAIN.
CAPTAIN ACIDULOUS, REPORT TO ME.
YES, GENERAL URO.
I WILL KEEP HER AMUSED.

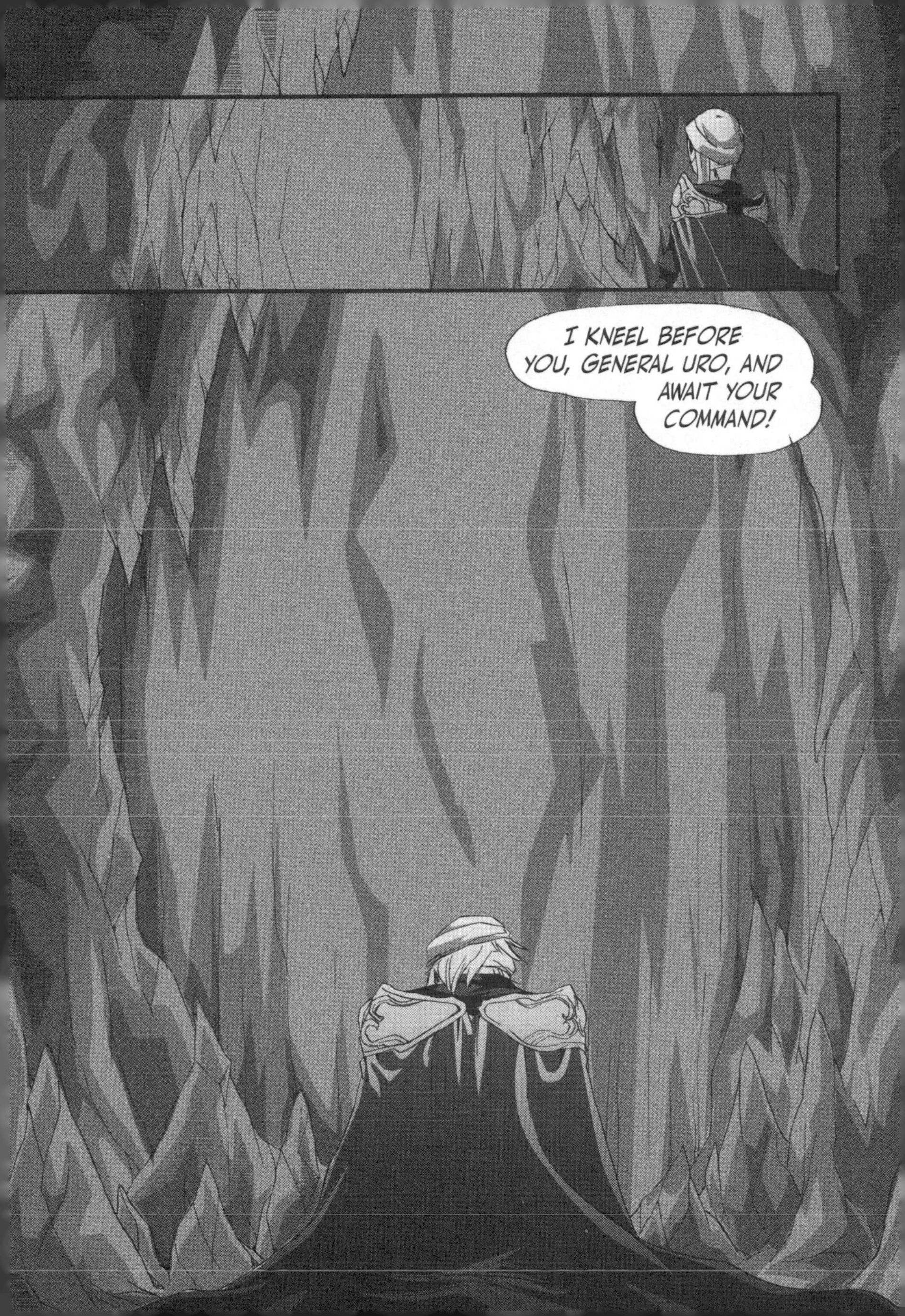
I KNEEL BEFORE YOU, GENERAL URO, AND AWAIT YOUR COMMAND!

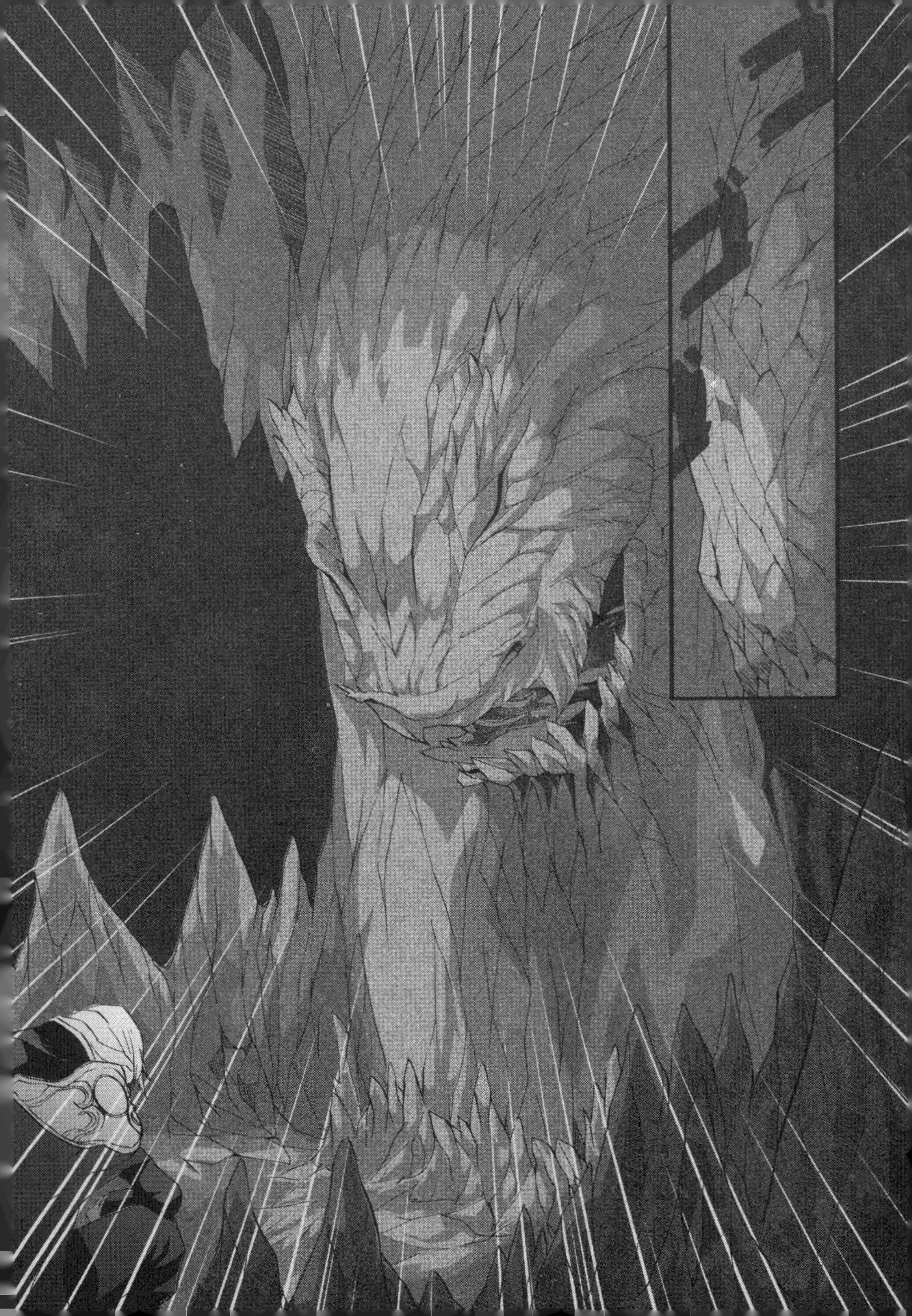

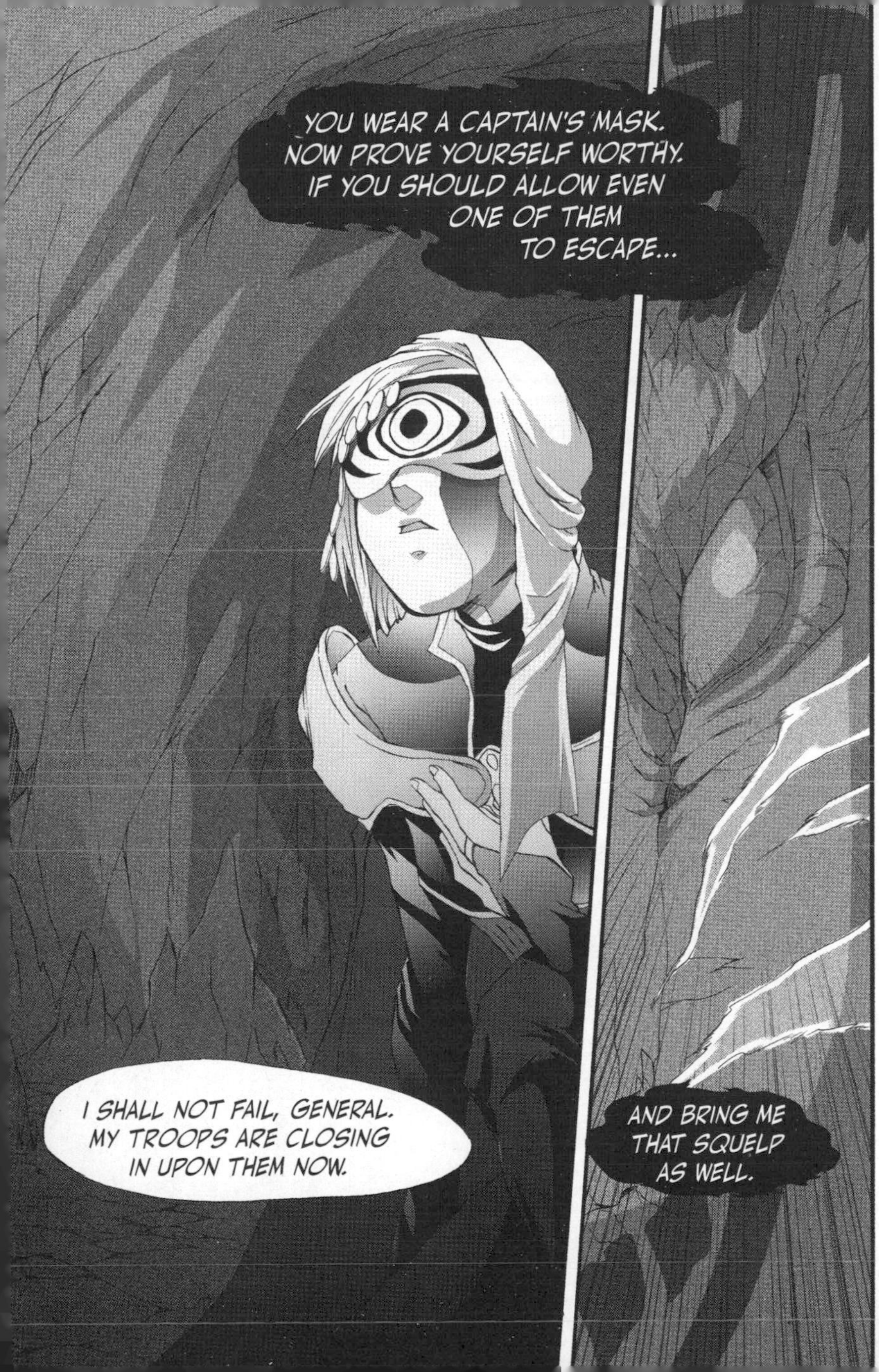
YOU WEAR A CAPTAIN'S MASK. NOW PROVE YOURSELF WORTHY. IF YOU SHOULD ALLOW EVEN ONE OF THEM TO ESCAPE...
I SHALL NOT FAIL, GENERAL. MY TROOPS ARE CLOSING IN UPON THEM NOW.
AND BRING ME THAT SQUELP AS WELL.

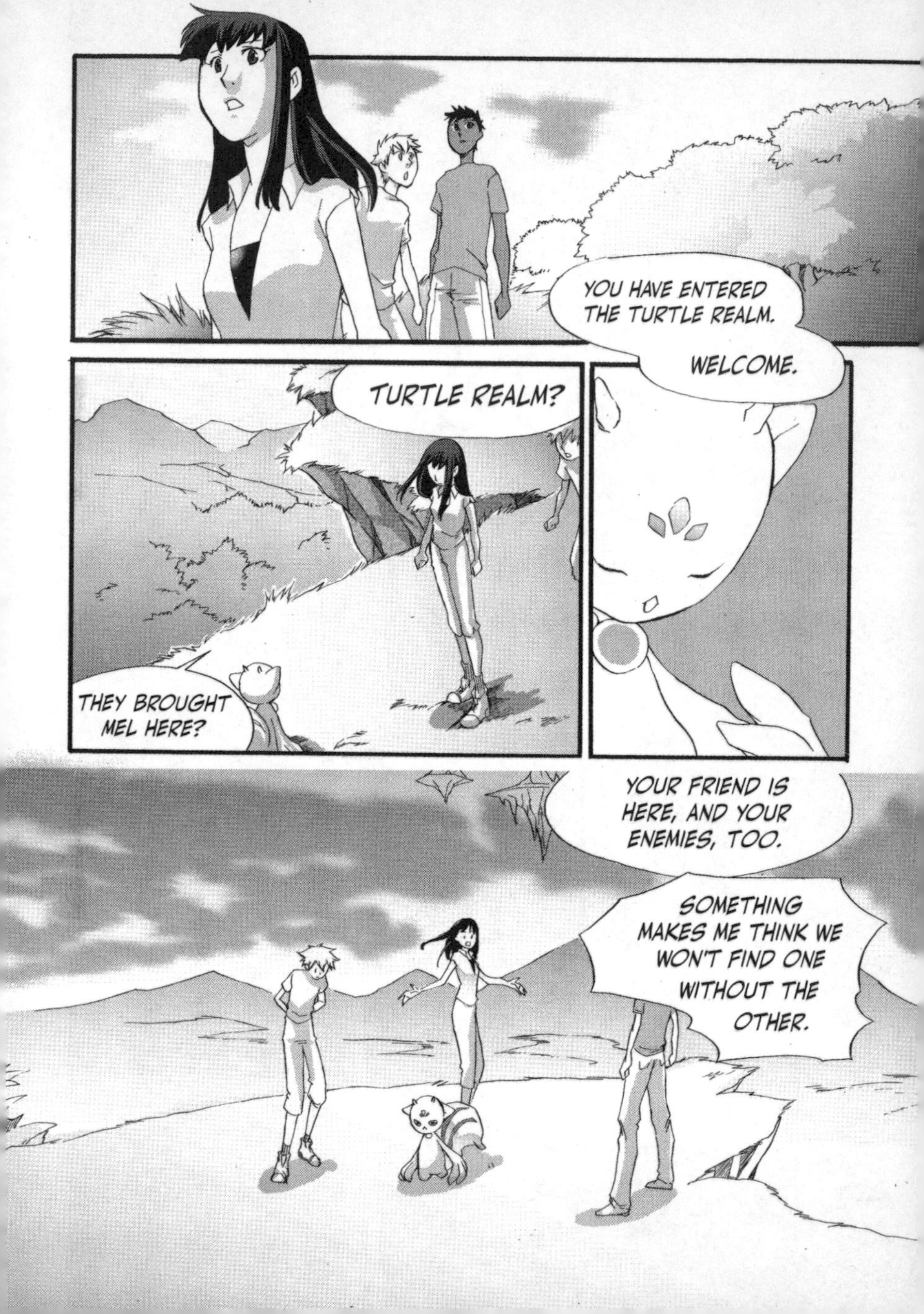
YOU HAVE ENTERED THE TURTLE REALM.
WELCOME.
TURTLE REALM?
THEY BROUGHT MEL HERE?
YOUR FRIEND IS HERE, AND YOUR ENEMIES, TOO.
SOMETHING MAKES ME THINK WE WON'T FIND ONE WITHOUT THE OTHER.

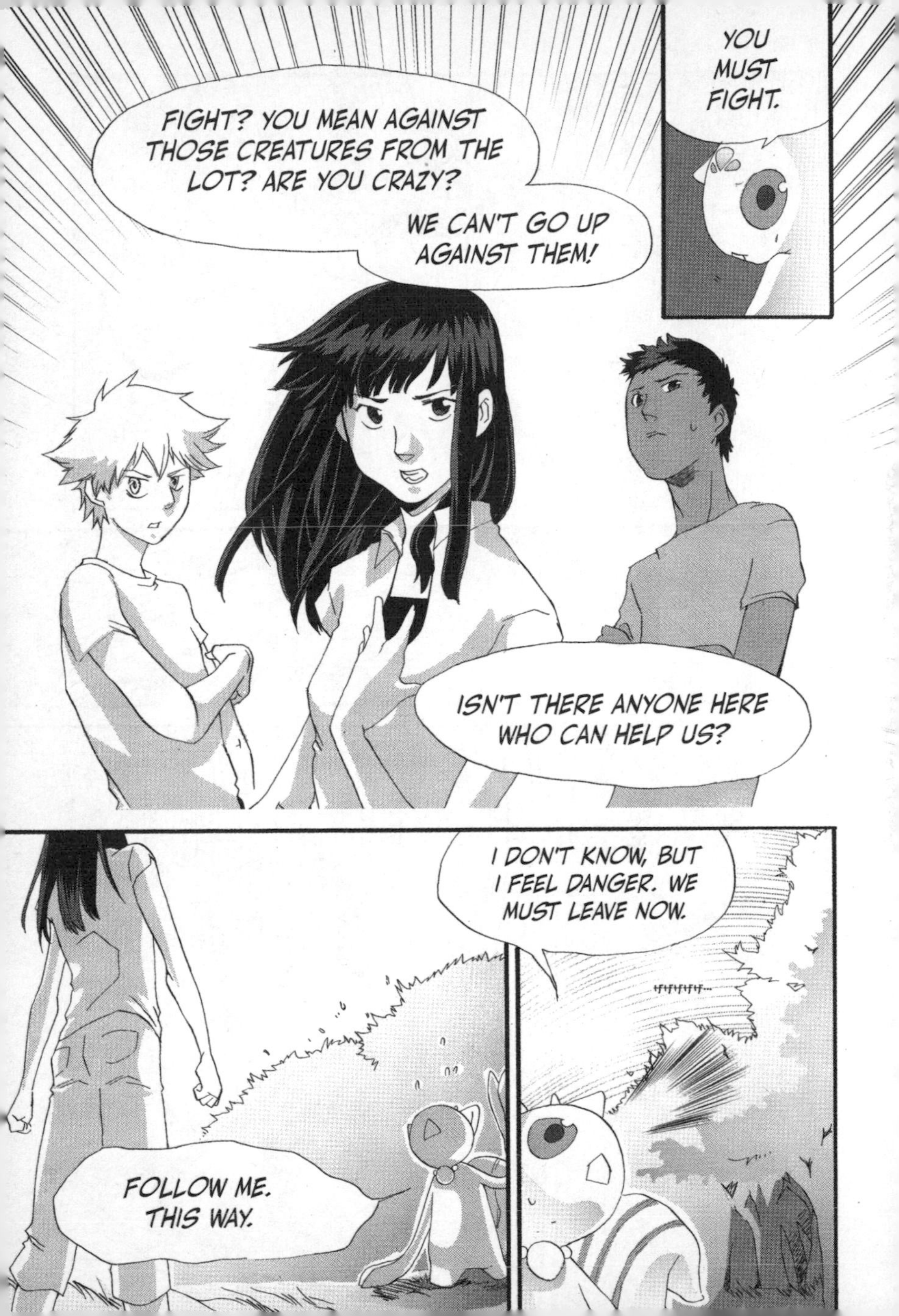
YOU MUST FIGHT.
FIGHT? YOU MEAN AGAINST THOSE CREATURES FROM THE LOT? ARE YOU CRAZY?
WE CAN'T GO UP AGAINST THEM!
ISN'T THERE ANYONE HERE WHO CAN HELP US?
I DON'T KNOW, BUT I FEEL DANGER. WE MUST LEAVE NOW.
FOLLOW ME. THIS WAY.

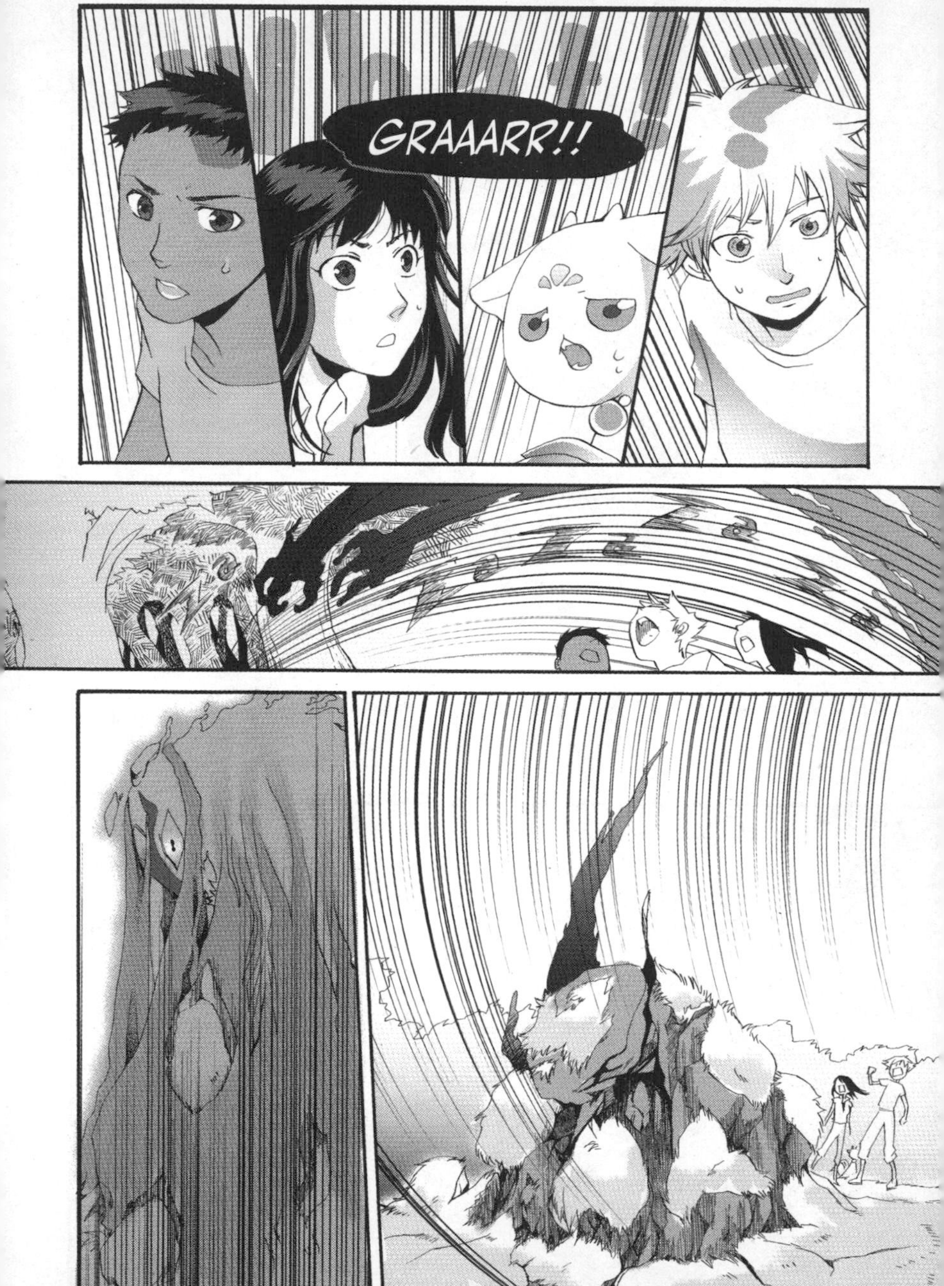
GRAAARR!!

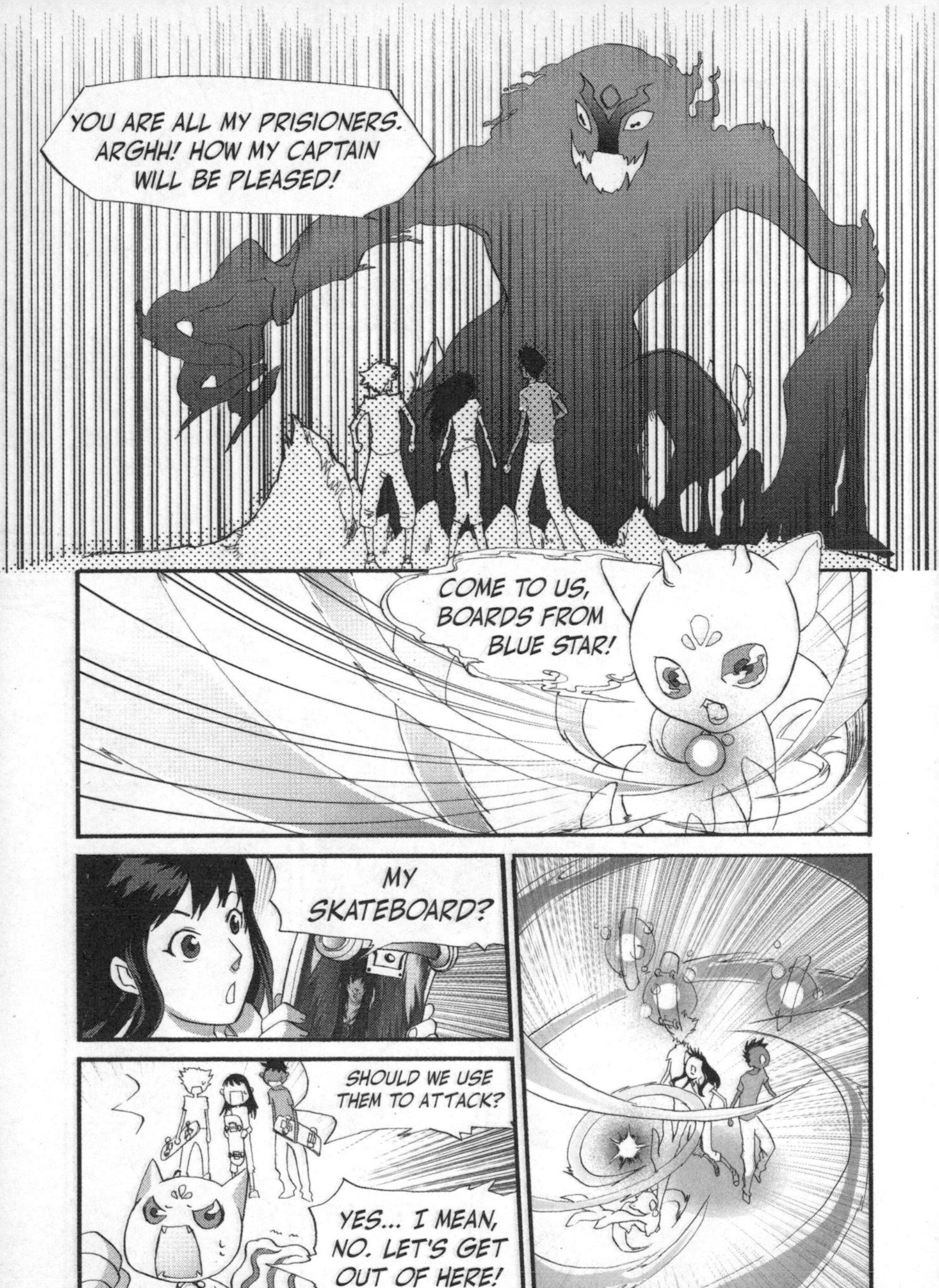
YOU ARE ALL MY PRISIONERS. ARGHH! HOW MY CAPTAIN WILL BE PLEASED!
COME TO US, BOARDS FROM BLUE STAR!
MY SKATEBOARD?
SHOULD WE USE THEM TO ATTACK?
YES... I MEAN, NO. LET'S GET OUT OF HERE!

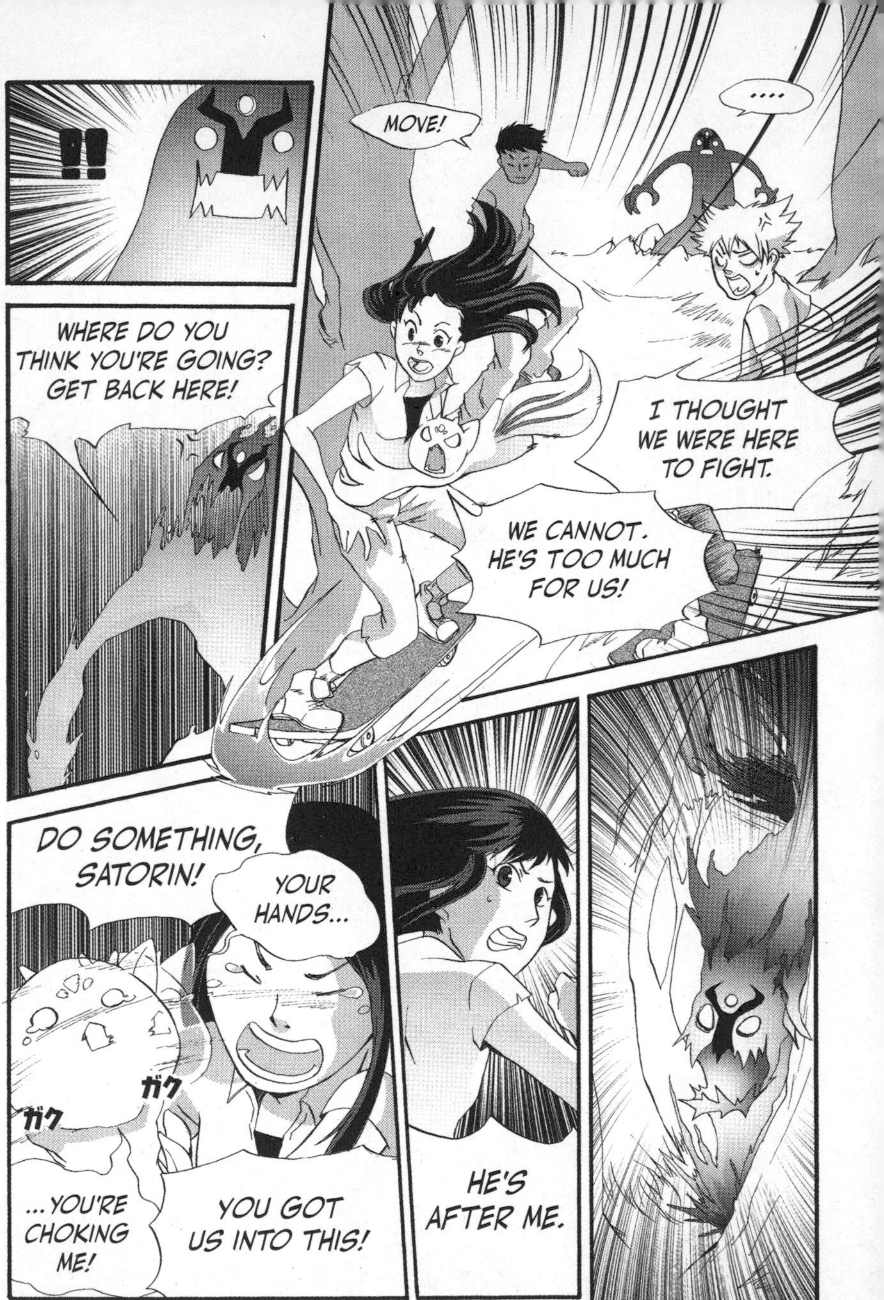
!!
MOVE!
....
WHERE DO YOU THINK YOU'RE GOING? GET BACK HERE!
I THOUGHT WE WERE HERE TO FIGHT.
WE CANNOT. HE'S TOO MUCH FOR US!
DO SOMETHING, SATORIN!
YOUR HANDS...
ガク
ガク
...YOU'RE CHOKING ME!
YOU GOT US INTO THIS!
HE'S AFTER ME.

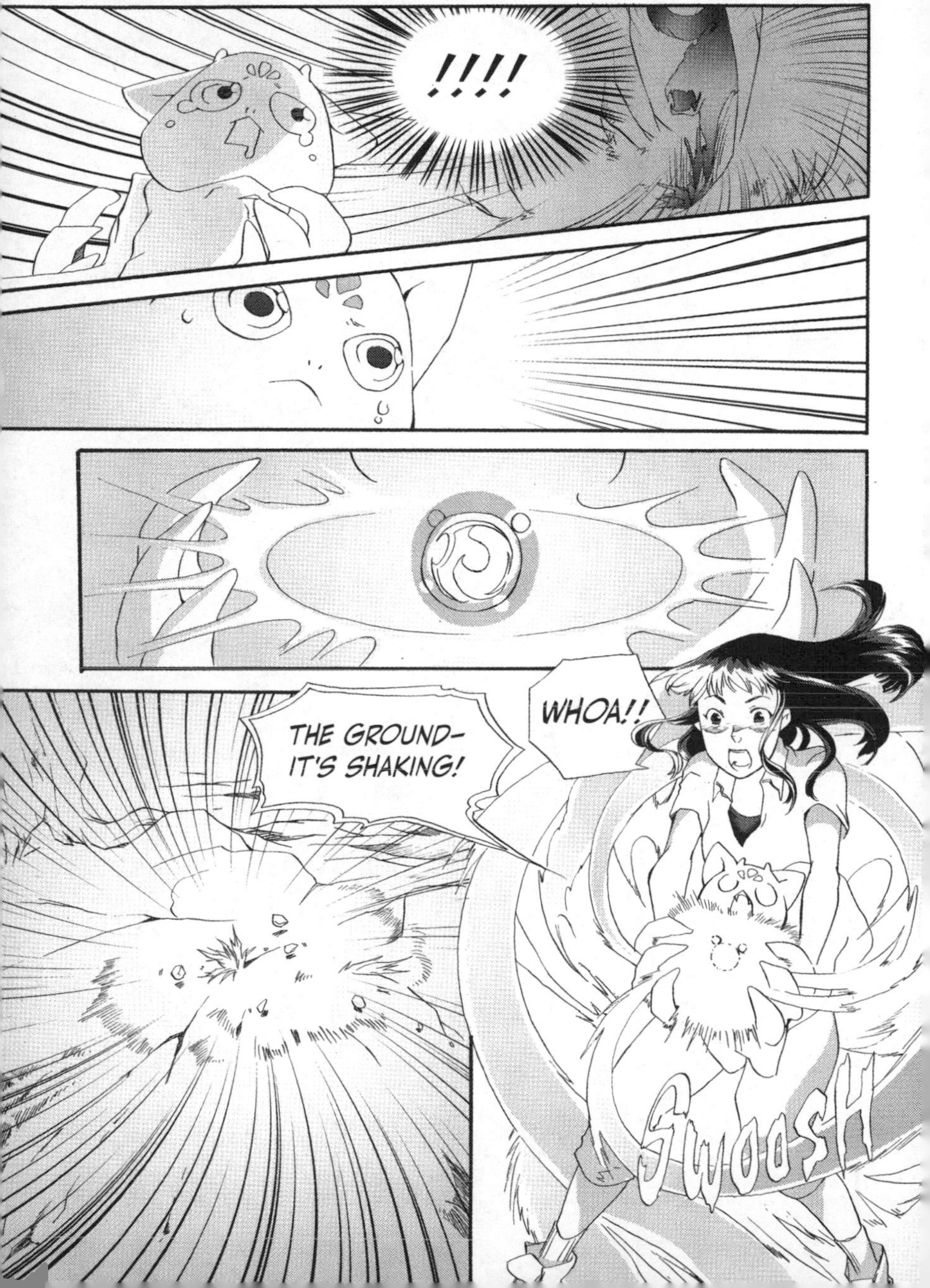
!!!!
WHOA!!
THE GROUND-
IT'S SHAKING!
SWOOSH

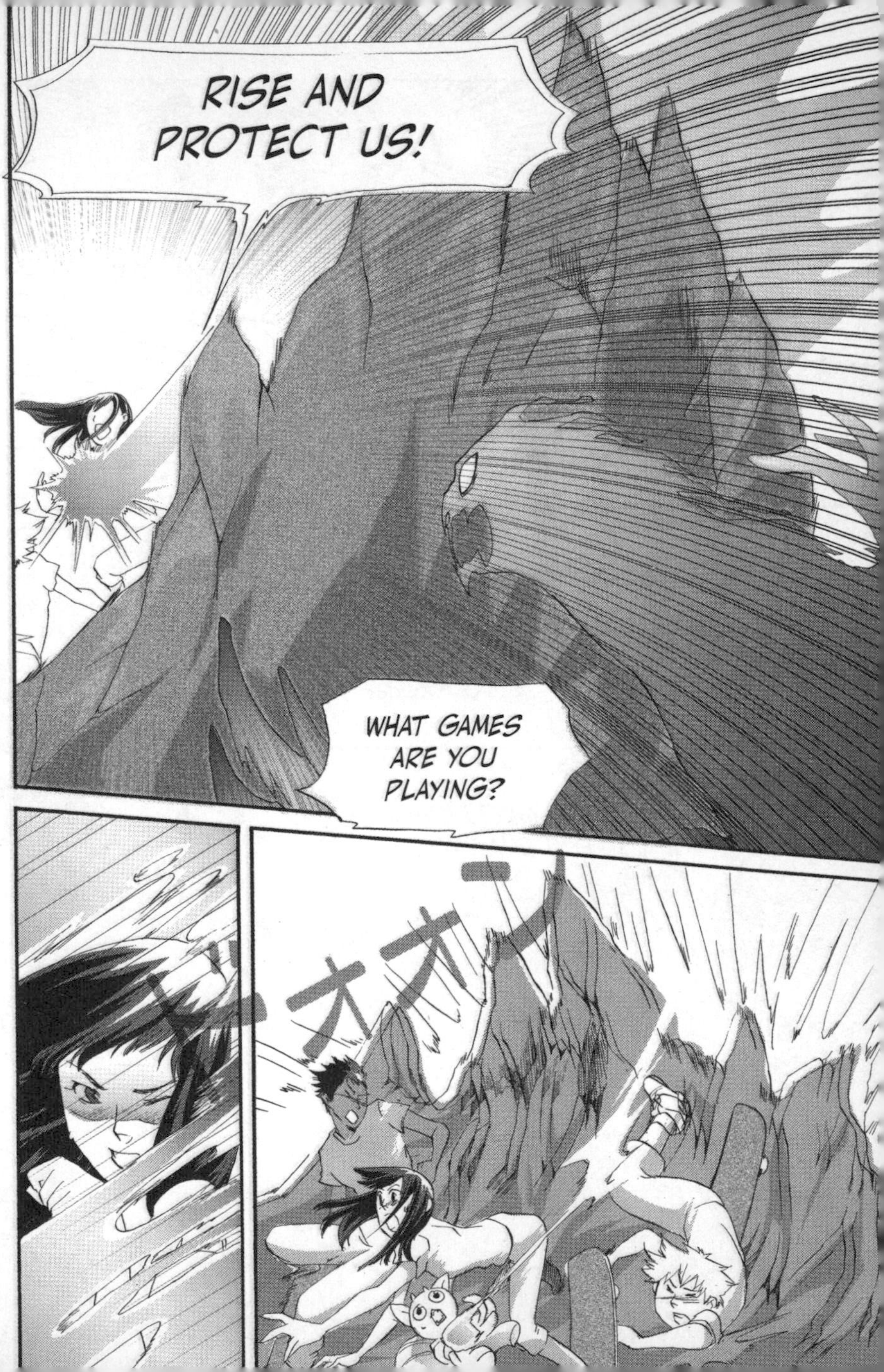
RISE AND PROTECT US!
WHAT GAMES ARE YOU PLAYING?

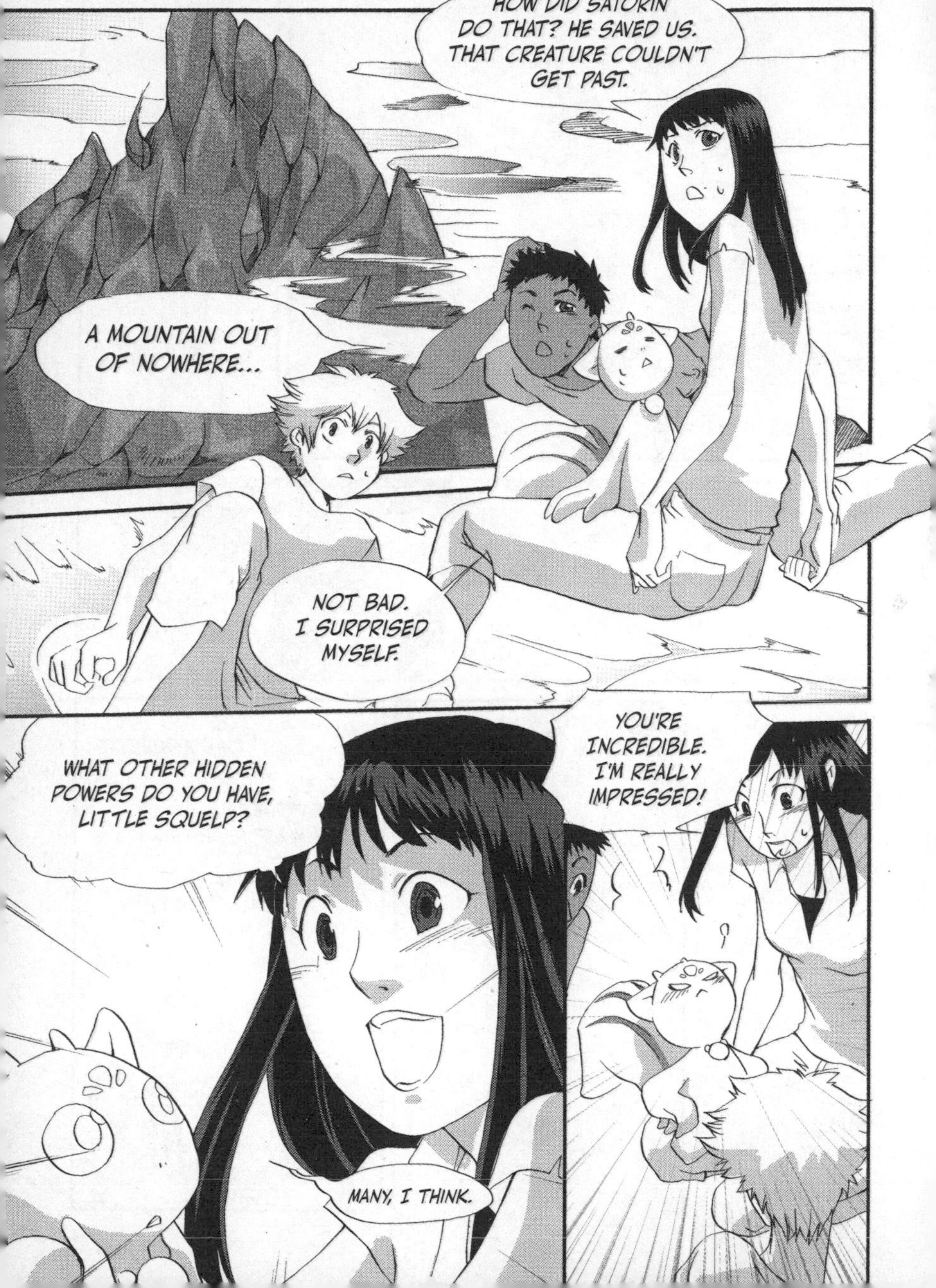
HOW DID SATORIN DO THAT? HE SAVED US. THAT CREATURE COULDN'T GET PAST.
A MOUNTAIN OUT OF NOWHERE...
NOT BAD. I SURPRISED MYSELF.
WHAT OTHER HIDDEN POWERS DO YOU HAVE, LITTLE SQUELP?
MANY, I THINK.
YOU'RE INCREDIBLE. I'M REALLY IMPRESSED!

....?

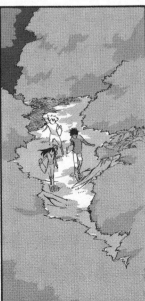

DO YOU SEE THIS FOREST?

I MADE IT TOO. I GROW MORE POWERFUL WITH YOUR HELP.

YOU'VE GOT THE MAGIC, SATORIN. WHICH WAY NOW?

真 102

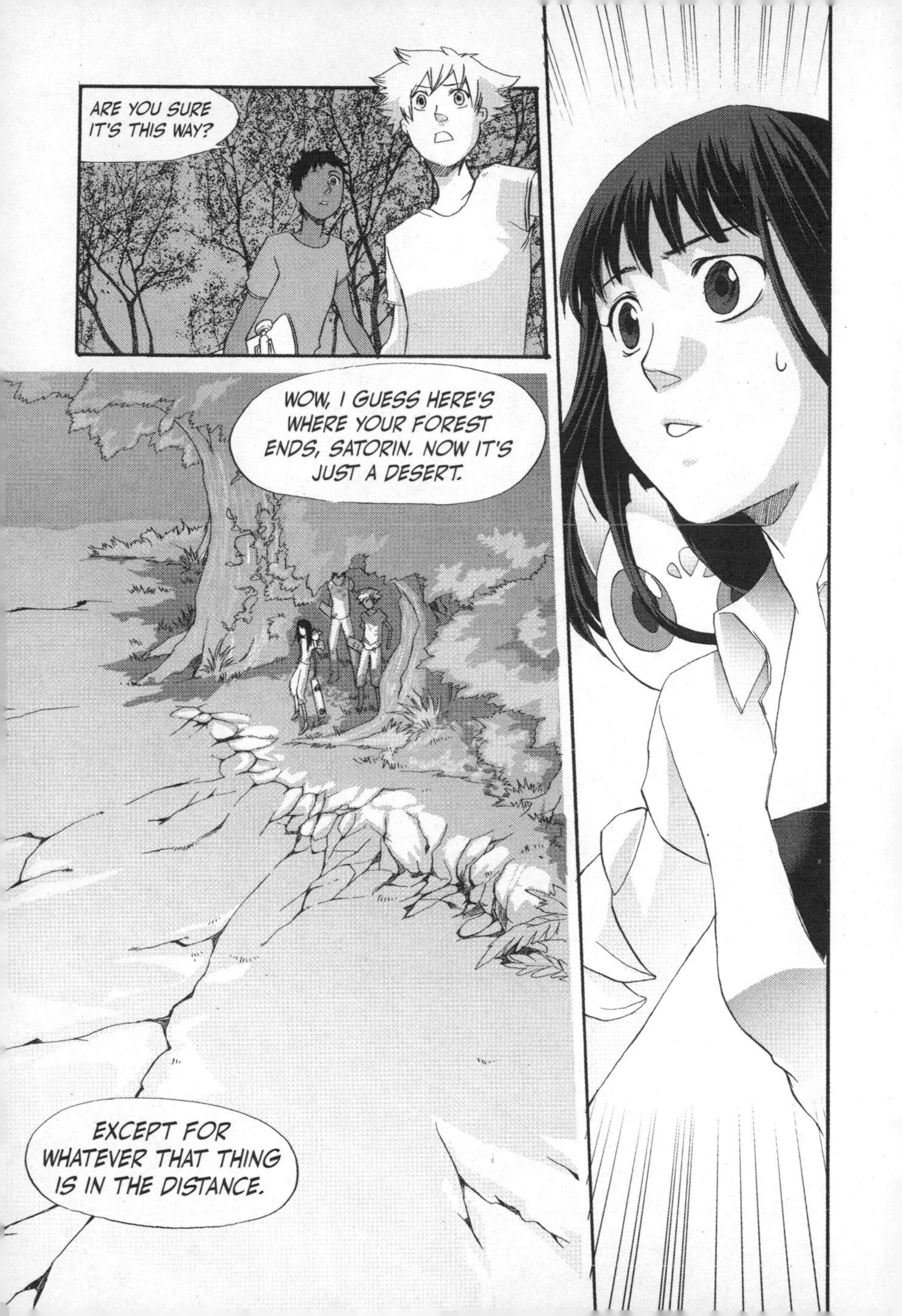
ARE YOU SURE IT'S THIS WAY?
WOW, I GUESS HERE'S WHERE YOUR FOREST ENDS, SATORIN. NOW IT'S JUST A DESERT.
EXCEPT FOR WHATEVER THAT THING IS IN THE DISTANCE.

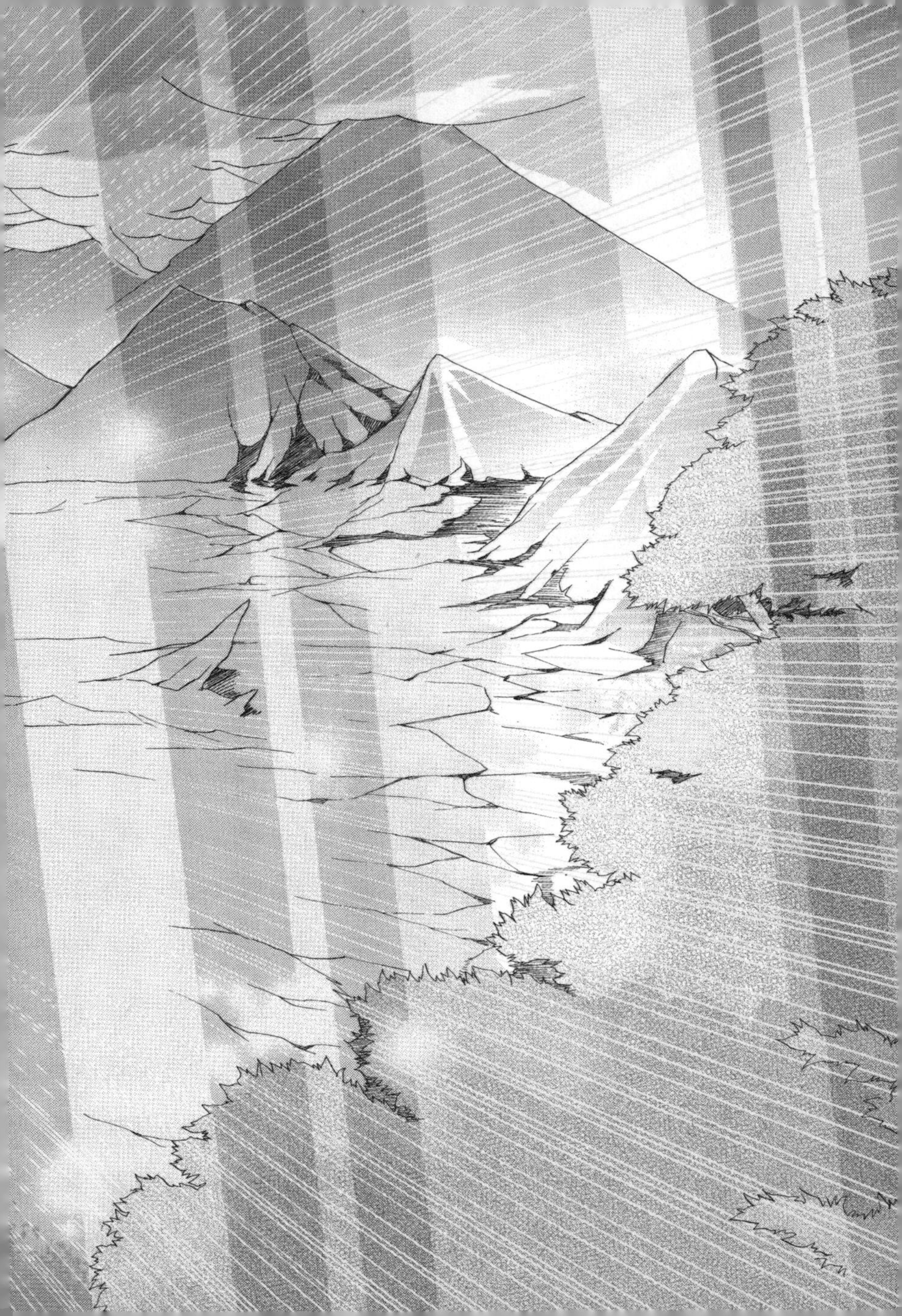

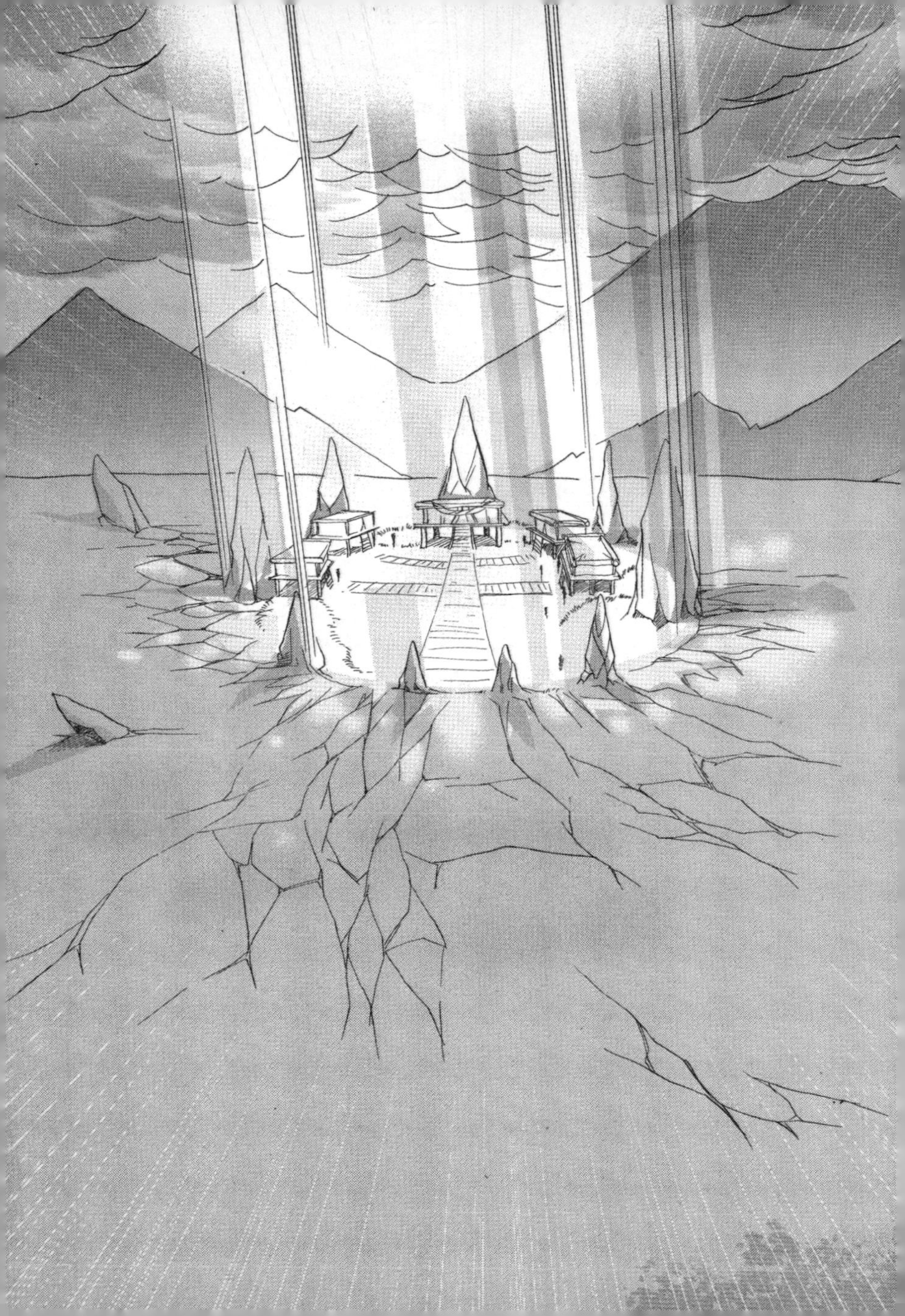

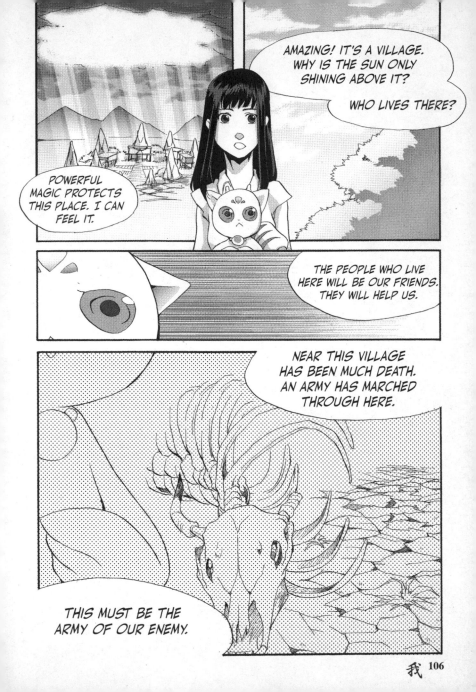

AMAZING! IT'S A VILLAGE. WHY IS THE SUN ONLY SHINING ABOVE IT?

WHO LIVES THERE?

POWERFUL MAGIC PROTECTS THIS PLACE. I CAN FEEL IT.

THE PEOPLE WHO LIVE HERE WILL BE OUR FRIENDS. THEY WILL HELP US.

NEAR THIS VILLAGE HAS BEEN MUCH DEATH. AN ARMY HAS MARCHED THROUGH HERE.

THIS MUST BE THE ARMY OF OUR ENEMY.

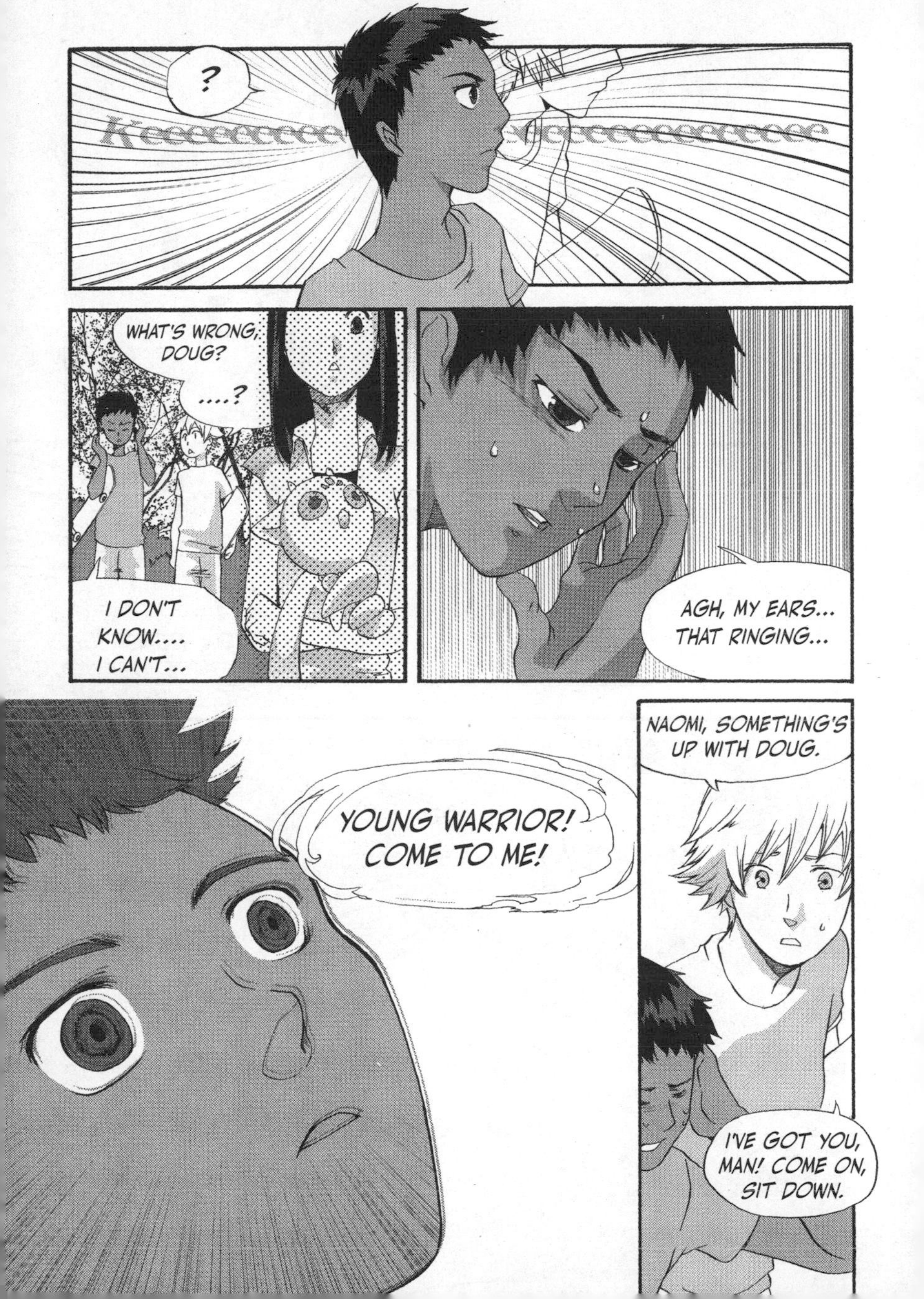
?
Keeeeeeeeeeeeeeeeeeeeeeeeeeeeee
WHAT'S WRONG, DOUG?
....?
I DON'T KNOW.... I CAN'T...
AGH, MY EARS... THAT RINGING...
YOUNG WARRIOR! COME TO ME!
NAOMI, SOMETHING'S UP WITH DOUG.
I'VE GOT YOU, MAN! COME ON, SIT DOWN.

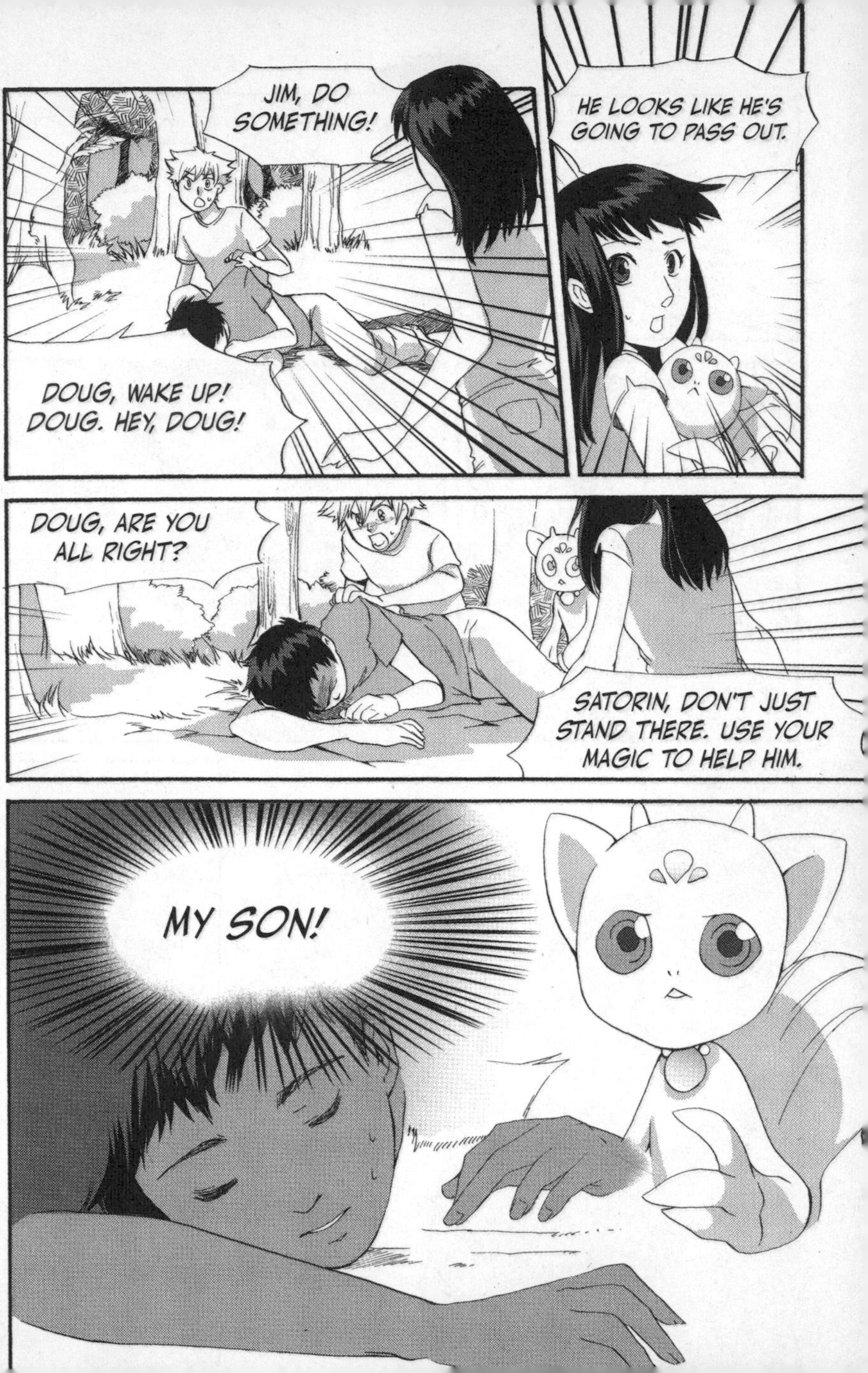
JIM, DO SOMETHING!
HE LOOKS LIKE HE'S GOING TO PASS OUT.
DOUG, WAKE UP! DOUG. HEY, DOUG!
DOUG, ARE YOU ALL RIGHT?
SATORIN, DON'T JUST STAND THERE. USE YOUR MAGIC TO HELP HIM.
MY SON!

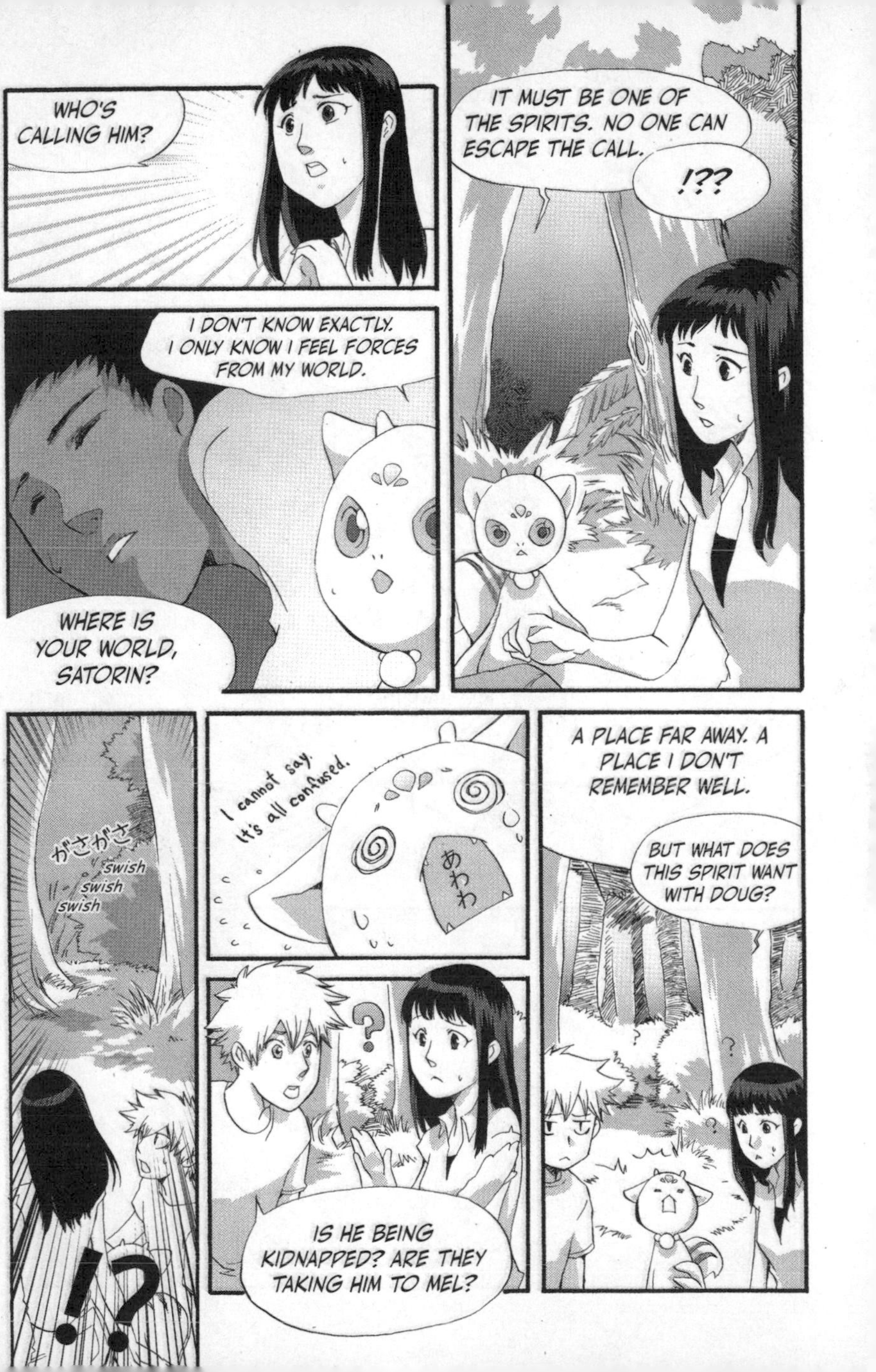
WHO'S CALLING HIM?
IT MUST BE ONE OF THE SPIRITS. NO ONE CAN ESCAPE THE CALL.
!??
I DON'T KNOW EXACTLY. I ONLY KNOW I FEEL FORCES FROM MY WORLD.
WHERE IS YOUR WORLD, SATORIN?
A PLACE FAR AWAY. A PLACE I DON'T REMEMBER WELL.
BUT WHAT DOES THIS SPIRIT WANT WITH DOUG?
I cannot say. It's all confused.
あわわ
がさがさ
swish swish swish
?
IS HE BEING KIDNAPPED? ARE THEY TAKING HIM TO MEL?
!?

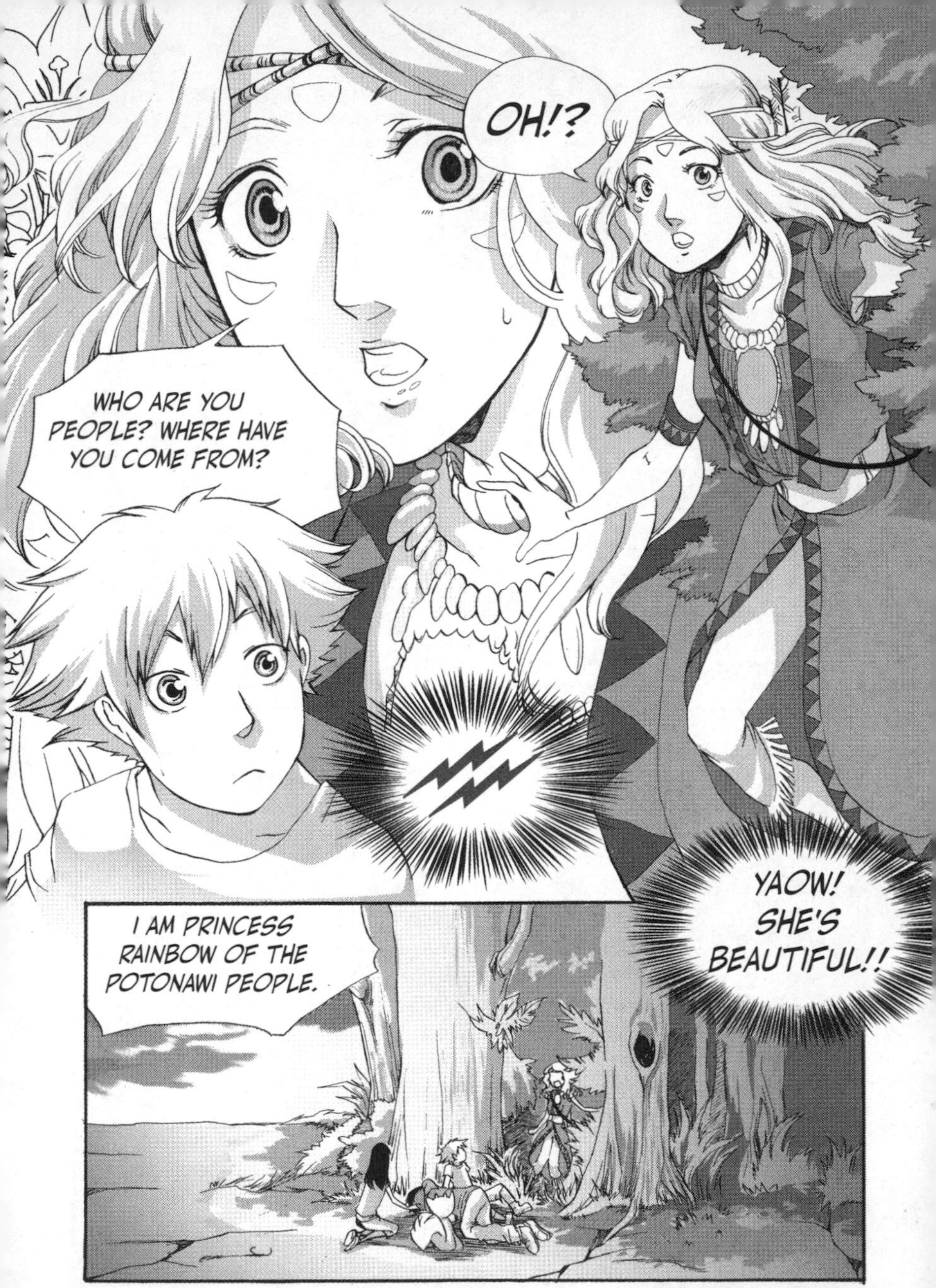
OH!?
WHO ARE YOU PEOPLE? WHERE HAVE YOU COME FROM?
YAOW! SHE'S BEAUTIFUL!!
I AM PRINCESS RAINBOW OF THE POTONAWI PEOPLE.

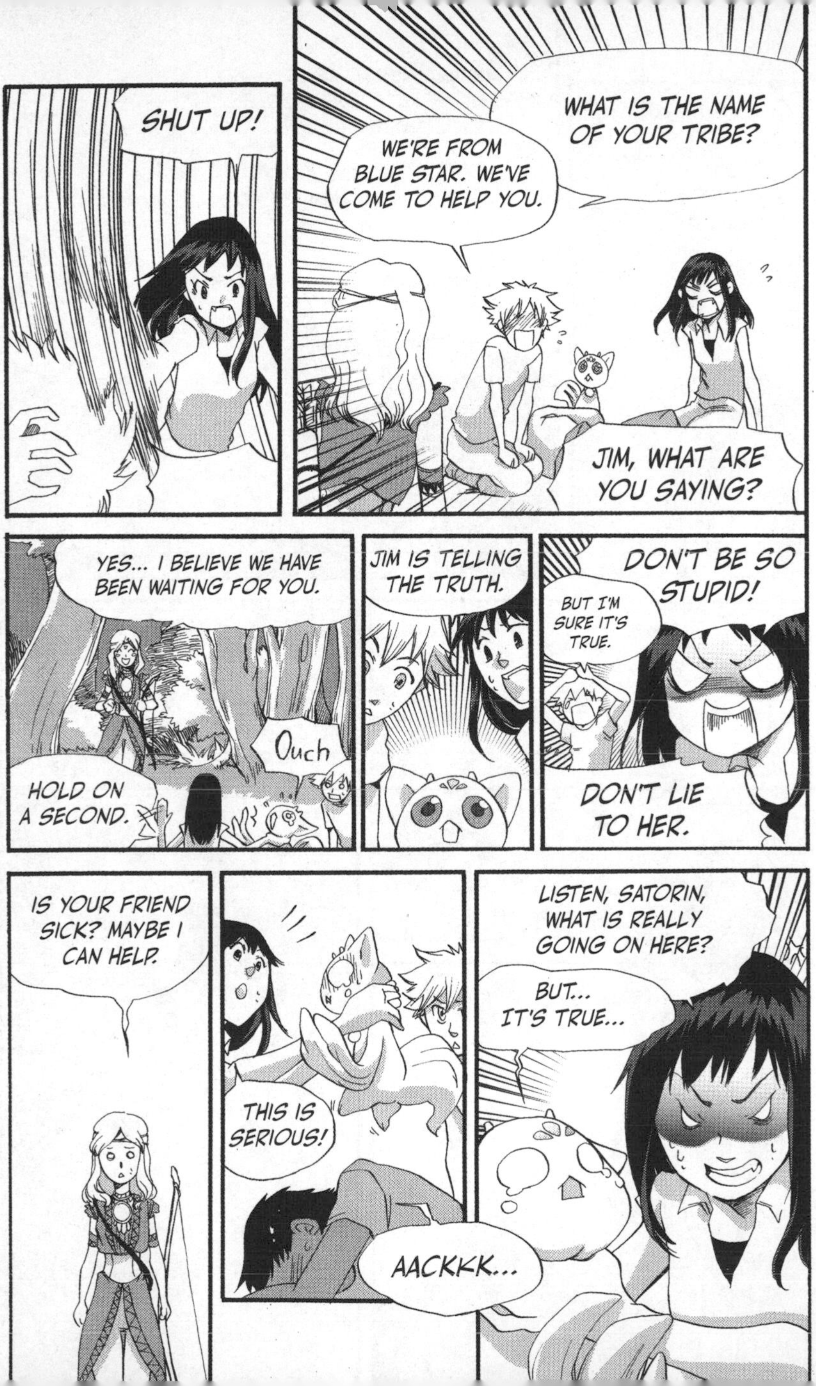
SHUT UP!
WHAT IS THE NAME OF YOUR TRIBE?
WE'RE FROM BLUE STAR. WE'VE COME TO HELP YOU.
JIM, WHAT ARE YOU SAYING?
YES... I BELIEVE WE HAVE BEEN WAITING FOR YOU.
HOLD ON A SECOND.
Ouch
JIM IS TELLING THE TRUTH.
DON'T BE SO STUPID!
BUT I'M SURE IT'S TRUE.
DON'T LIE TO HER.
IS YOUR FRIEND SICK? MAYBE I CAN HELP.
THIS IS SERIOUS!
AACKKK...
LISTEN, SATORIN, WHAT IS REALLY GOING ON HERE?
BUT... IT'S TRUE...

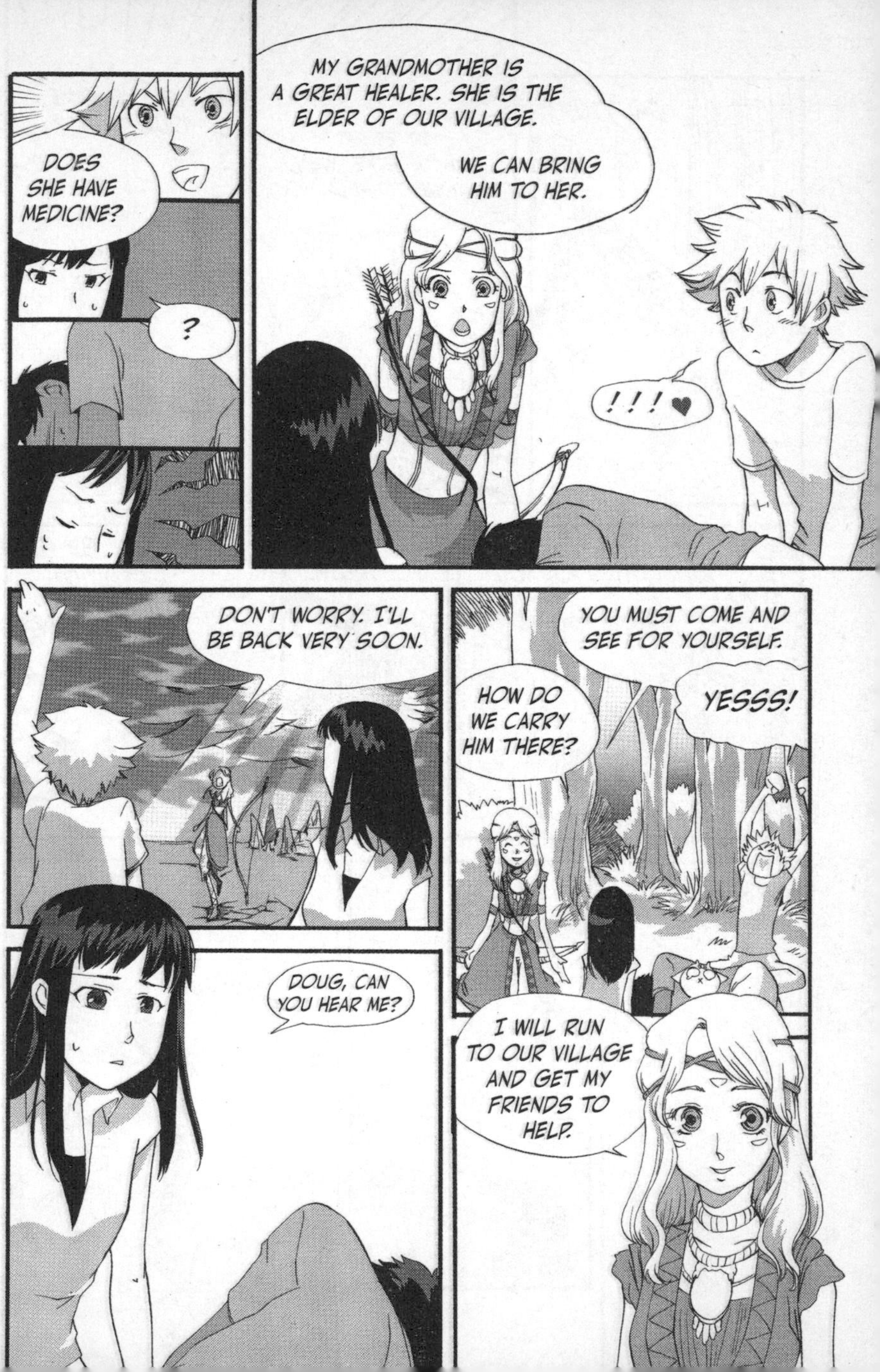
MY GRANDMOTHER IS A GREAT HEALER. SHE IS THE ELDER OF OUR VILLAGE.
WE CAN BRING HIM TO HER.
DOES SHE HAVE MEDICINE?
?
!!!♥
YOU MUST COME AND SEE FOR YOURSELF.
HOW DO WE CARRY HIM THERE?
YESSS!
DON'T WORRY. I'LL BE BACK VERY SOON.
I WILL RUN TO OUR VILLAGE AND GET MY FRIENDS TO HELP.
DOUG, CAN YOU HEAR ME?

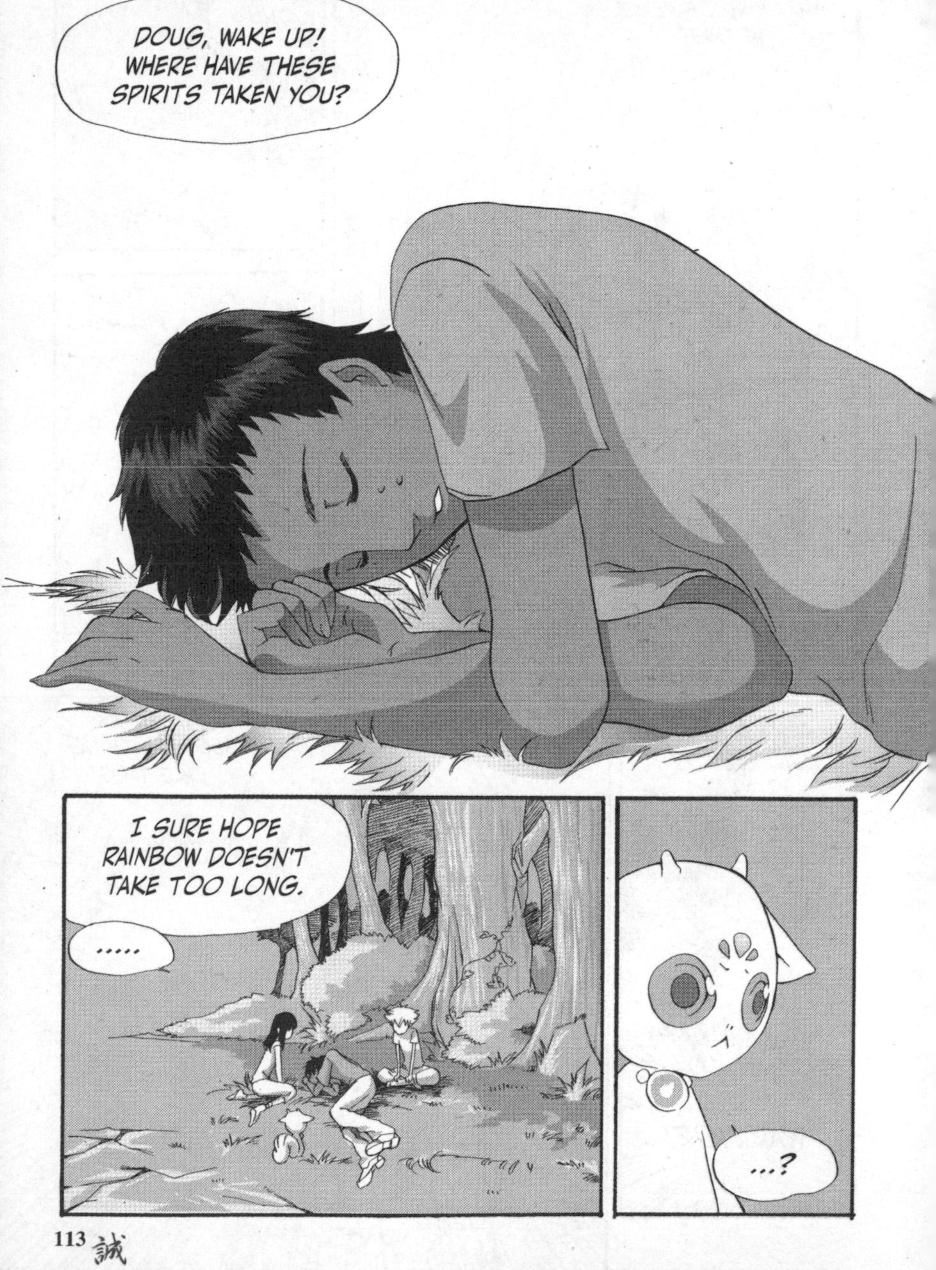
DOUG, WAKE UP! WHERE HAVE THESE SPIRITS TAKEN YOU?
I SURE HOPE RAINBOW DOESN'T TAKE TOO LONG.
......
...?

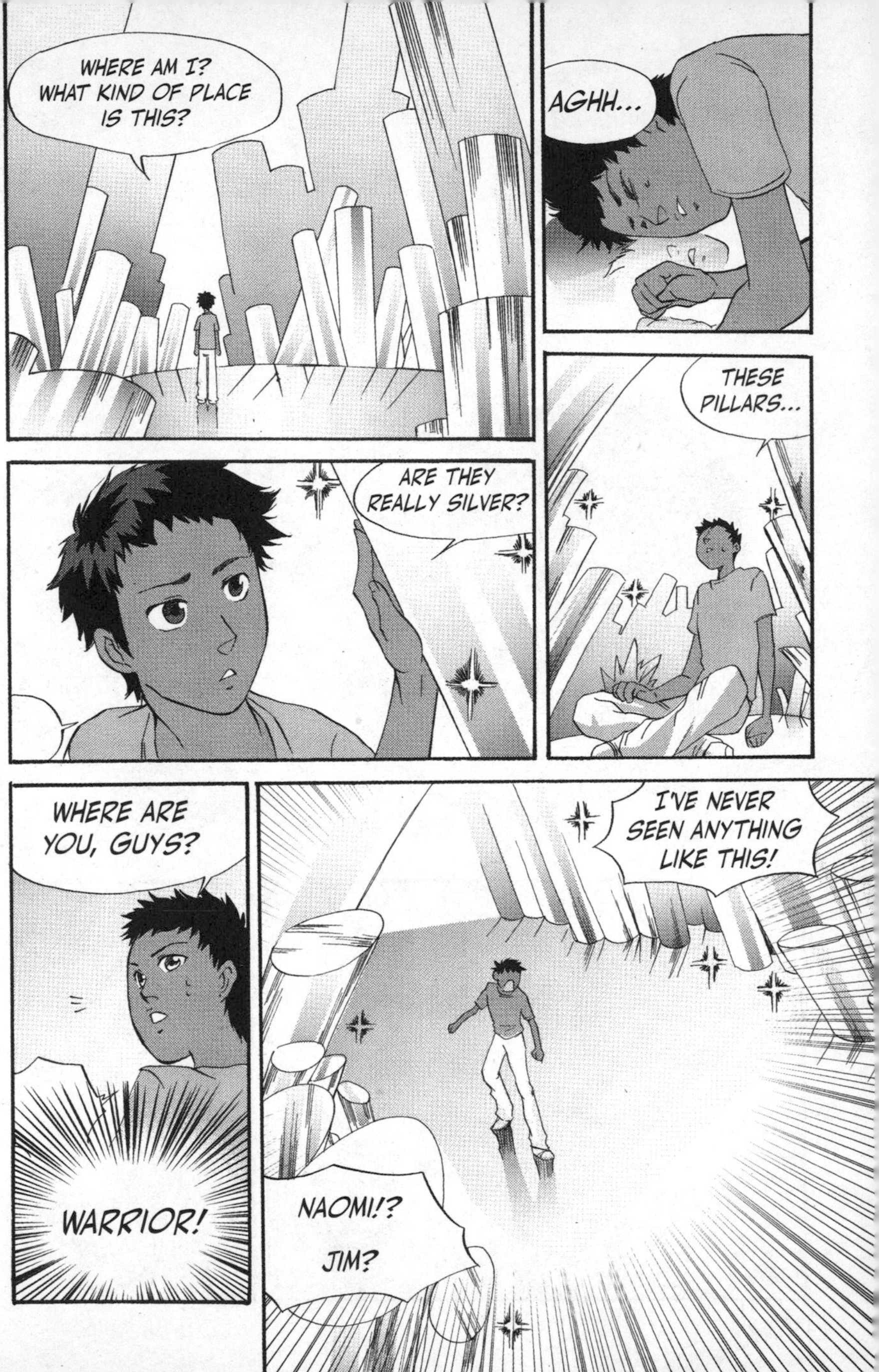
WHERE AM I? WHAT KIND OF PLACE IS THIS?
AGHH...
THESE PILLARS...
ARE THEY REALLY SILVER?
WHERE ARE YOU, GUYS?
WARRIOR!
I'VE NEVER SEEN ANYTHING LIKE THIS!
NAOMI!?
JIM?

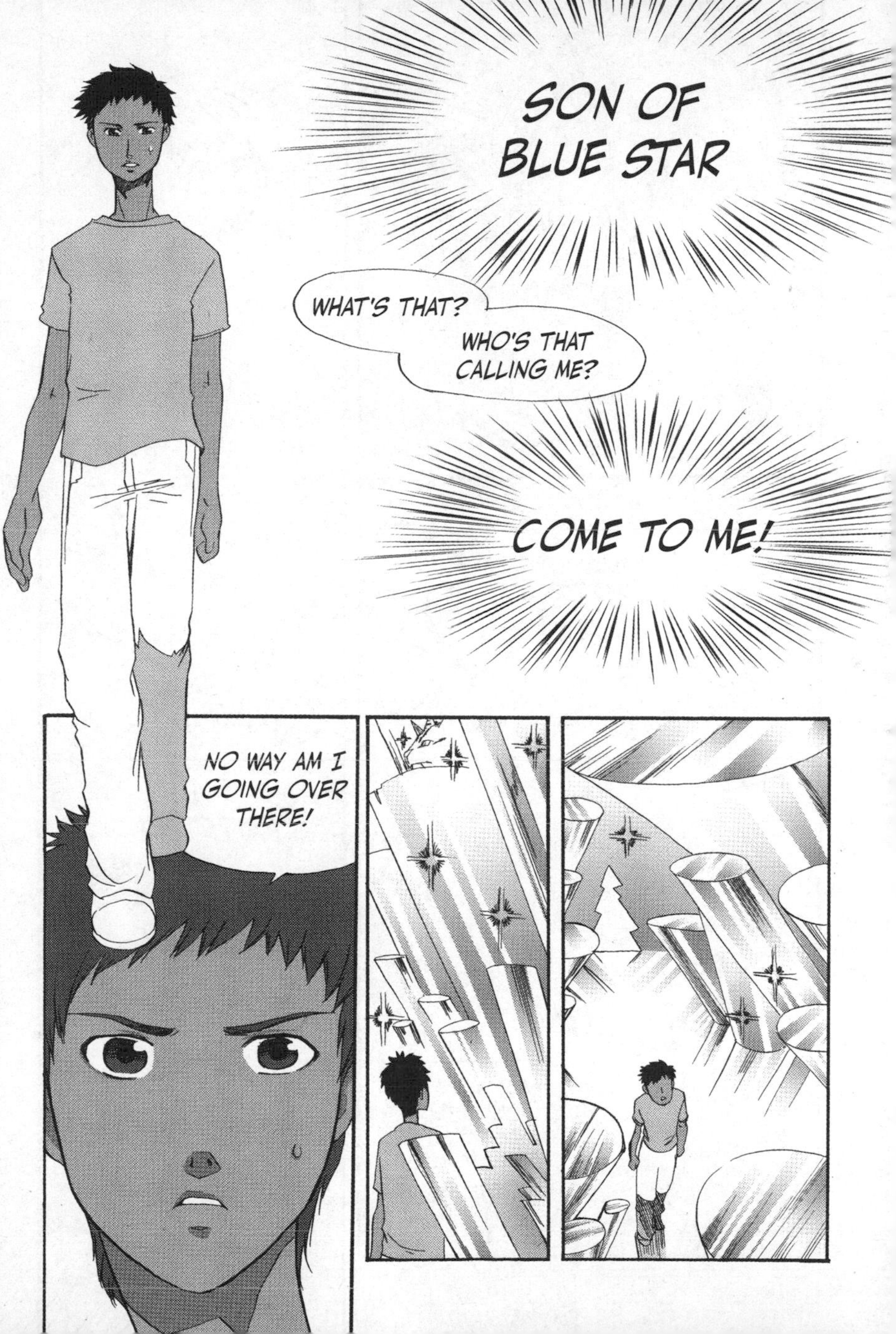
SON OF BLUE STAR
WHAT'S THAT?
WHO'S THAT CALLING ME?
COME TO ME!
NO WAY AM I GOING OVER THERE!

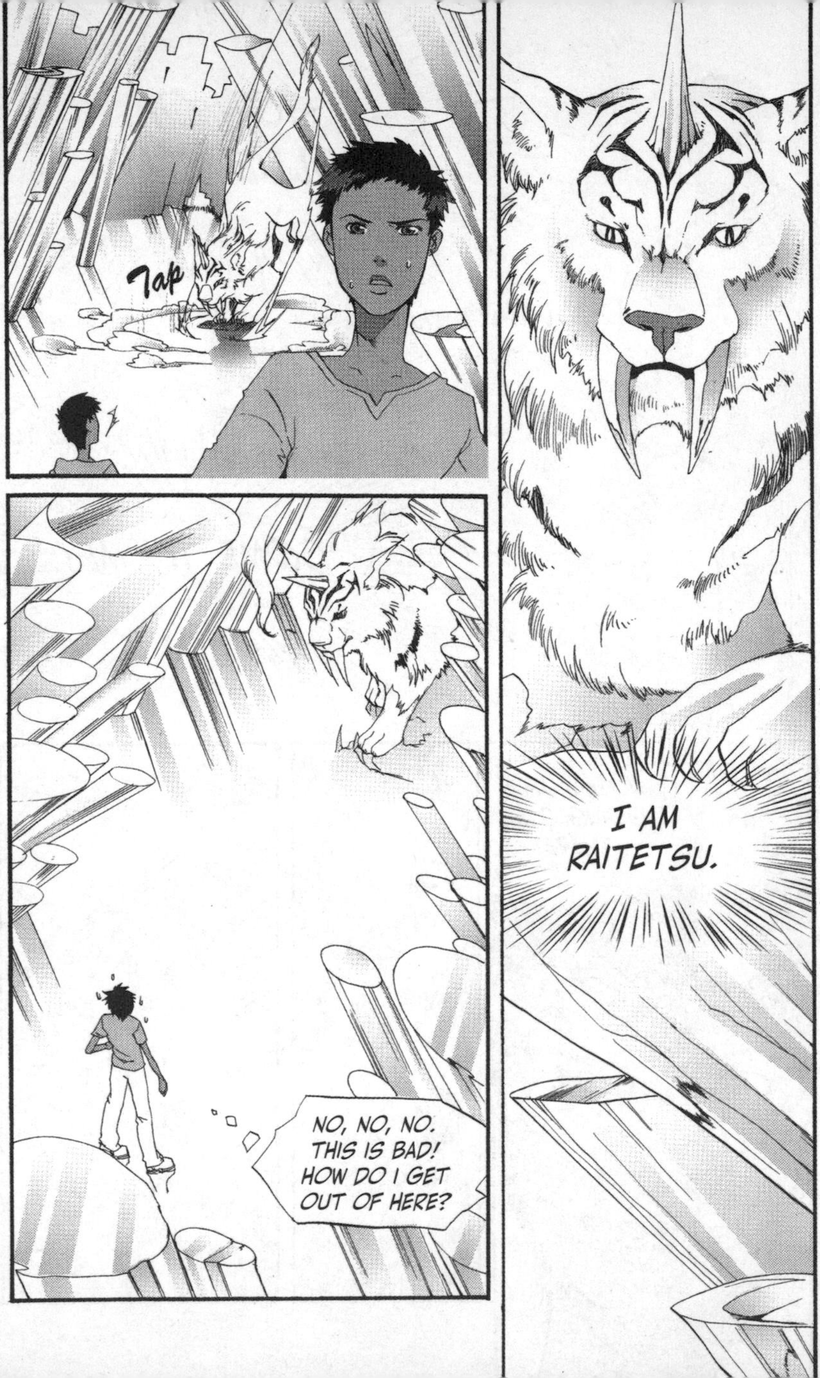
Tap
I AM RAITETSU.
NO, NO, NO. THIS IS BAD! HOW DO I GET OUT OF HERE?

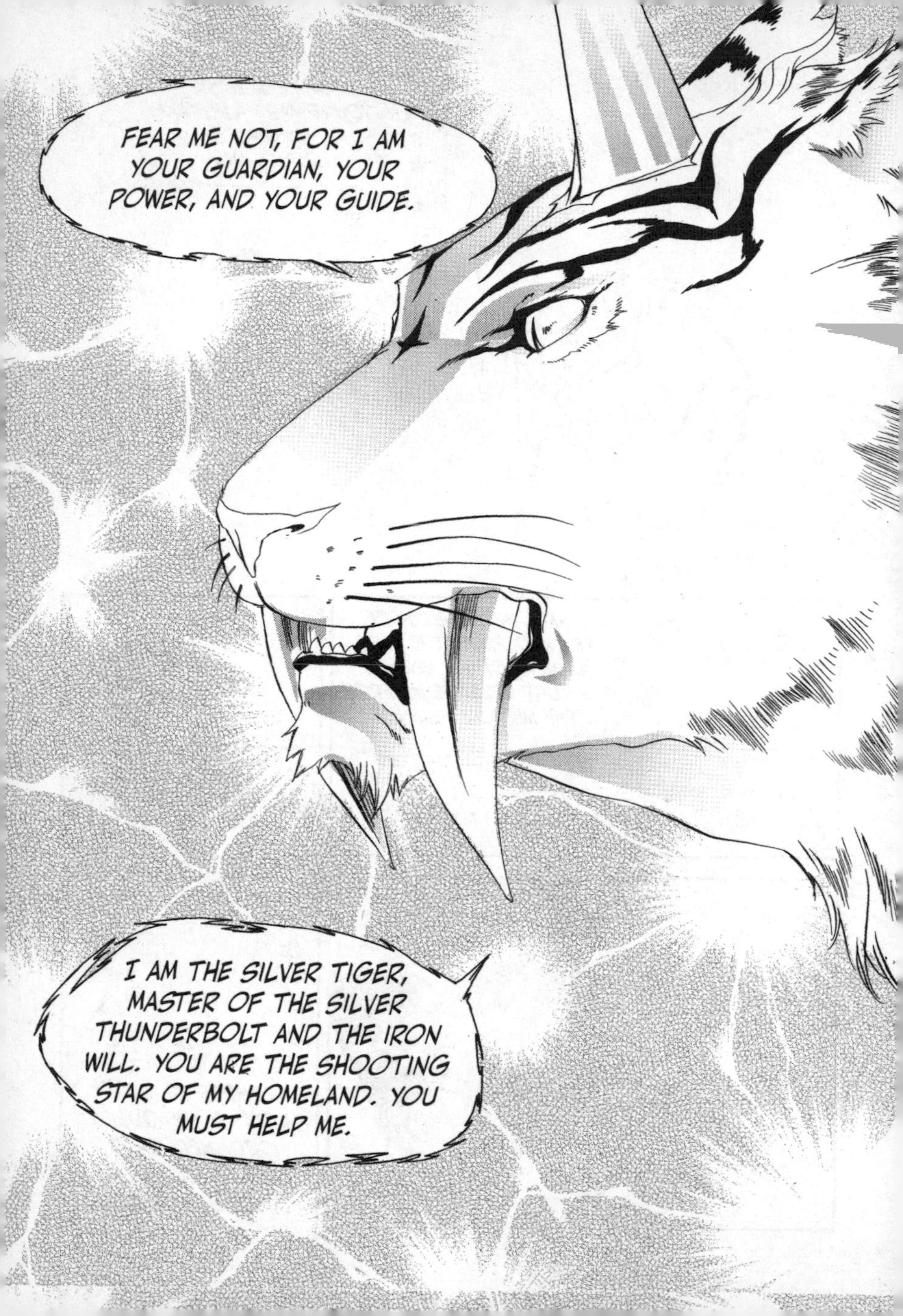
FEAR ME NOT, FOR I AM YOUR GUARDIAN, YOUR POWER, AND YOUR GUIDE.
I AM THE SILVER TIGER, MASTER OF THE SILVER THUNDERBOLT AND THE IRON WILL. YOU ARE THE SHOOTING STAR OF MY HOMELAND. YOU MUST HELP ME.

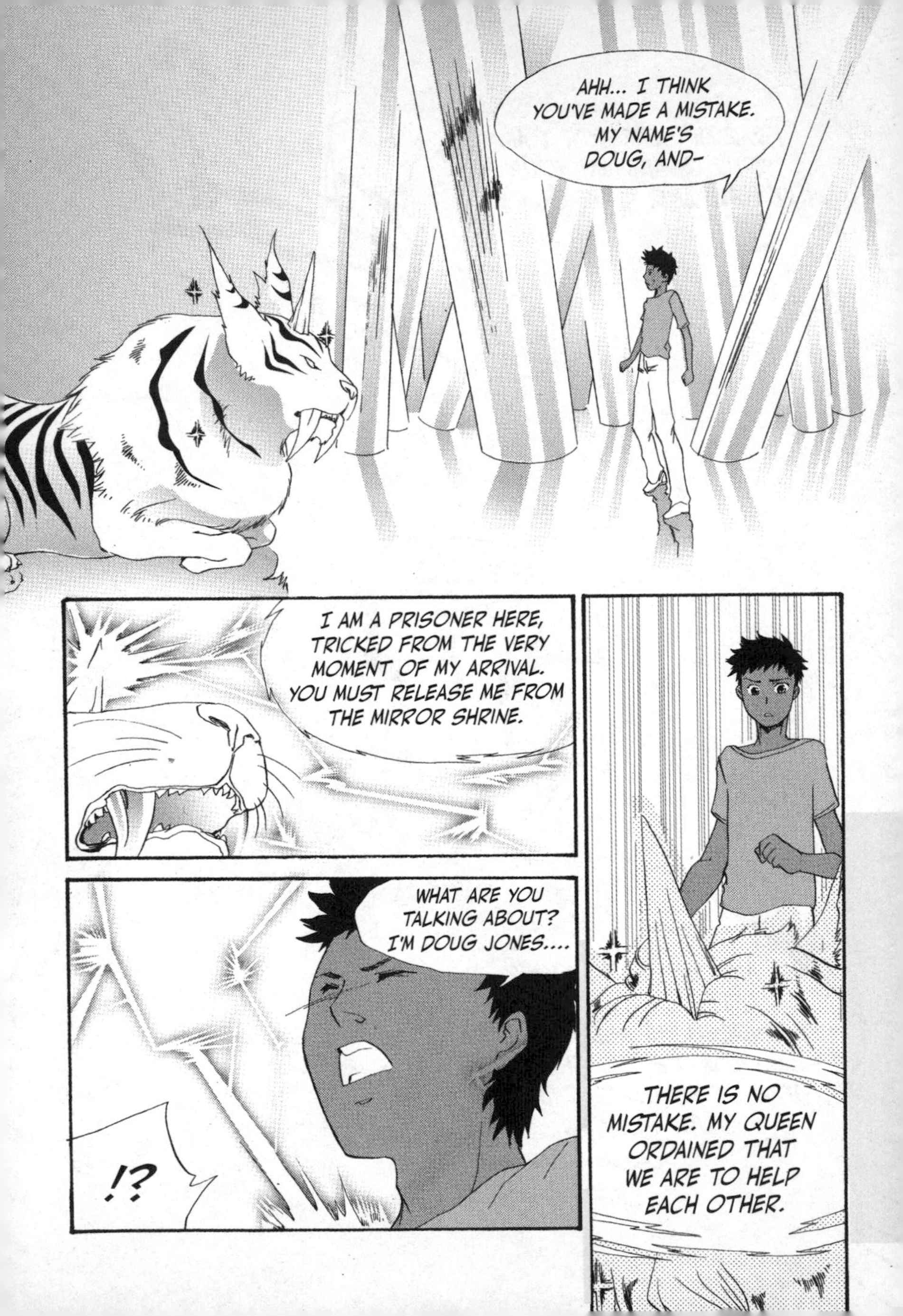
AHH... I THINK YOU'VE MADE A MISTAKE. MY NAME'S DOUG, AND-
I AM A PRISONER HERE, TRICKED FROM THE VERY MOMENT OF MY ARRIVAL. YOU MUST RELEASE ME FROM THE MIRROR SHRINE.
WHAT ARE YOU TALKING ABOUT? I'M DOUG JONES....
!?
THERE IS NO MISTAKE. MY QUEEN ORDAINED THAT WE ARE TO HELP EACH OTHER.

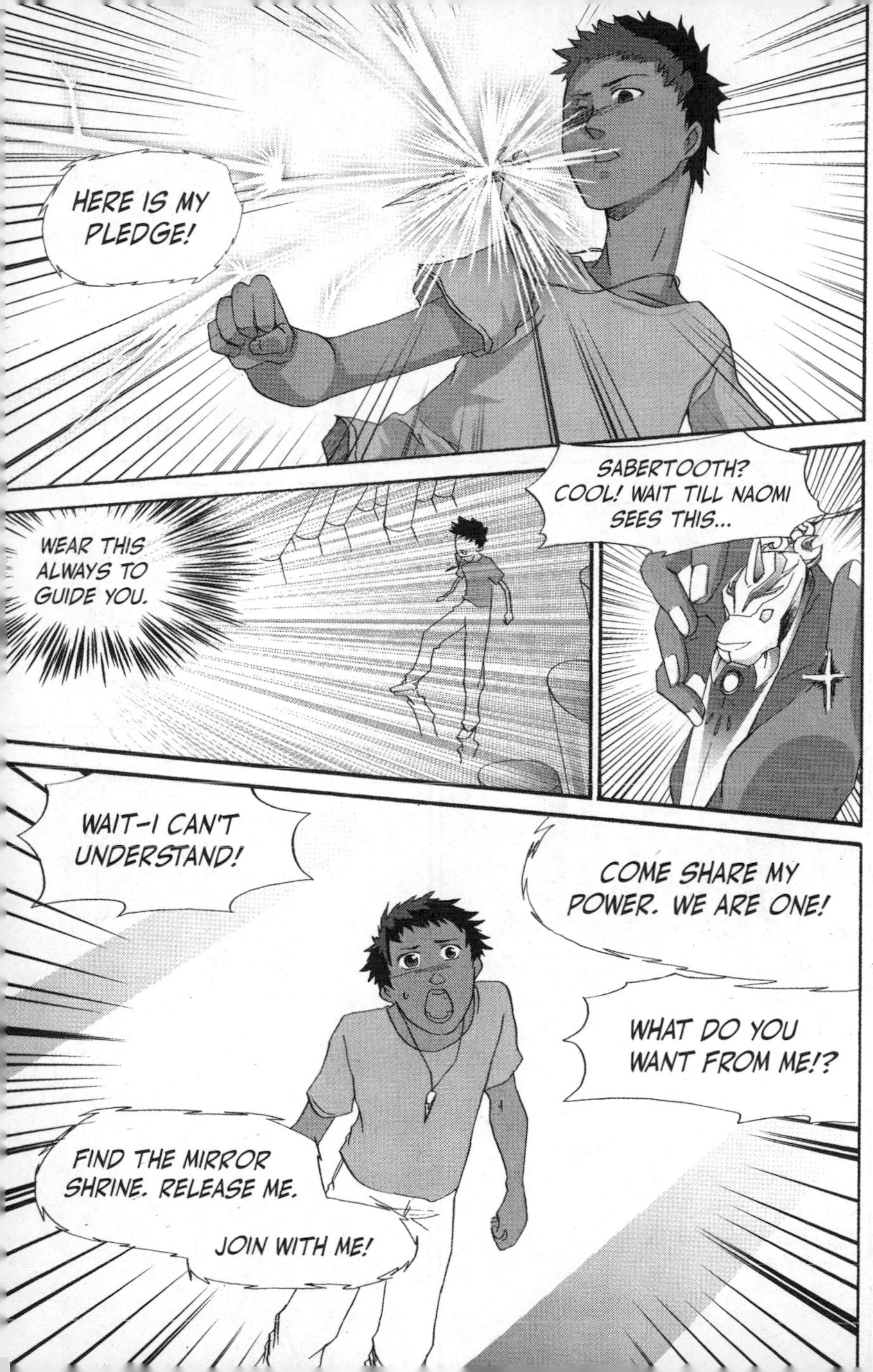
HERE IS MY PLEDGE!
WEAR THIS ALWAYS TO GUIDE YOU.
SABERTOOTH? COOL! WAIT TILL NAOMI SEES THIS...
WAIT—I CAN'T UNDERSTAND!
COME SHARE MY POWER. WE ARE ONE!
WHAT DO YOU WANT FROM ME!?
FIND THE MIRROR SHRINE. RELEASE ME.
JOIN WITH ME!

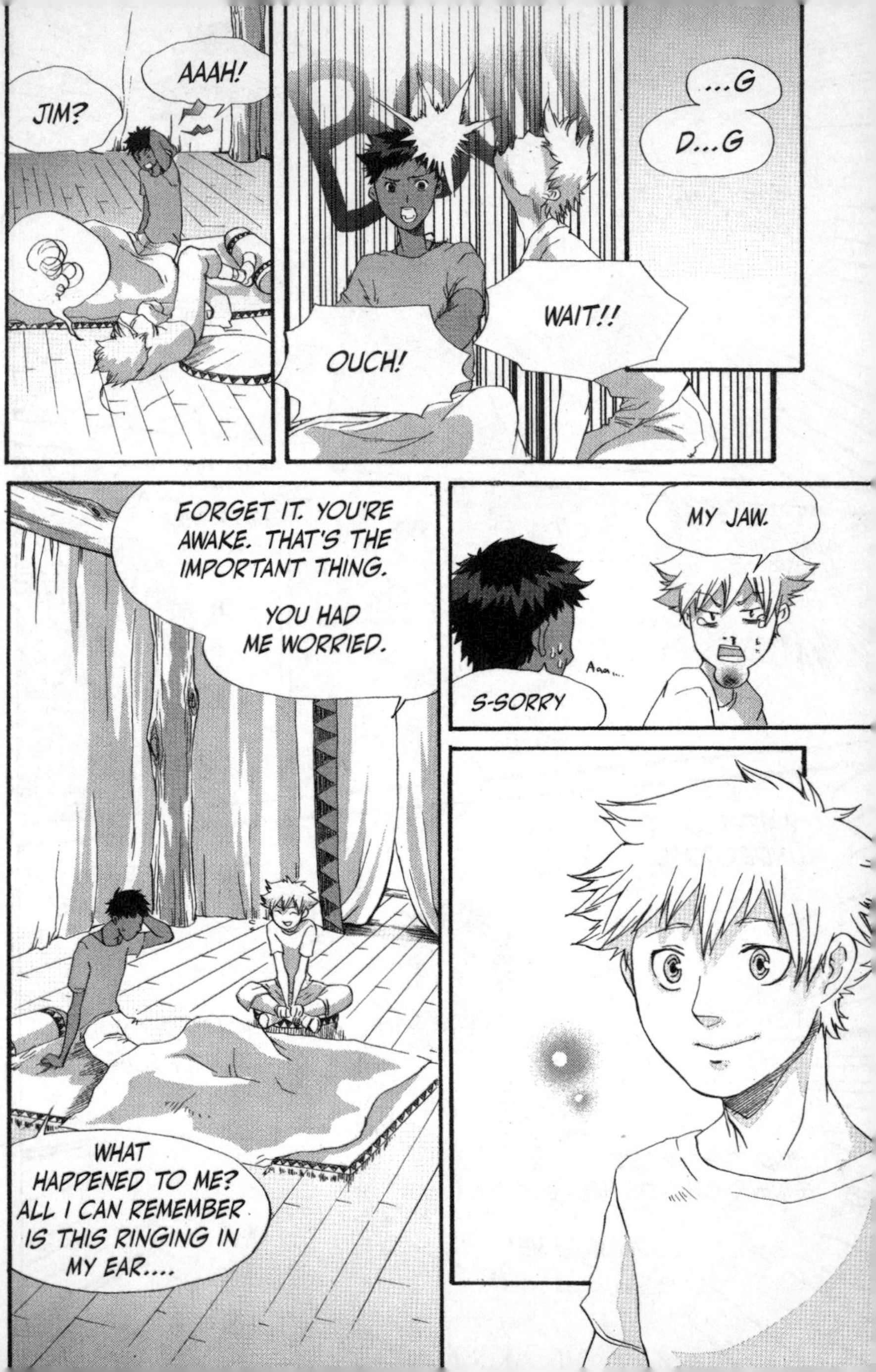
JIM?
AAAH!
OUCH!
WAIT!!
...G
D...G
FORGET IT. YOU'RE AWAKE. THAT'S THE IMPORTANT THING.
YOU HAD ME WORRIED.
MY JAW.
S-SORRY
Aaa...
WHAT HAPPENED TO ME? ALL I CAN REMEMBER IS THIS RINGING IN MY EAR....

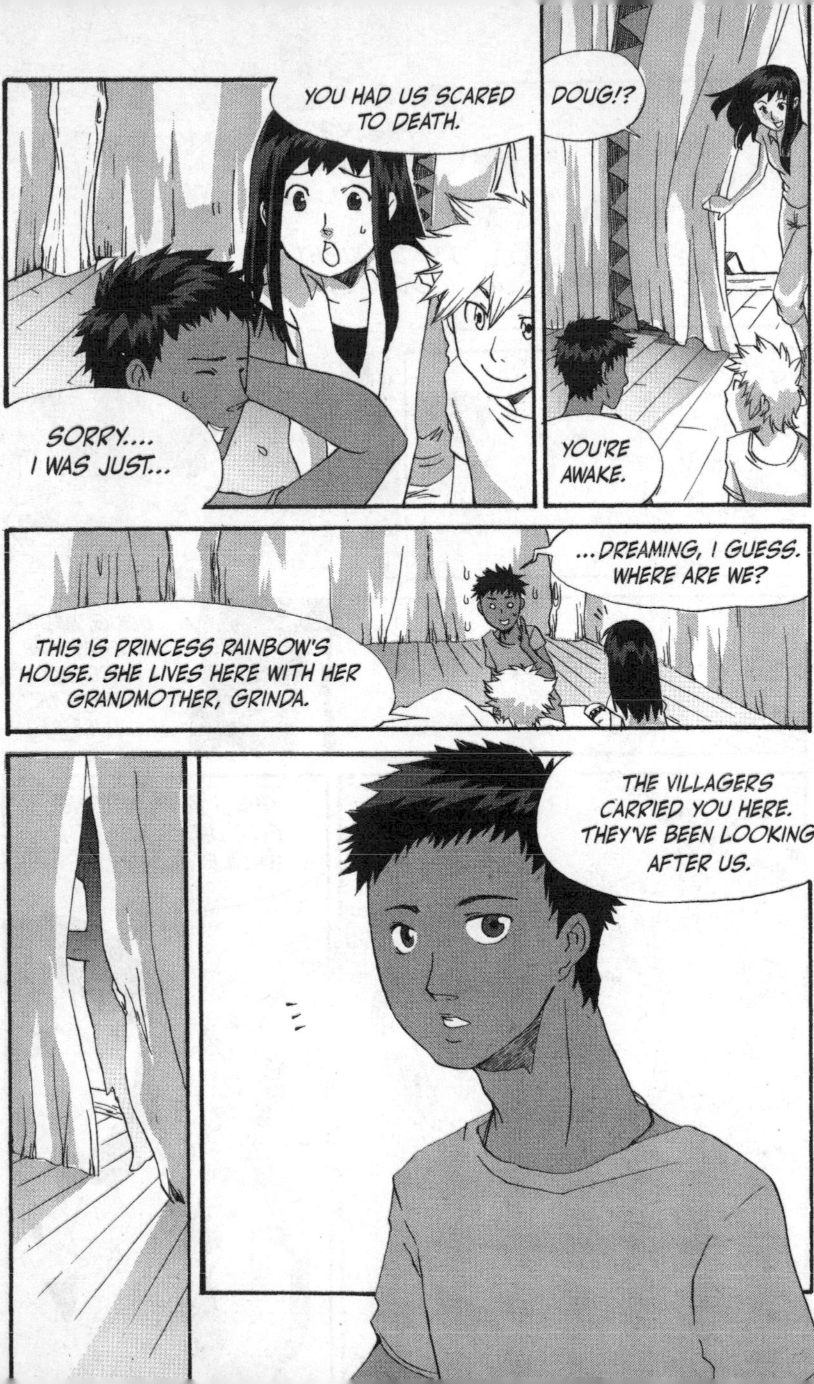
DOUG!?
YOU'RE AWAKE.
YOU HAD US SCARED TO DEATH.
SORRY.... I WAS JUST...
...DREAMING, I GUESS. WHERE ARE WE?
THIS IS PRINCESS RAINBOW'S HOUSE. SHE LIVES HERE WITH HER GRANDMOTHER, GRINDA.
THE VILLAGERS CARRIED YOU HERE. THEY'VE BEEN LOOKING AFTER US.

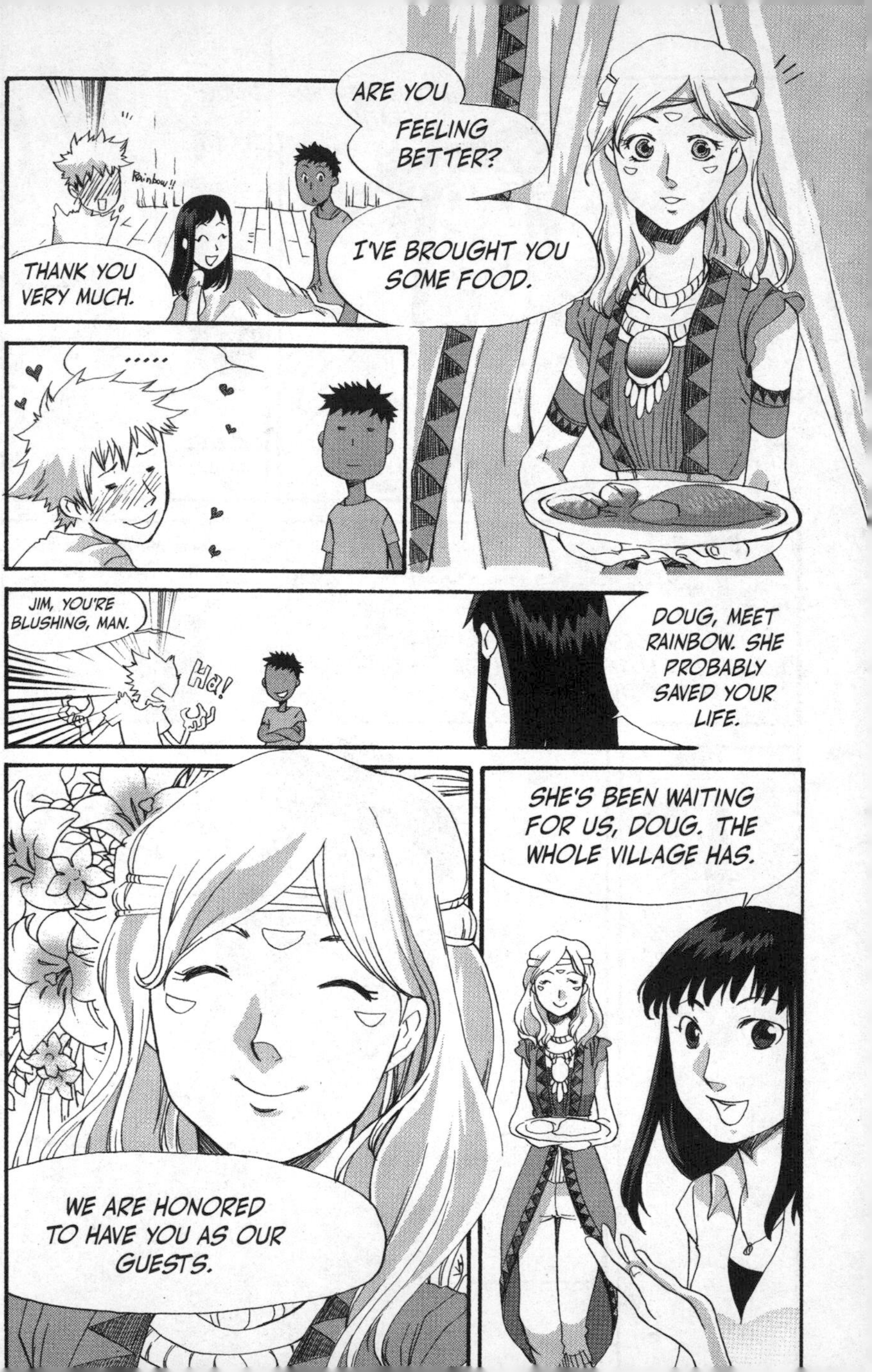
ARE YOU
FEELING BETTER?
I'VE BROUGHT YOU SOME FOOD.
Rainbow!!
THANK YOU VERY MUCH.
.....
JIM, YOU'RE BLUSHING, MAN.
Ha!
DOUG, MEET RAINBOW. SHE PROBABLY SAVED YOUR LIFE.
SHE'S BEEN WAITING FOR US, DOUG. THE WHOLE VILLAGE HAS.
WE ARE HONORED TO HAVE YOU AS OUR GUESTS.

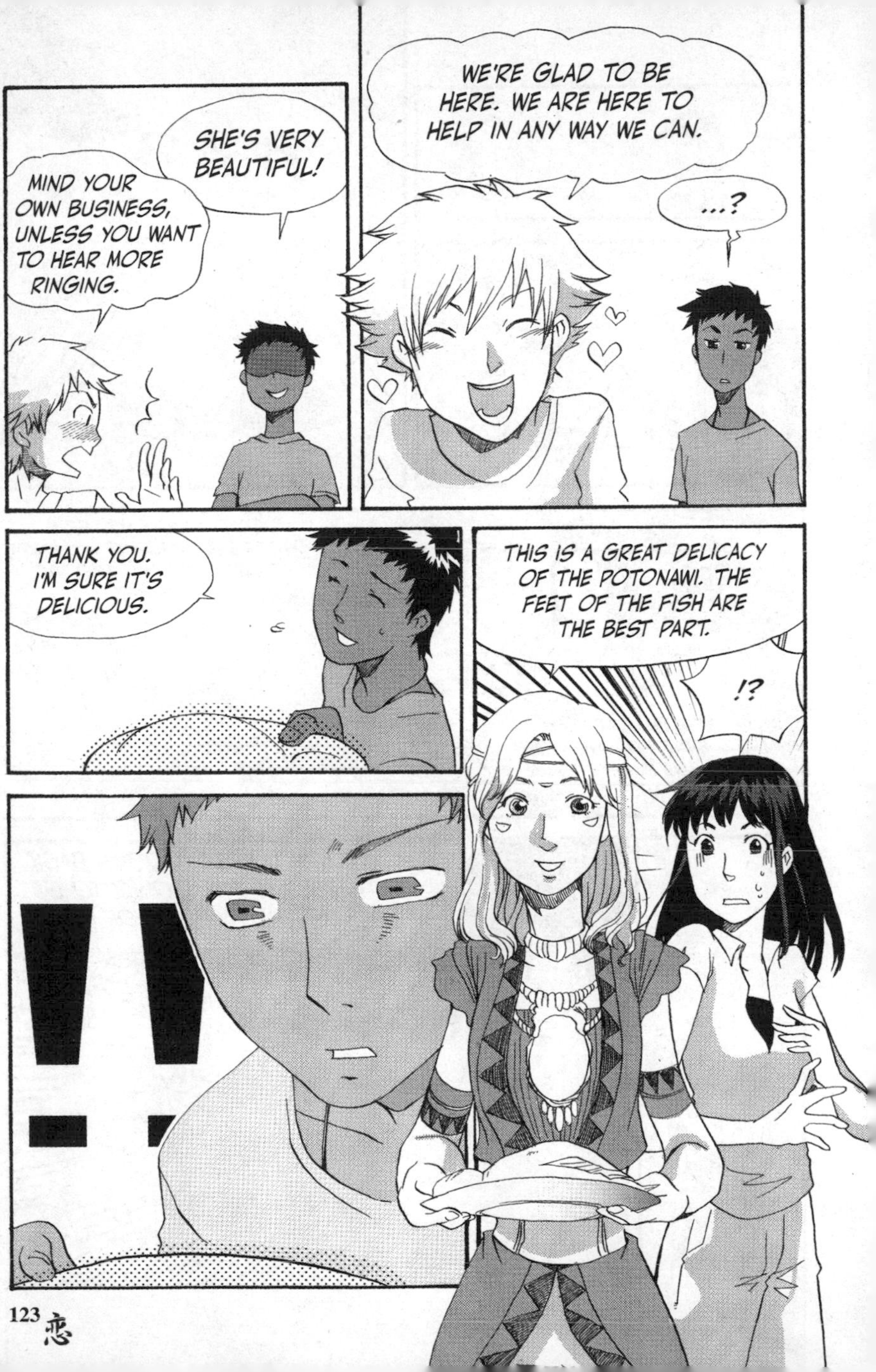
SHE'S VERY BEAUTIFUL!
MIND YOUR OWN BUSINESS, UNLESS YOU WANT TO HEAR MORE RINGING.
WE'RE GLAD TO BE HERE. WE ARE HERE TO HELP IN ANY WAY WE CAN.
...?
THANK YOU. I'M SURE IT'S DELICIOUS.
THIS IS A GREAT DELICACY OF THE POTONAWI. THE FEET OF THE FISH ARE THE BEST PART.
!?
!!

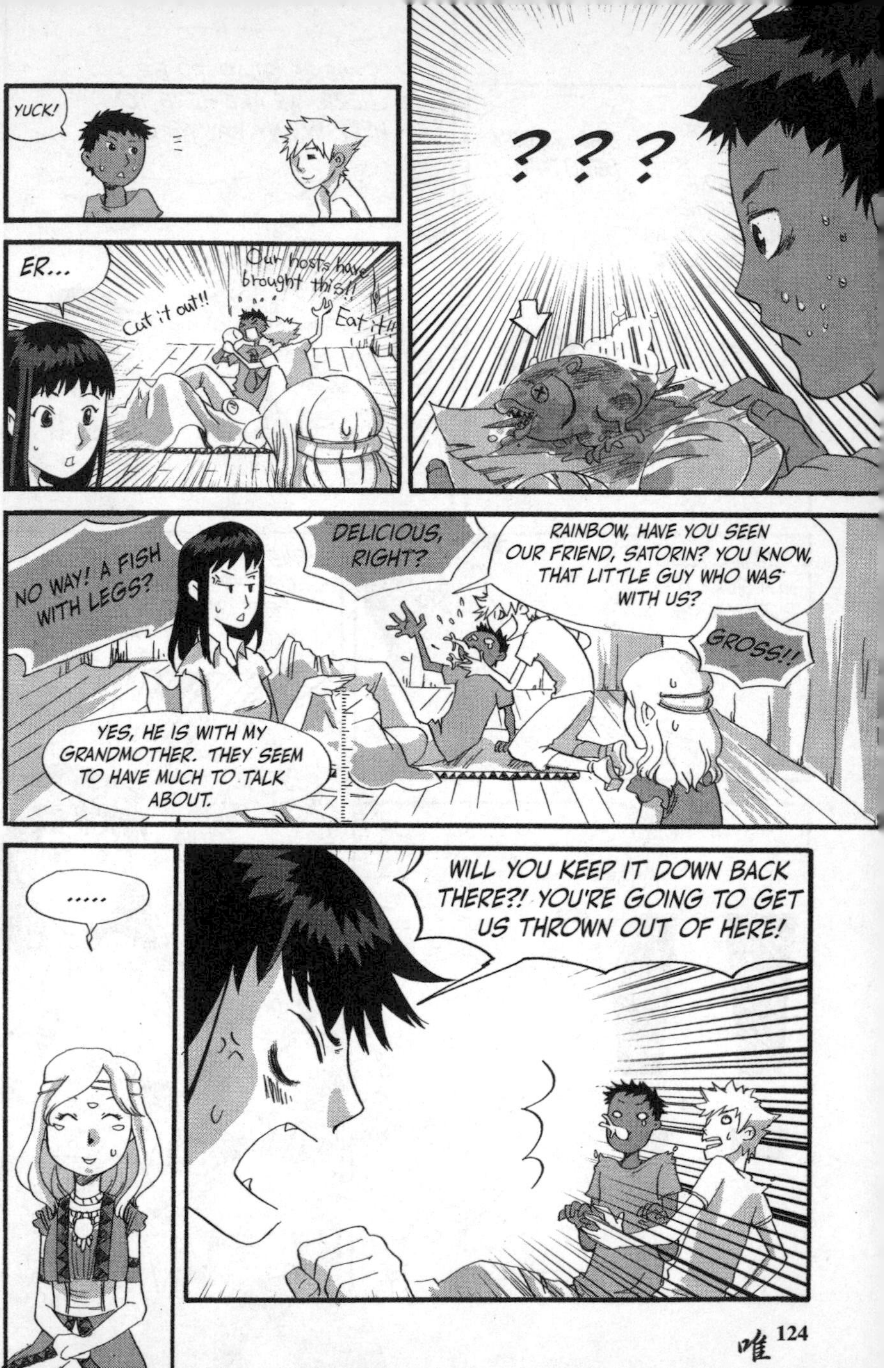
???
YUCK!
ER...
Our hosts have brought this!!
Cut it out!!
Eat it!!
NO WAY! A FISH WITH LEGS?
DELICIOUS, RIGHT?
RAINBOW, HAVE YOU SEEN OUR FRIEND, SATORIN? YOU KNOW, THAT LITTLE GUY WHO WAS WITH US?
GROSS!!
YES, HE IS WITH MY GRANDMOTHER. THEY SEEM TO HAVE MUCH TO TALK ABOUT.
WILL YOU KEEP IT DOWN BACK THERE?! YOU'RE GOING TO GET US THROWN OUT OF HERE!
......

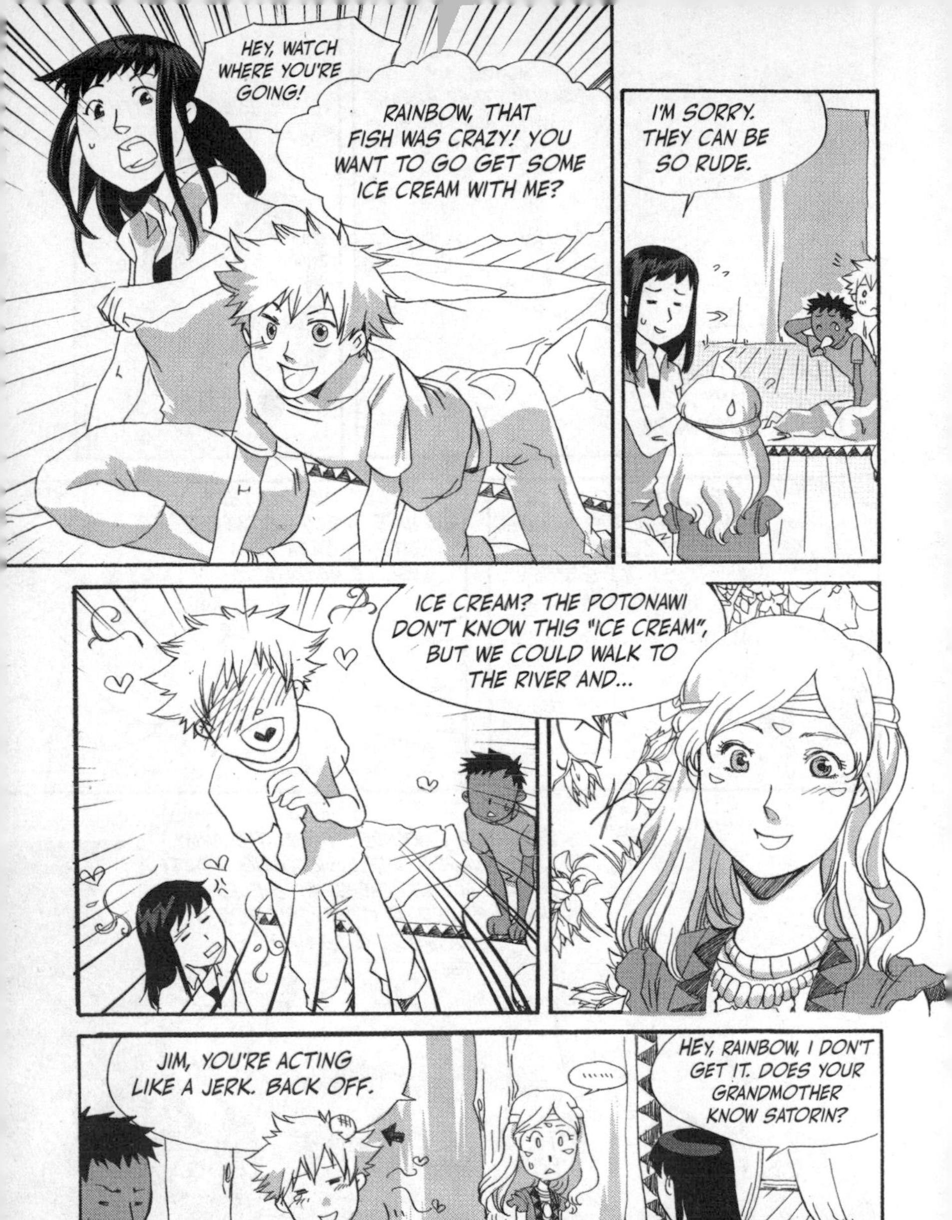

HEY, WATCH WHERE YOU'RE GOING!
RAINBOW, THAT FISH WAS CRAZY! YOU WANT TO GO GET SOME ICE CREAM WITH ME?
I'M SORRY. THEY CAN BE SO RUDE.
ICE CREAM? THE POTONAWI DON'T KNOW THIS "ICE CREAM", BUT WE COULD WALK TO THE RIVER AND...
JIM, YOU'RE ACTING LIKE A JERK. BACK OFF.
.....
HEY, RAINBOW, I DON'T GET IT. DOES YOUR GRANDMOTHER KNOW SATORIN?
Jim...

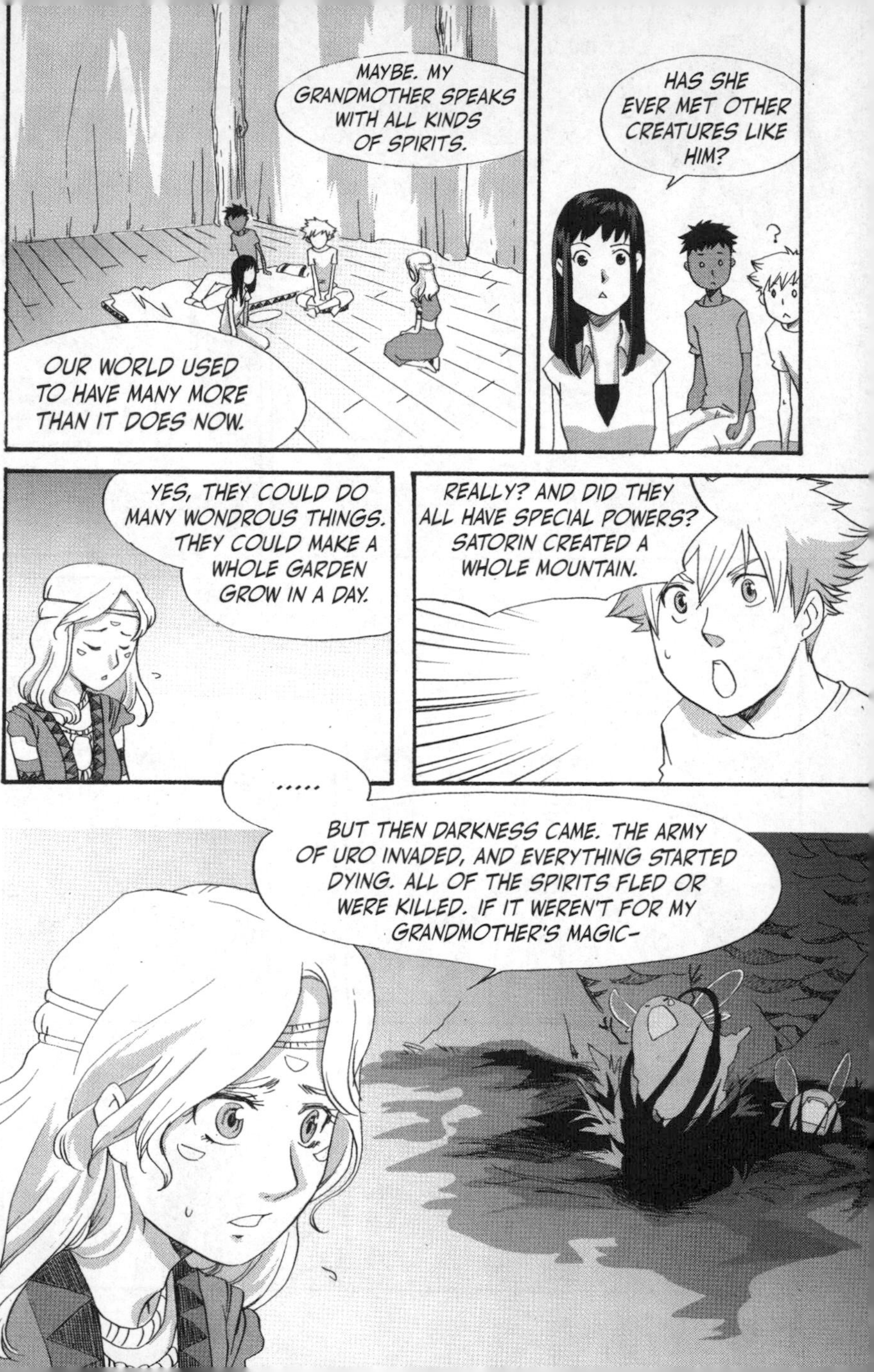
MAYBE. MY GRANDMOTHER SPEAKS WITH ALL KINDS OF SPIRITS.
OUR WORLD USED TO HAVE MANY MORE THAN IT DOES NOW.
HAS SHE EVER MET OTHER CREATURES LIKE HIM?
YES, THEY COULD DO MANY WONDROUS THINGS. THEY COULD MAKE A WHOLE GARDEN GROW IN A DAY.
REALLY? AND DID THEY ALL HAVE SPECIAL POWERS? SATORIN CREATED A WHOLE MOUNTAIN.
......
BUT THEN DARKNESS CAME. THE ARMY OF URO INVADED, AND EVERYTHING STARTED DYING. ALL OF THE SPIRITS FLED OR WERE KILLED. IF IT WEREN'T FOR MY GRANDMOTHER'S MAGIC-

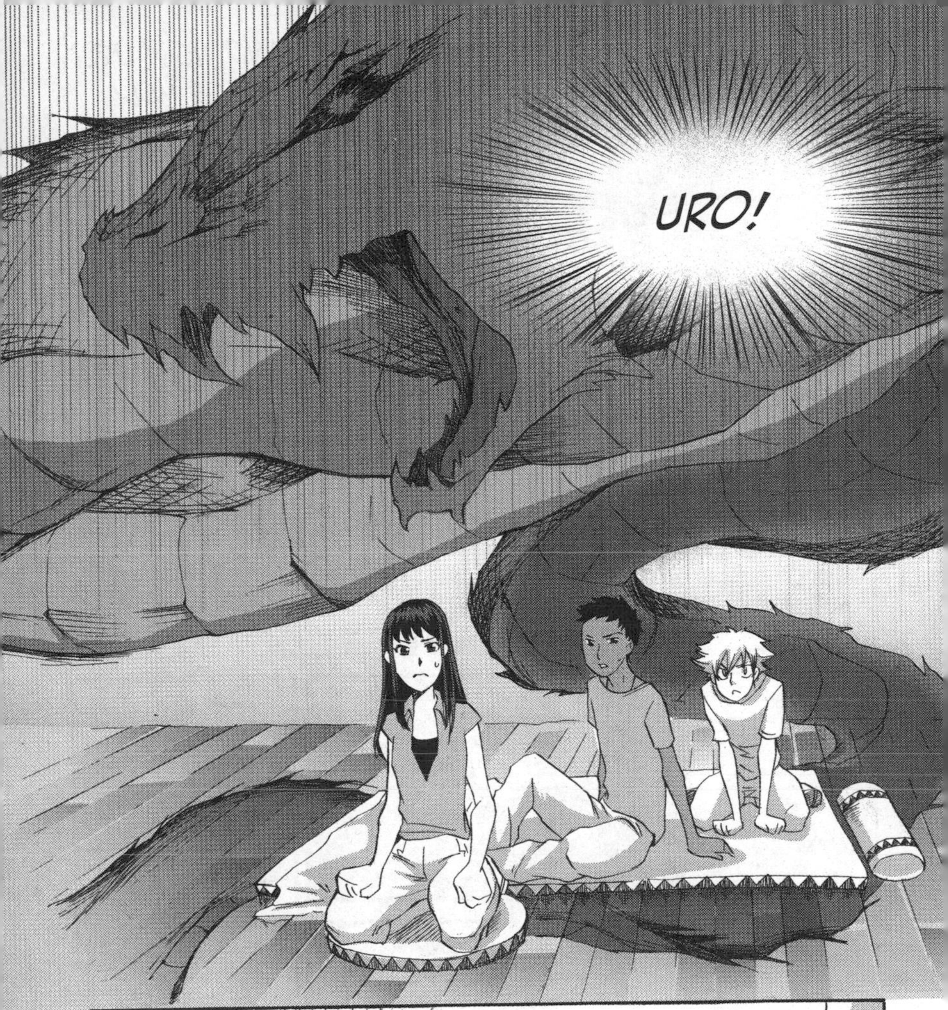
URO!

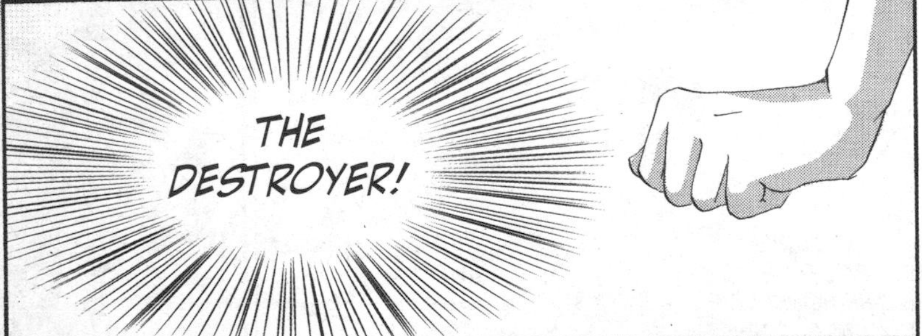
THE DESTROYER!

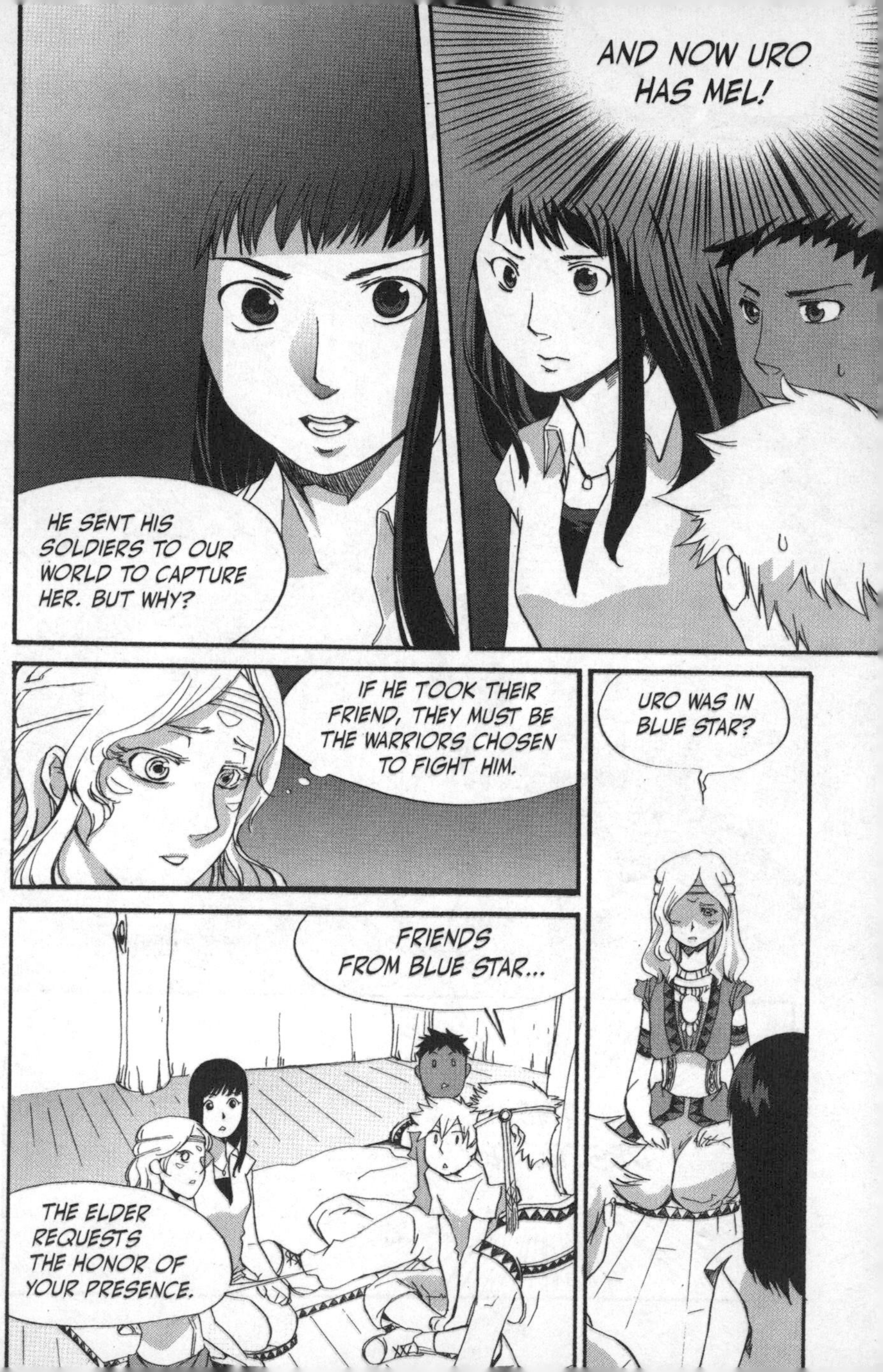
AND NOW URO HAS MEL!
HE SENT HIS SOLDIERS TO OUR WORLD TO CAPTURE HER. BUT WHY?
IF HE TOOK THEIR FRIEND, THEY MUST BE THE WARRIORS CHOSEN TO FIGHT HIM.
URO WAS IN BLUE STAR?
FRIENDS FROM BLUE STAR...
THE ELDER REQUESTS THE HONOR OF YOUR PRESENCE.

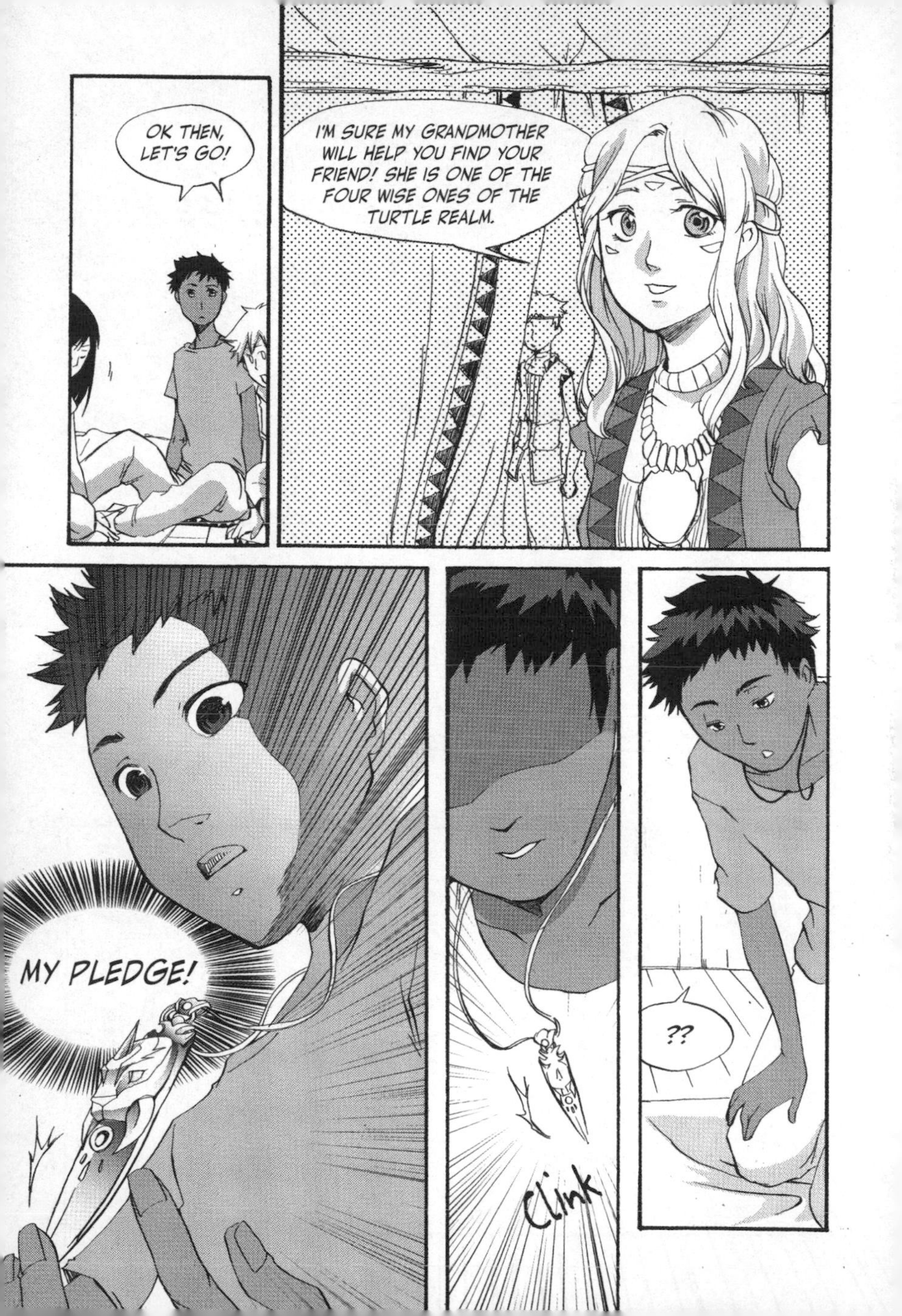
I'M SURE MY GRANDMOTHER WILL HELP YOU FIND YOUR FRIEND! SHE IS ONE OF THE FOUR WISE ONES OF THE TURTLE REALM.
OK THEN, LET'S GO!
MY PLEDGE!
Clink
??

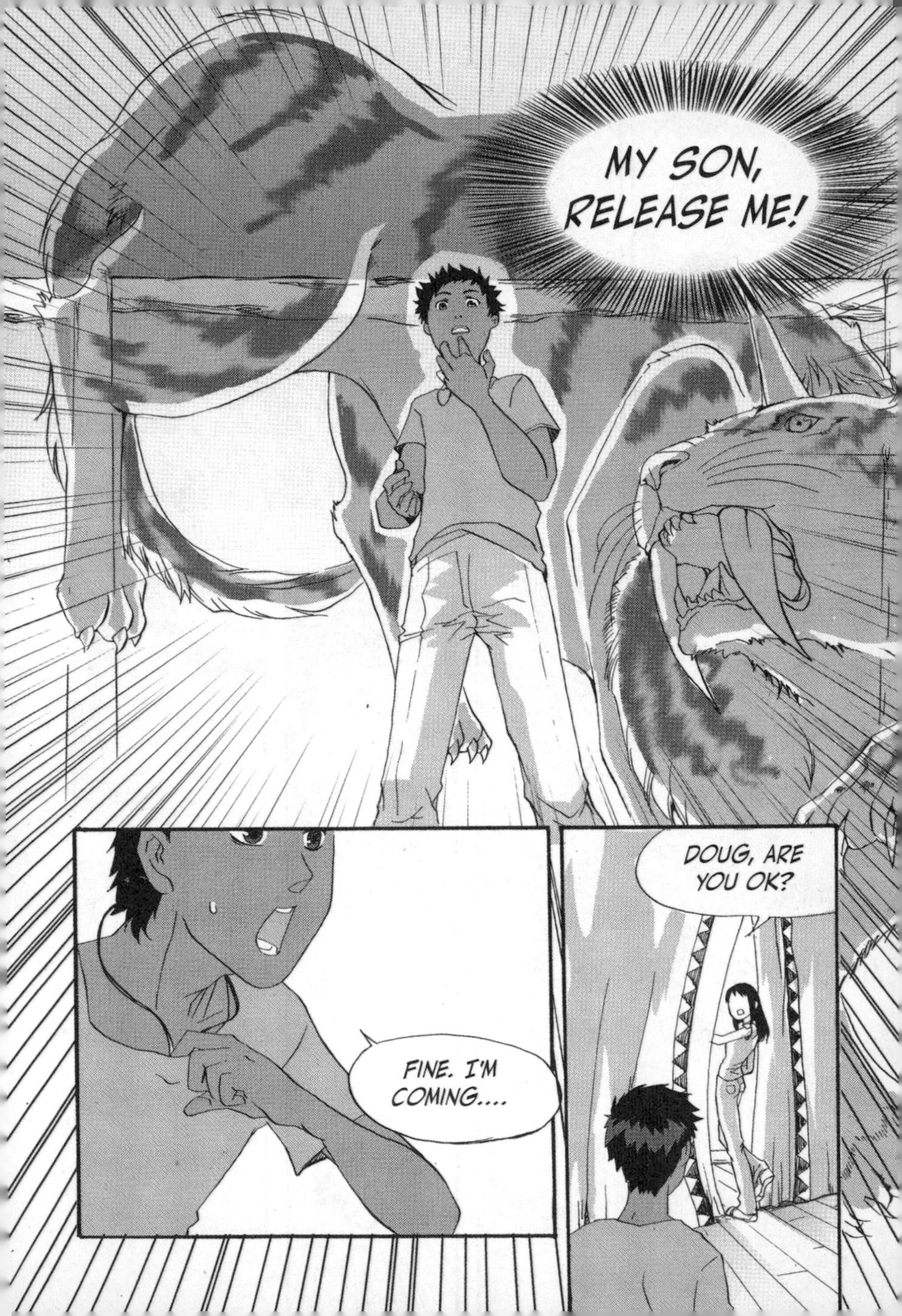
MY SON, RELEASE ME!
DOUG, ARE YOU OK?
FINE. I'M COMING....

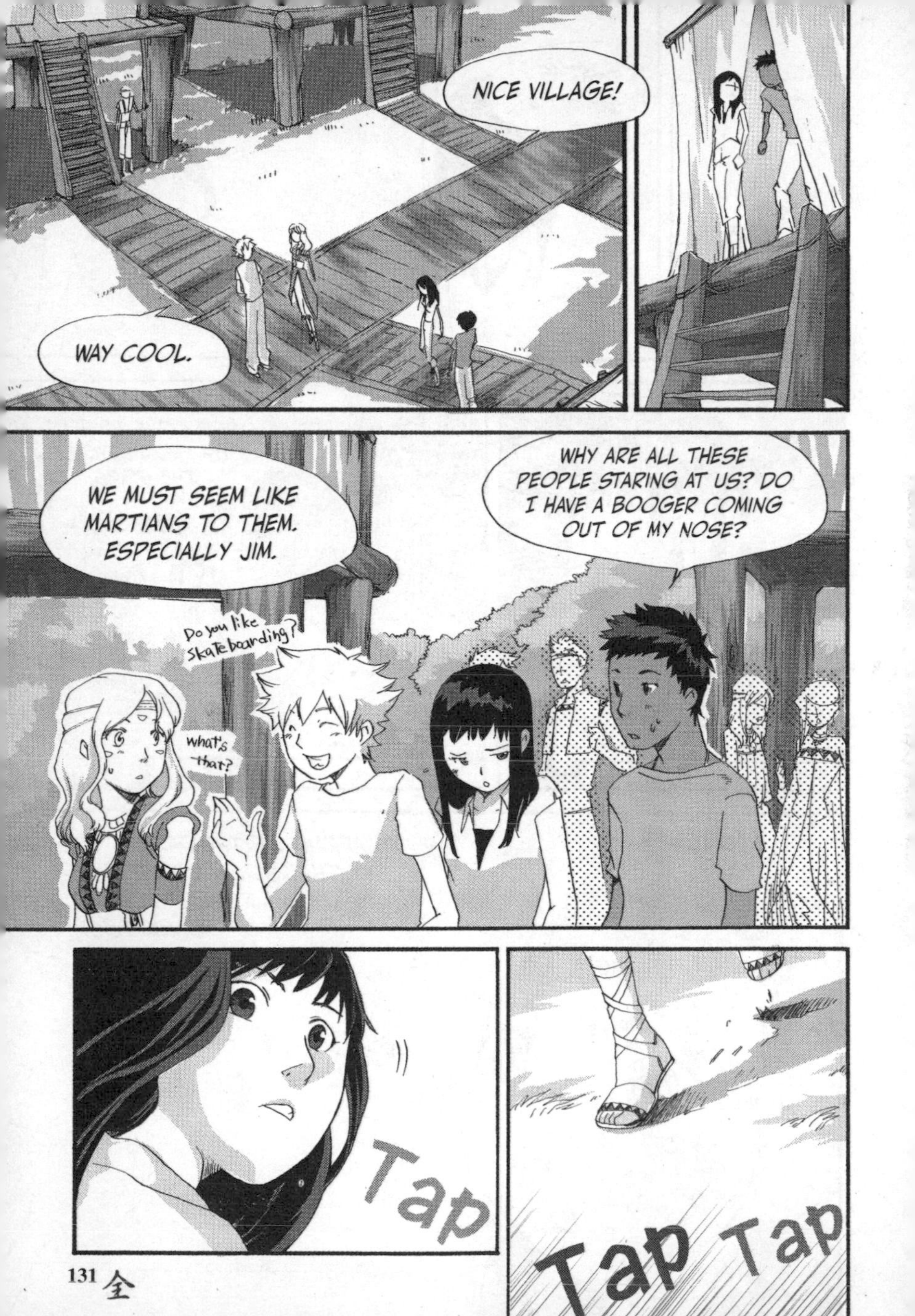
NICE VILLAGE!
WAY COOL.
WHY ARE ALL THESE PEOPLE STARING AT US? DO I HAVE A BOOGER COMING OUT OF MY NOSE?
WE MUST SEEM LIKE MARTIANS TO THEM. ESPECIALLY JIM.
Do you like skateboarding?
what's that?
Tap
Tap Tap

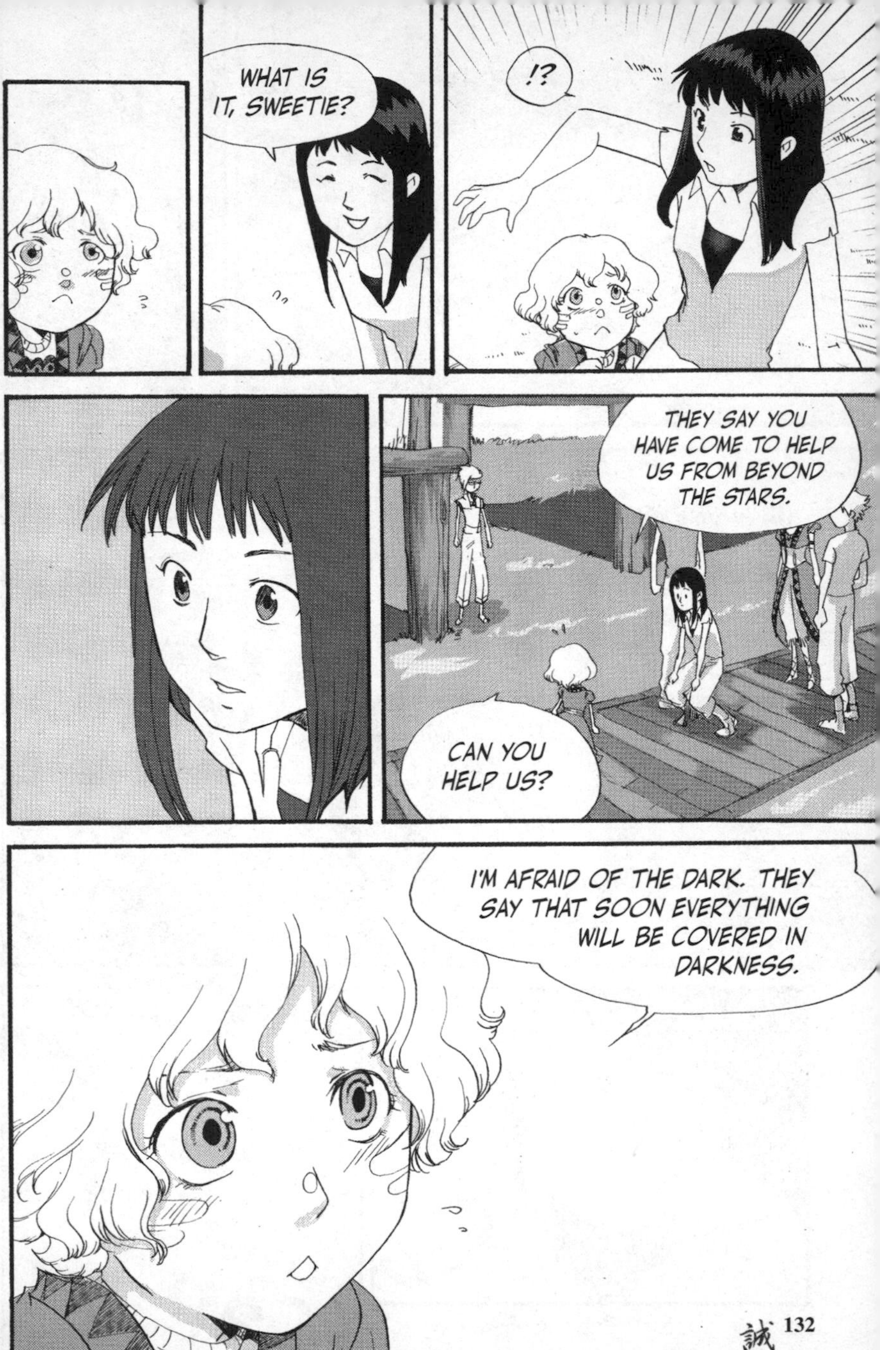
WHAT IS IT, SWEETIE?
!?
THEY SAY YOU HAVE COME TO HELP US FROM BEYOND THE STARS.
CAN YOU HELP US?
I'M AFRAID OF THE DARK. THEY SAY THAT SOON EVERYTHING WILL BE COVERED IN DARKNESS.

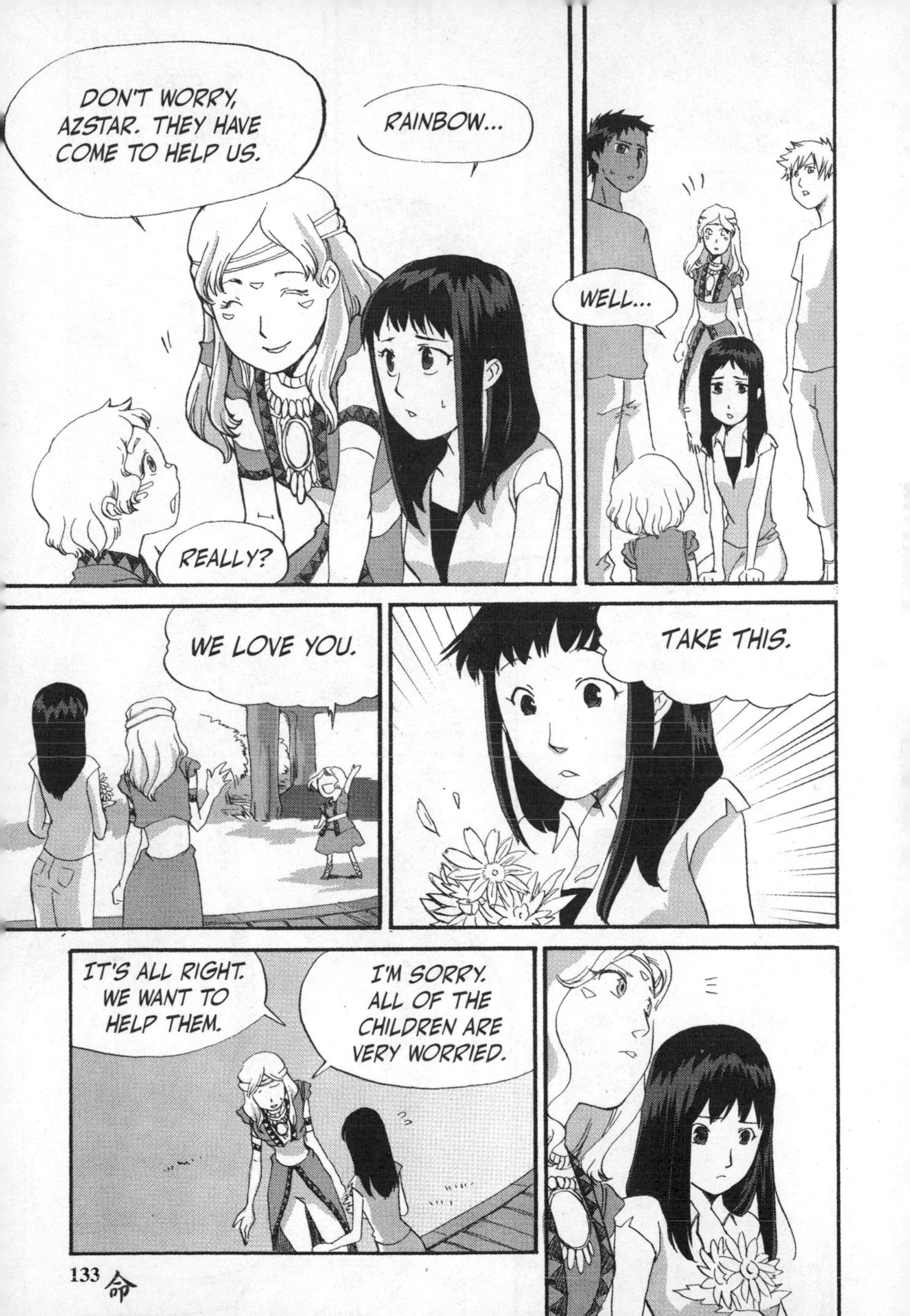
DON'T WORRY, AZSTAR. THEY HAVE COME TO HELP US.
RAINBOW...
REALLY?
WELL...
WE LOVE YOU.
TAKE THIS.
I'M SORRY. ALL OF THE CHILDREN ARE VERY WORRIED.
IT'S ALL RIGHT. WE WANT TO HELP THEM.

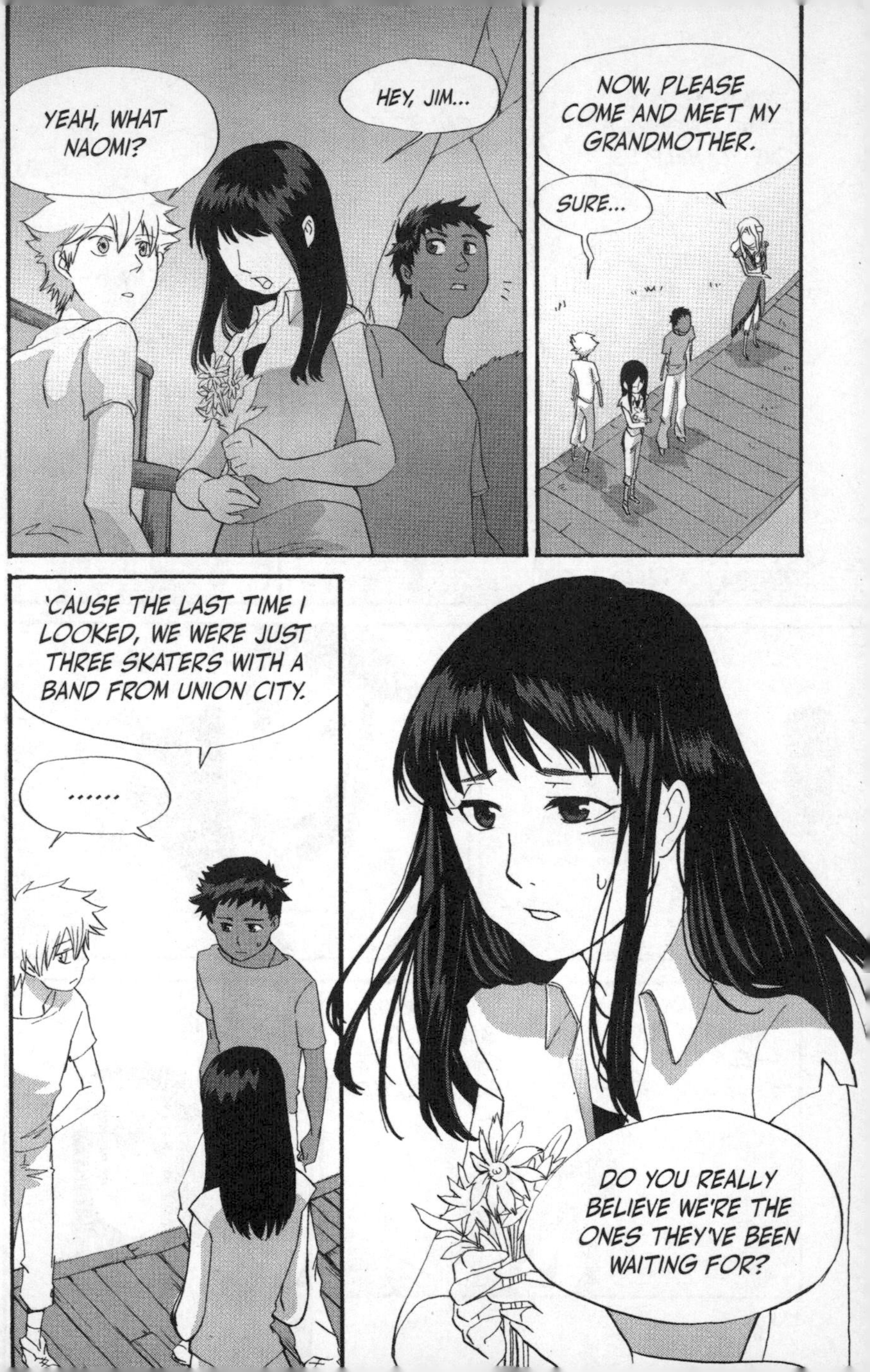
YEAH, WHAT NAOMI?
HEY, JIM...
NOW, PLEASE COME AND MEET MY GRANDMOTHER.
SURE...
'CAUSE THE LAST TIME I LOOKED, WE WERE JUST THREE SKATERS WITH A BAND FROM UNION CITY.
......
DO YOU REALLY BELIEVE WE'RE THE ONES THEY'VE BEEN WAITING FOR?

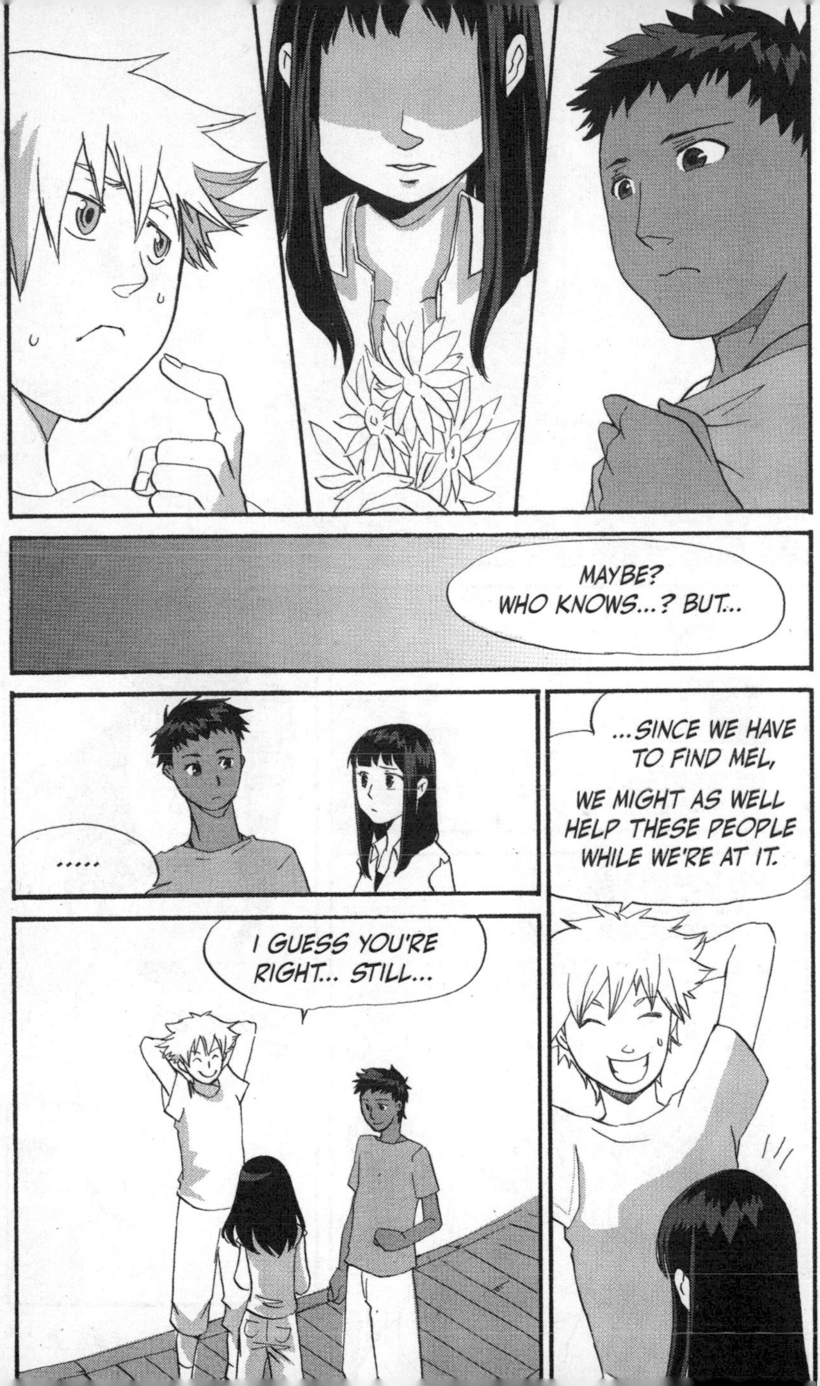

MAYBE? WHO KNOWS...? BUT...
...SINCE WE HAVE TO FIND MEL,
WE MIGHT AS WELL HELP THESE PEOPLE WHILE WE'RE AT IT.
.....
I GUESS YOU'RE RIGHT... STILL...

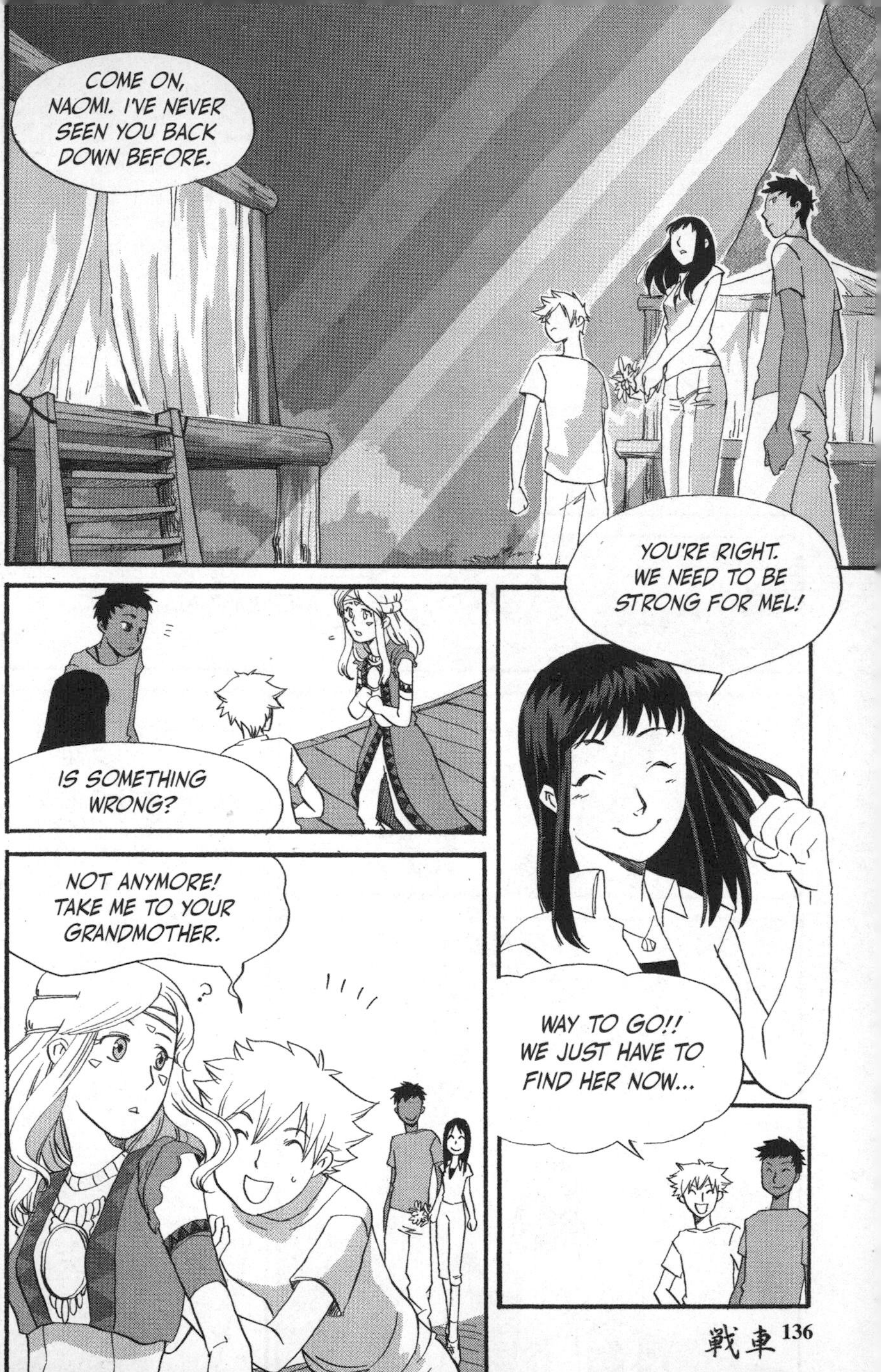
COME ON, NAOMI. I'VE NEVER SEEN YOU BACK DOWN BEFORE.
YOU'RE RIGHT. WE NEED TO BE STRONG FOR MEL!
IS SOMETHING WRONG?
NOT ANYMORE! TAKE ME TO YOUR GRANDMOTHER.
WAY TO GO!! WE JUST HAVE TO FIND HER NOW...

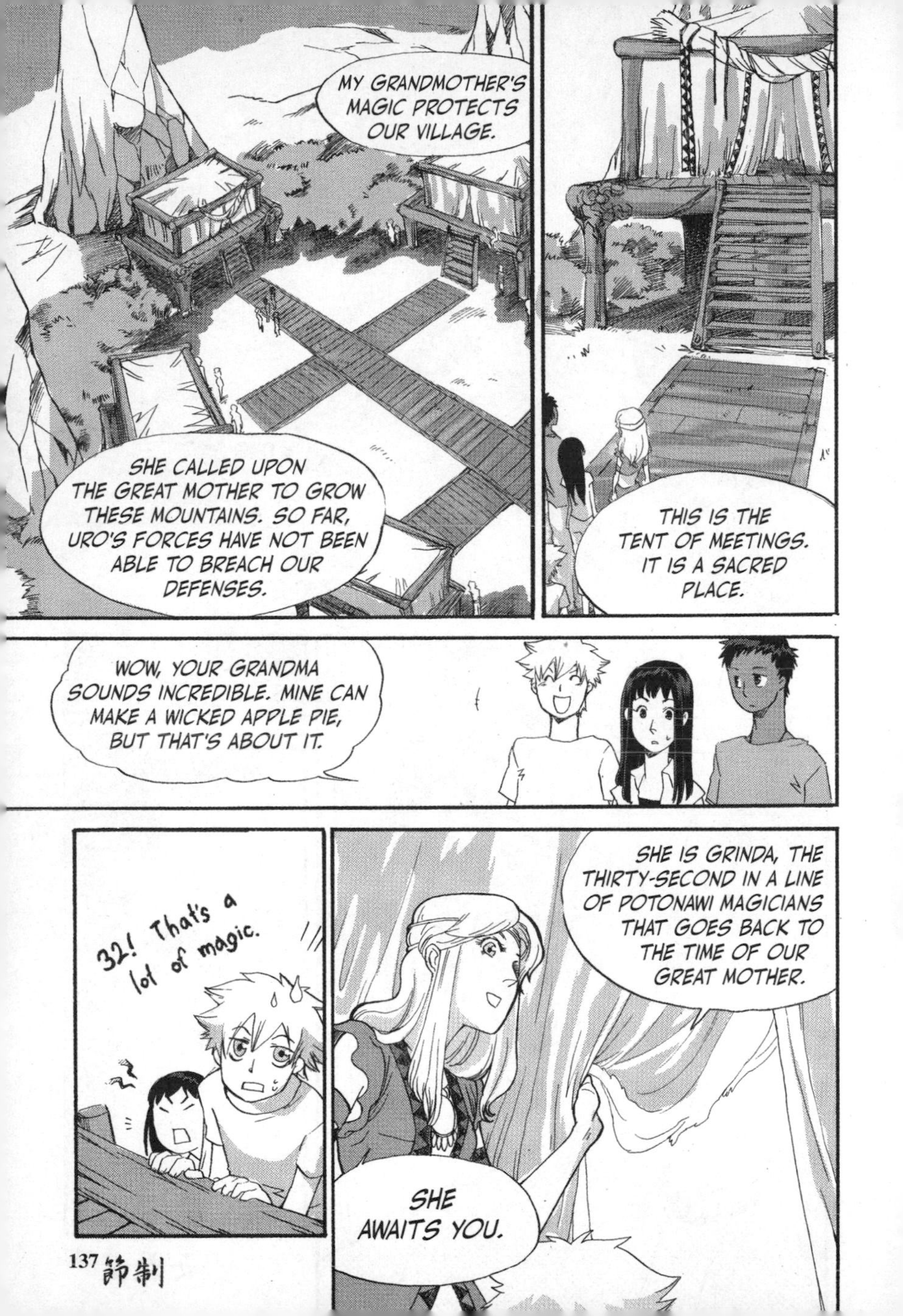
MY GRANDMOTHER'S MAGIC PROTECTS OUR VILLAGE.
SHE CALLED UPON THE GREAT MOTHER TO GROW THESE MOUNTAINS. SO FAR, URO'S FORCES HAVE NOT BEEN ABLE TO BREACH OUR DEFENSES.
THIS IS THE TENT OF MEETINGS. IT IS A SACRED PLACE.
WOW, YOUR GRANDMA SOUNDS INCREDIBLE. MINE CAN MAKE A WICKED APPLE PIE, BUT THAT'S ABOUT IT.
SHE IS GRINDA, THE THIRTY-SECOND IN A LINE OF POTONAWI MAGICIANS THAT GOES BACK TO THE TIME OF OUR GREAT MOTHER.
32! That's a lot of magic.
SHE AWAITS YOU.

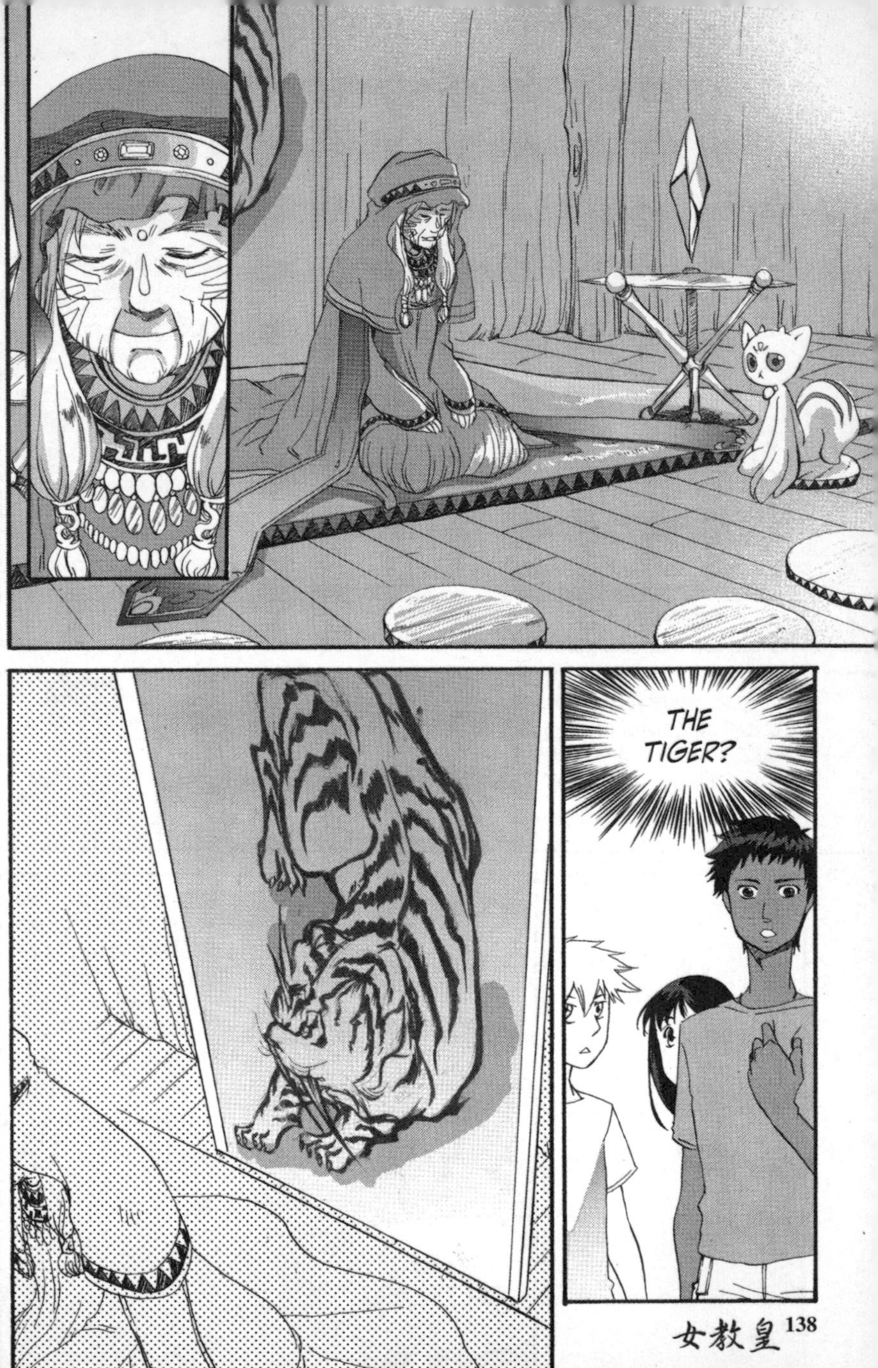
THE TIGER?

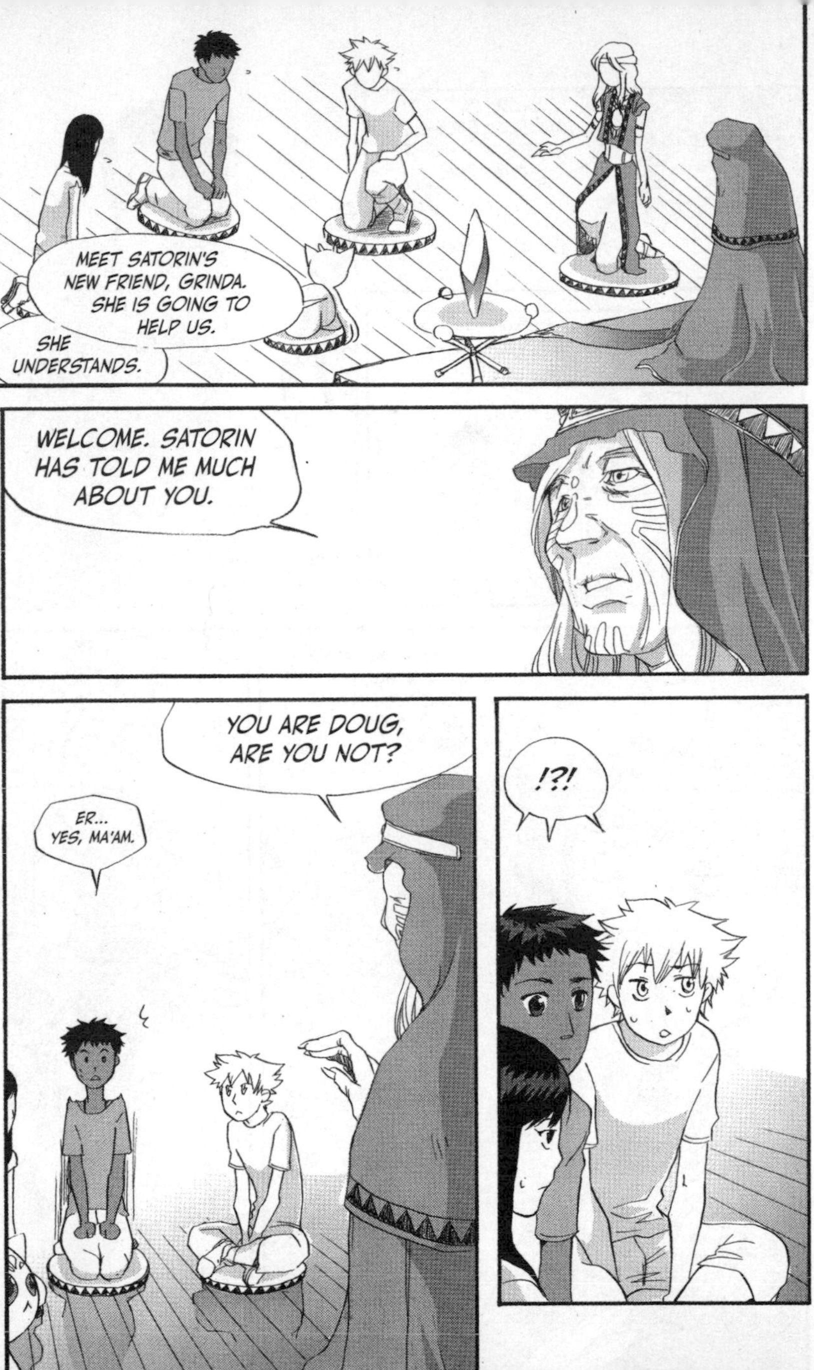
MEET SATORIN'S NEW FRIEND, GRINDA. SHE IS GOING TO HELP US.
SHE UNDERSTANDS.
WELCOME. SATORIN HAS TOLD ME MUCH ABOUT YOU.
YOU ARE DOUG, ARE YOU NOT?
ER... YES, MA'AM.
!?!

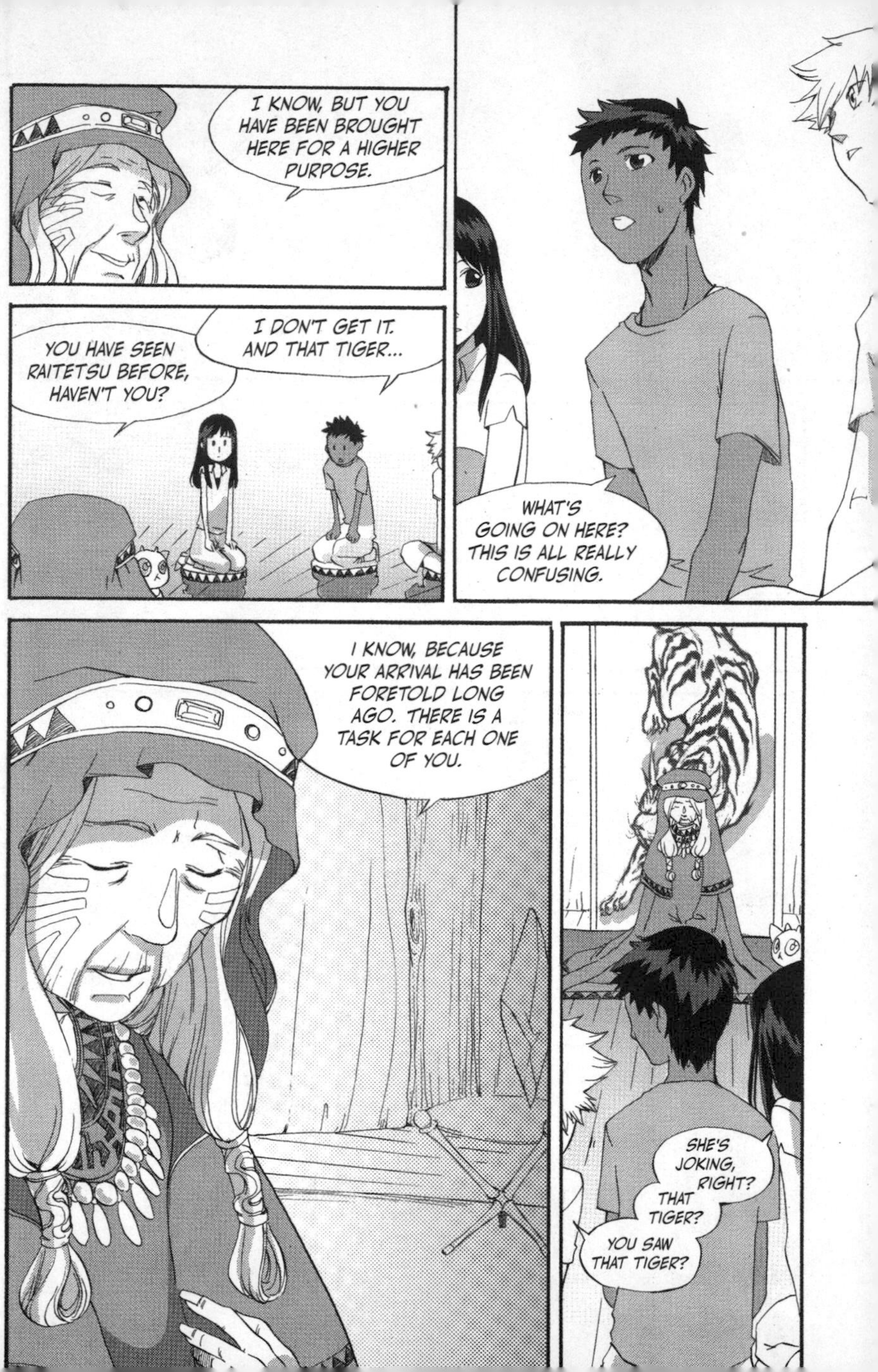
I KNOW, BUT YOU HAVE BEEN BROUGHT HERE FOR A HIGHER PURPOSE.
I DON'T GET IT. AND THAT TIGER...
YOU HAVE SEEN RAITETSU BEFORE, HAVEN'T YOU?
WHAT'S GOING ON HERE? THIS IS ALL REALLY CONFUSING.
I KNOW, BECAUSE YOUR ARRIVAL HAS BEEN FORETOLD LONG AGO. THERE IS A TASK FOR EACH ONE OF YOU.
SHE'S JOKING, RIGHT?
THAT TIGER?
YOU SAW THAT TIGER?

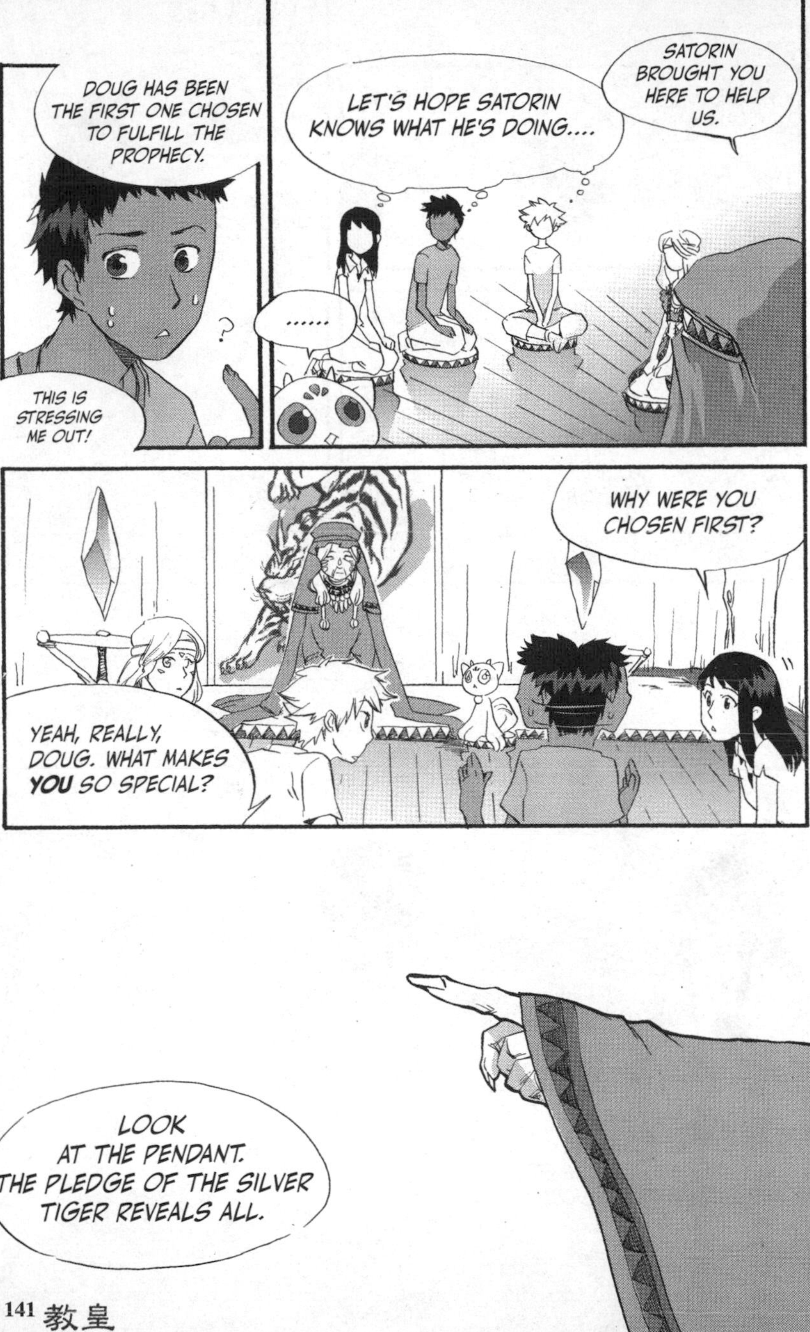
DOUG HAS BEEN THE FIRST ONE CHOSEN TO FULFILL THE PROPHECY.
THIS IS STRESSING ME OUT!
?
SATORIN BROUGHT YOU HERE TO HELP US.
LET'S HOPE SATORIN KNOWS WHAT HE'S DOING....
......
WHY WERE YOU CHOSEN FIRST?
YEAH, REALLY, DOUG. WHAT MAKES **YOU** SO SPECIAL?
LOOK AT THE PENDANT. THE PLEDGE OF THE SILVER TIGER REVEALS ALL.

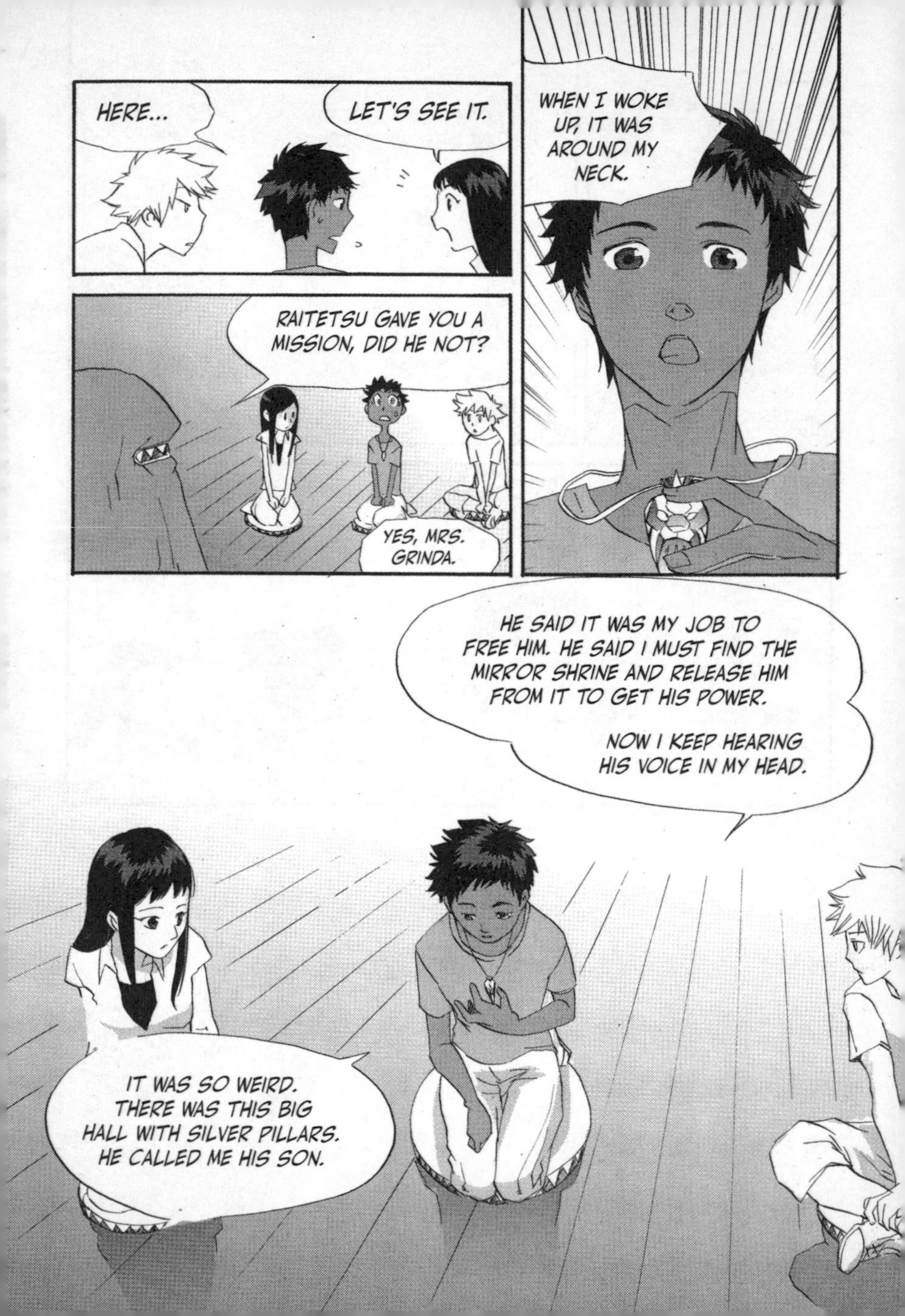
HERE...
LET'S SEE IT.
WHEN I WOKE UP, IT WAS AROUND MY NECK.
RAITETSU GAVE YOU A MISSION, DID HE NOT?
YES, MRS. GRINDA.
HE SAID IT WAS MY JOB TO FREE HIM. HE SAID I MUST FIND THE MIRROR SHRINE AND RELEASE HIM FROM IT TO GET HIS POWER.
NOW I KEEP HEARING HIS VOICE IN MY HEAD.
IT WAS SO WEIRD. THERE WAS THIS BIG HALL WITH SILVER PILLARS. HE CALLED ME HIS SON.

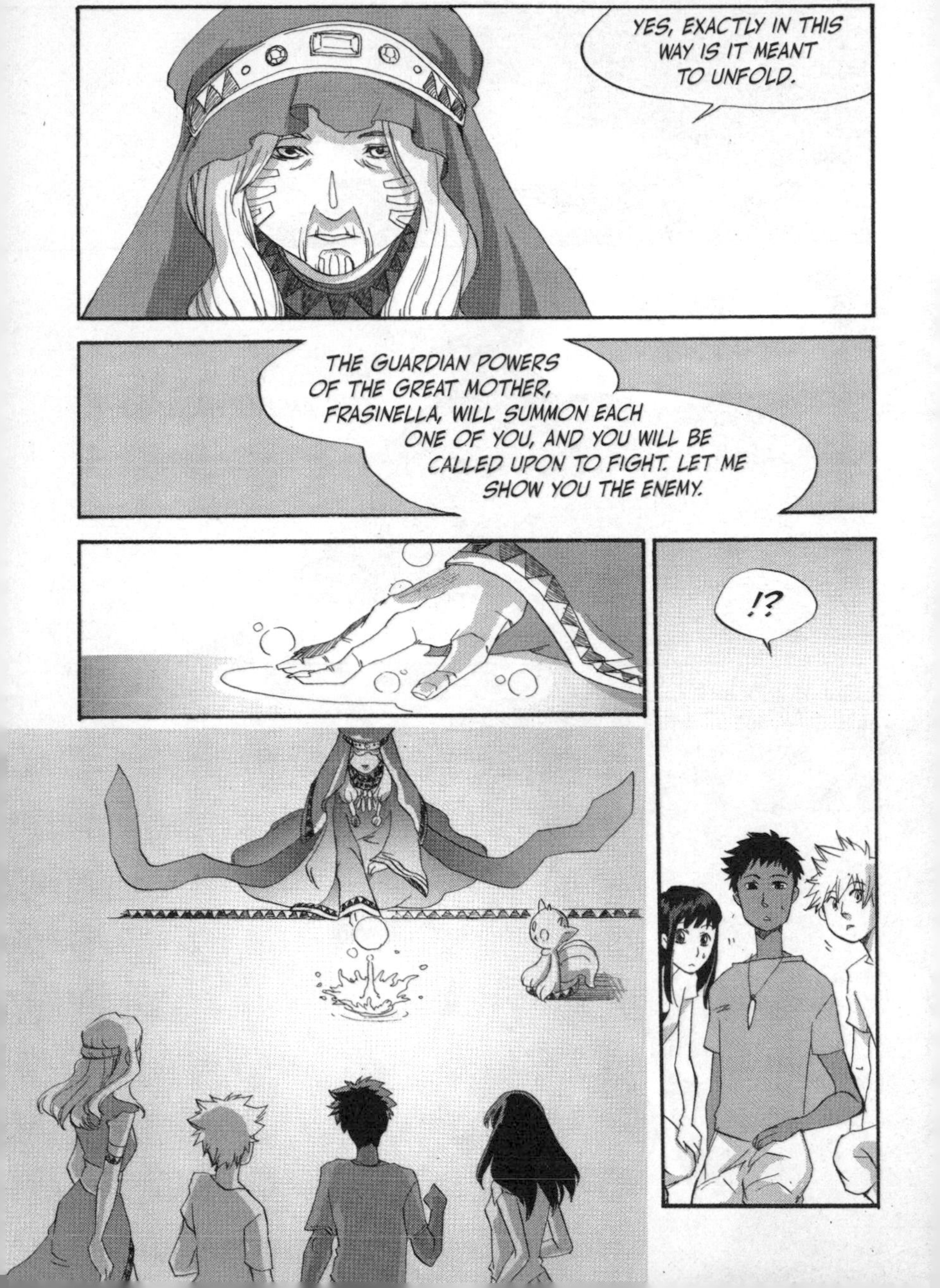
YES, EXACTLY IN THIS WAY IS IT MEANT TO UNFOLD.
THE GUARDIAN POWERS OF THE GREAT MOTHER, FRASINELLA, WILL SUMMON EACH ONE OF YOU, AND YOU WILL BE CALLED UPON TO FIGHT. LET ME SHOW YOU THE ENEMY.
!?

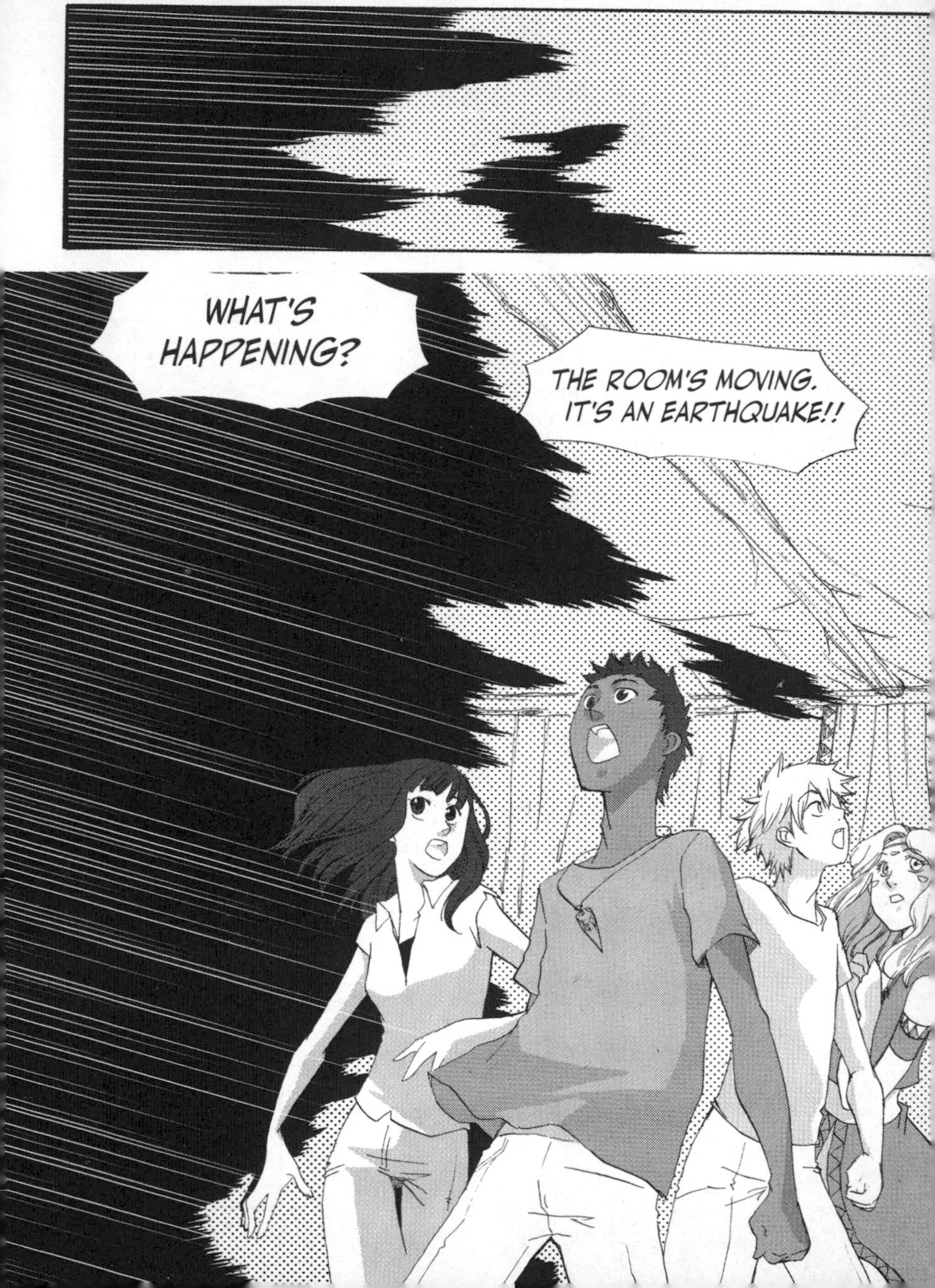
WHAT'S HAPPENING?
THE ROOM'S MOVING. IT'S AN EARTHQUAKE!!

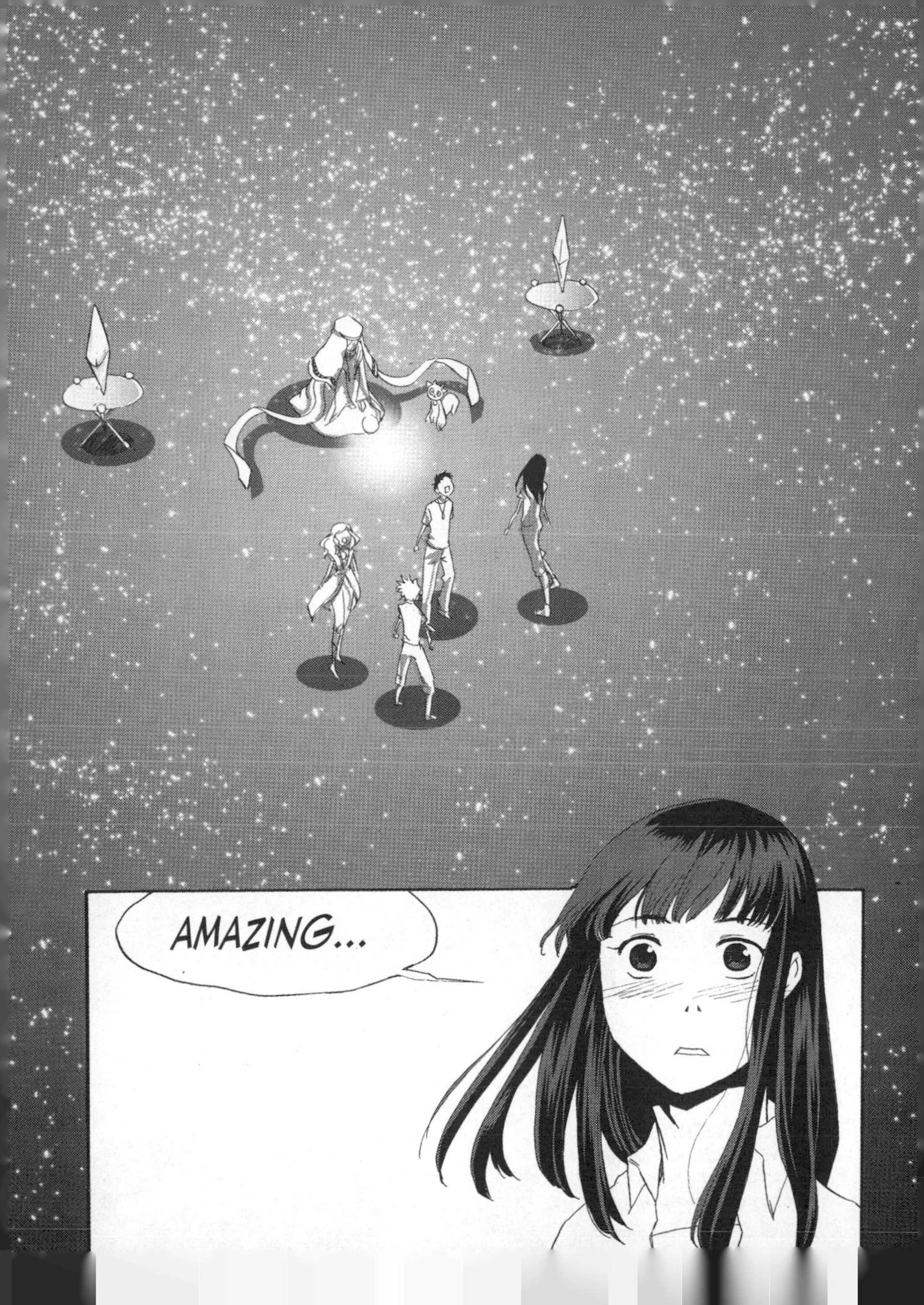
AMAZING...

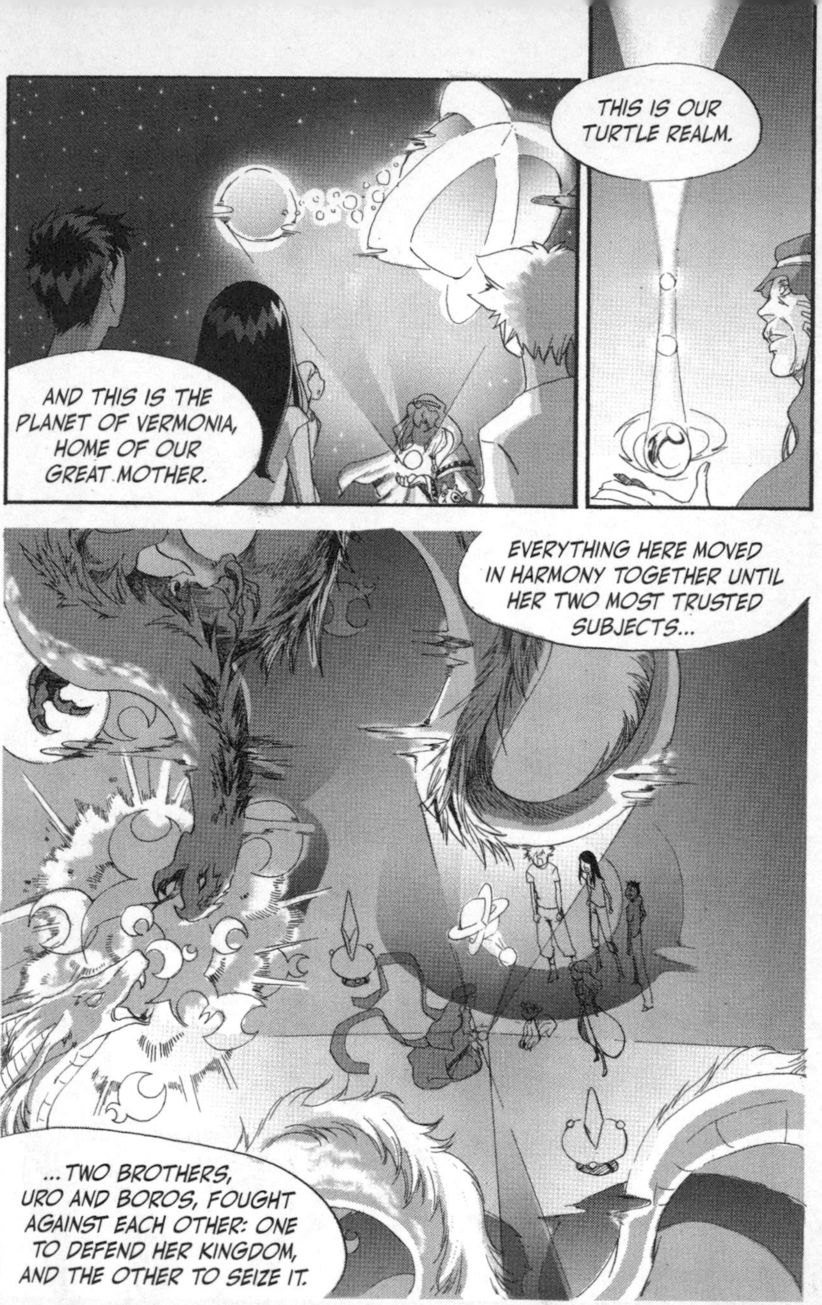
THIS IS OUR TURTLE REALM.
AND THIS IS THE PLANET OF VERMONIA, HOME OF OUR GREAT MOTHER.
EVERYTHING HERE MOVED IN HARMONY TOGETHER UNTIL HER TWO MOST TRUSTED SUBJECTS...
...TWO BROTHERS, URO AND BOROS, FOUGHT AGAINST EACH OTHER: ONE TO DEFEND HER KINGDOM, AND THE OTHER TO SEIZE IT.

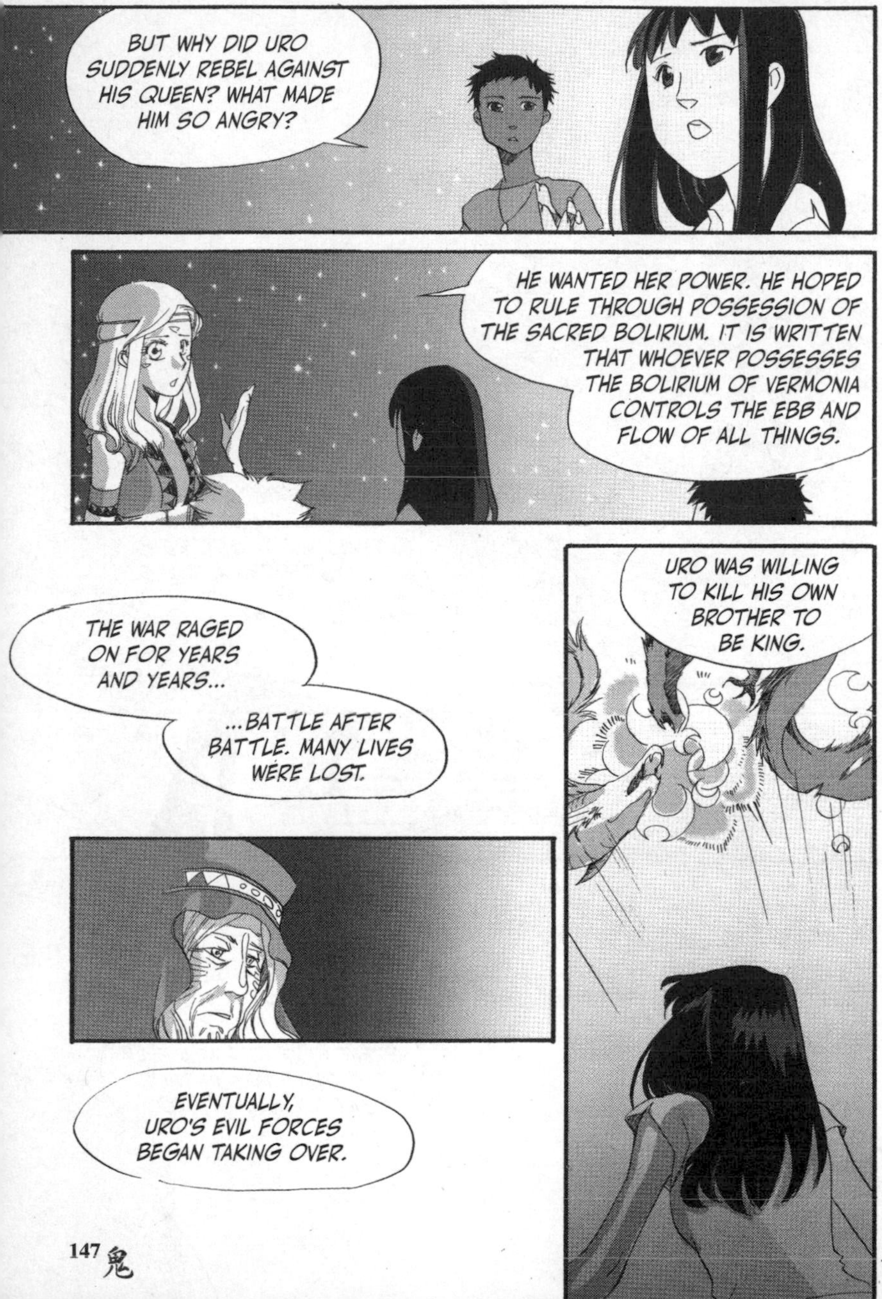
BUT WHY DID URO SUDDENLY REBEL AGAINST HIS QUEEN? WHAT MADE HIM SO ANGRY?
HE WANTED HER POWER. HE HOPED TO RULE THROUGH POSSESSION OF THE SACRED BOLIRIUM. IT IS WRITTEN THAT WHOEVER POSSESSES THE BOLIRIUM OF VERMONIA CONTROLS THE EBB AND FLOW OF ALL THINGS.
URO WAS WILLING TO KILL HIS OWN BROTHER TO BE KING.
THE WAR RAGED ON FOR YEARS AND YEARS...
...BATTLE AFTER BATTLE. MANY LIVES WERE LOST.
EVENTUALLY, URO'S EVIL FORCES BEGAN TAKING OVER.

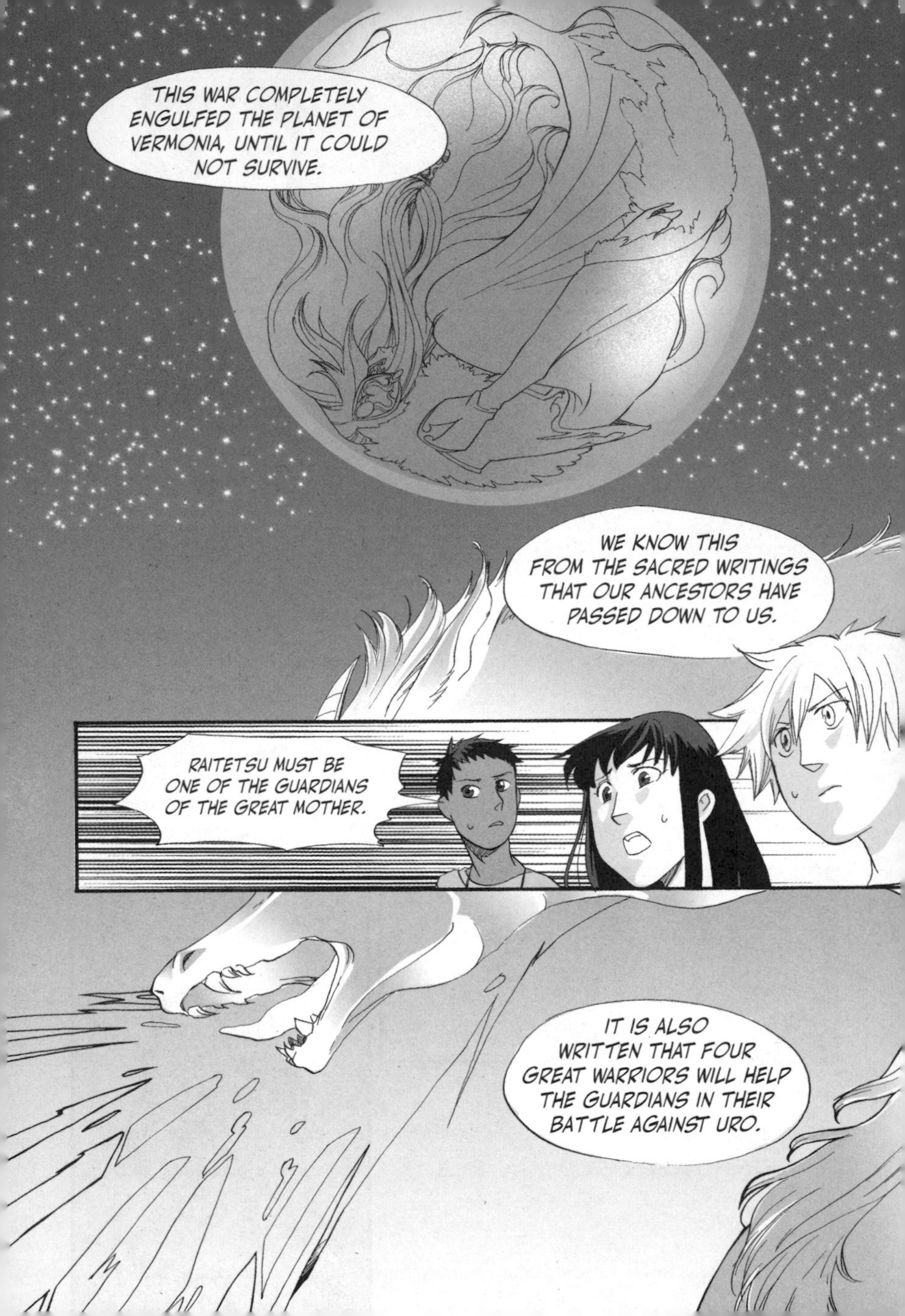
THIS WAR COMPLETELY ENGULFED THE PLANET OF VERMONIA, UNTIL IT COULD NOT SURVIVE.
WE KNOW THIS FROM THE SACRED WRITINGS THAT OUR ANCESTORS HAVE PASSED DOWN TO US.
RAITETSU MUST BE ONE OF THE GUARDIANS OF THE GREAT MOTHER.
IT IS ALSO WRITTEN THAT FOUR GREAT WARRIORS WILL HELP THE GUARDIANS IN THEIR BATTLE AGAINST URO.

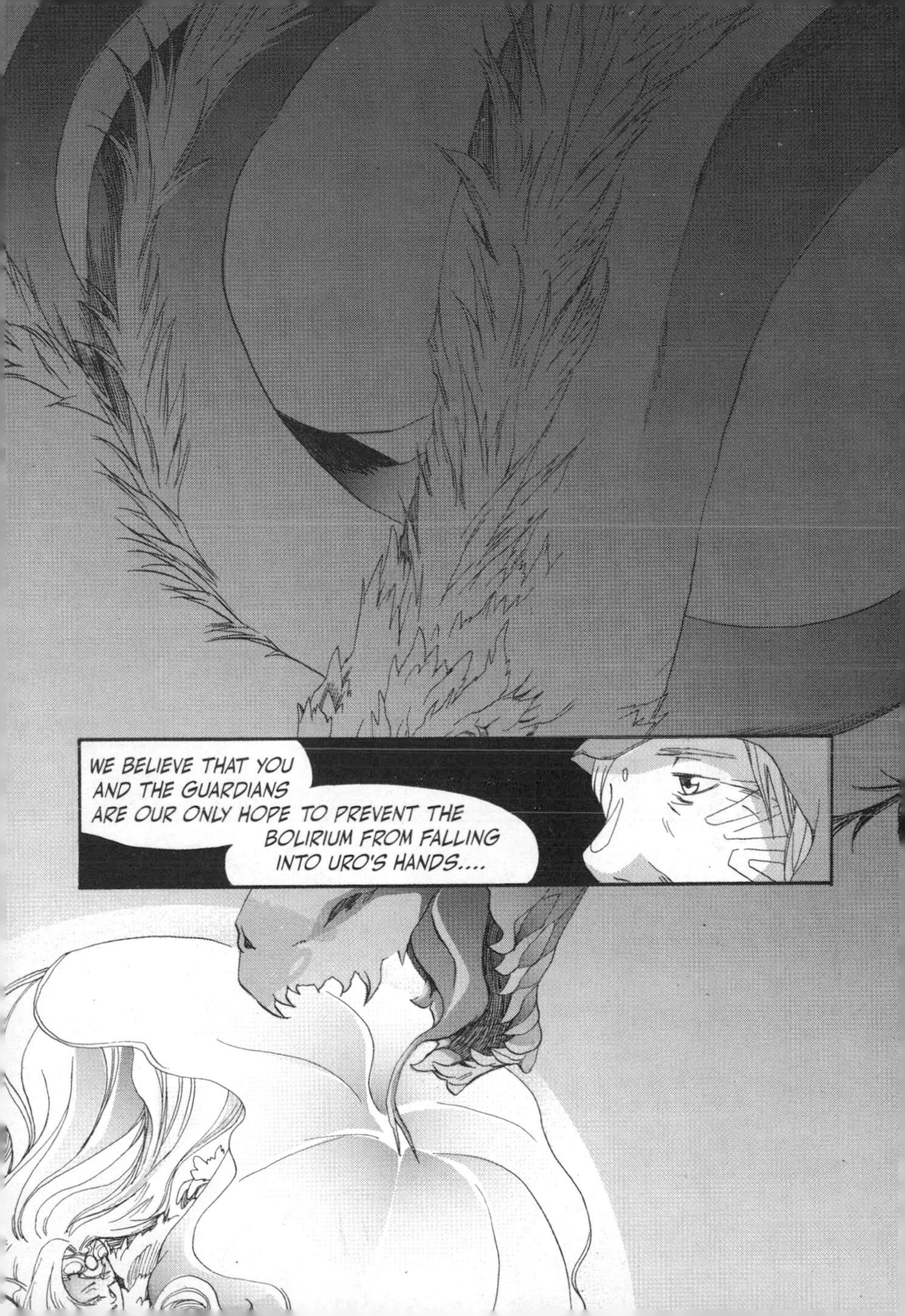
WE BELIEVE THAT YOU AND THE GUARDIANS ARE OUR ONLY HOPE TO PREVENT THE BOLIRIUM FROM FALLING INTO URO'S HANDS....

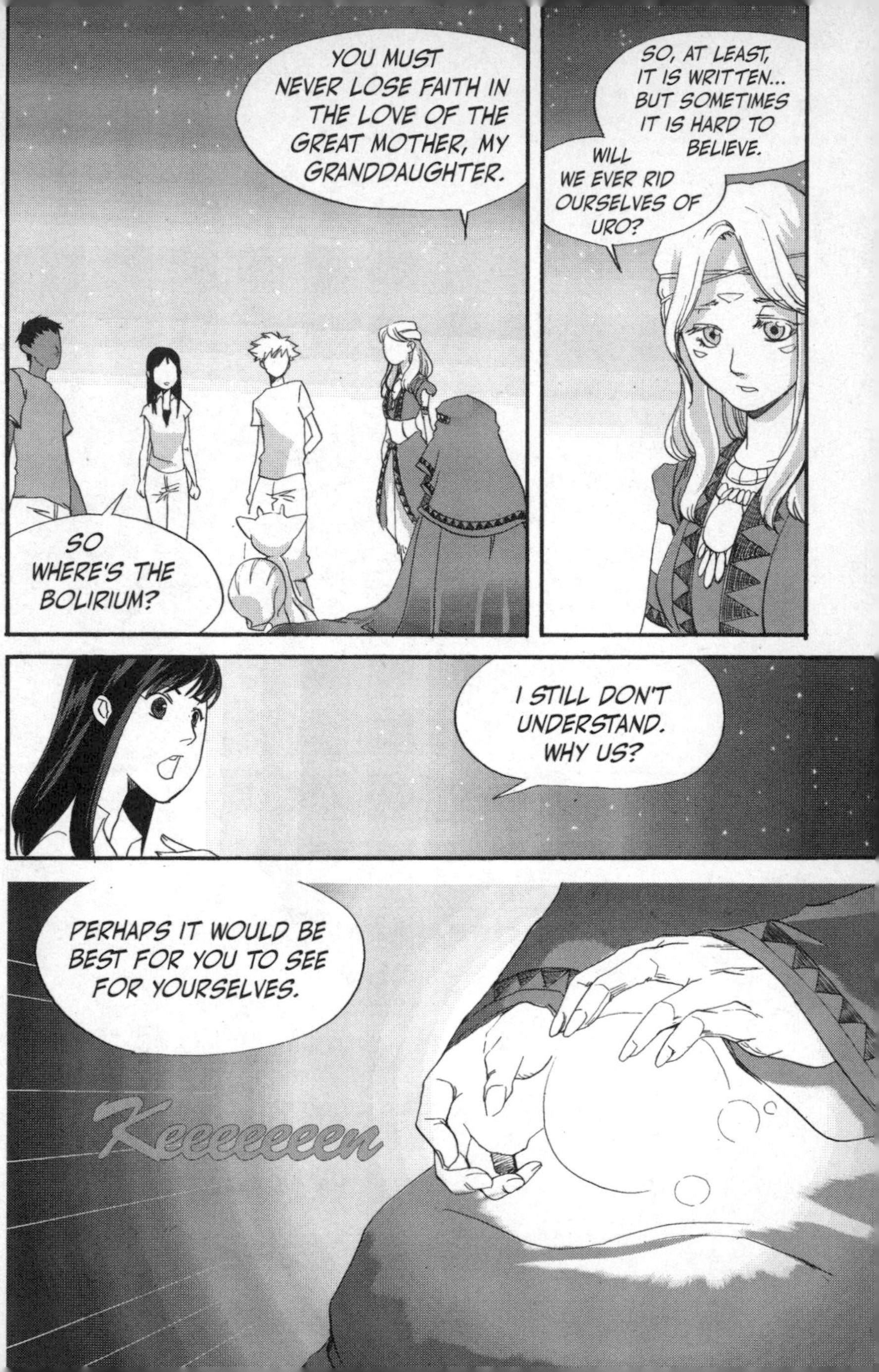
YOU MUST NEVER LOSE FAITH IN THE LOVE OF THE GREAT MOTHER, MY GRANDDAUGHTER.
SO WHERE'S THE BOLIRIUM?
SO, AT LEAST, IT IS WRITTEN... BUT SOMETIMES IT IS HARD TO BELIEVE.
WILL WE EVER RID OURSELVES OF URO?
I STILL DON'T UNDERSTAND. WHY US?
PERHAPS IT WOULD BE BEST FOR YOU TO SEE FOR YOURSELVES.
Keeeeeeen

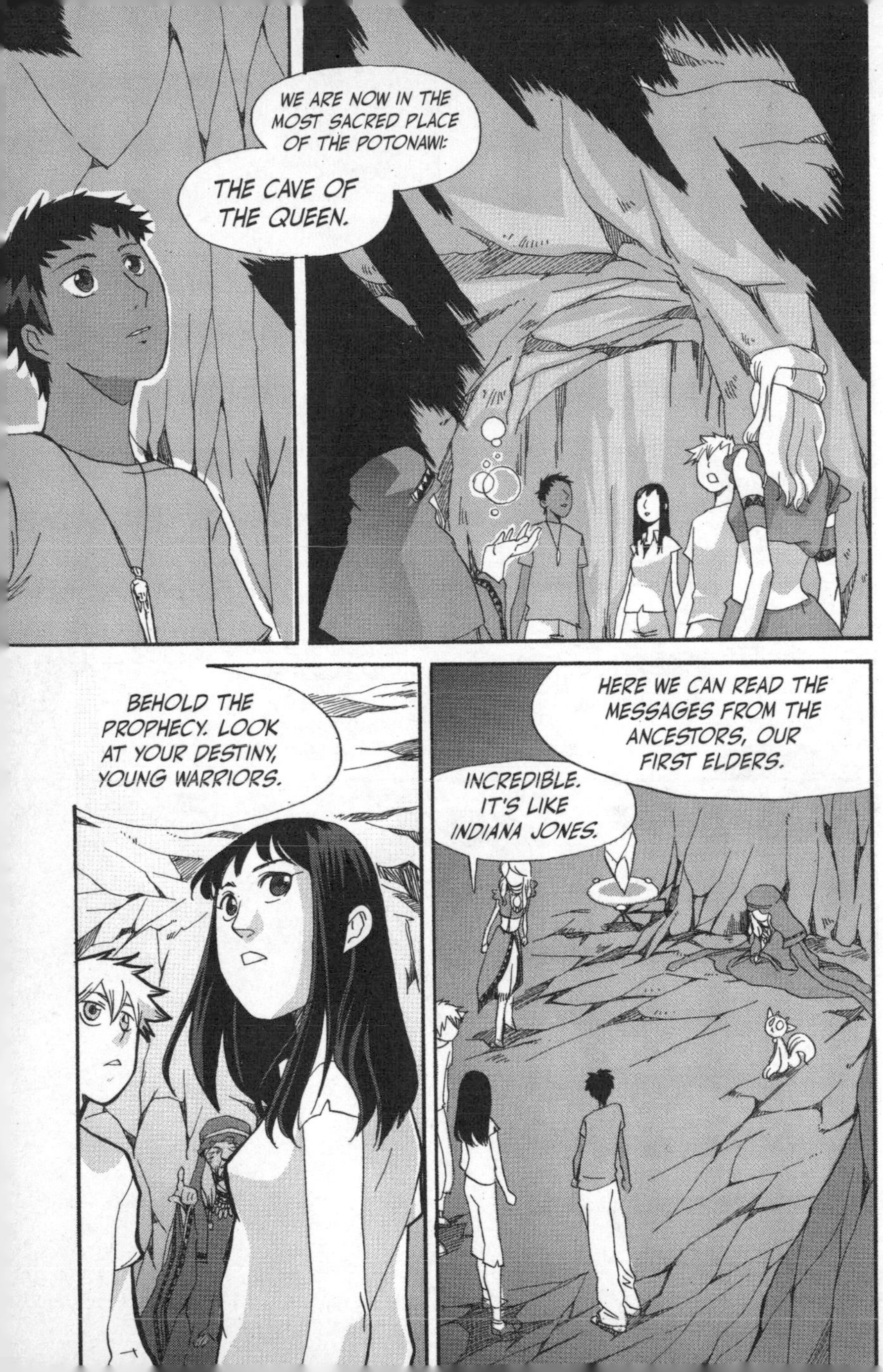
WE ARE NOW IN THE MOST SACRED PLACE OF THE POTONAWI:
THE CAVE OF THE QUEEN.
BEHOLD THE PROPHECY. LOOK AT YOUR DESTINY, YOUNG WARRIORS.
HERE WE CAN READ THE MESSAGES FROM THE ANCESTORS, OUR FIRST ELDERS.
INCREDIBLE. IT'S LIKE INDIANA JONES.

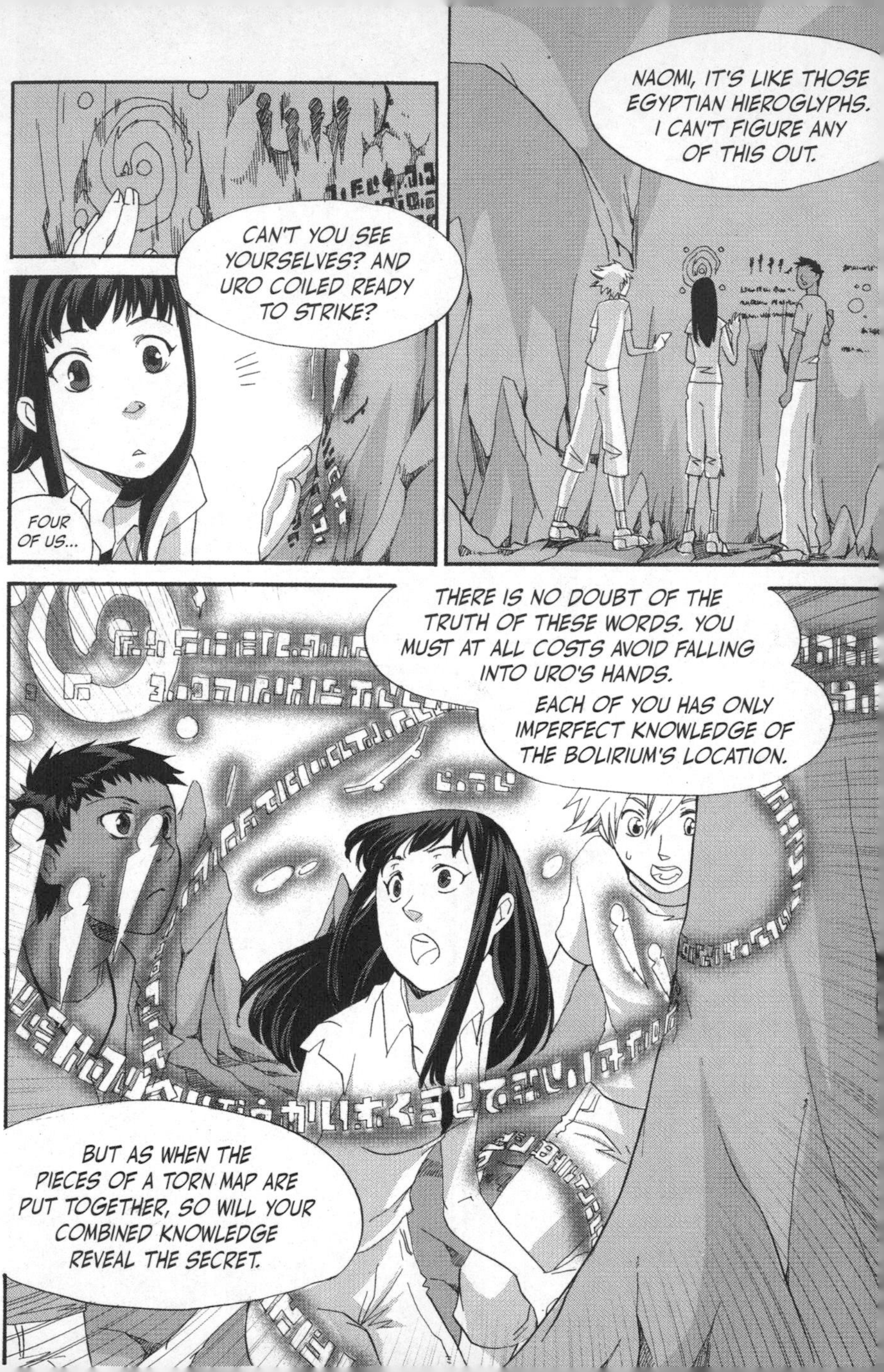
CAN'T YOU SEE YOURSELVES? AND URO COILED READY TO STRIKE?
FOUR OF US...
NAOMI, IT'S LIKE THOSE EGYPTIAN HIEROGLYPHS. I CAN'T FIGURE ANY OF THIS OUT.
THERE IS NO DOUBT OF THE TRUTH OF THESE WORDS. YOU MUST AT ALL COSTS AVOID FALLING INTO URO'S HANDS.
EACH OF YOU HAS ONLY IMPERFECT KNOWLEDGE OF THE BOLIRIUM'S LOCATION.
BUT AS WHEN THE PIECES OF A TORN MAP ARE PUT TOGETHER, SO WILL YOUR COMBINED KNOWLEDGE REVEAL THE SECRET.

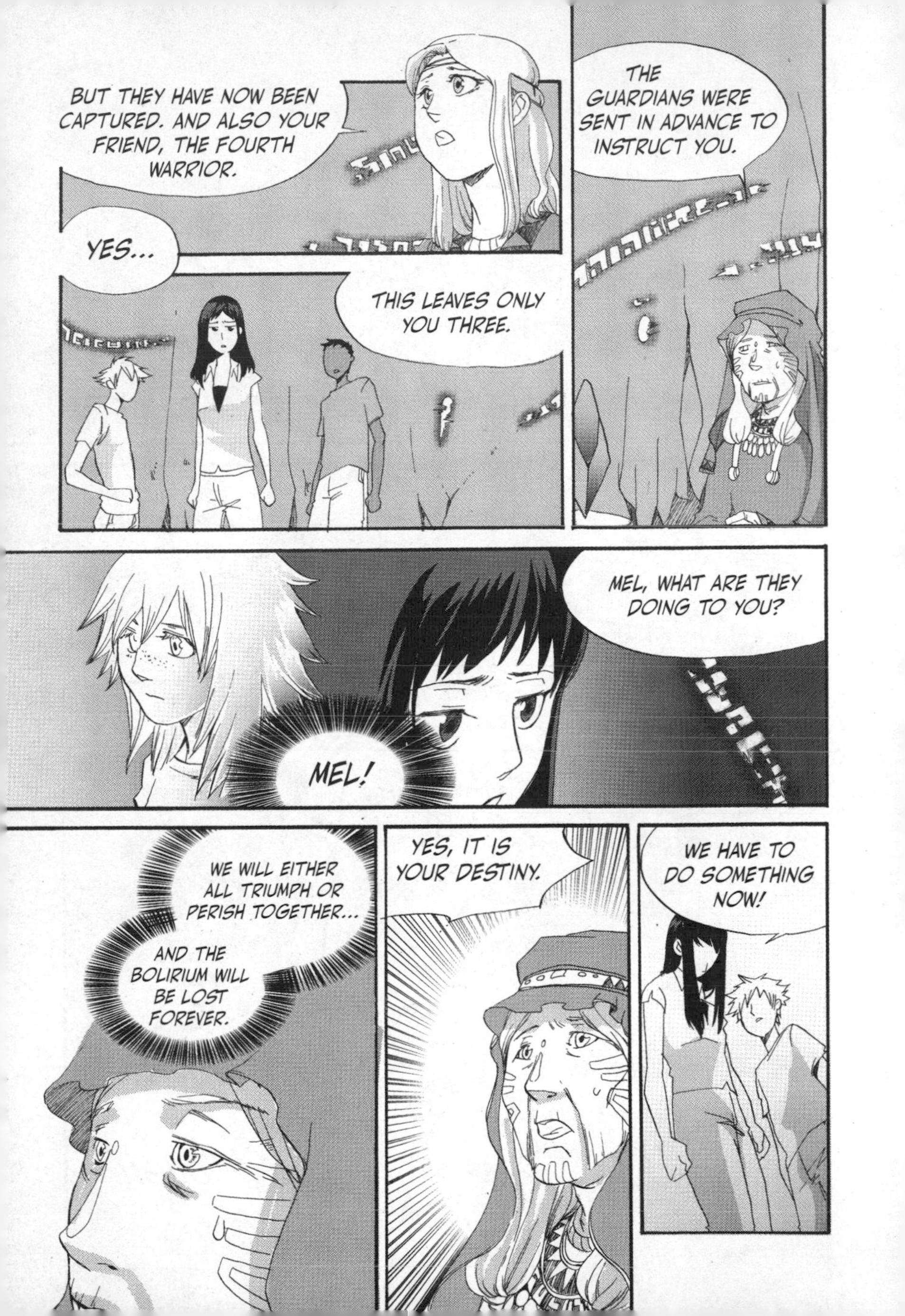
BUT THEY HAVE NOW BEEN CAPTURED. AND ALSO YOUR FRIEND, THE FOURTH WARRIOR.
THE GUARDIANS WERE SENT IN ADVANCE TO INSTRUCT YOU.
YES...
THIS LEAVES ONLY YOU THREE.
MEL, WHAT ARE THEY DOING TO YOU?
MEL!
WE WILL EITHER ALL TRIUMPH OR PERISH TOGETHER...
AND THE BOLIRIUM WILL BE LOST FOREVER.
YES, IT IS YOUR DESTINY.
WE HAVE TO DO SOMETHING NOW!

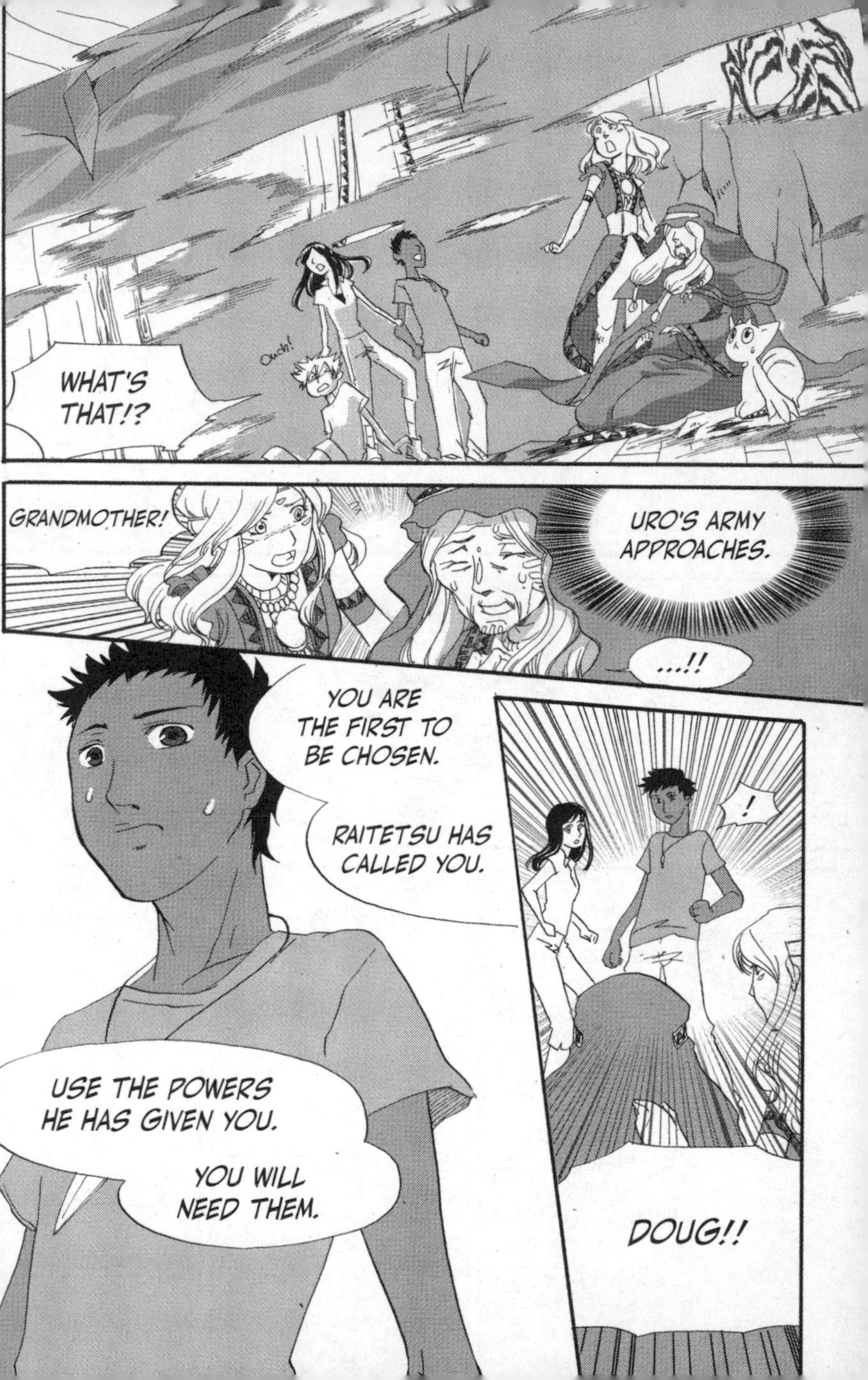
Ouch!
WHAT'S THAT!?
GRANDMOTHER!
URO'S ARMY APPROACHES.
...!!
YOU ARE THE FIRST TO BE CHOSEN.
RAITETSU HAS CALLED YOU.
!
USE THE POWERS HE HAS GIVEN YOU.
YOU WILL NEED THEM.
DOUG!!

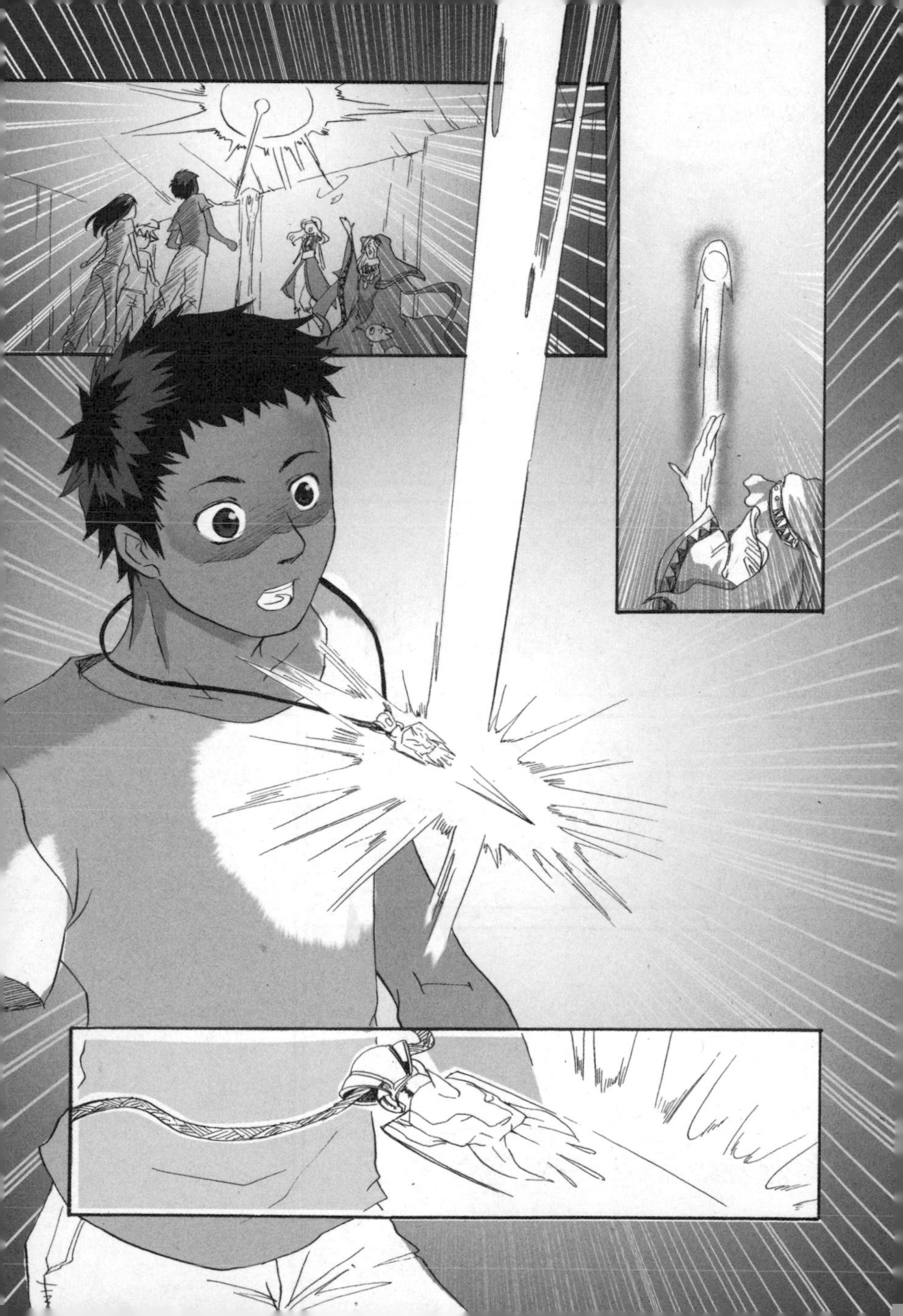

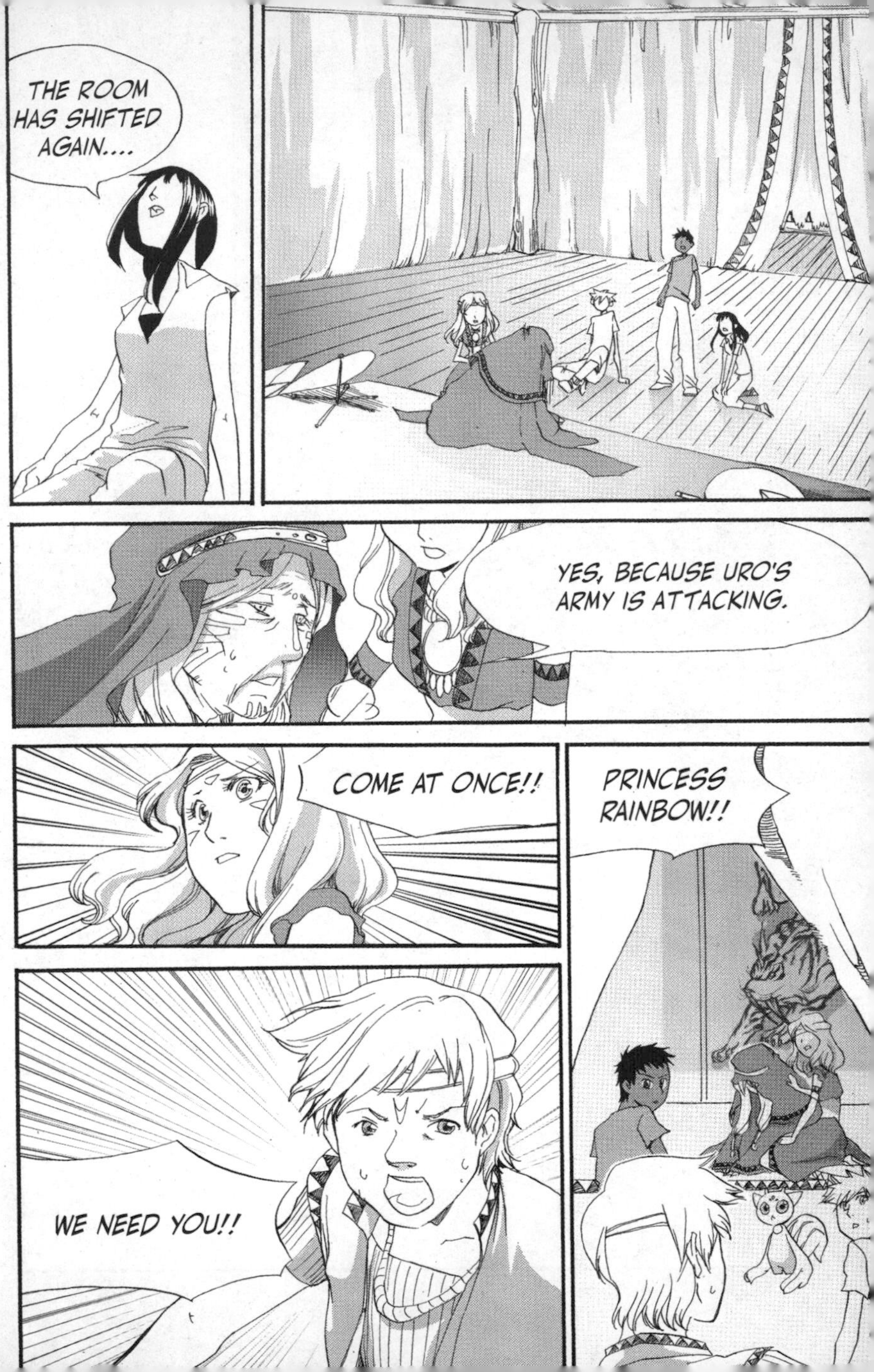
THE ROOM HAS SHIFTED AGAIN....
YES, BECAUSE URO'S ARMY IS ATTACKING.
COME AT ONCE!!
PRINCESS RAINBOW!!
WE NEED YOU!!

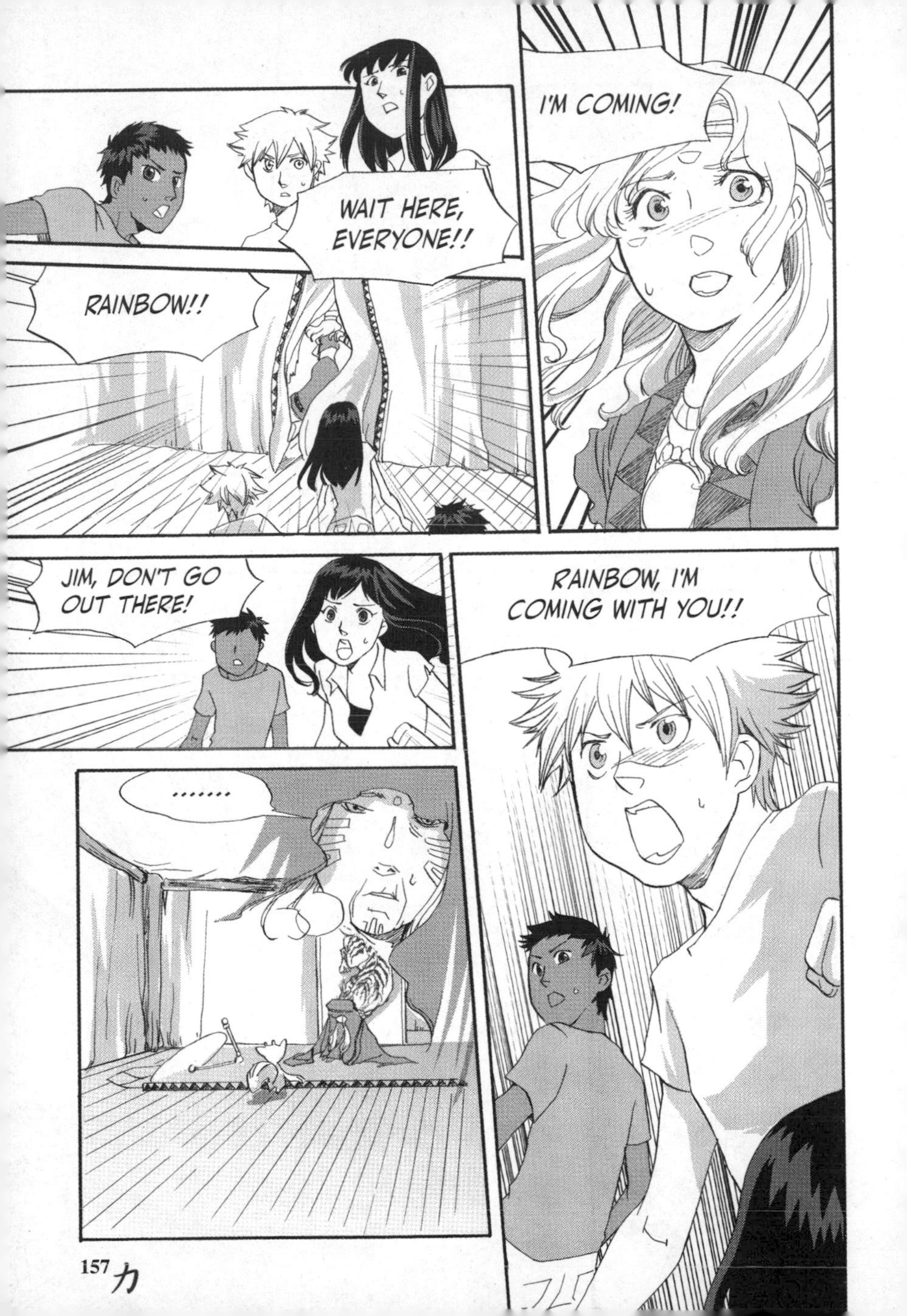

I'M COMING!
WAIT HERE, EVERYONE!!
RAINBOW!!
RAINBOW, I'M COMING WITH YOU!!
JIM, DON'T GO OUT THERE!
....

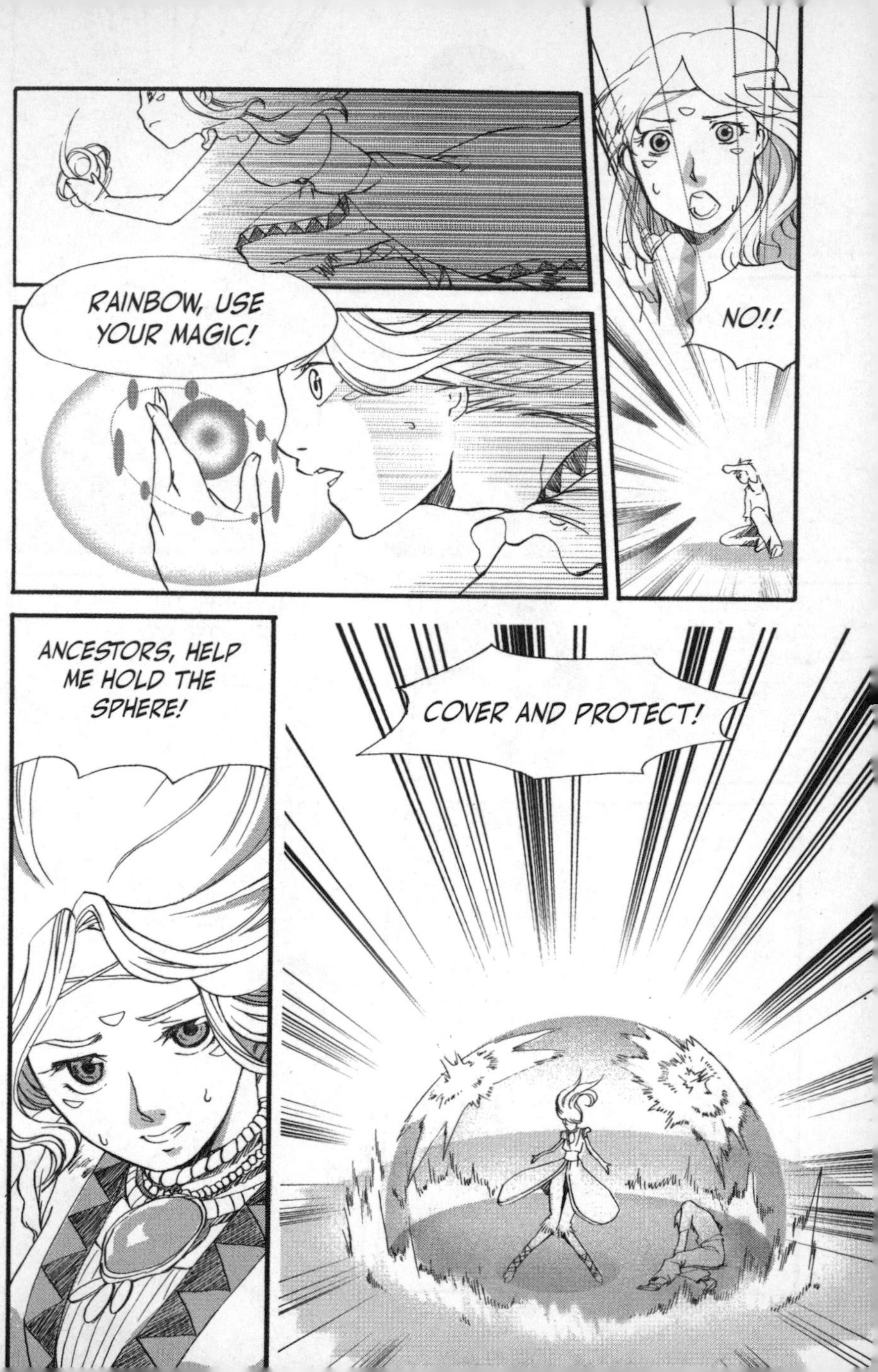
NO!!
RAINBOW, USE YOUR MAGIC!
ANCESTORS, HELP ME HOLD THE SPHERE!
COVER AND PROTECT!

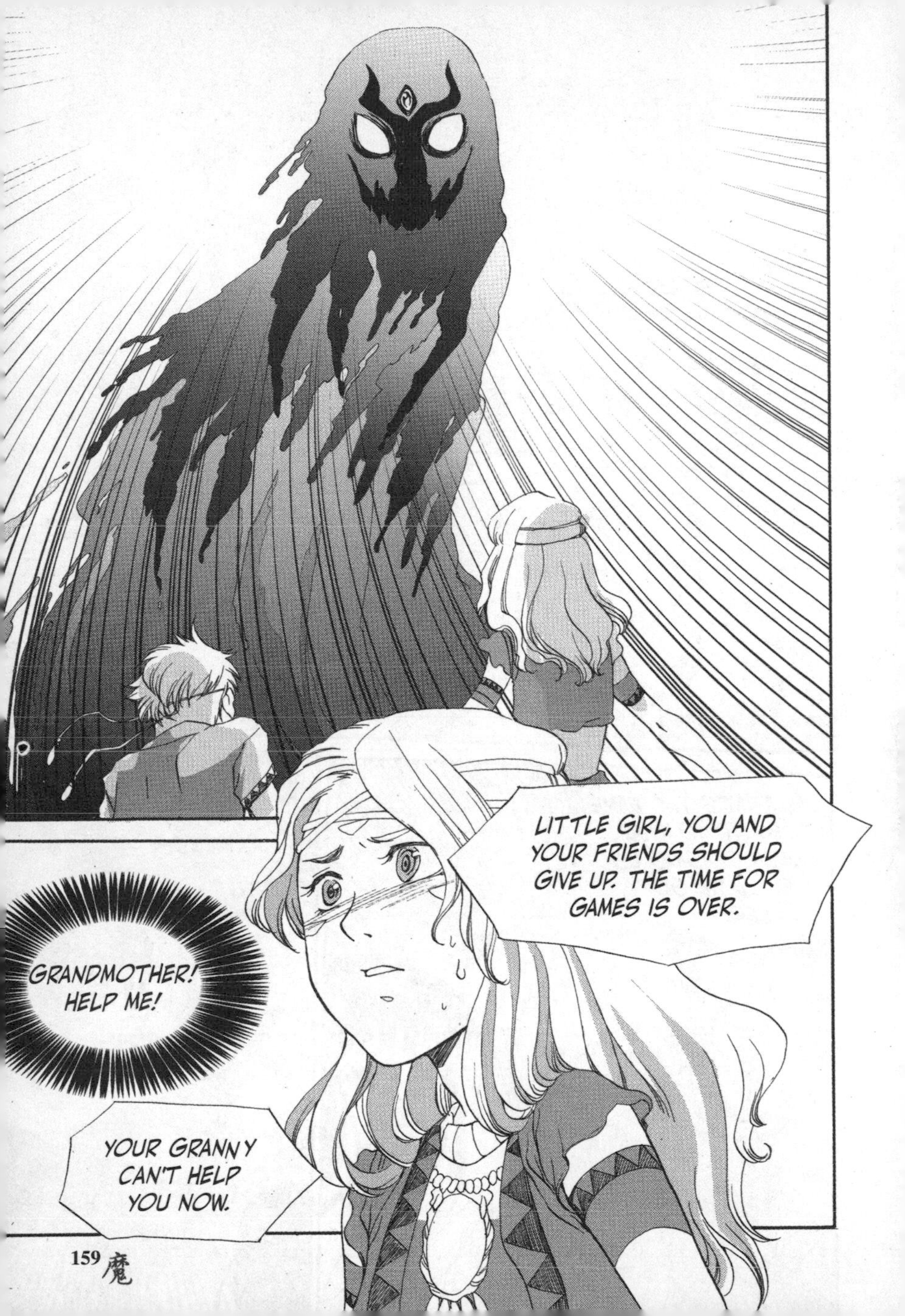
LITTLE GIRL, YOU AND YOUR FRIENDS SHOULD GIVE UP. THE TIME FOR GAMES IS OVER.
GRANDMOTHER! HELP ME!
YOUR GRANNY CAN'T HELP YOU NOW.

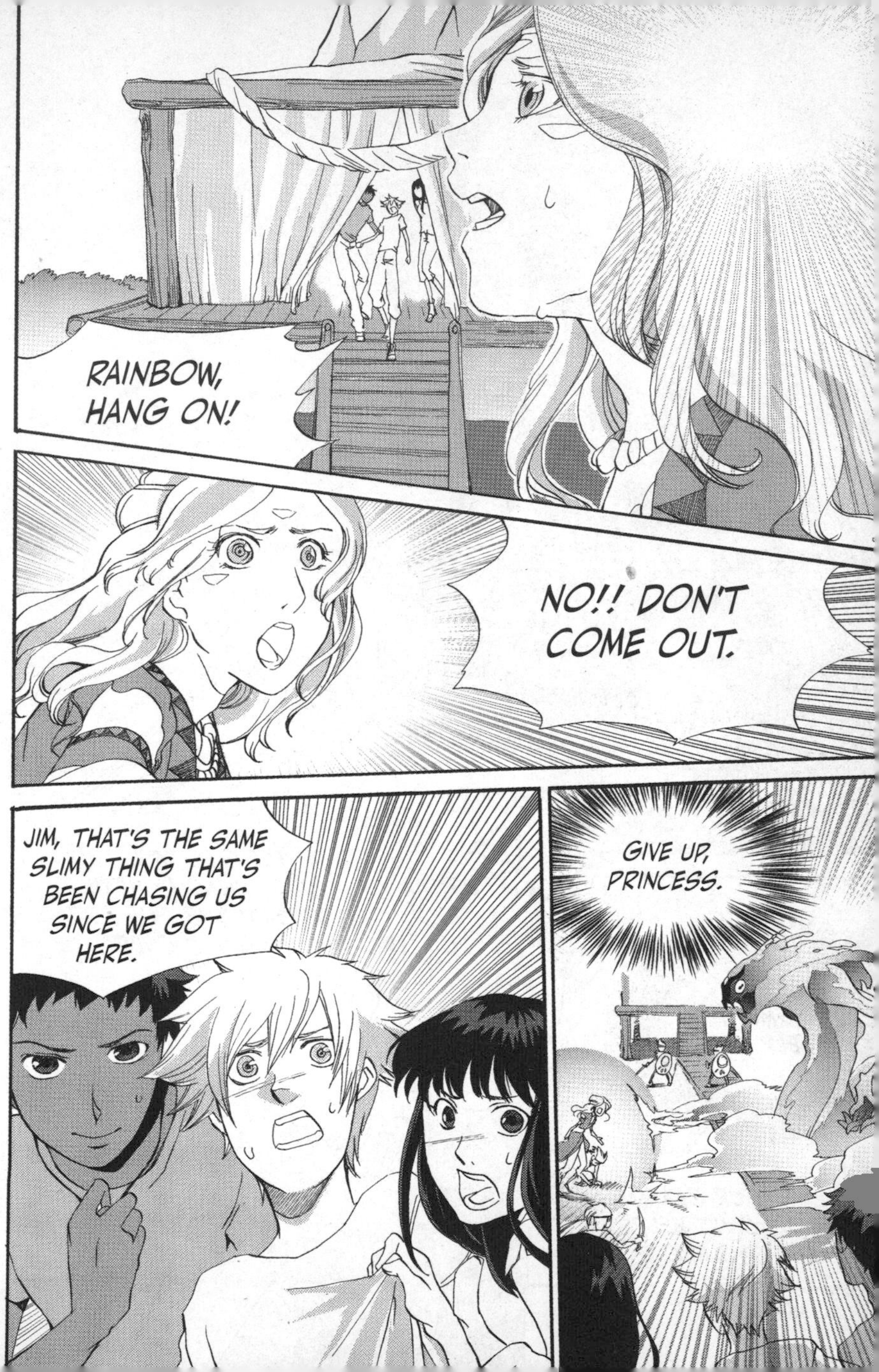
RAINBOW, HANG ON!
NO!! DON'T COME OUT.
JIM, THAT'S THE SAME SLIMY THING THAT'S BEEN CHASING US SINCE WE GOT HERE.
GIVE UP, PRINCESS.

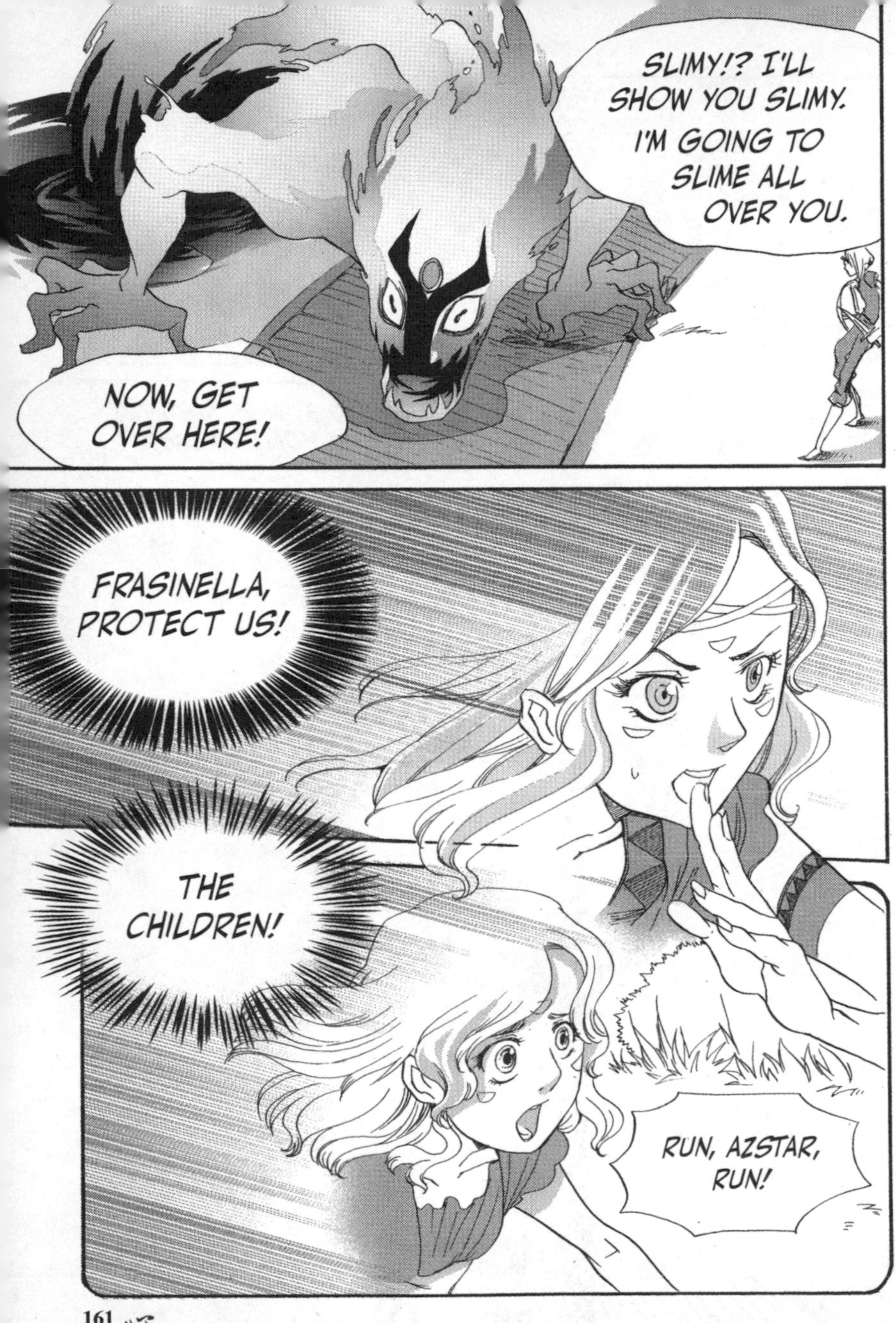
SLIMY!? I'LL SHOW YOU SLIMY. I'M GOING TO SLIME ALL OVER YOU.
NOW, GET OVER HERE!
FRASINELLA, PROTECT US!
THE CHILDREN!
RUN, AZSTAR, RUN!

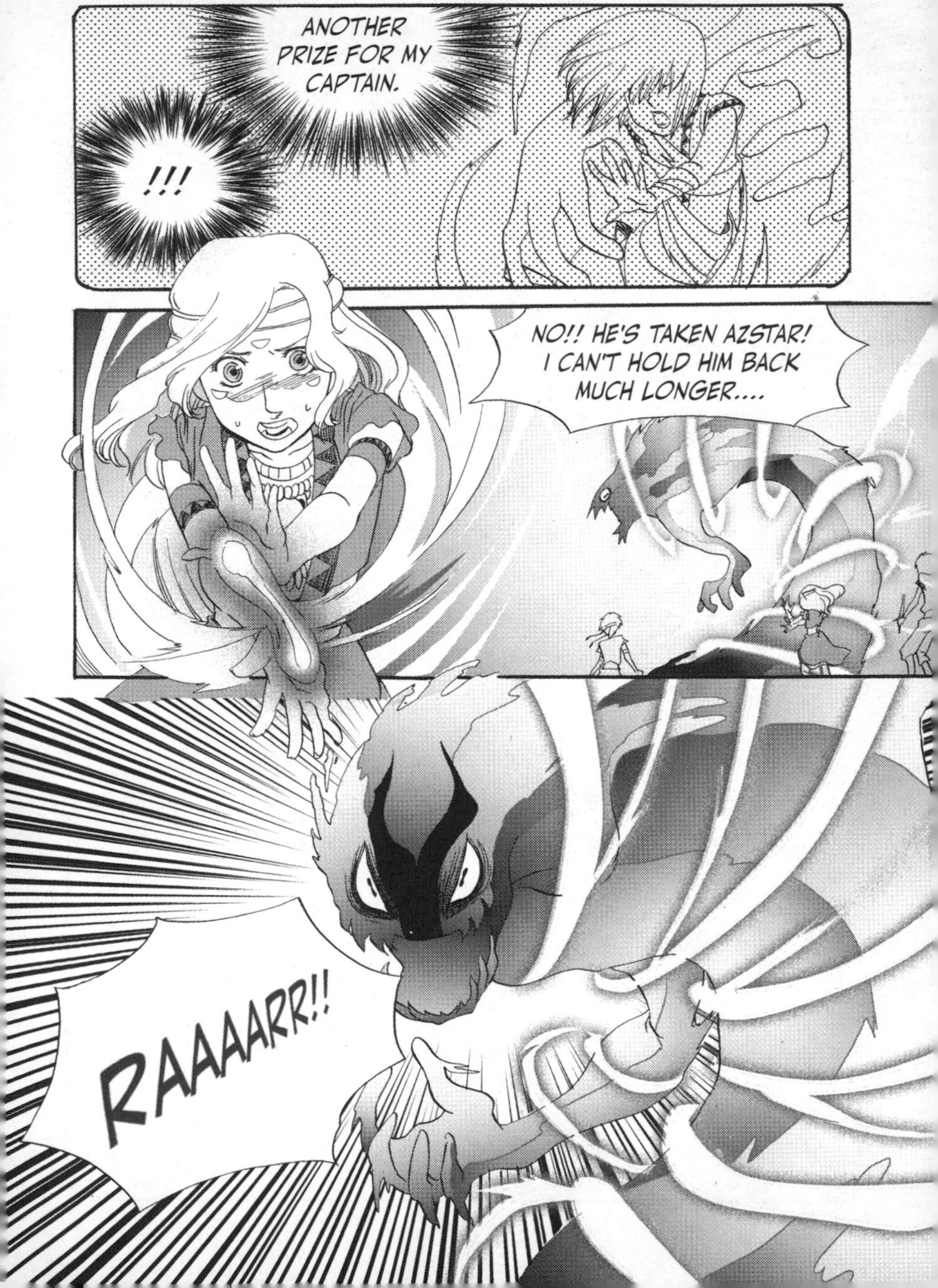
ANOTHER PRIZE FOR MY CAPTAIN.
!!!
NO!! HE'S TAKEN AZSTAR! I CAN'T HOLD HIM BACK MUCH LONGER....
RAAAARR!!

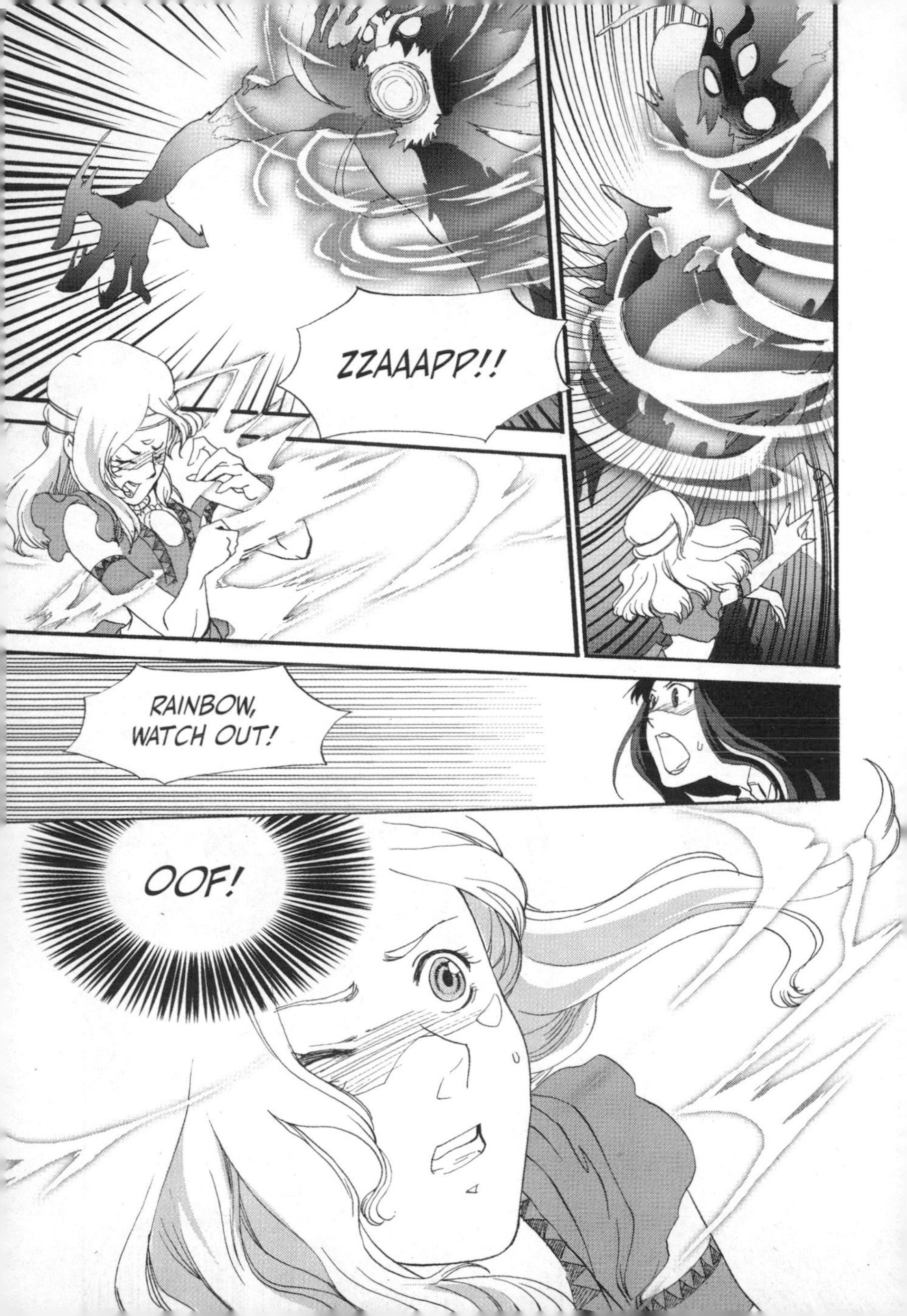
ZZAAAPP!!
RAINBOW, WATCH OUT!
OOF!

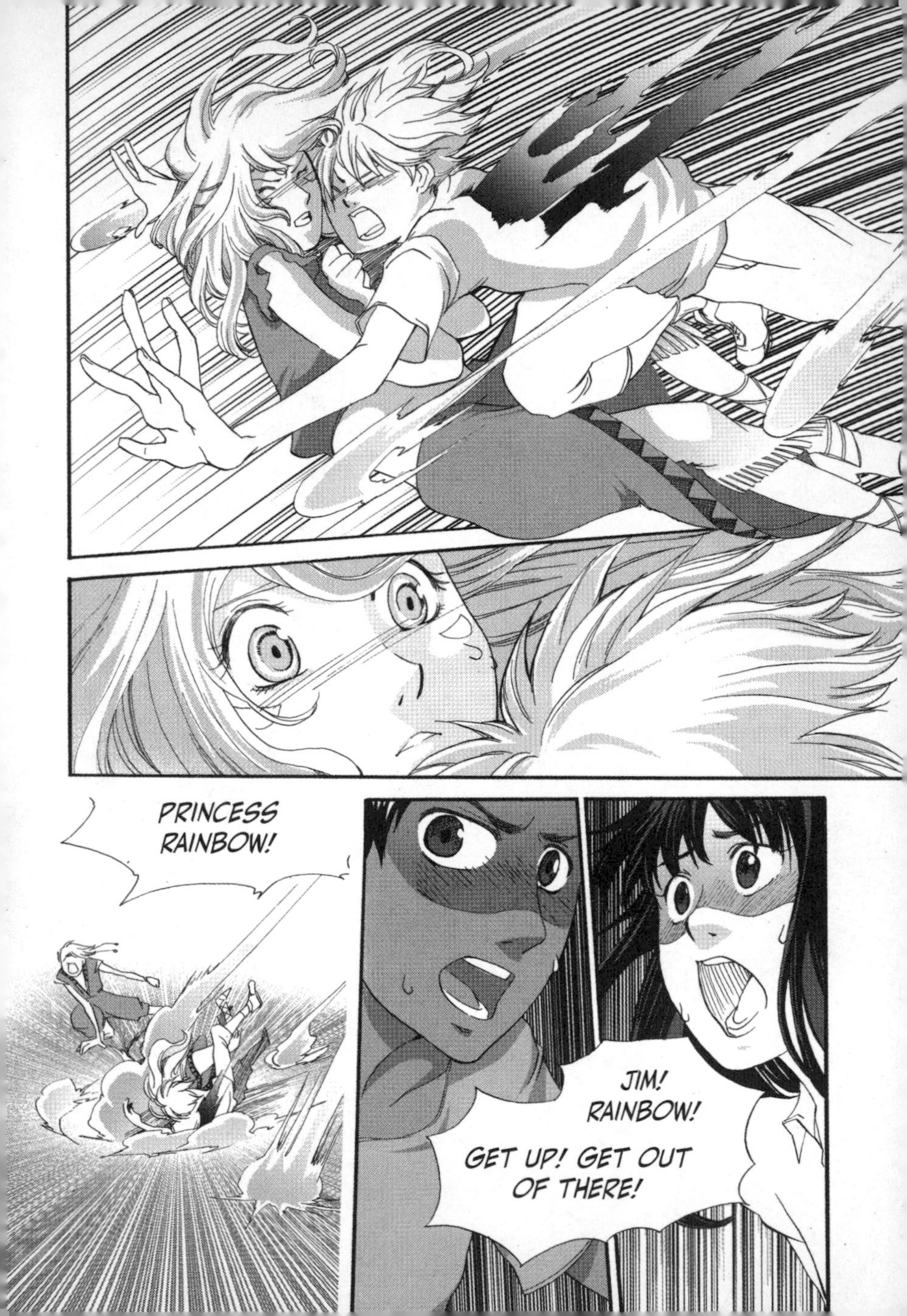
PRINCESS RAINBOW!
JIM! RAINBOW!
GET UP! GET OUT OF THERE!

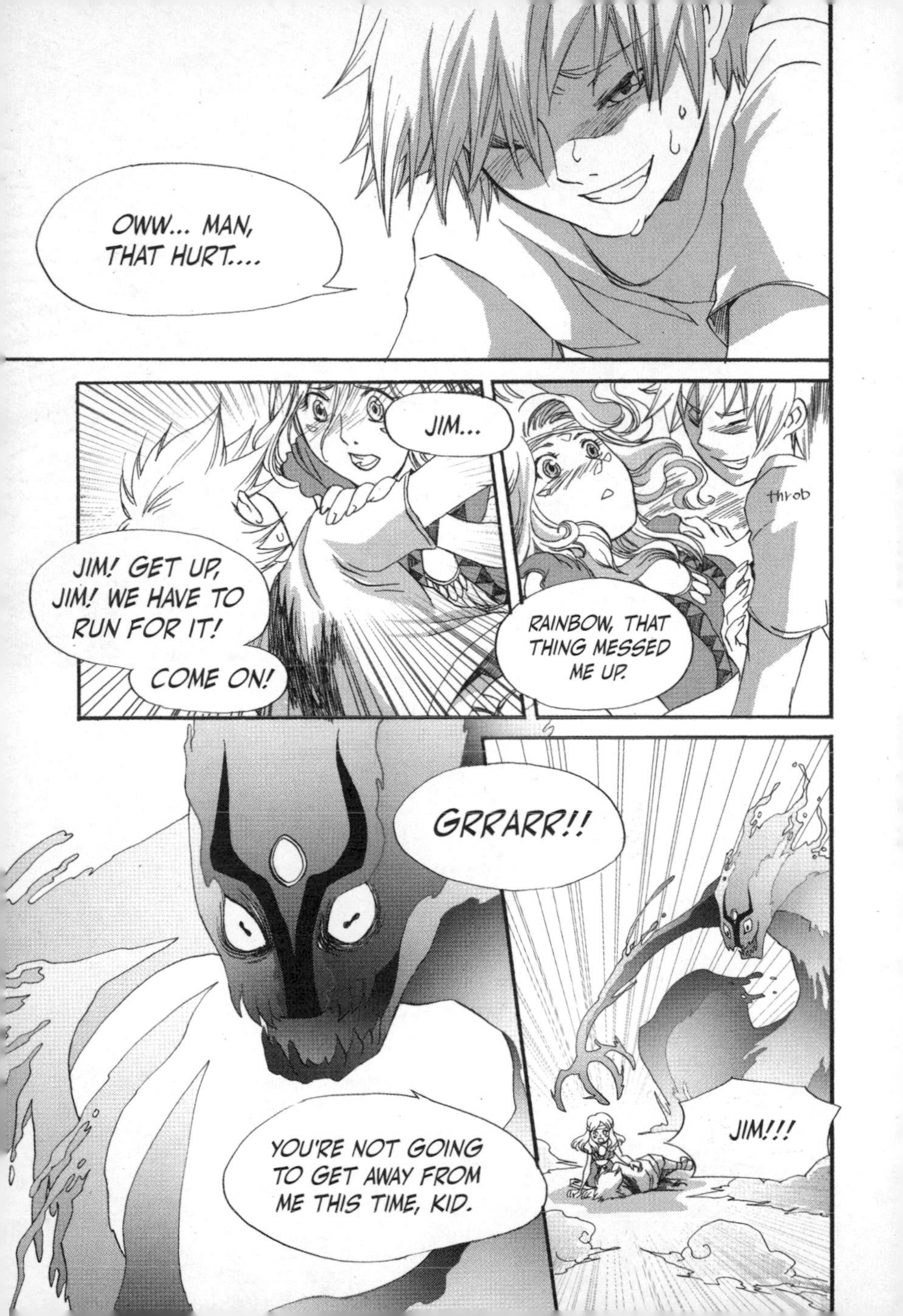
OWW... MAN, THAT HURT....
JIM...
JIM! GET UP, JIM! WE HAVE TO RUN FOR IT!
COME ON!
throb
RAINBOW, THAT THING MESSED ME UP.
GRRARR!!
YOU'RE NOT GOING TO GET AWAY FROM ME THIS TIME, KID.
JIM!!!

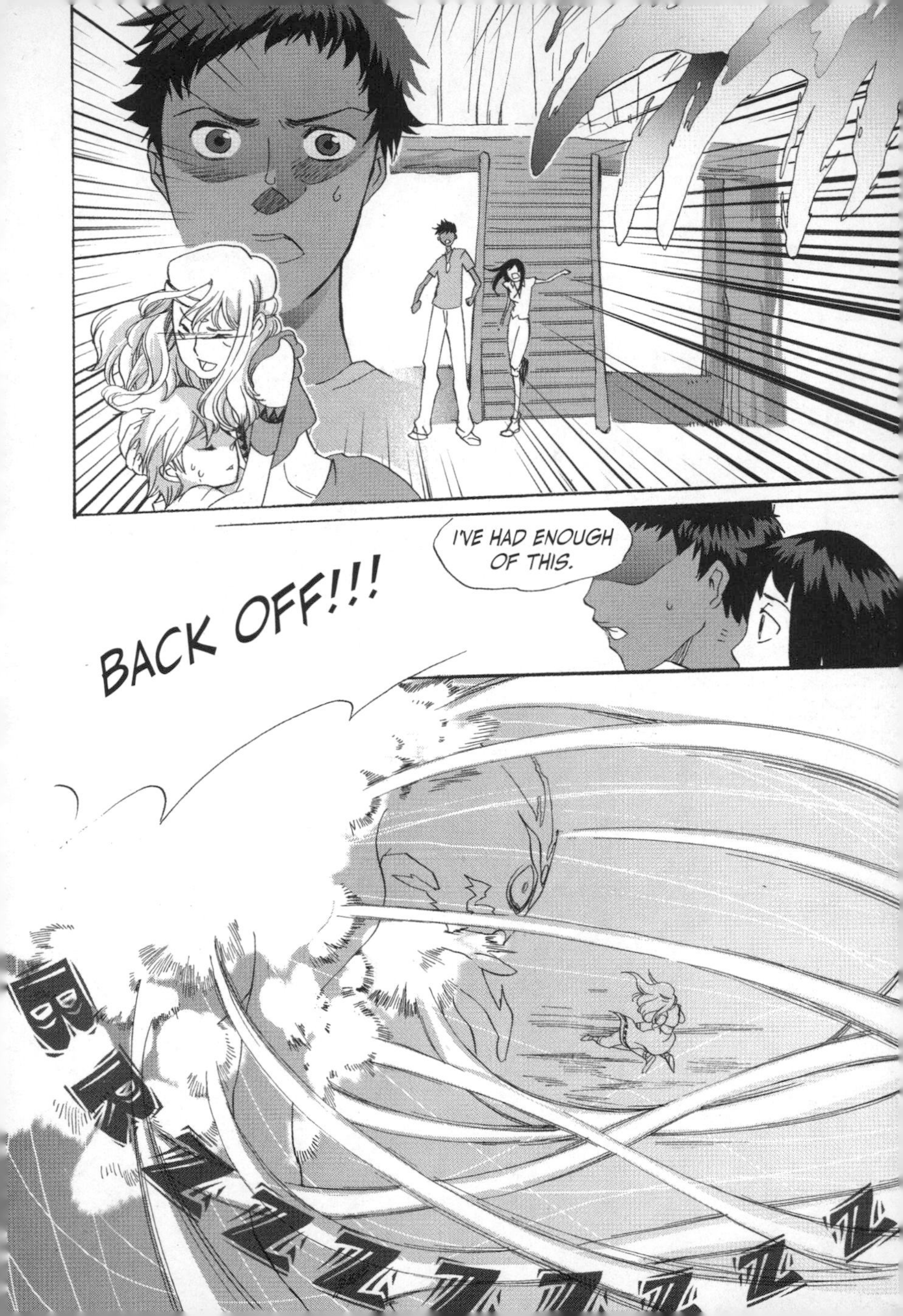
I'VE HAD ENOUGH OF THIS.
BACK OFF!!!

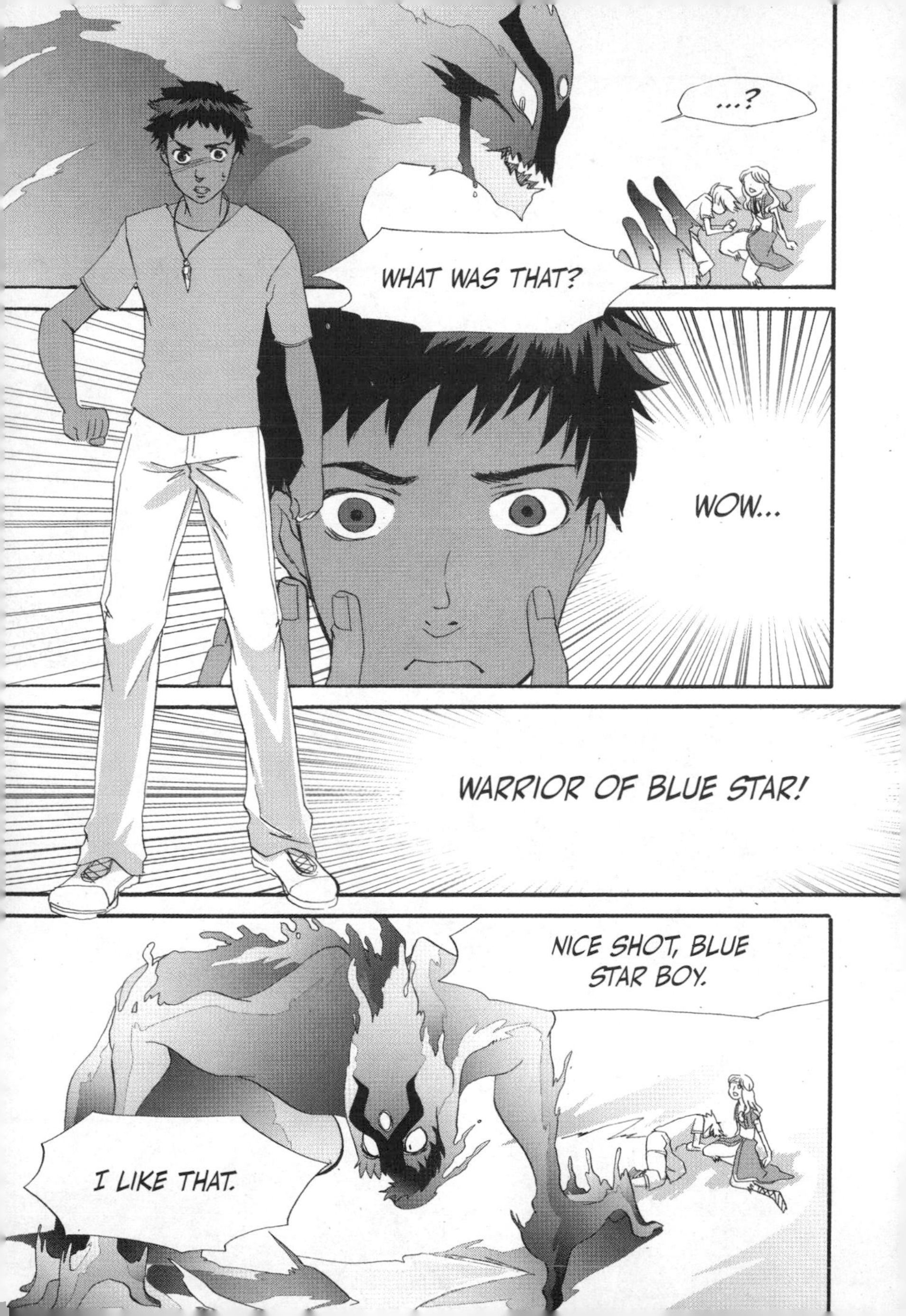
...?
WHAT WAS THAT?
WOW...
WARRIOR OF BLUE STAR!
NICE SHOT, BLUE STAR BOY.
I LIKE THAT.

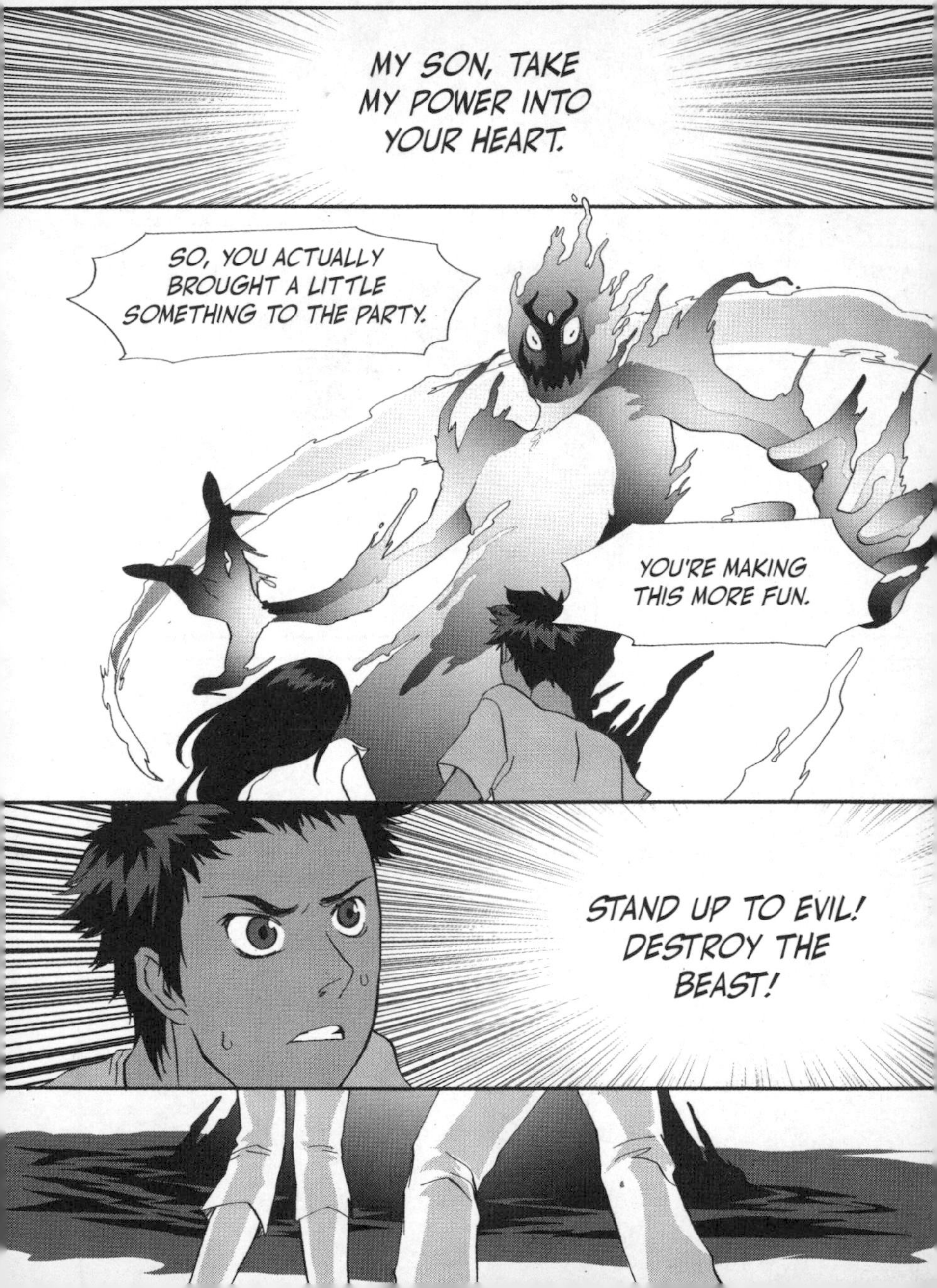
MY SON, TAKE MY POWER INTO YOUR HEART.
SO, YOU ACTUALLY BROUGHT A LITTLE SOMETHING TO THE PARTY.
YOU'RE MAKING THIS MORE FUN.
STAND UP TO EVIL! DESTROY THE BEAST!

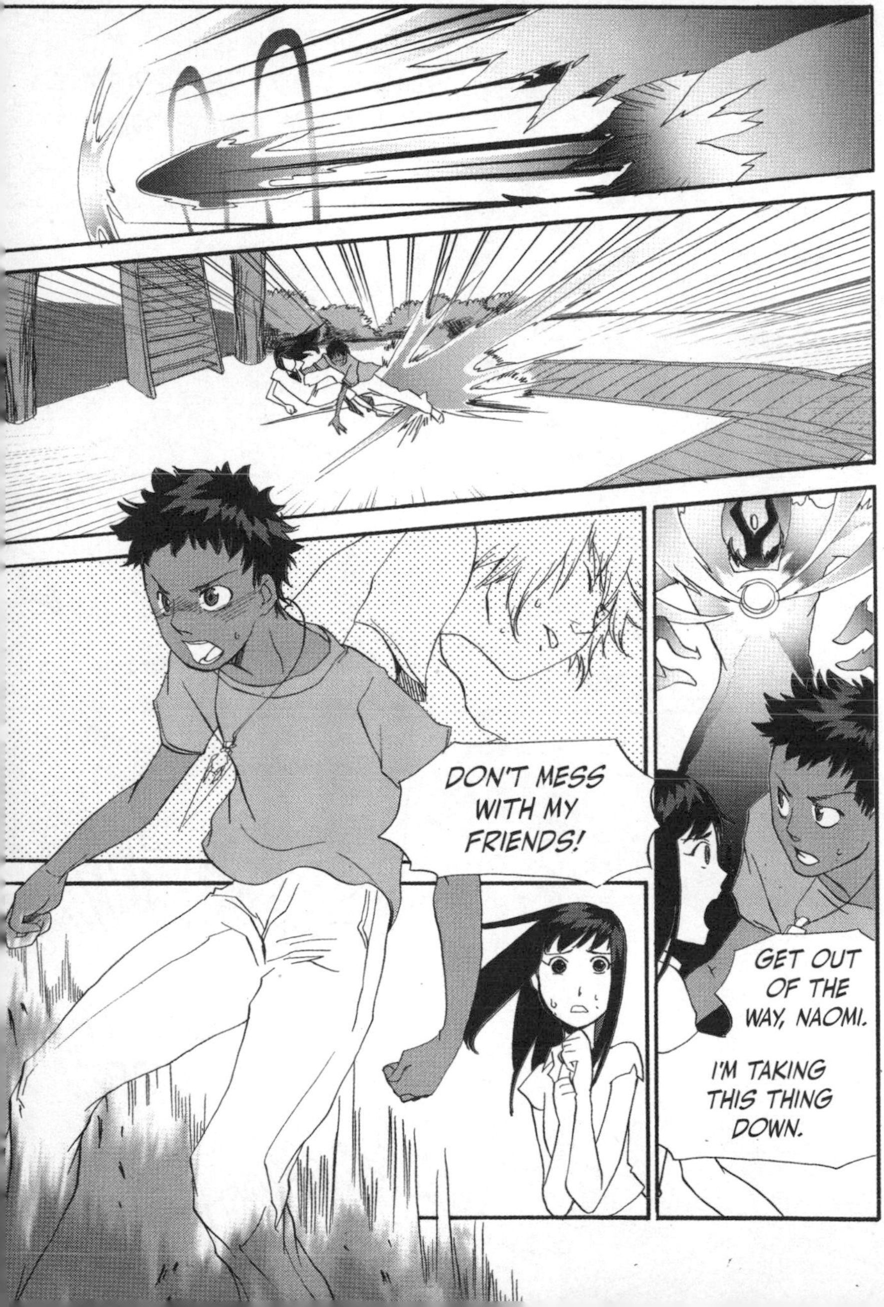
DON'T MESS WITH MY FRIENDS!
GET OUT OF THE WAY, NAOMI.
I'M TAKING THIS THING DOWN.

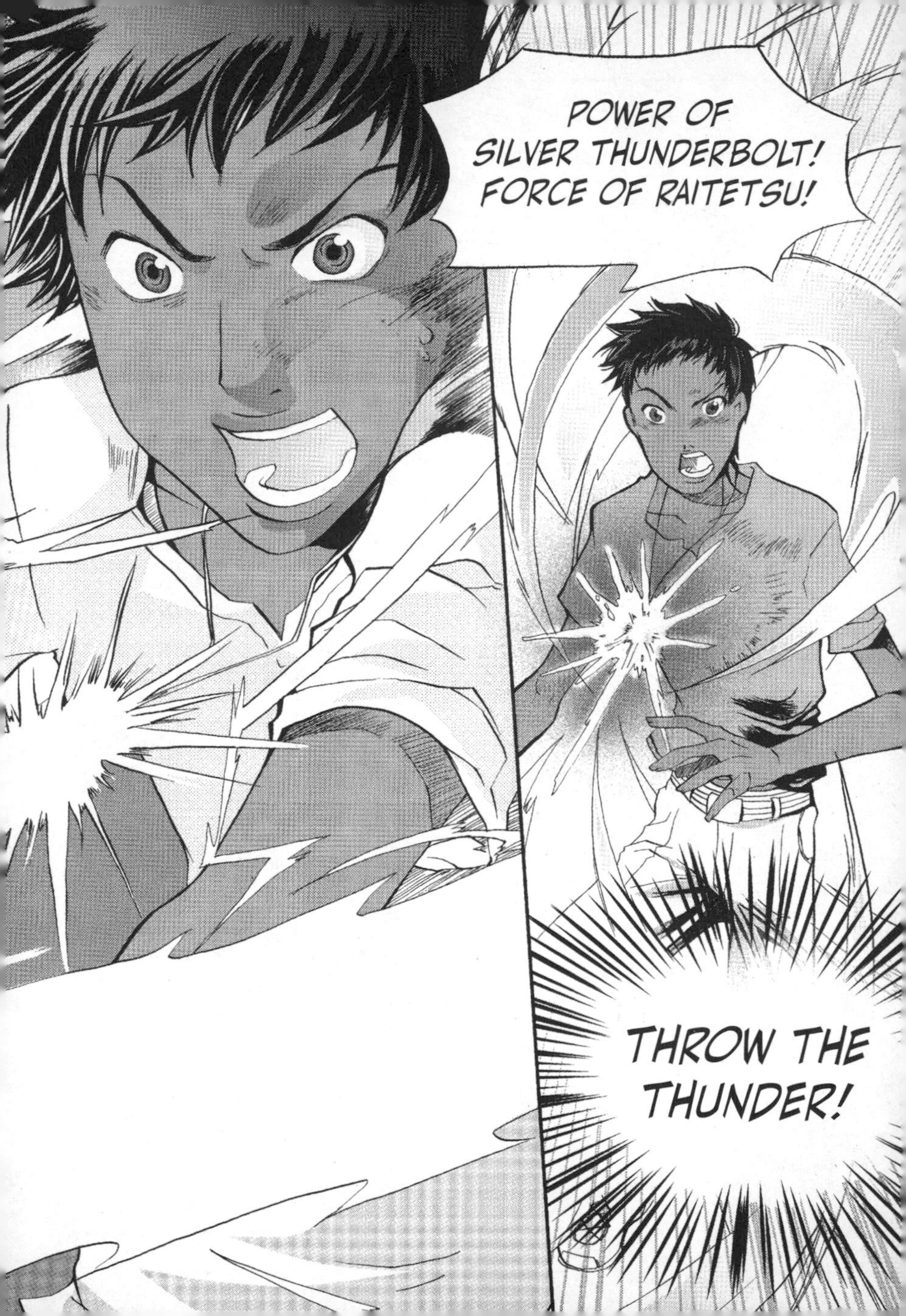
POWER OF SILVER THUNDERBOLT! FORCE OF RAITETSU!
THROW THE THUNDER!

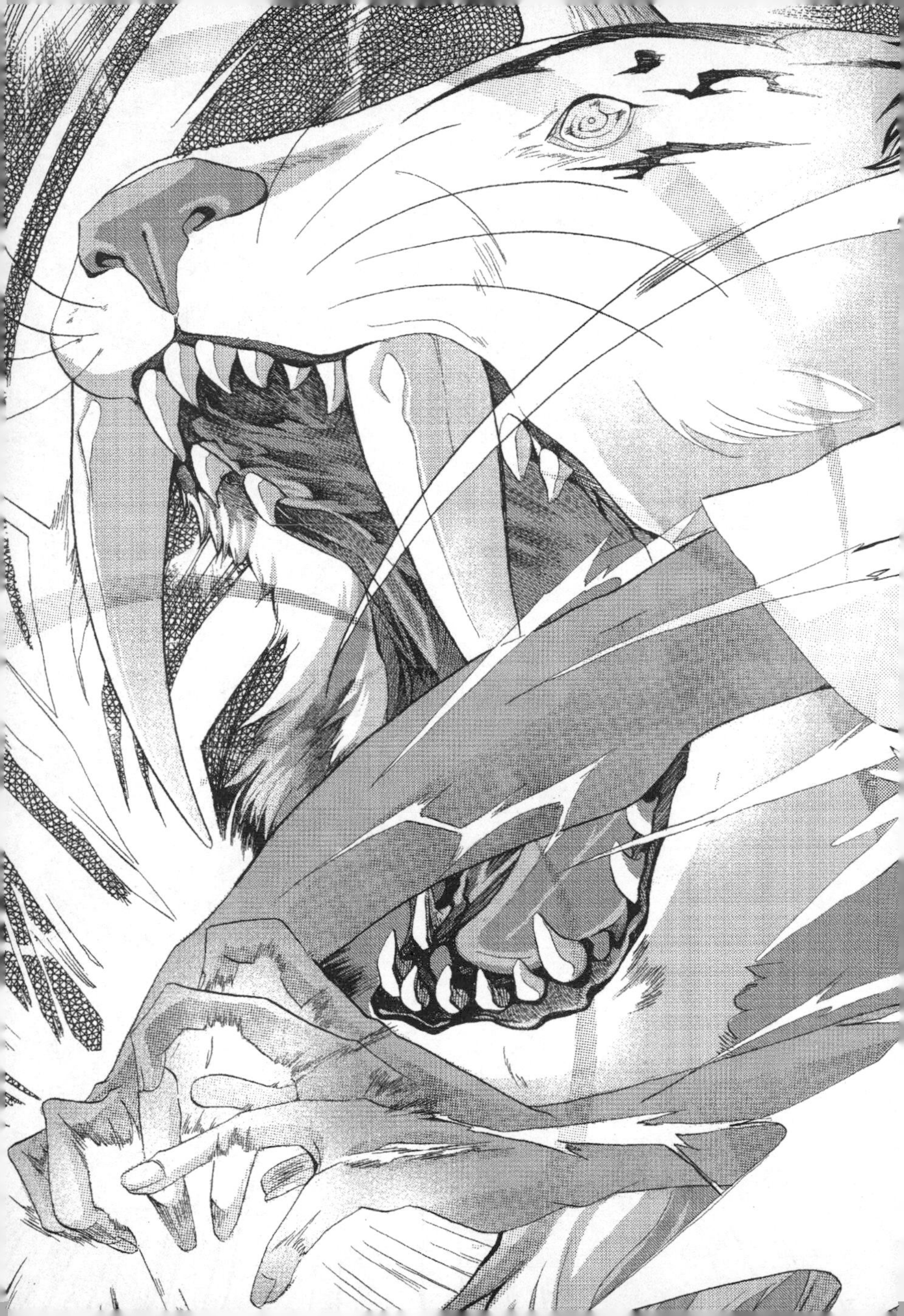

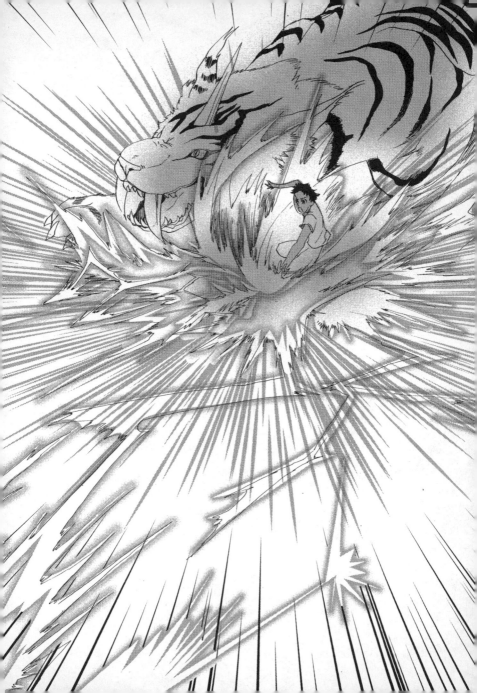

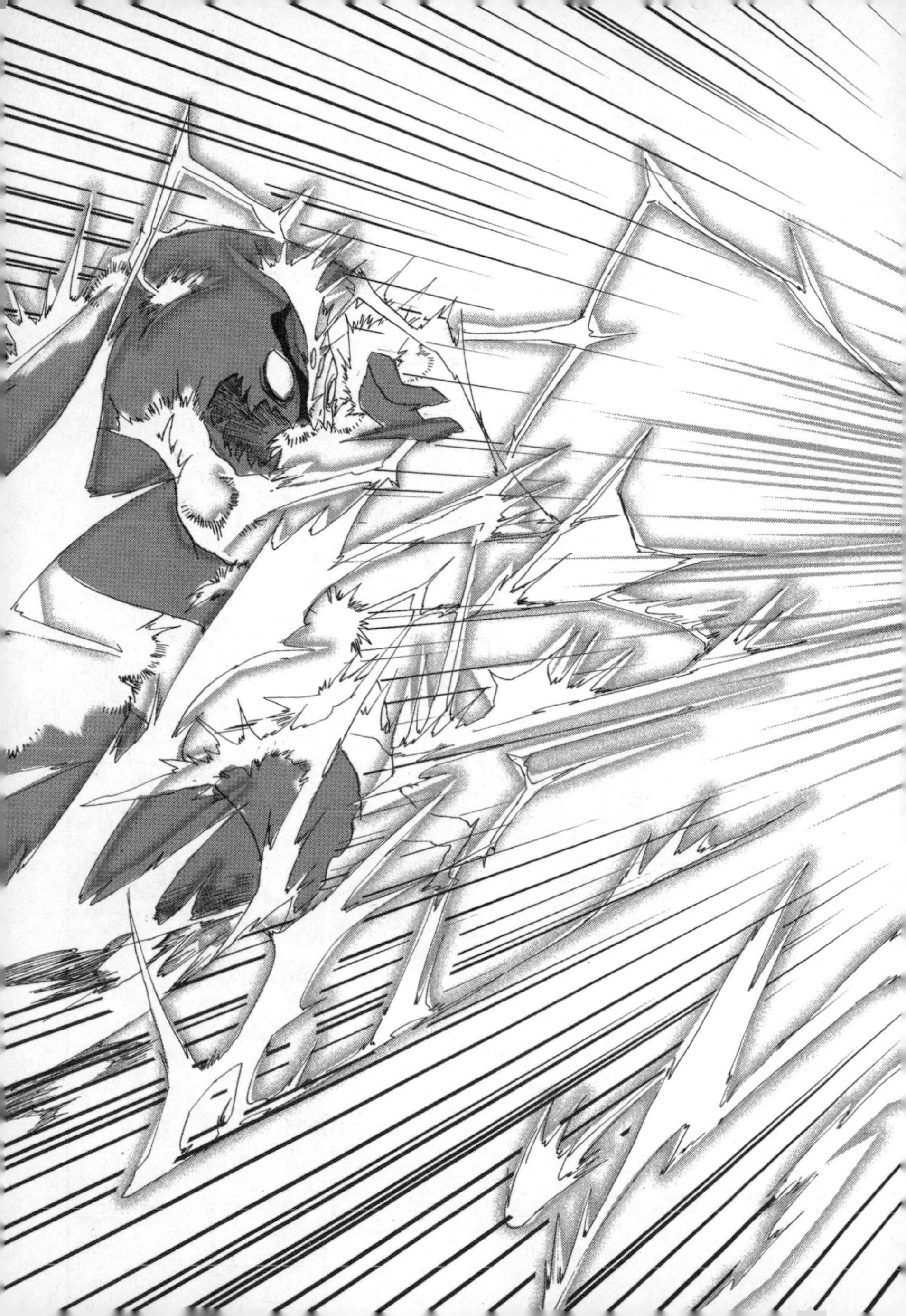

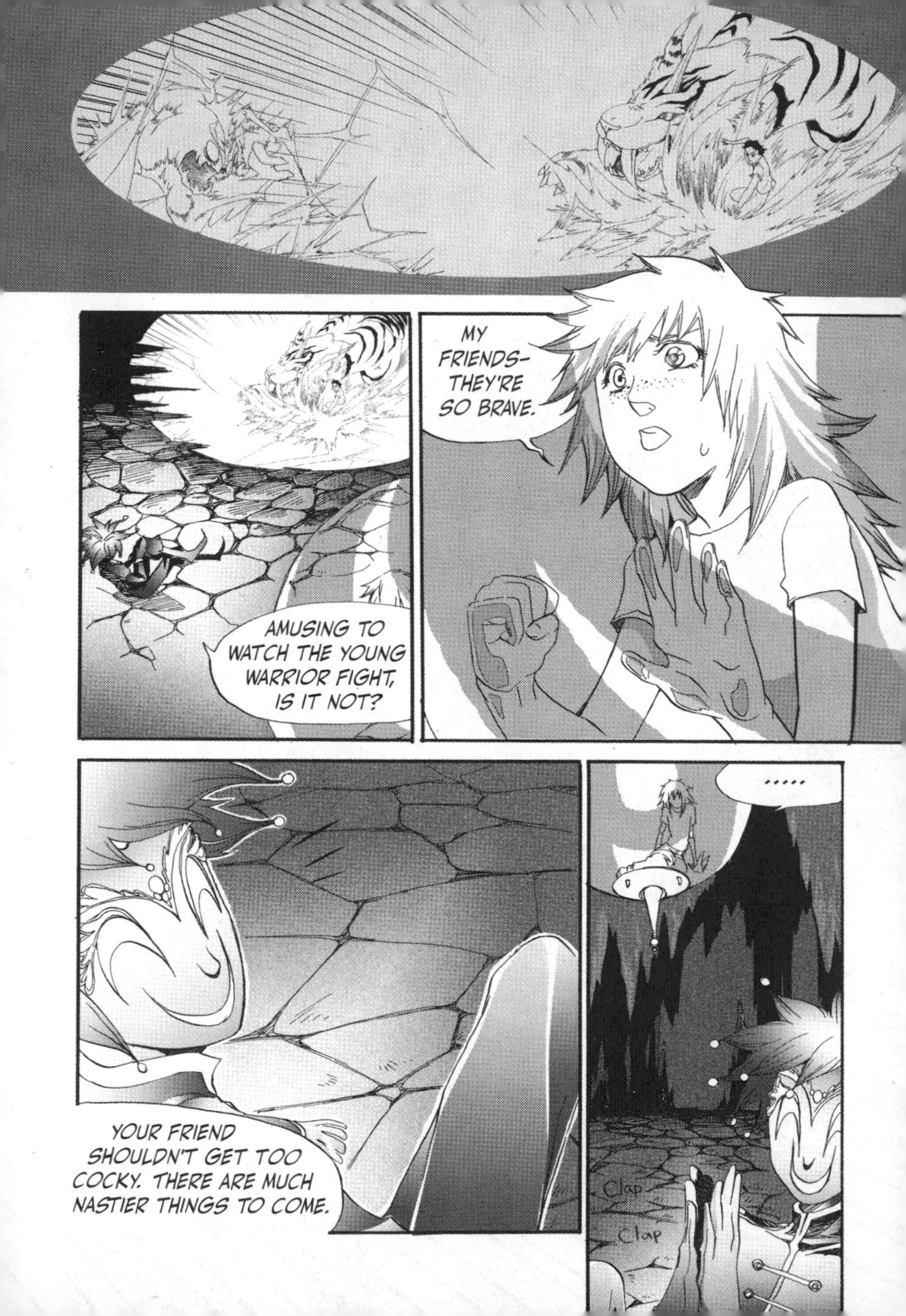
MY FRIENDS- THEY'RE SO BRAVE.
AMUSING TO WATCH THE YOUNG WARRIOR FIGHT, IS IT NOT?
.....
YOUR FRIEND SHOULDN'T GET TOO COCKY. THERE ARE MUCH NASTIER THINGS TO COME.
Clap
Clap

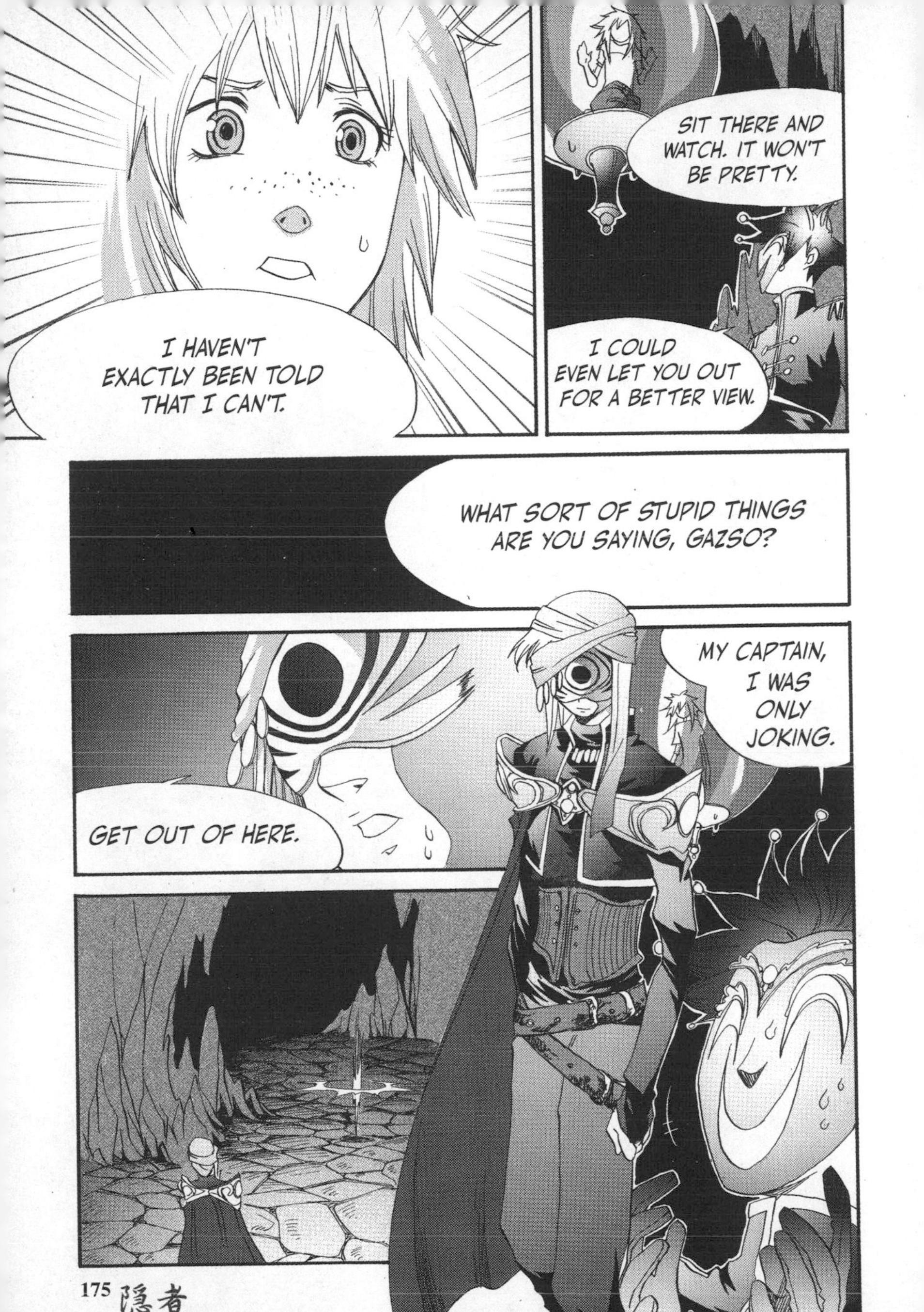
SIT THERE AND WATCH. IT WON'T BE PRETTY.
I COULD EVEN LET YOU OUT FOR A BETTER VIEW.
I HAVEN'T EXACTLY BEEN TOLD THAT I CAN'T.
WHAT SORT OF STUPID THINGS ARE YOU SAYING, GAZSO?
MY CAPTAIN, I WAS ONLY JOKING.
GET OUT OF HERE.

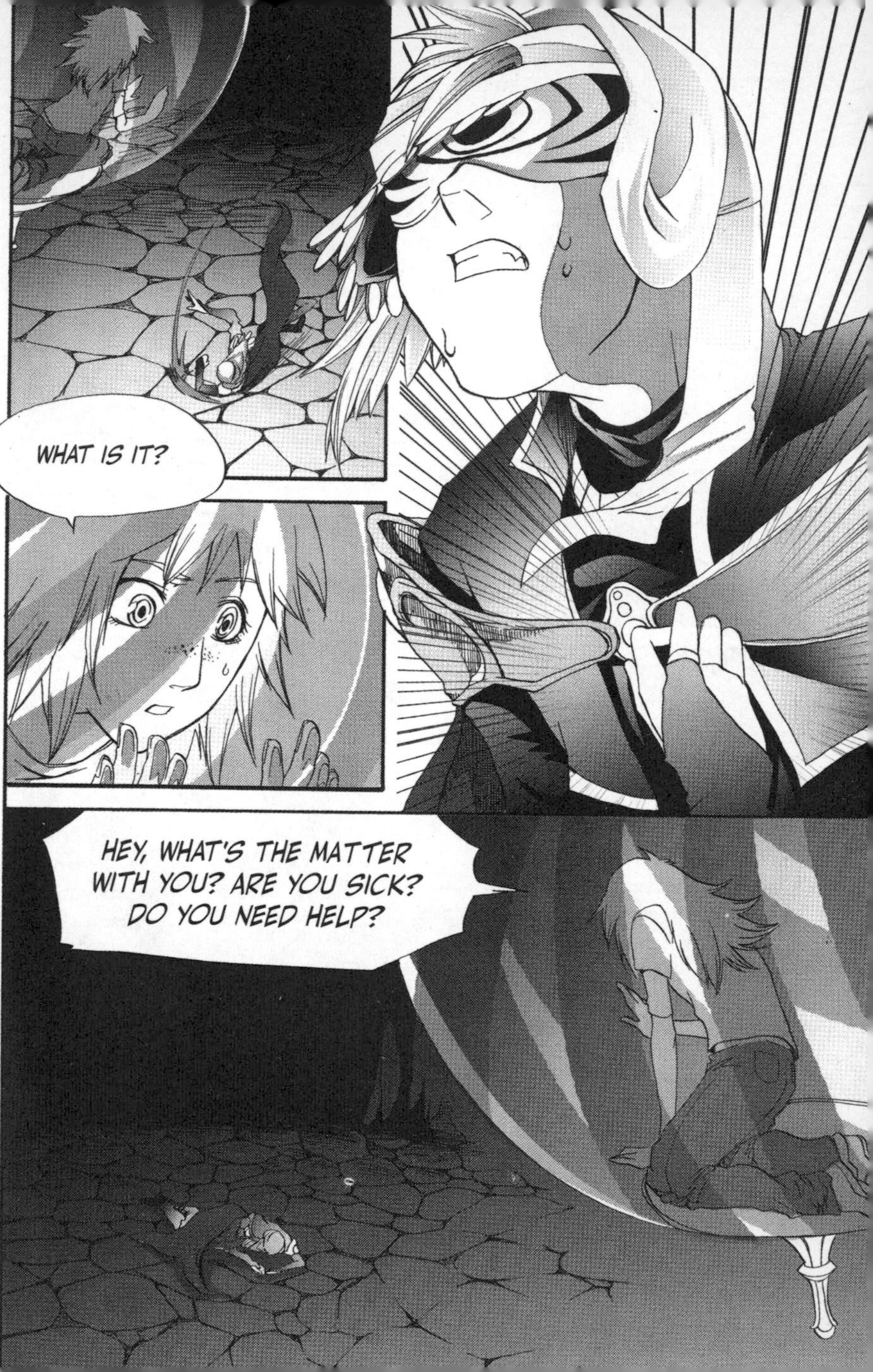
WHAT IS IT?
HEY, WHAT'S THE MATTER WITH YOU? ARE YOU SICK? DO YOU NEED HELP?

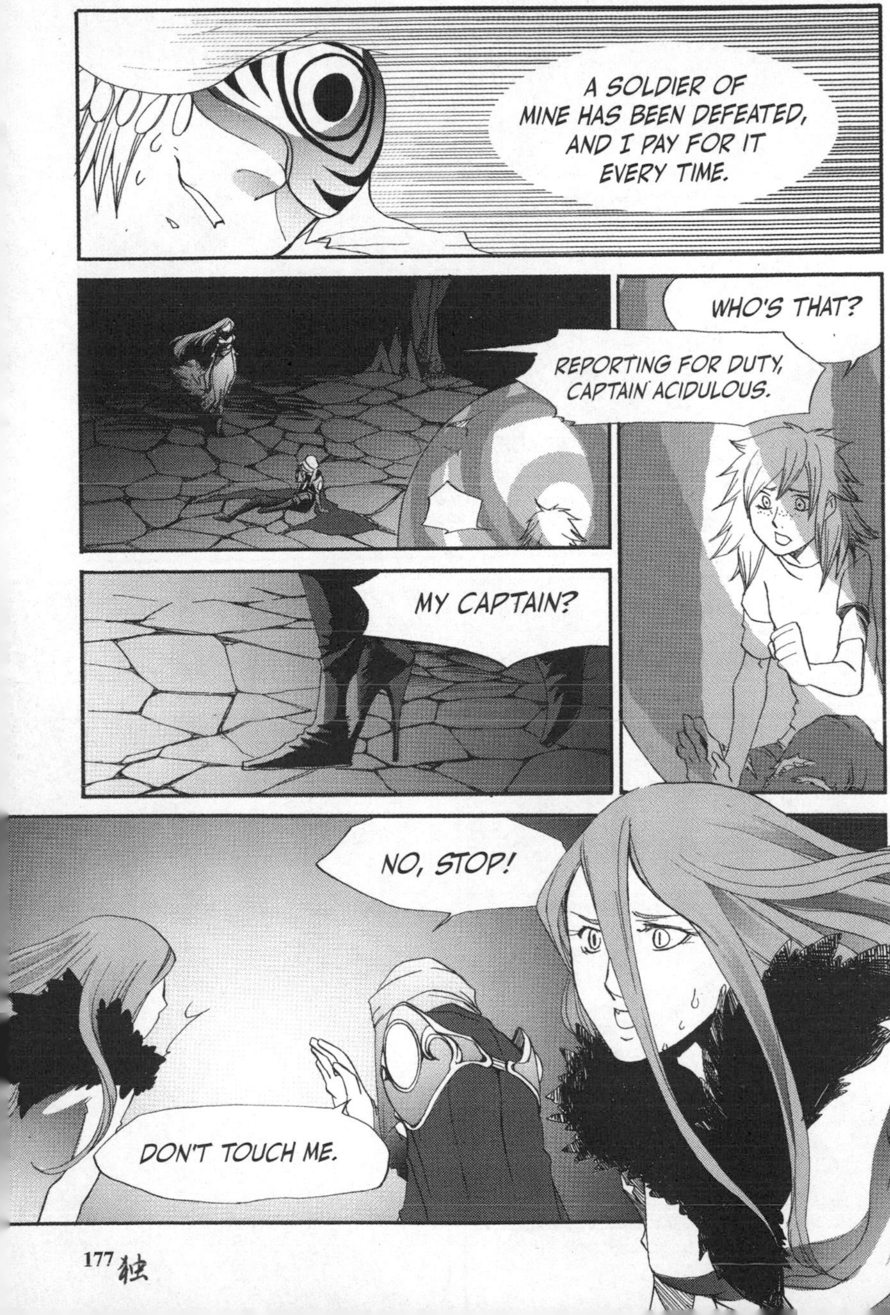
A SOLDIER OF MINE HAS BEEN DEFEATED, AND I PAY FOR IT EVERY TIME.
WHO'S THAT?
REPORTING FOR DUTY, CAPTAIN ACIDULOUS.
MY CAPTAIN?
NO, STOP!
DON'T TOUCH ME.

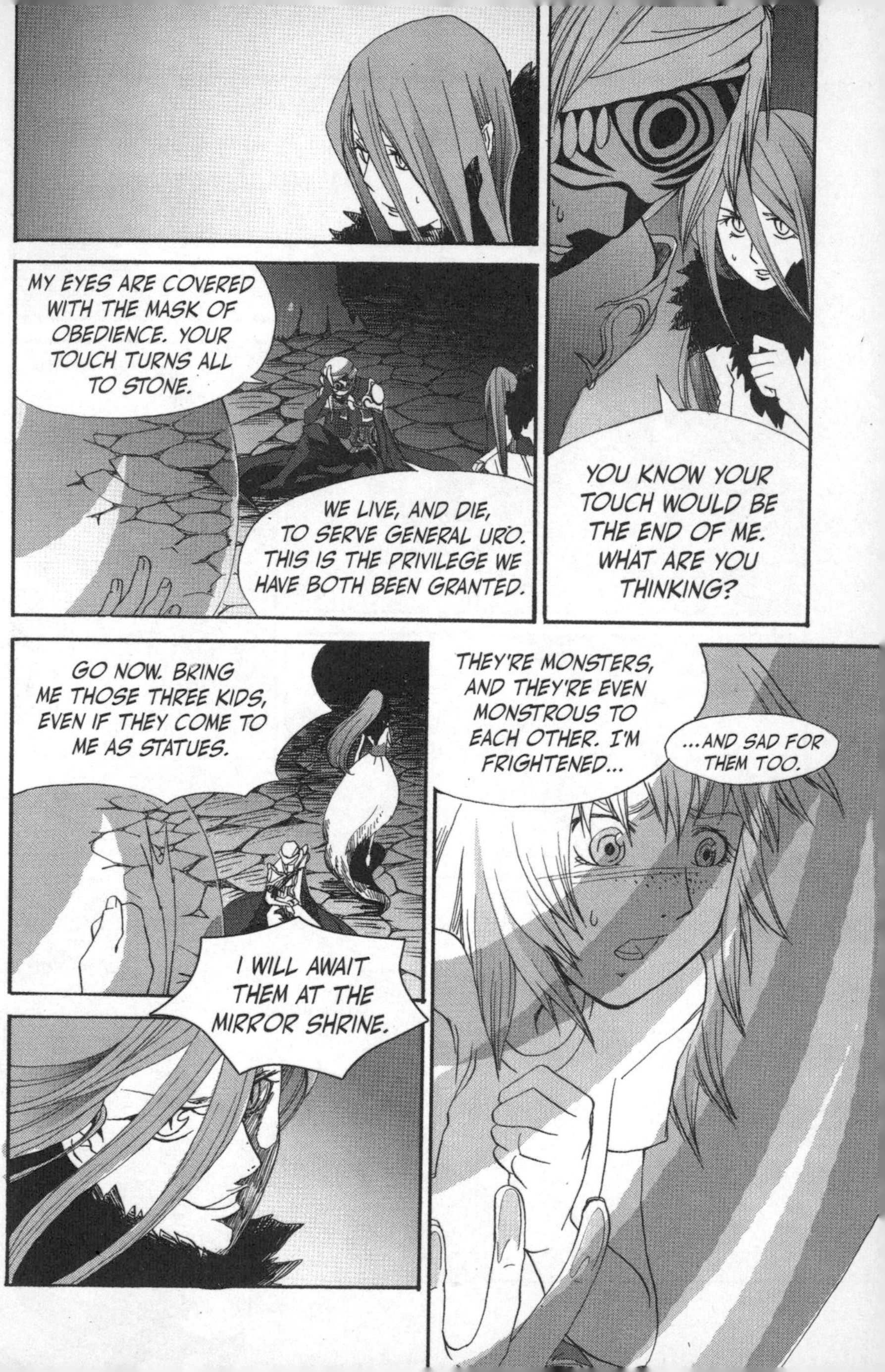
MY EYES ARE COVERED WITH THE MASK OF OBEDIENCE. YOUR TOUCH TURNS ALL TO STONE.
WE LIVE, AND DIE, TO SERVE GENERAL URO. THIS IS THE PRIVILEGE WE HAVE BOTH BEEN GRANTED.
YOU KNOW YOUR TOUCH WOULD BE THE END OF ME. WHAT ARE YOU THINKING?
GO NOW. BRING ME THOSE THREE KIDS, EVEN IF THEY COME TO ME AS STATUES.
I WILL AWAIT THEM AT THE MIRROR SHRINE.
THEY'RE MONSTERS, AND THEY'RE EVEN MONSTROUS TO EACH OTHER. I'M FRIGHTENED...
...AND SAD FOR THEM TOO.

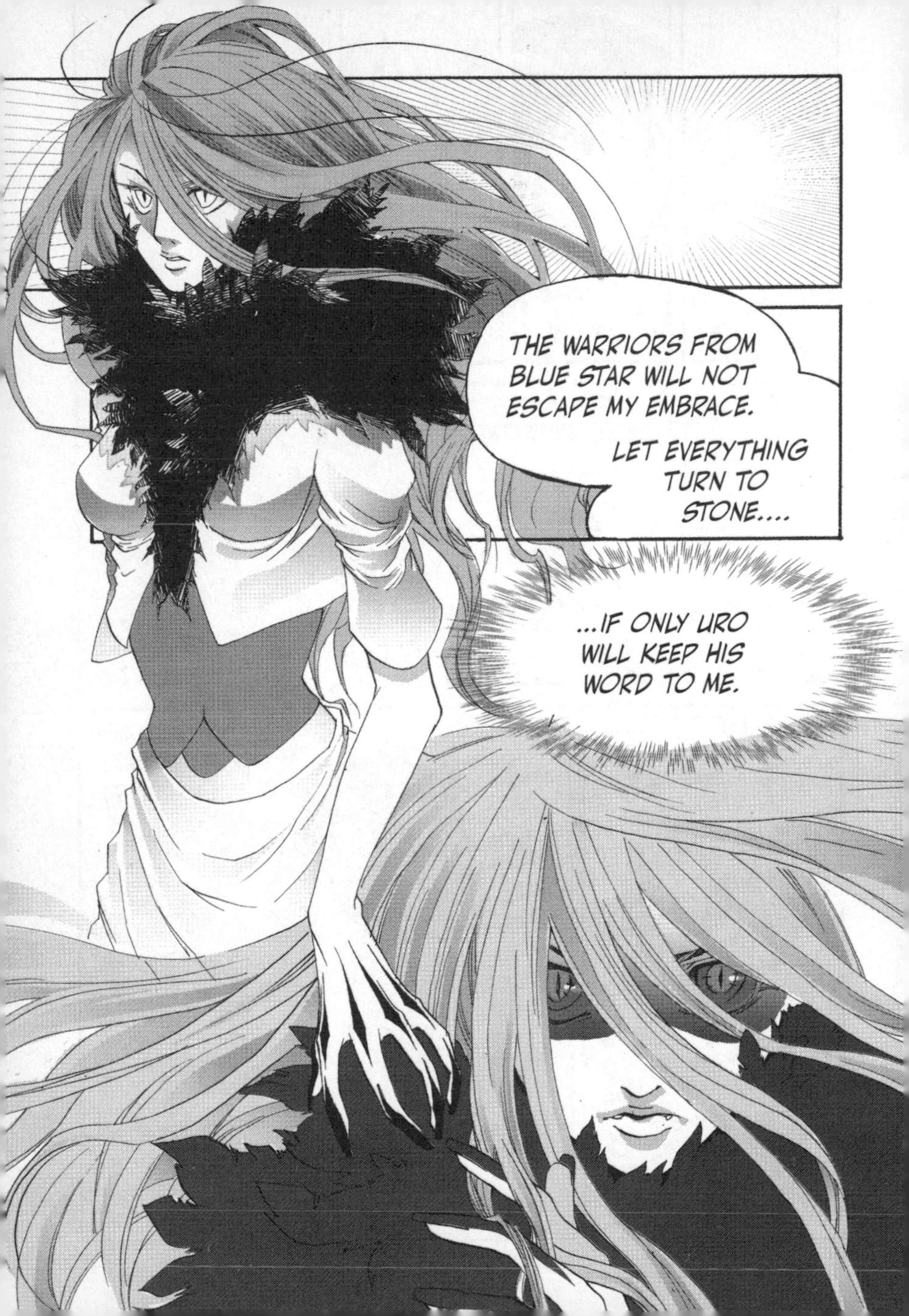
THE WARRIORS FROM BLUE STAR WILL NOT ESCAPE MY EMBRACE.
LET EVERYTHING TURN TO STONE....
...IF ONLY URO WILL KEEP HIS WORD TO ME.

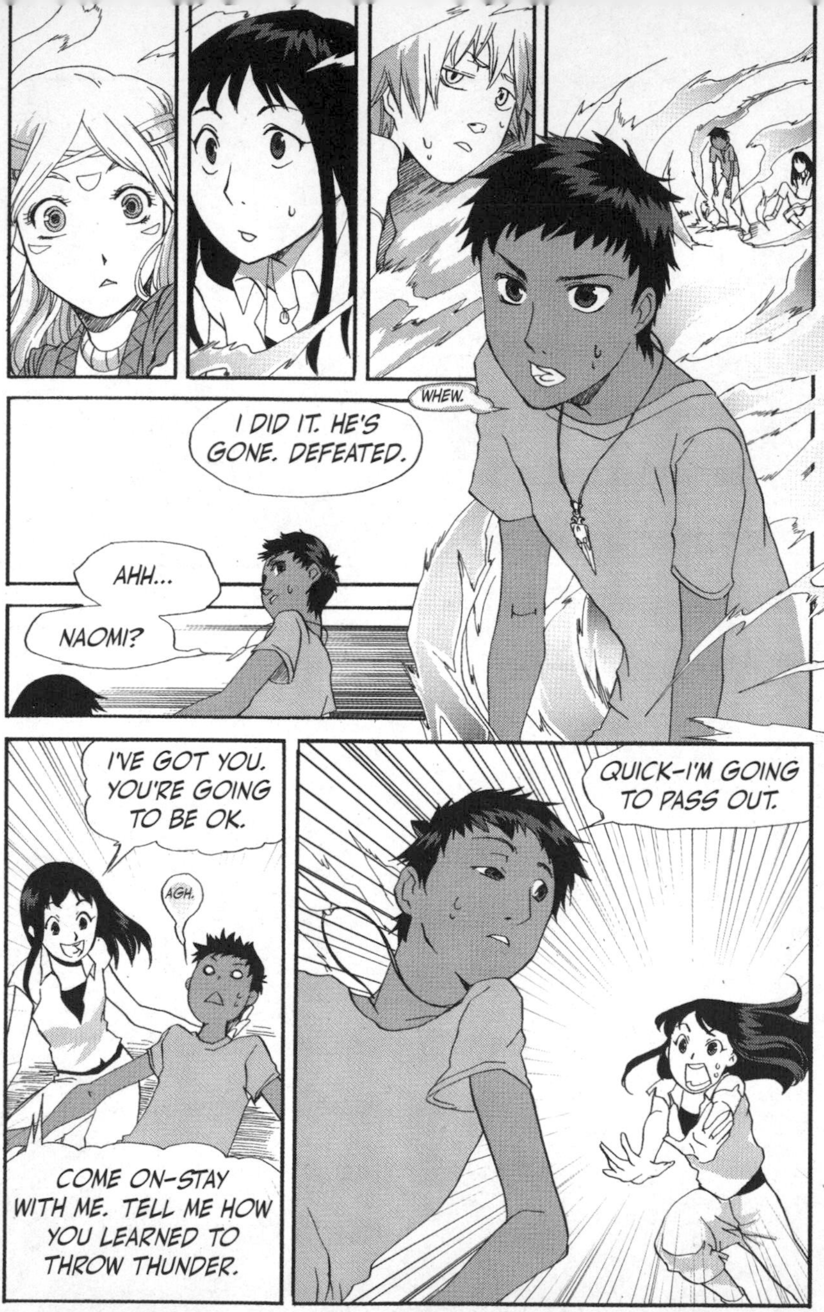
WHEW.
I DID IT. HE'S GONE. DEFEATED.
AHH...
NAOMI?
QUICK–I'M GOING TO PASS OUT.
I'VE GOT YOU. YOU'RE GOING TO BE OK.
AGH.
COME ON–STAY WITH ME. TELL ME HOW YOU LEARNED TO THROW THUNDER.

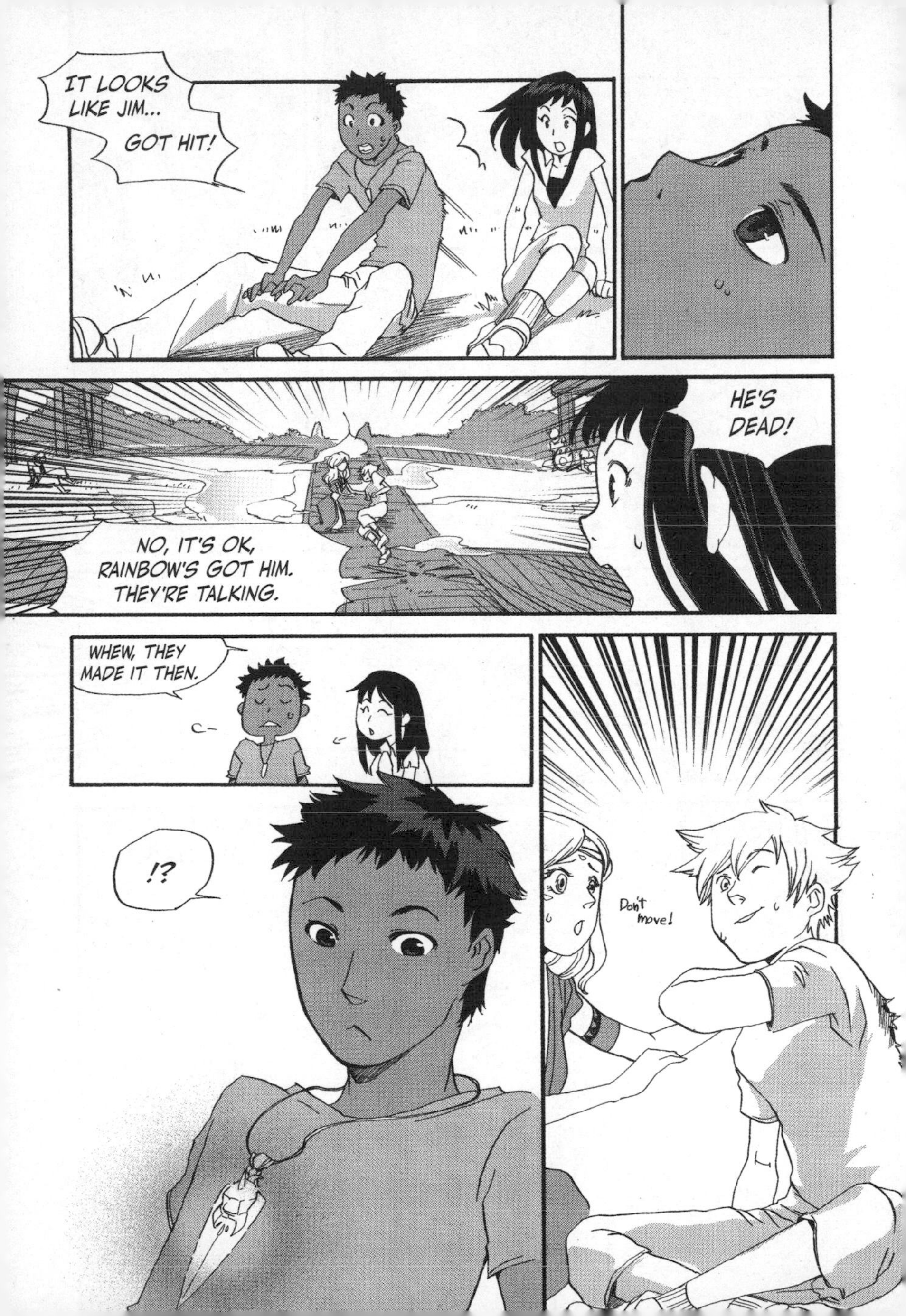
IT LOOKS LIKE JIM...
GOT HIT!
HE'S DEAD!
NO, IT'S OK, RAINBOW'S GOT HIM. THEY'RE TALKING.
WHEW, THEY MADE IT THEN.
!?
Don't move!

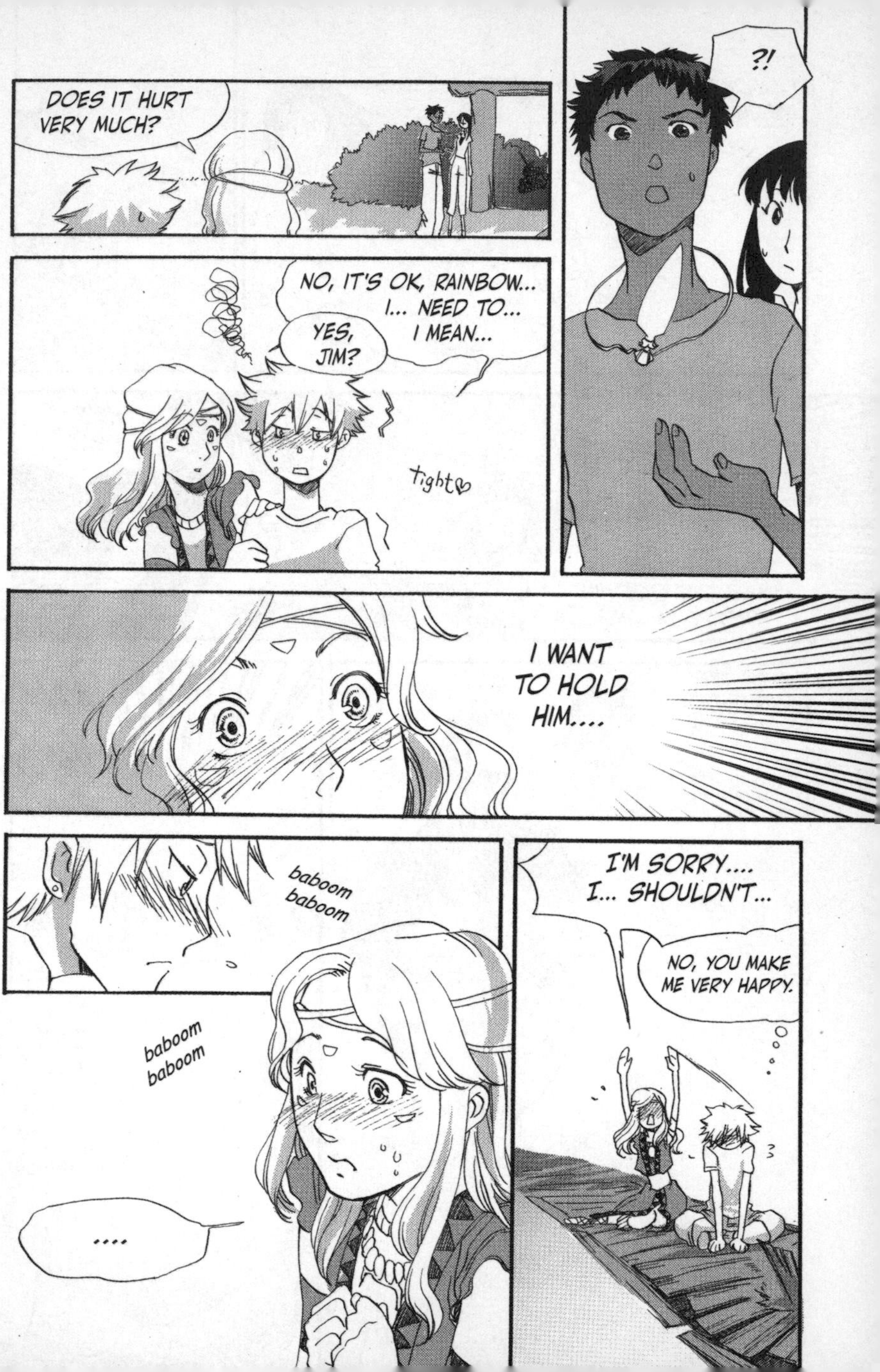

DOES IT HURT VERY MUCH?
?!
NO, IT'S OK, RAINBOW... I... NEED TO... I MEAN...
YES, JIM?
tight
I WANT TO HOLD HIM....
baboom baboom
baboom baboom
....
I'M SORRY.... I... SHOULDN'T...
NO, YOU MAKE ME VERY HAPPY.

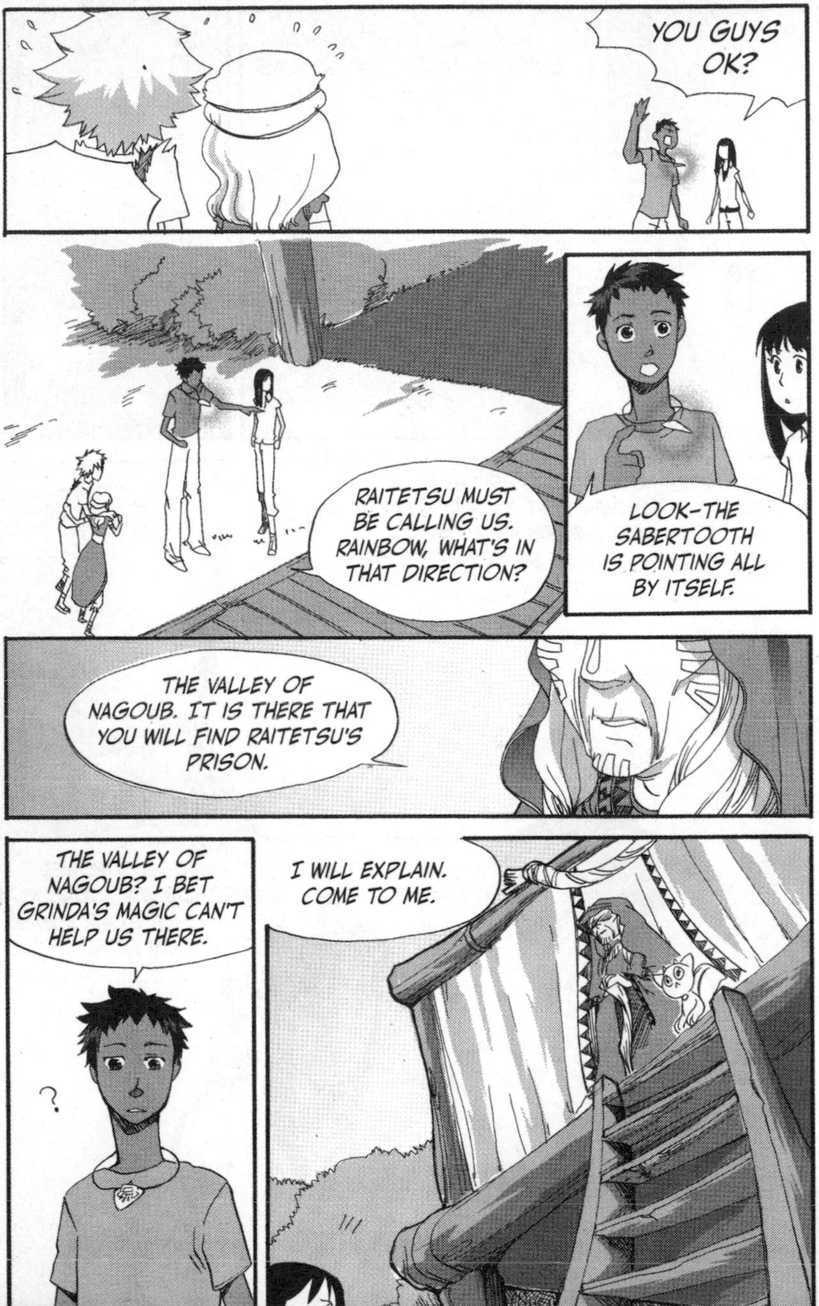
YOU GUYS OK?
RAITETSU MUST BE CALLING US. RAINBOW, WHAT'S IN THAT DIRECTION?
LOOK—THE SABERTOOTH IS POINTING ALL BY ITSELF.
THE VALLEY OF NAGOUB. IT IS THERE THAT YOU WILL FIND RAITETSU'S PRISON.
THE VALLEY OF NAGOUB? I BET GRINDA'S MAGIC CAN'T HELP US THERE.
I WILL EXPLAIN. COME TO ME.
?

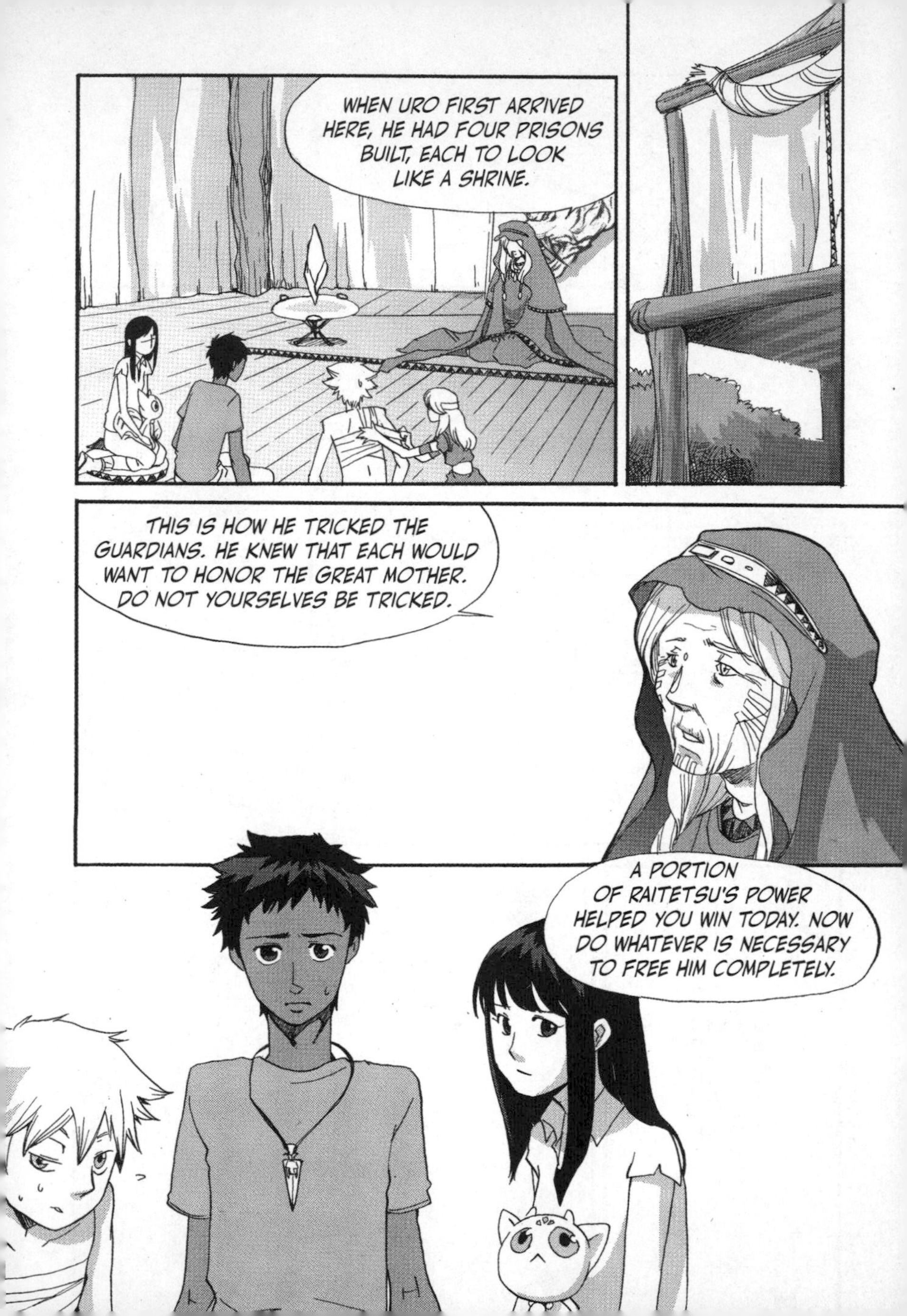
WHEN URO FIRST ARRIVED HERE, HE HAD FOUR PRISONS BUILT, EACH TO LOOK LIKE A SHRINE.
THIS IS HOW HE TRICKED THE GUARDIANS. HE KNEW THAT EACH WOULD WANT TO HONOR THE GREAT MOTHER. DO NOT YOURSELVES BE TRICKED.
A PORTION OF RAITETSU'S POWER HELPED YOU WIN TODAY. NOW DO WHATEVER IS NECESSARY TO FREE HIM COMPLETELY.

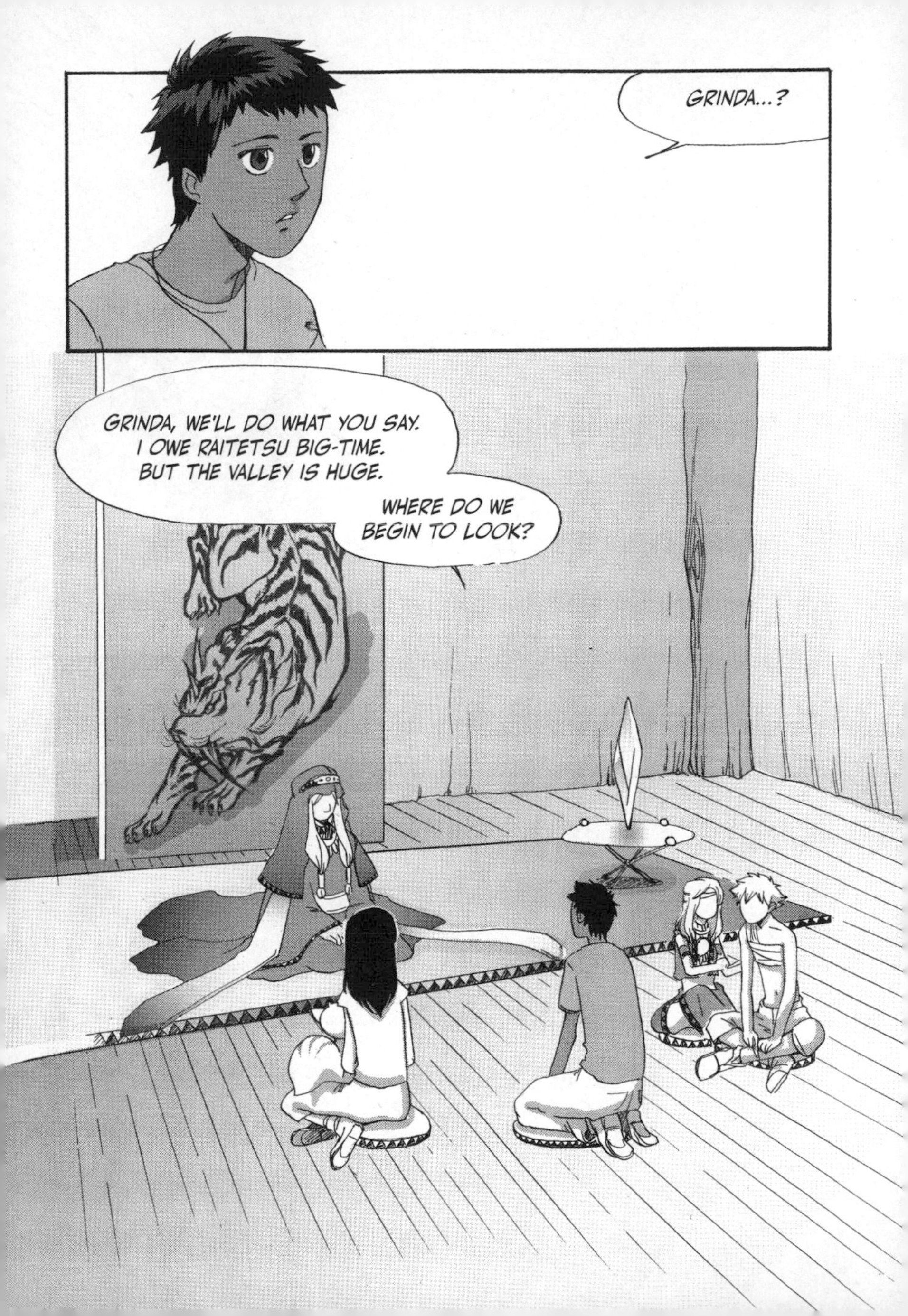
GRINDA...?
GRINDA, WE'LL DO WHAT YOU SAY. I OWE RAITETSU BIG-TIME. BUT THE VALLEY IS HUGE.
WHERE DO WE BEGIN TO LOOK?

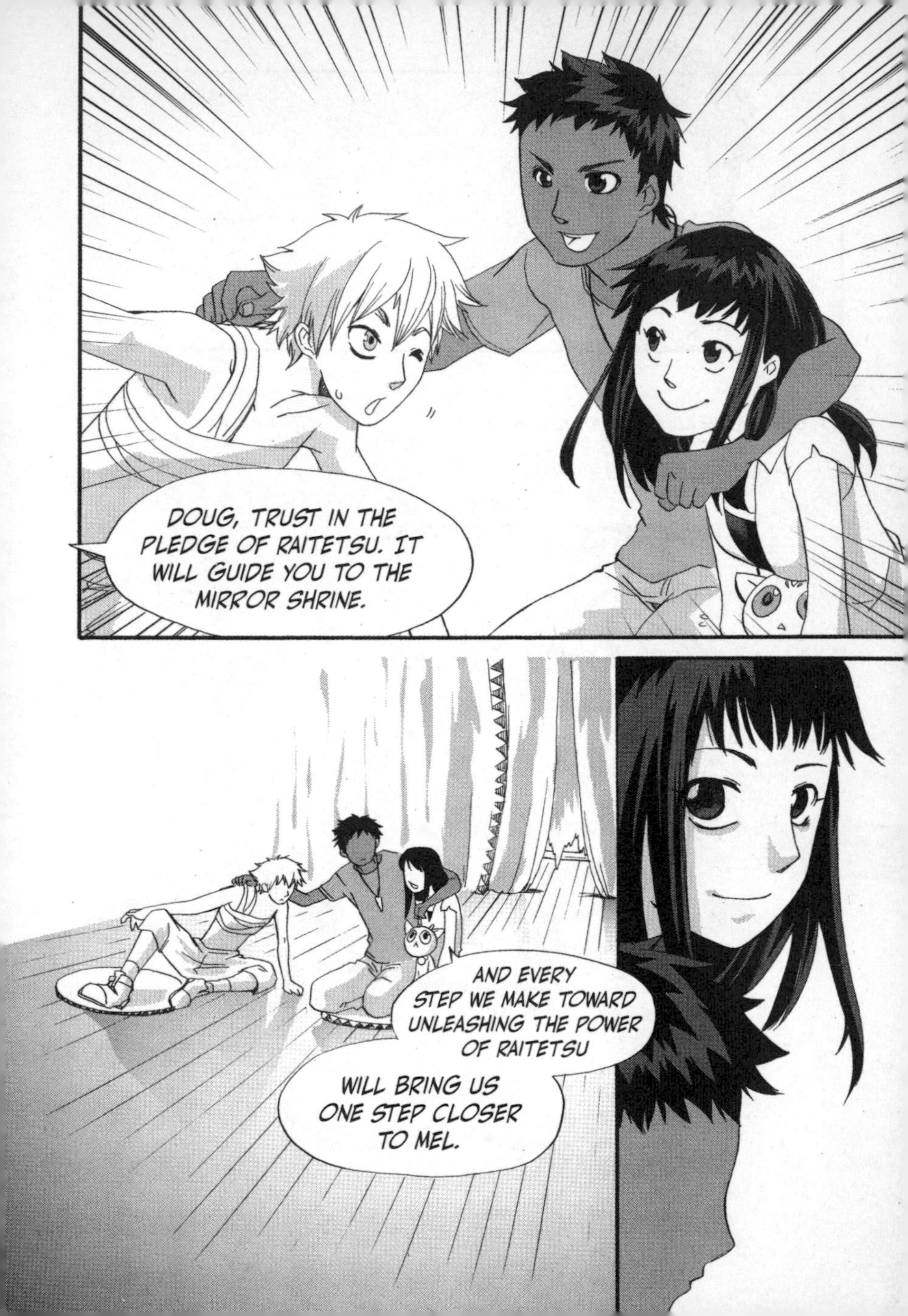
DOUG, TRUST IN THE PLEDGE OF RAITETSU. IT WILL GUIDE YOU TO THE MIRROR SHRINE.
AND EVERY STEP WE MAKE TOWARD UNLEASHING THE POWER OF RAITETSU
WILL BRING US ONE STEP CLOSER TO MEL.

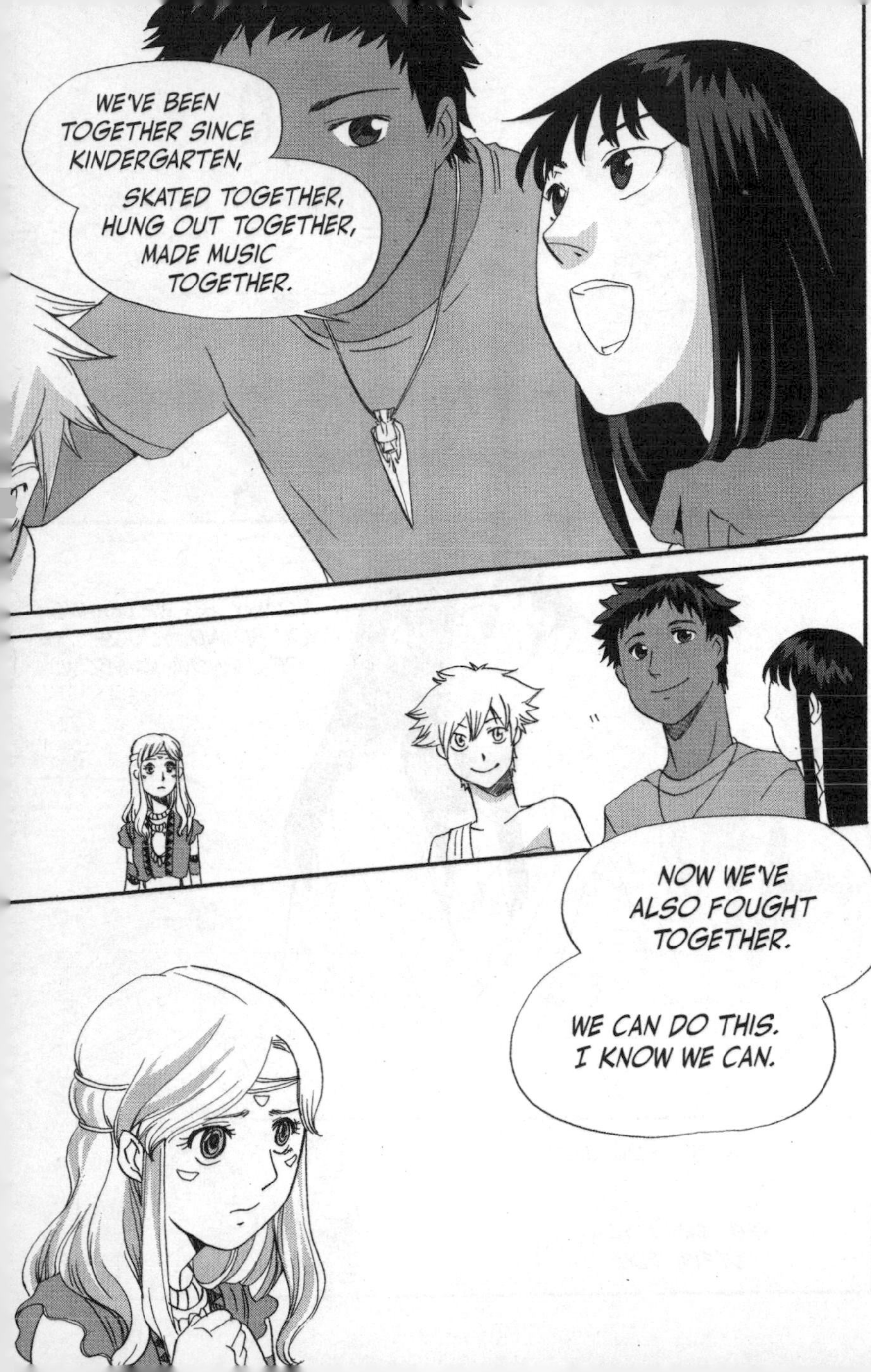
WE'VE BEEN TOGETHER SINCE KINDERGARTEN,
SKATED TOGETHER, HUNG OUT TOGETHER, MADE MUSIC TOGETHER.
NOW WE'VE ALSO FOUGHT TOGETHER.
WE CAN DO THIS. I KNOW WE CAN.

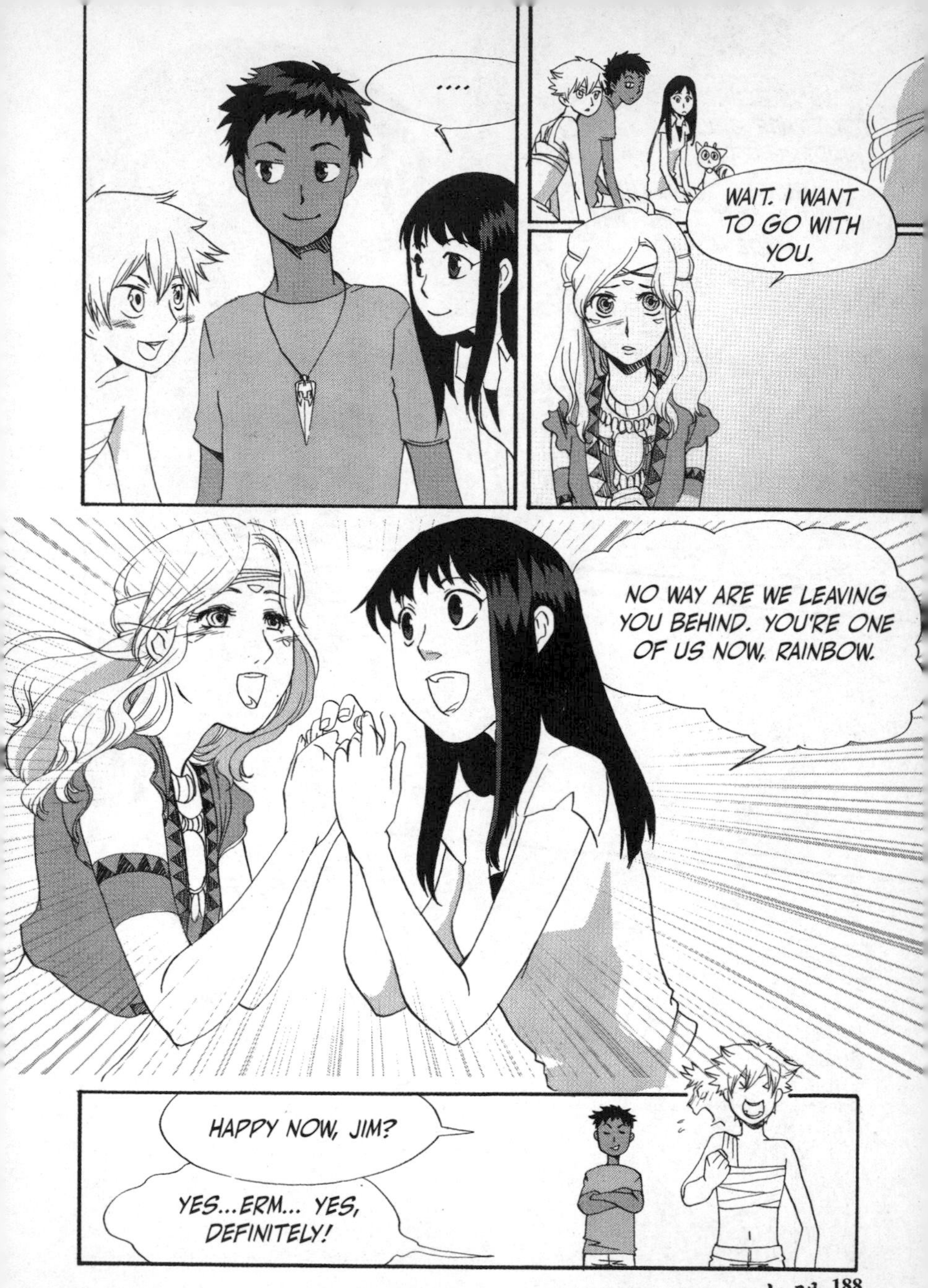
....
WAIT. I WANT TO GO WITH YOU.
NO WAY ARE WE LEAVING YOU BEHIND. YOU'RE ONE OF US NOW, RAINBOW.
HAPPY NOW, JIM?
YES...ERM... YES, DEFINITELY!

WARRIORS OF BLUE STAR: BATTLE STATIONS. IT'S TIME WE BRING THIS WAR TO URO!

MEL'S LISTENING. I KNOW IT. SHE KNOWS WE'RE COMING.

!?

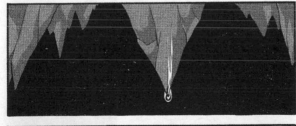

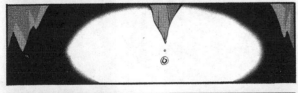

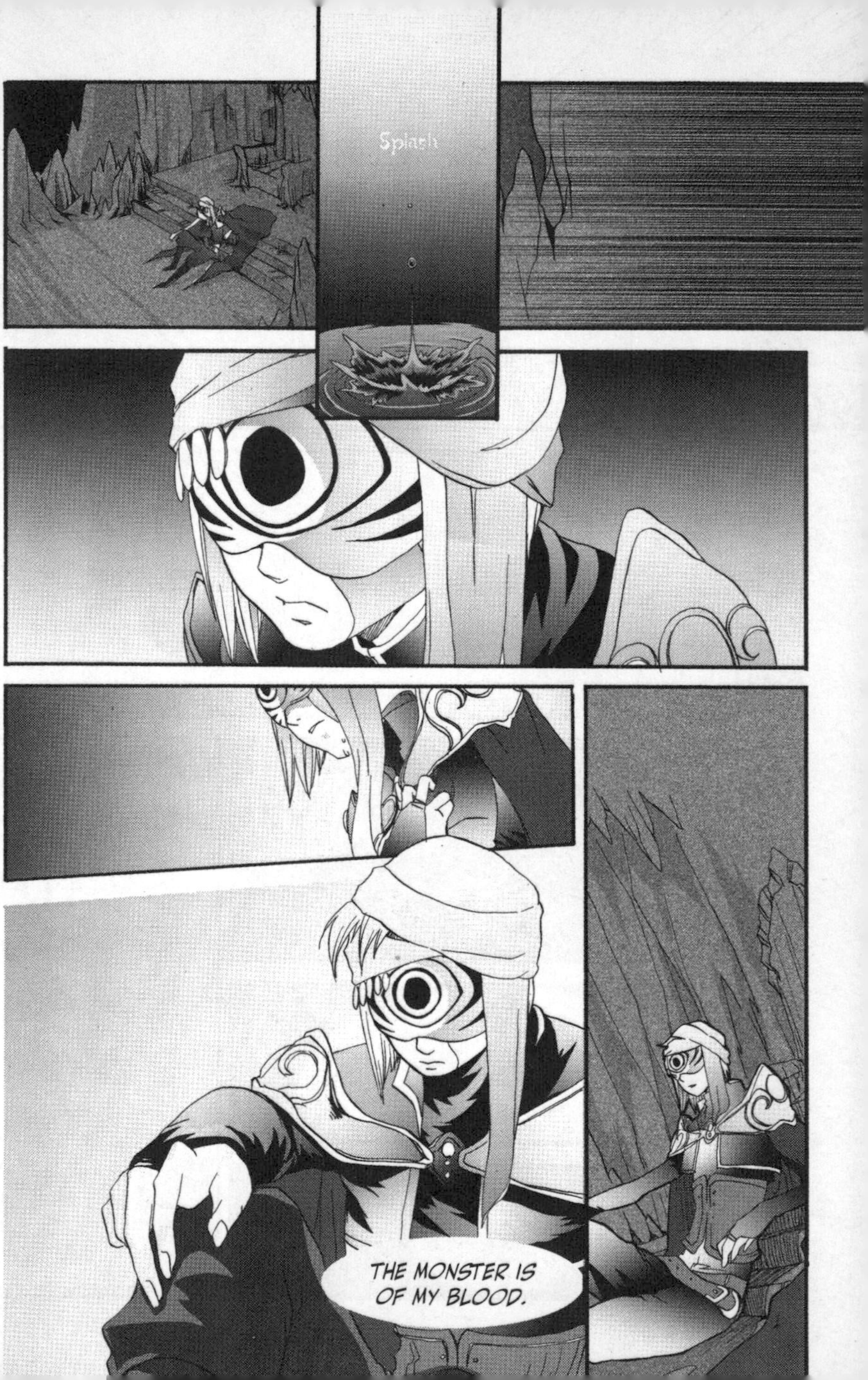

Splash
THE MONSTER IS OF MY BLOOD.

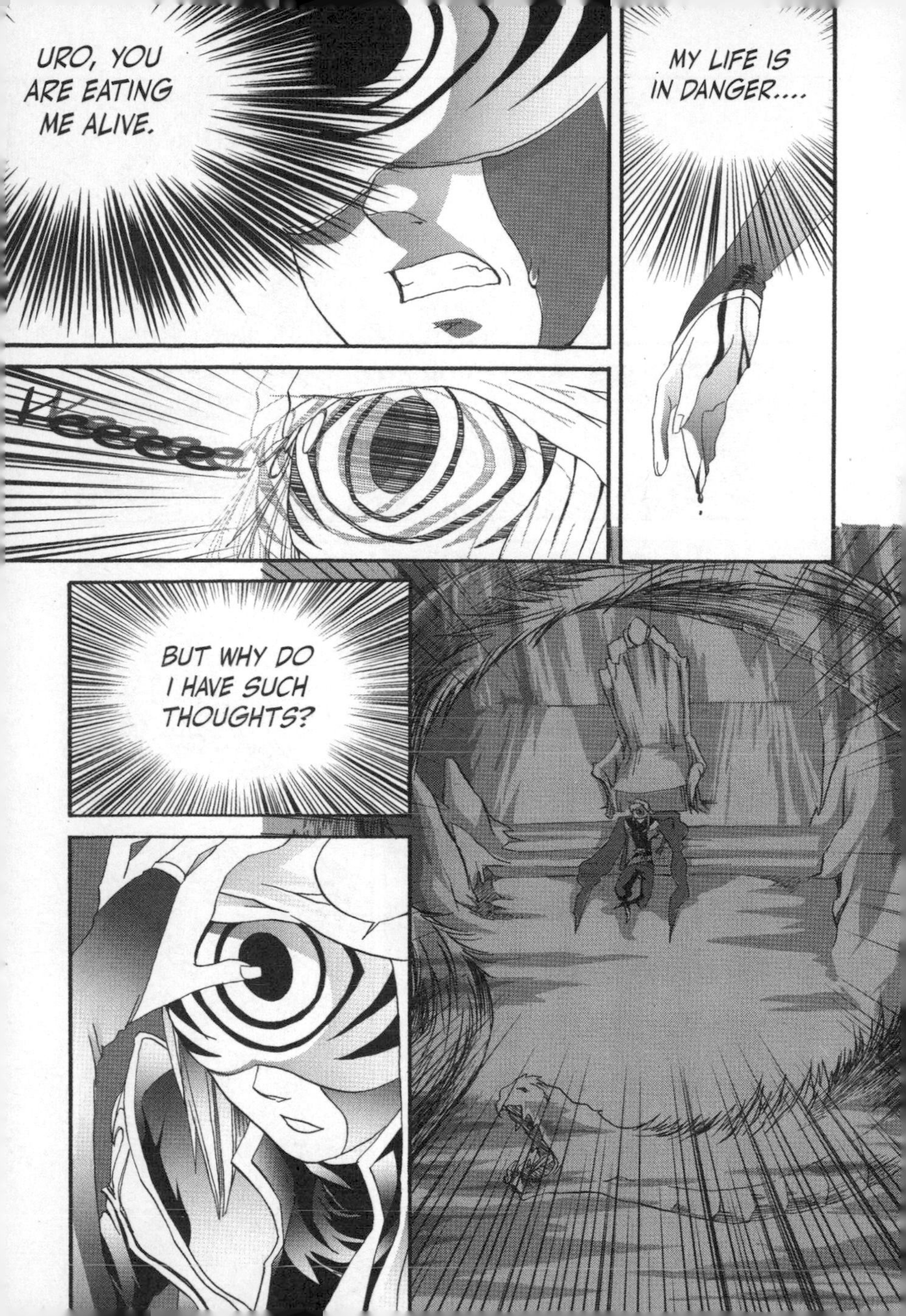
MY LIFE IS IN DANGER....
URO, YOU ARE EATING ME ALIVE.
BUT WHY DO I HAVE SUCH THOUGHTS?

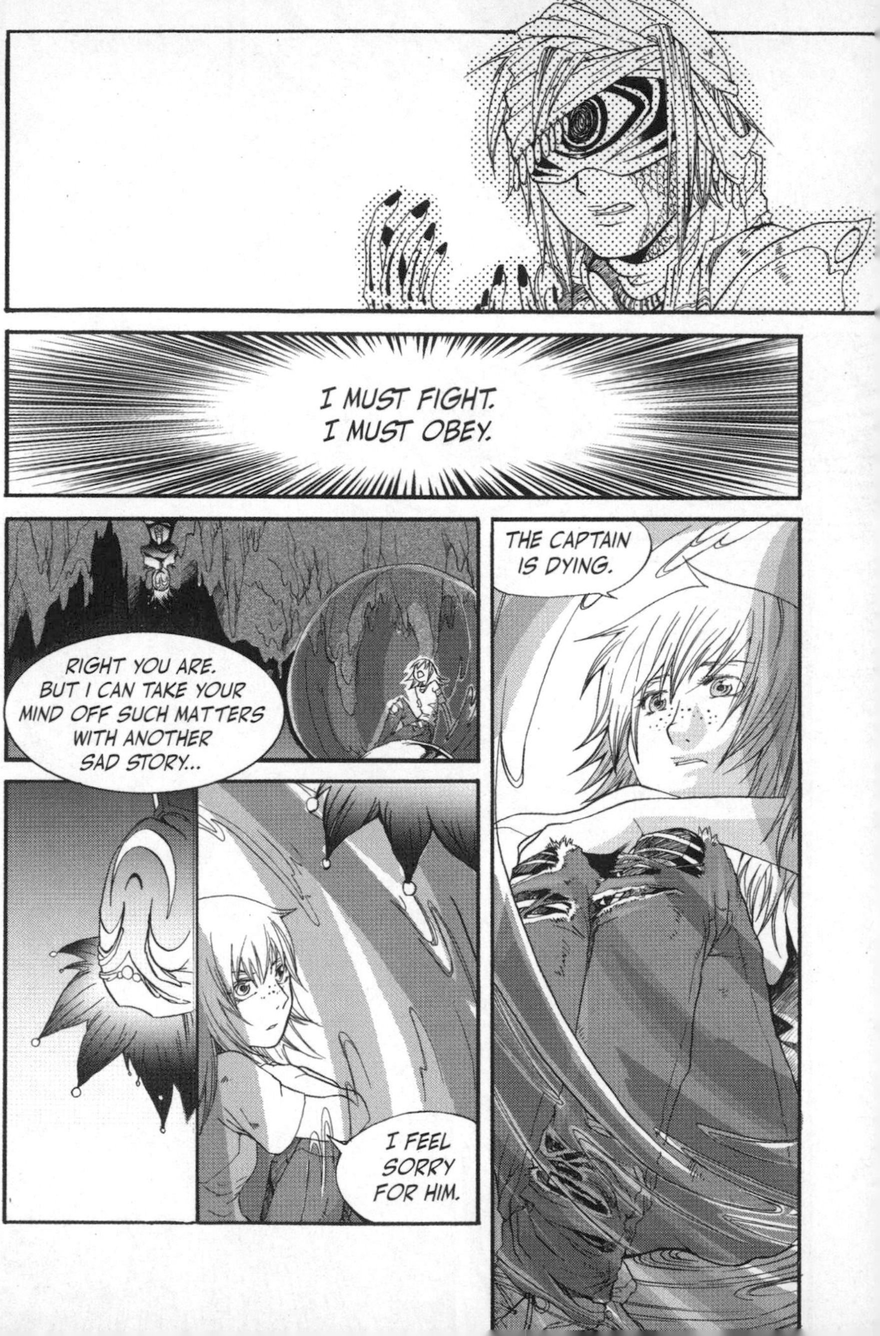
I MUST FIGHT.
I MUST OBEY.
THE CAPTAIN IS DYING.
RIGHT YOU ARE. BUT I CAN TAKE YOUR MIND OFF SUCH MATTERS WITH ANOTHER SAD STORY...
I FEEL SORRY FOR HIM.

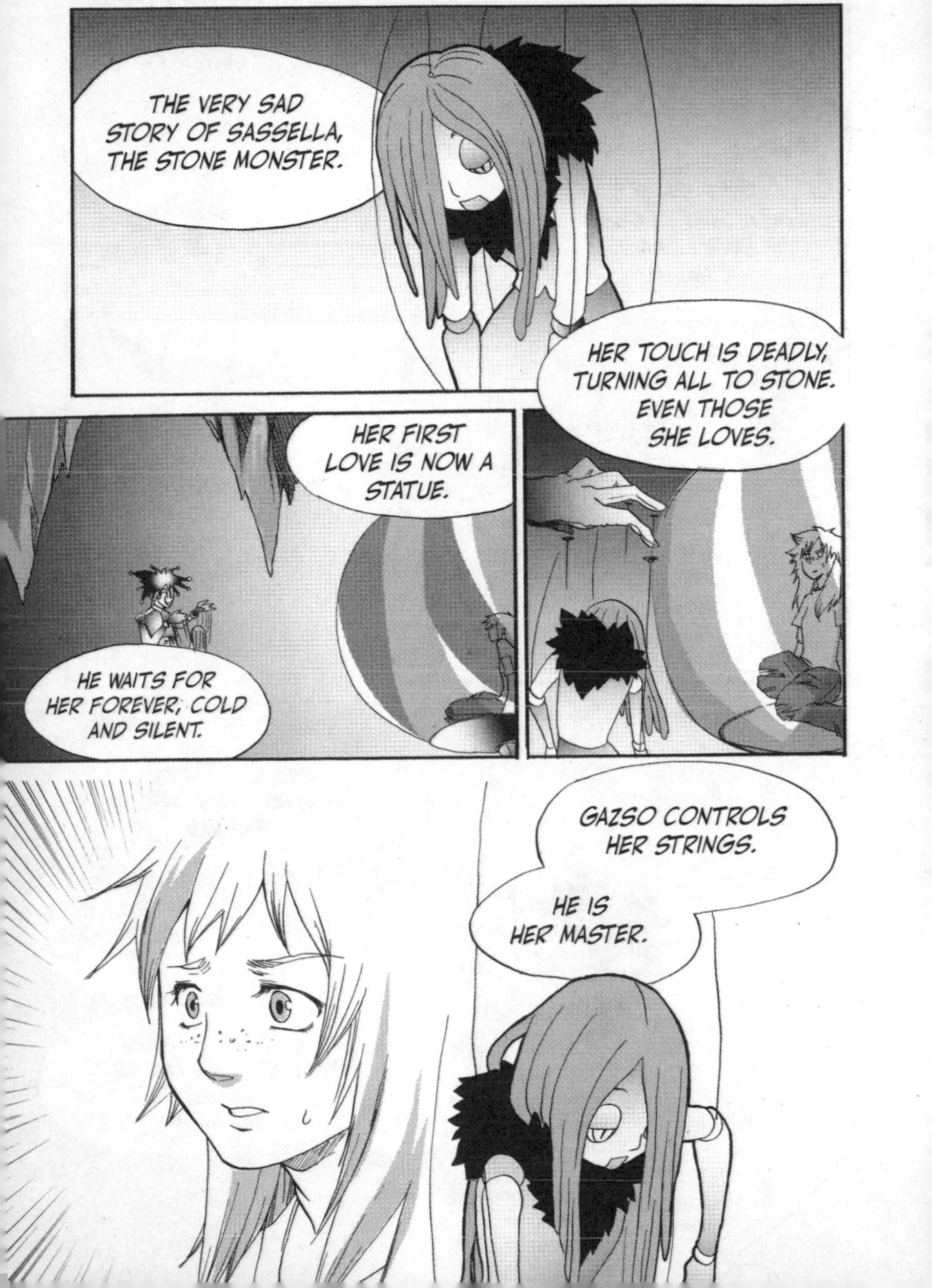
THE VERY SAD STORY OF SASSELLA, THE STONE MONSTER.
HER TOUCH IS DEADLY, TURNING ALL TO STONE. EVEN THOSE SHE LOVES.
HER FIRST LOVE IS NOW A STATUE.
HE WAITS FOR HER FOREVER, COLD AND SILENT.
GAZSO CONTROLS HER STRINGS.
HE IS HER MASTER.

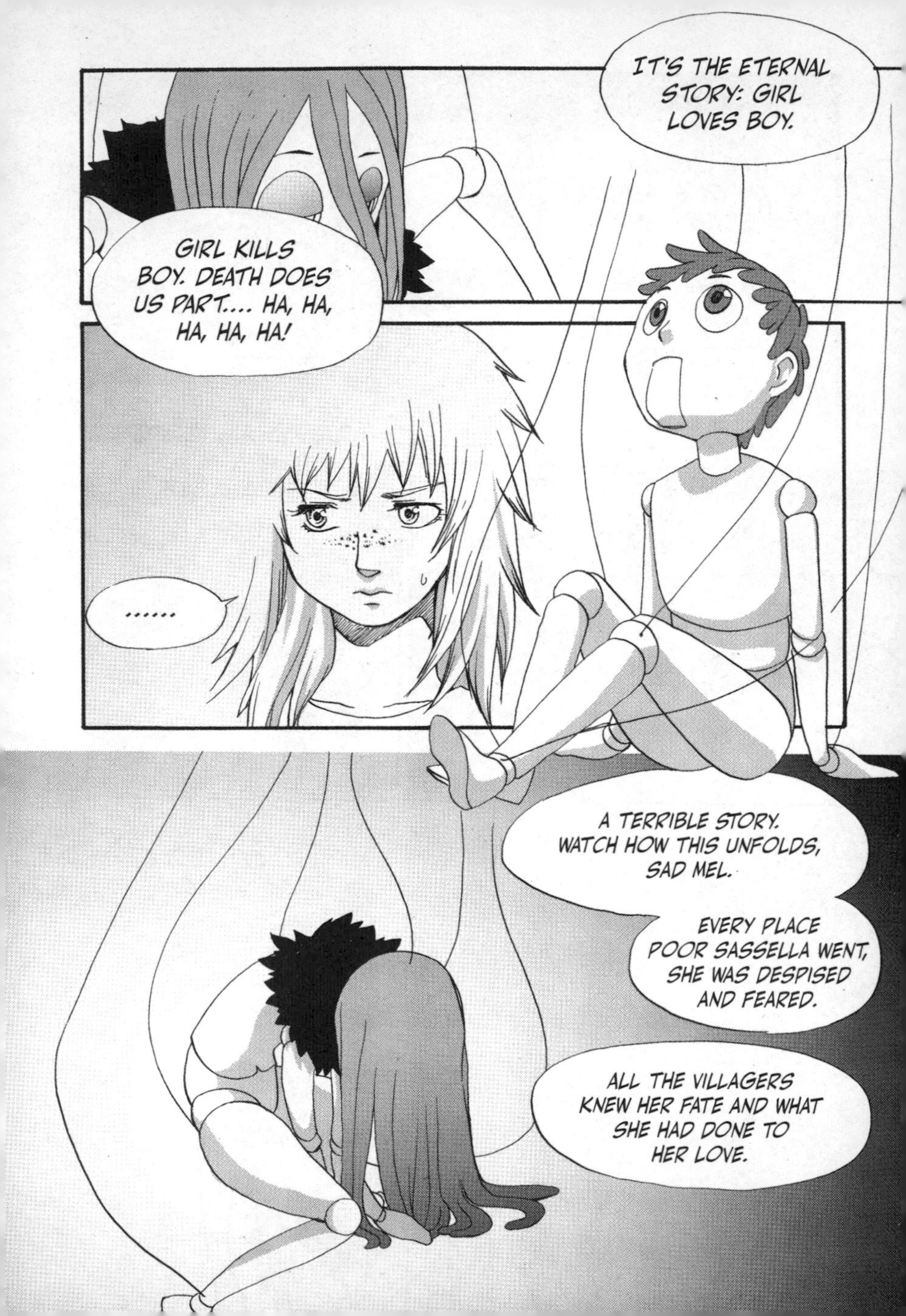
IT'S THE ETERNAL STORY: GIRL LOVES BOY.
GIRL KILLS BOY. DEATH DOES US PART.... HA, HA, HA, HA, HA!
......
A TERRIBLE STORY. WATCH HOW THIS UNFOLDS, SAD MEL.
EVERY PLACE POOR SASSELLA WENT, SHE WAS DESPISED AND FEARED.
ALL THE VILLAGERS KNEW HER FATE AND WHAT SHE HAD DONE TO HER LOVE.

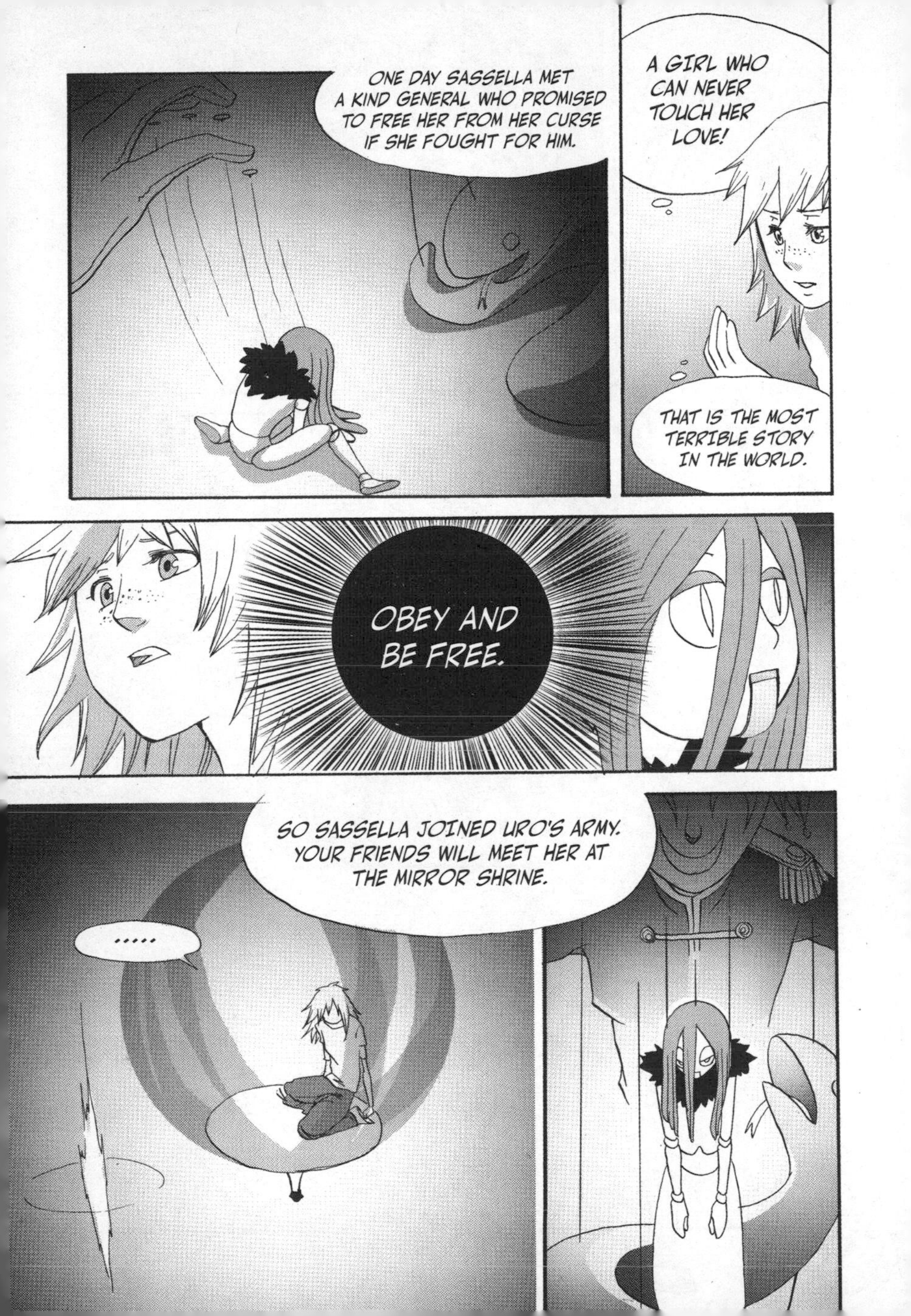
ONE DAY SASSELLA MET A KIND GENERAL WHO PROMISED TO FREE HER FROM HER CURSE IF SHE FOUGHT FOR HIM.
A GIRL WHO CAN NEVER TOUCH HER LOVE!
THAT IS THE MOST TERRIBLE STORY IN THE WORLD.
OBEY AND BE FREE.
SO SASSELLA JOINED URO'S ARMY. YOUR FRIENDS WILL MEET HER AT THE MIRROR SHRINE.
.....

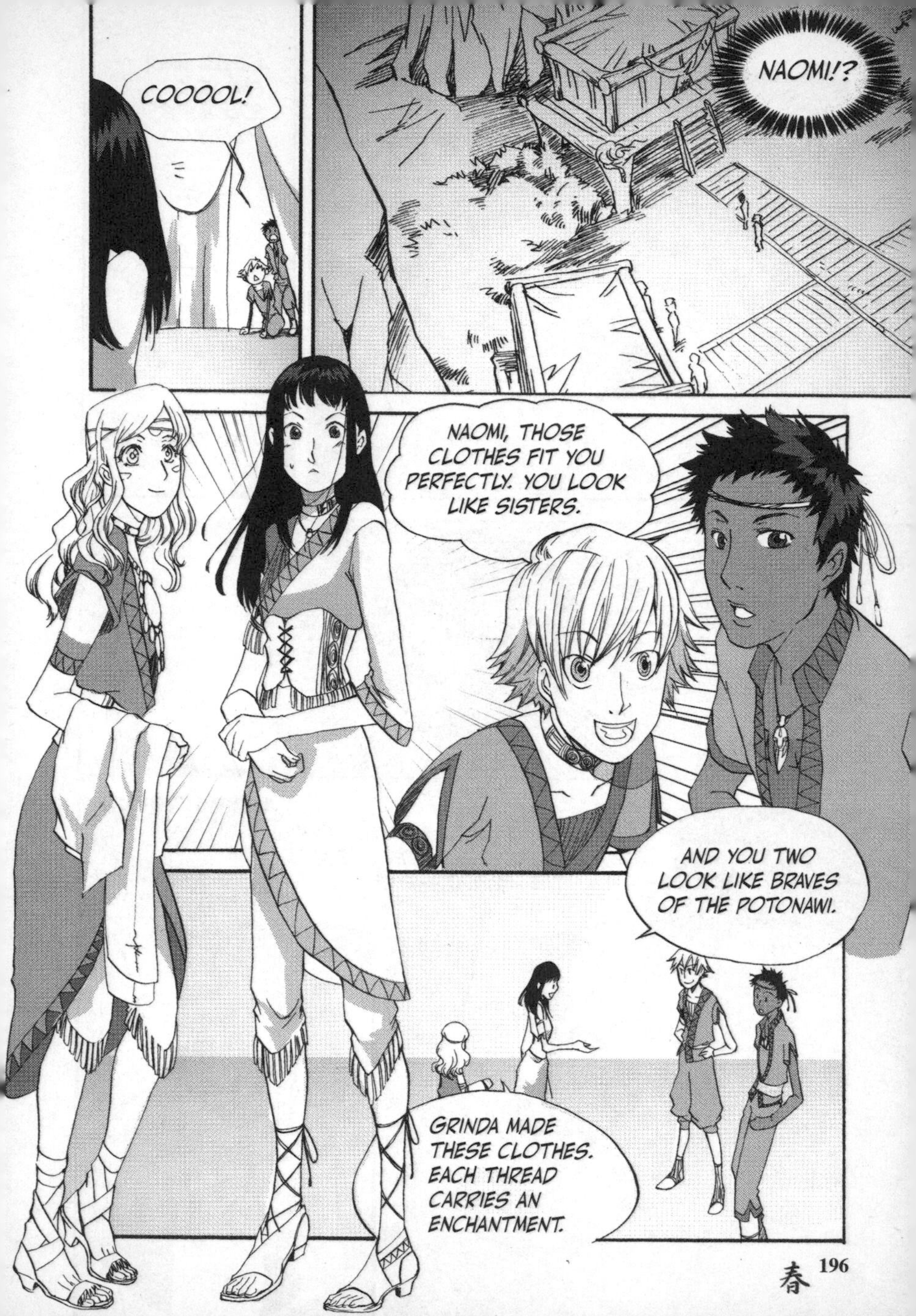
COOOOL!
NAOMI!?
NAOMI, THOSE CLOTHES FIT YOU PERFECTLY. YOU LOOK LIKE SISTERS.
AND YOU TWO LOOK LIKE BRAVES OF THE POTONAWI.
GRINDA MADE THESE CLOTHES. EACH THREAD CARRIES AN ENCHANTMENT.

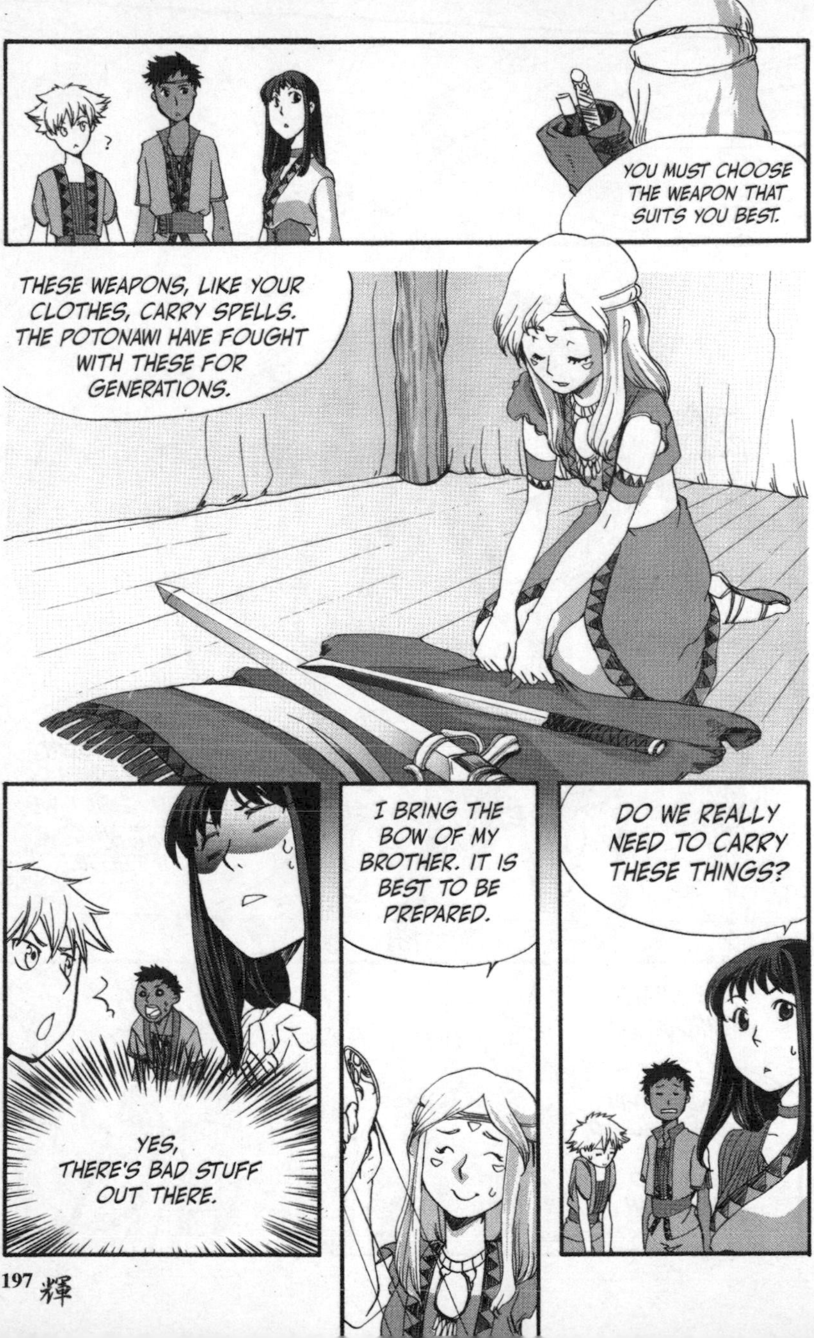
YOU MUST CHOOSE THE WEAPON THAT SUITS YOU BEST.
THESE WEAPONS, LIKE YOUR CLOTHES, CARRY SPELLS. THE POTONAWI HAVE FOUGHT WITH THESE FOR GENERATIONS.
YES, THERE'S BAD STUFF OUT THERE.
I BRING THE BOW OF MY BROTHER. IT IS BEST TO BE PREPARED.
DO WE REALLY NEED TO CARRY THESE THINGS?

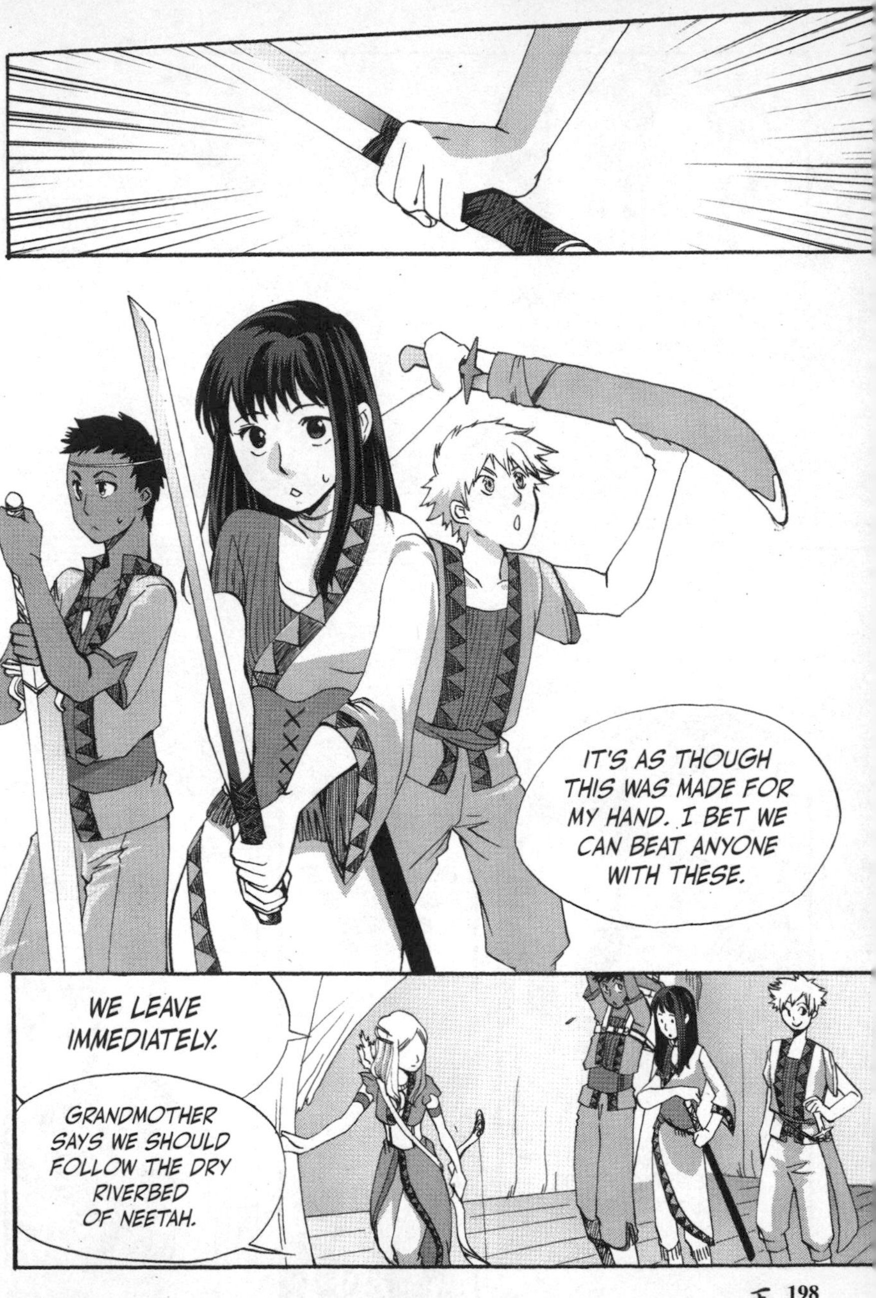
IT'S AS THOUGH THIS WAS MADE FOR MY HAND. I BET WE CAN BEAT ANYONE WITH THESE.
WE LEAVE IMMEDIATELY.
GRANDMOTHER SAYS WE SHOULD FOLLOW THE DRY RIVERBED OF NEETAH.

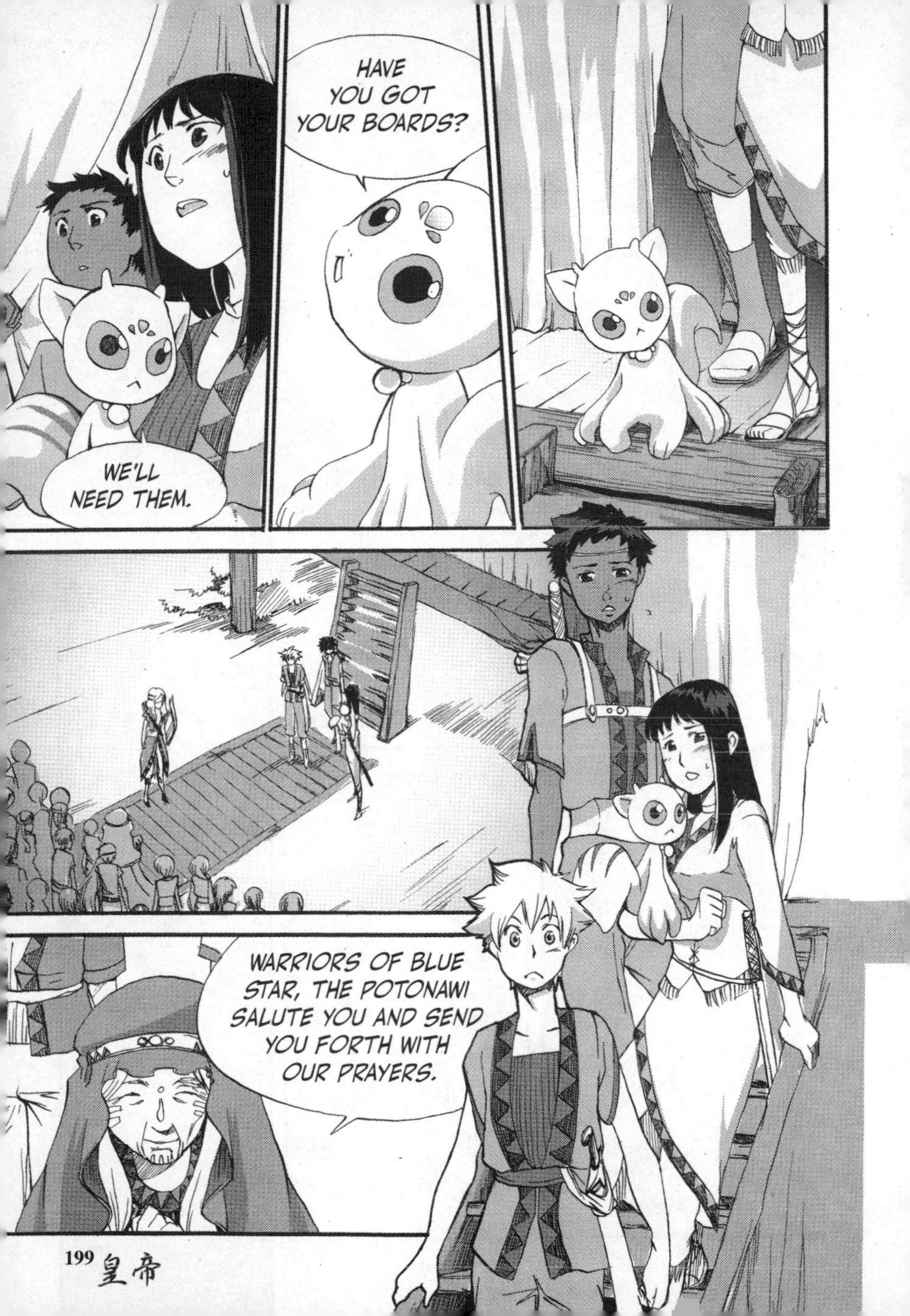
HAVE YOU GOT YOUR BOARDS?
WE'LL NEED THEM.
WARRIORS OF BLUE STAR, THE POTONAWI SALUTE YOU AND SEND YOU FORTH WITH OUR PRAYERS.

HAS ANYONE FIGURED OUT HOW WE ARE GOING TO FIND THIS SHRINE?

I SEE ONLY ROCKS AND MORE ROCKS.

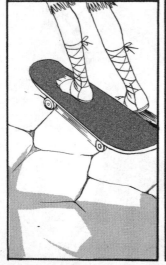

THERE USED TO BE A BEAUTIFUL FOREST HERE.

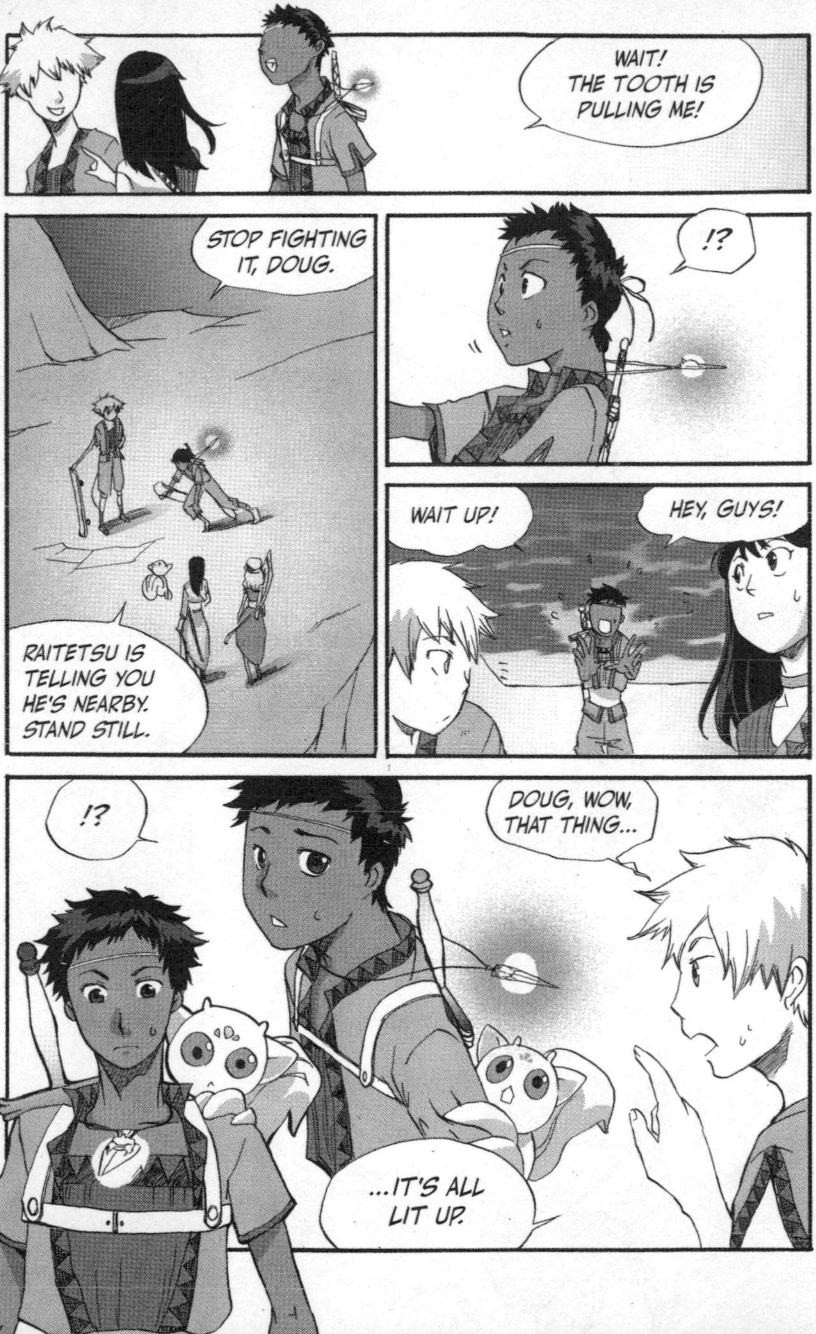
WAIT! THE TOOTH IS PULLING ME!
STOP FIGHTING IT, DOUG.
RAITETSU IS TELLING YOU HE'S NEARBY. STAND STILL.
!?
WAIT UP!
HEY, GUYS!
!?
DOUG, WOW, THAT THING...
...IT'S ALL LIT UP.

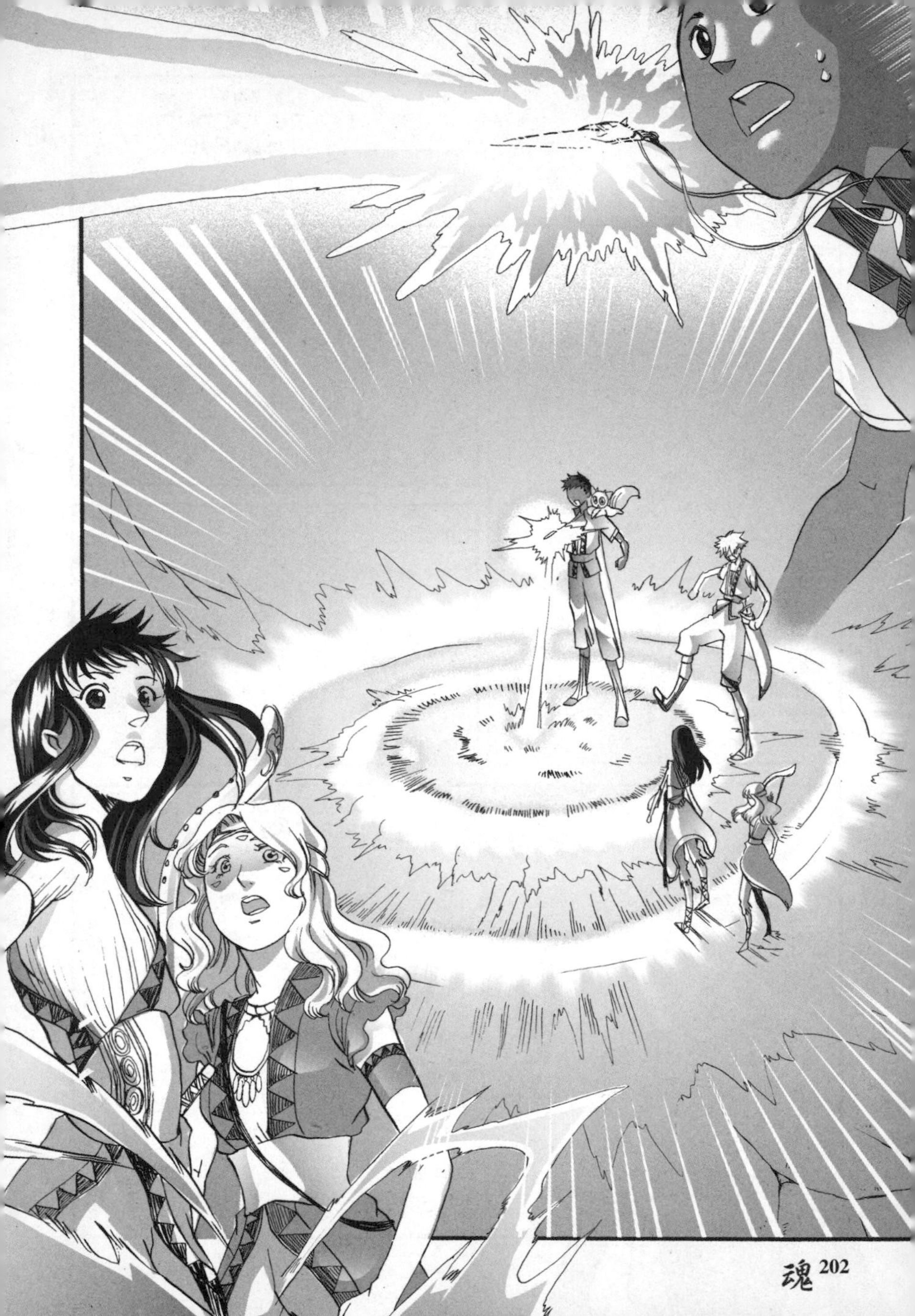

WOW. EVERYTHING'S BEEN CLEARED AWAY.

??

UNBELIEVABLE!

LOOK DOWN!

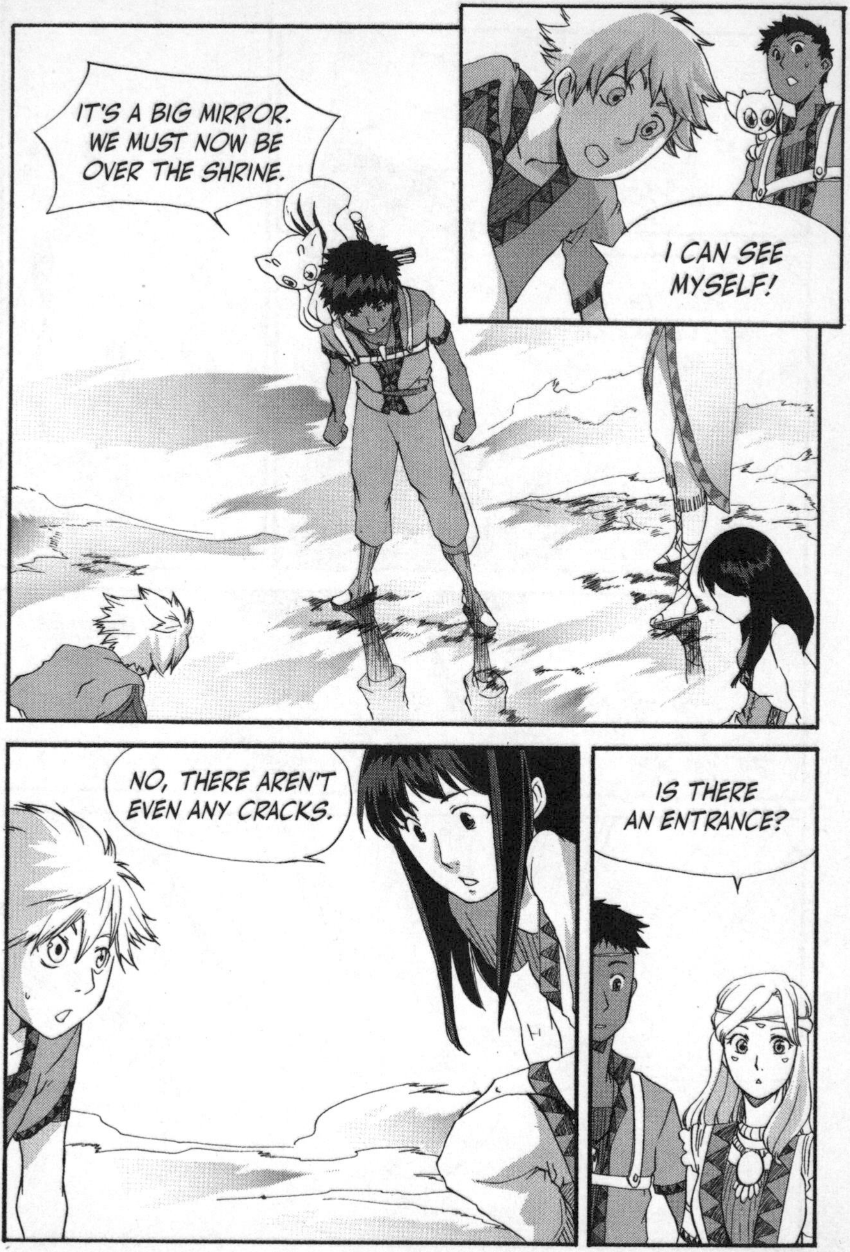
IT'S A BIG MIRROR. WE MUST NOW BE OVER THE SHRINE.
I CAN SEE MYSELF!
NO, THERE AREN'T EVEN ANY CRACKS.
IS THERE AN ENTRANCE?

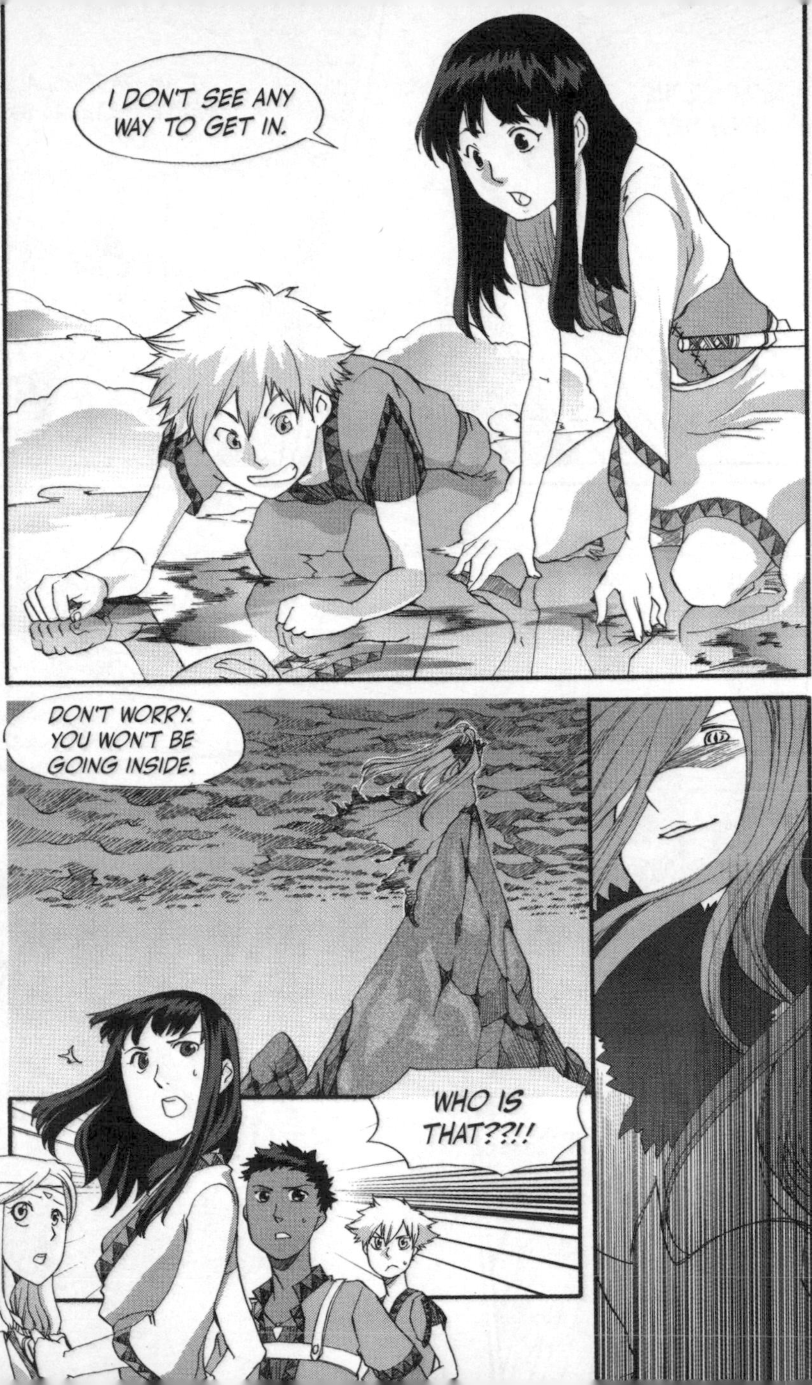
I DON'T SEE ANY WAY TO GET IN.
DON'T WORRY. YOU WON'T BE GOING INSIDE.
WHO IS THAT??!!

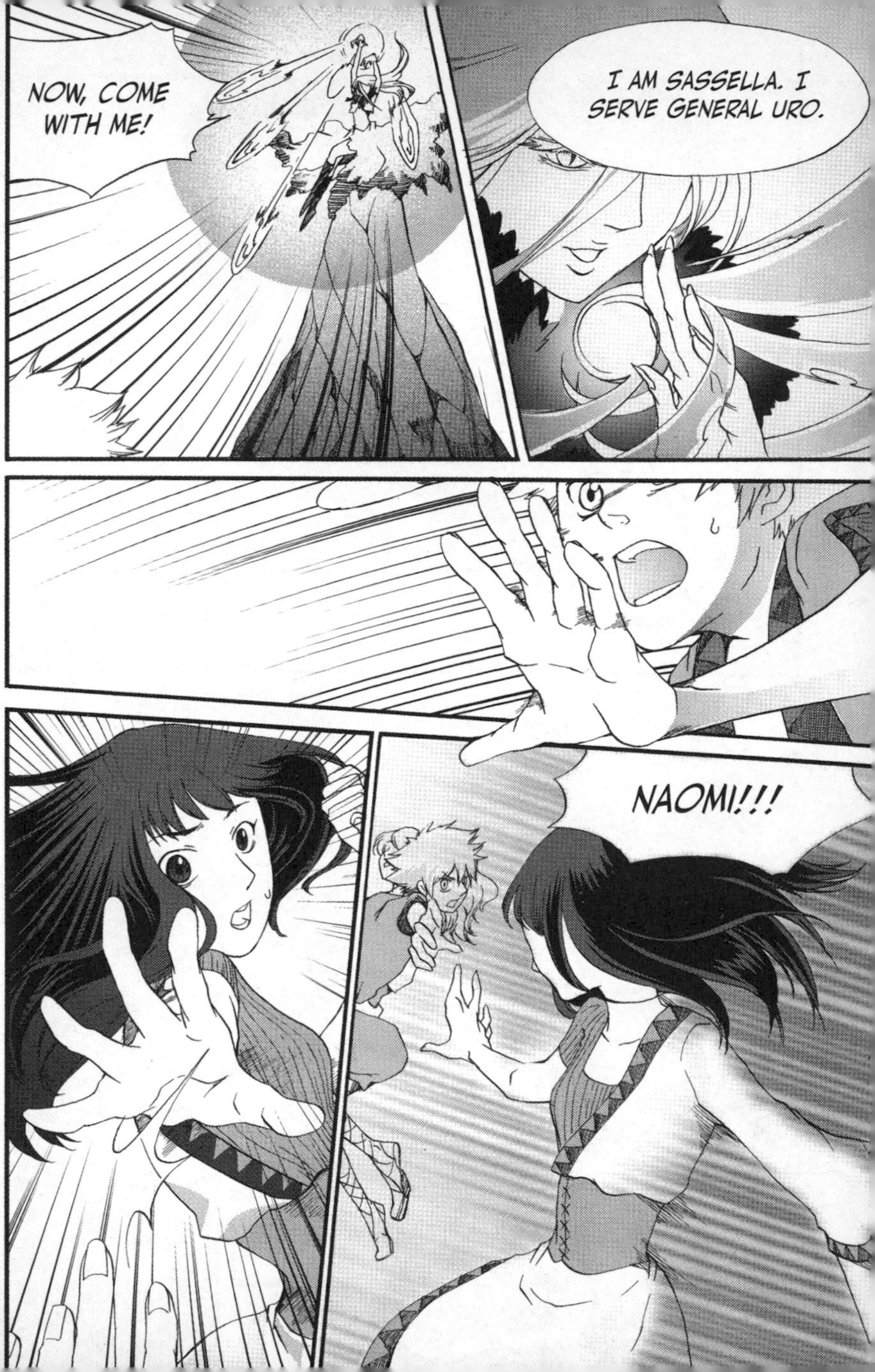
NOW, COME WITH ME!
I AM SASSELLA. I SERVE GENERAL URO.
NAOMI!!!

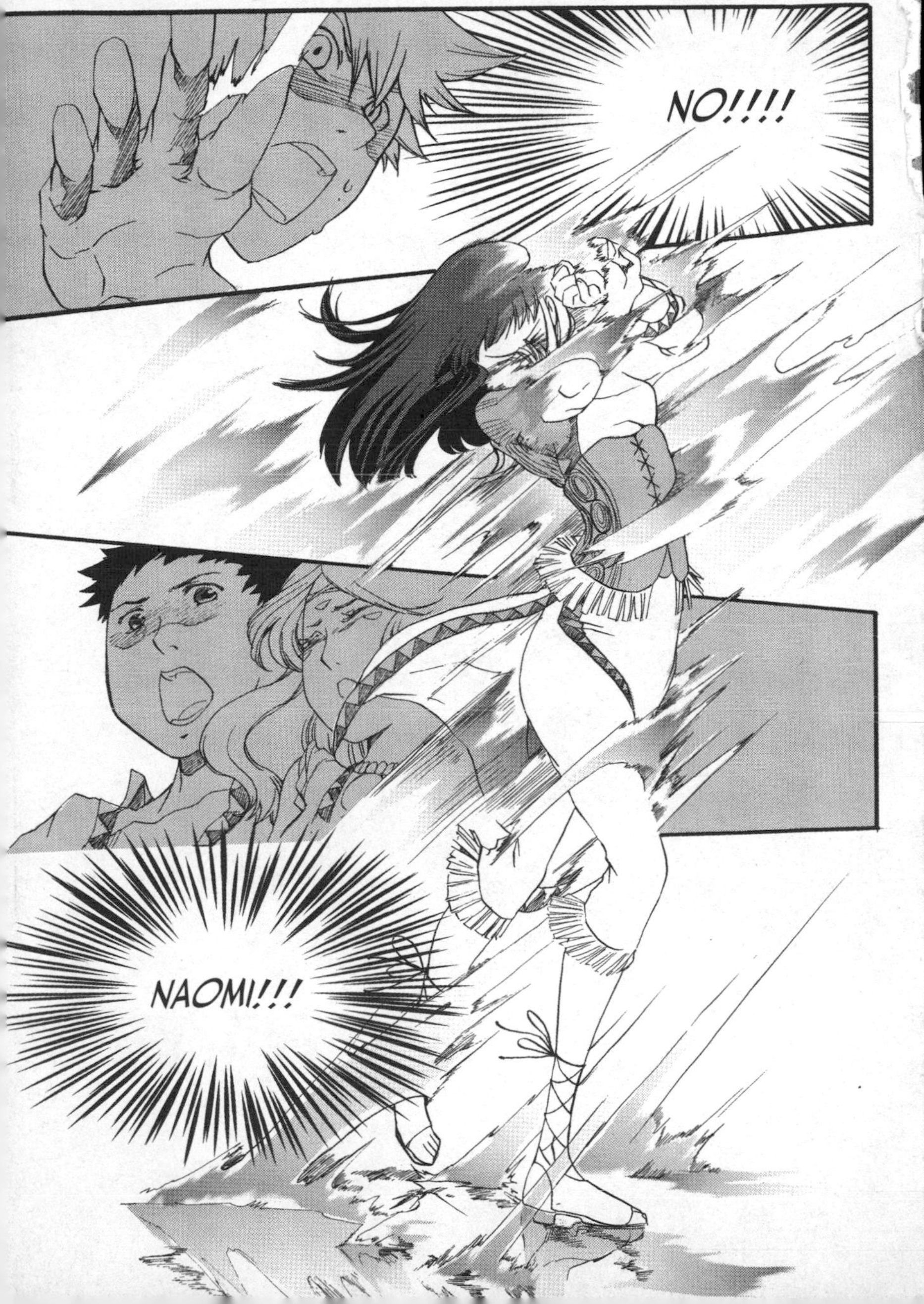
NO!!!!
NAOMI!!!

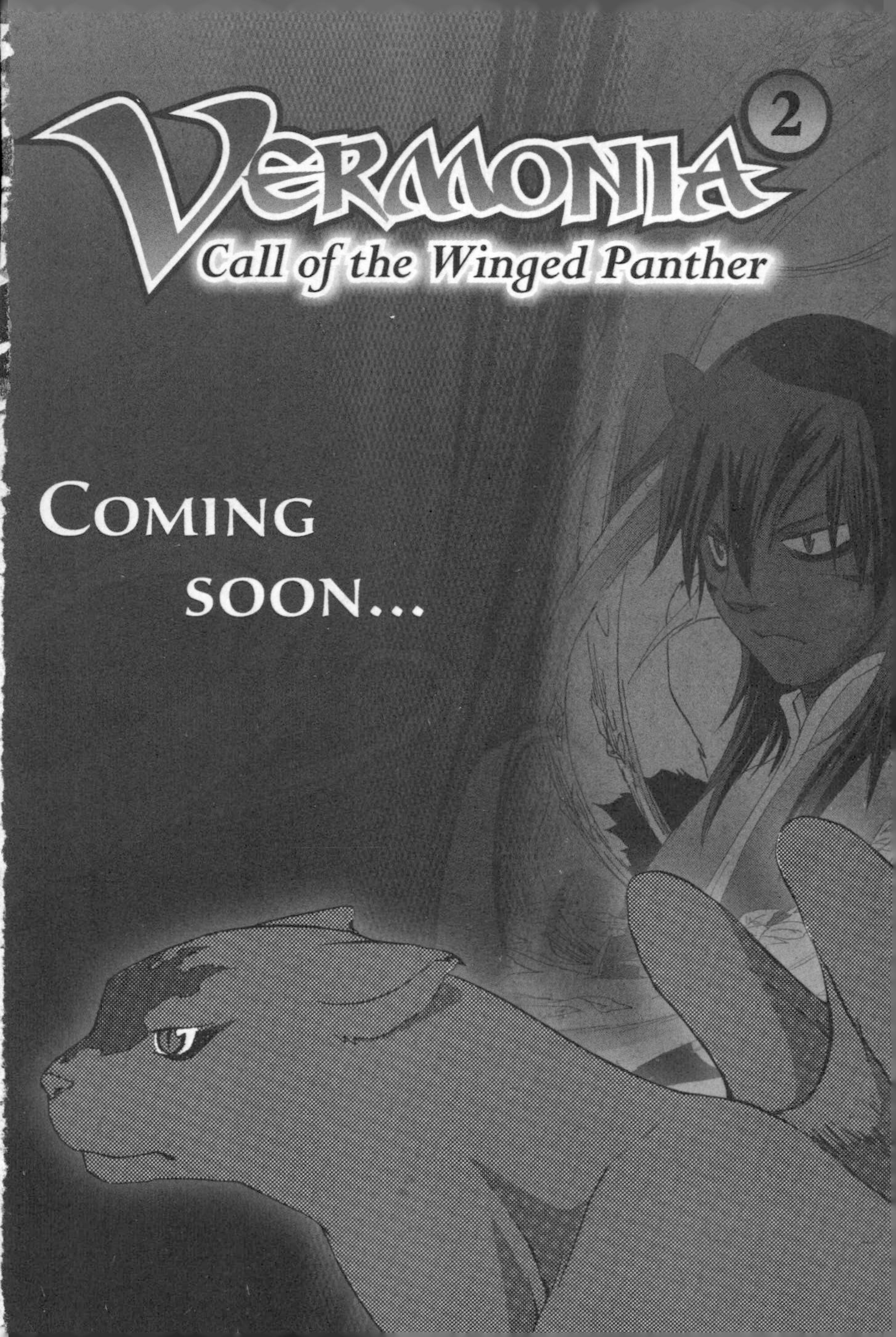
Vermonia 2
Call of the Winged Panther
Coming soon...

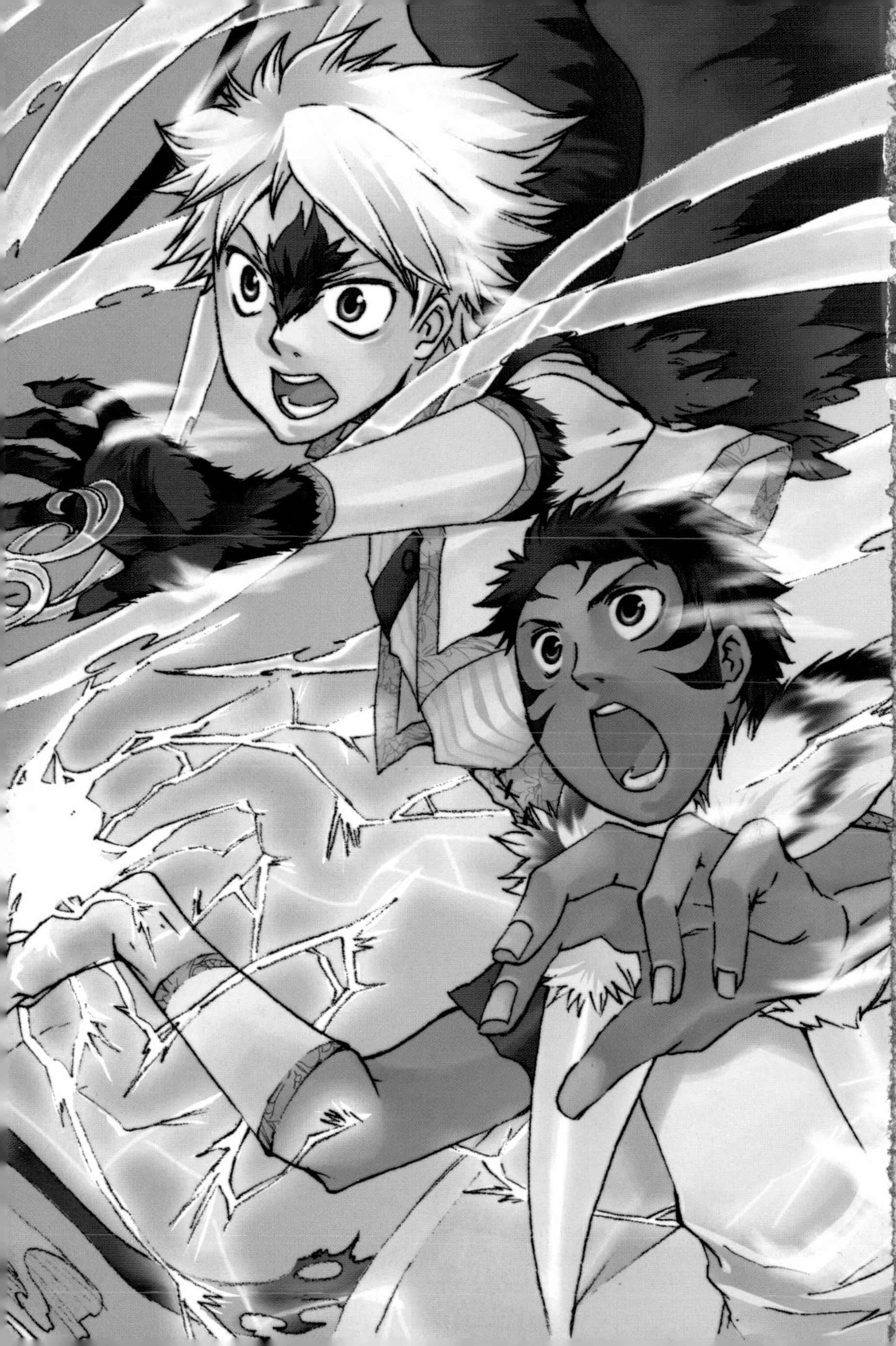

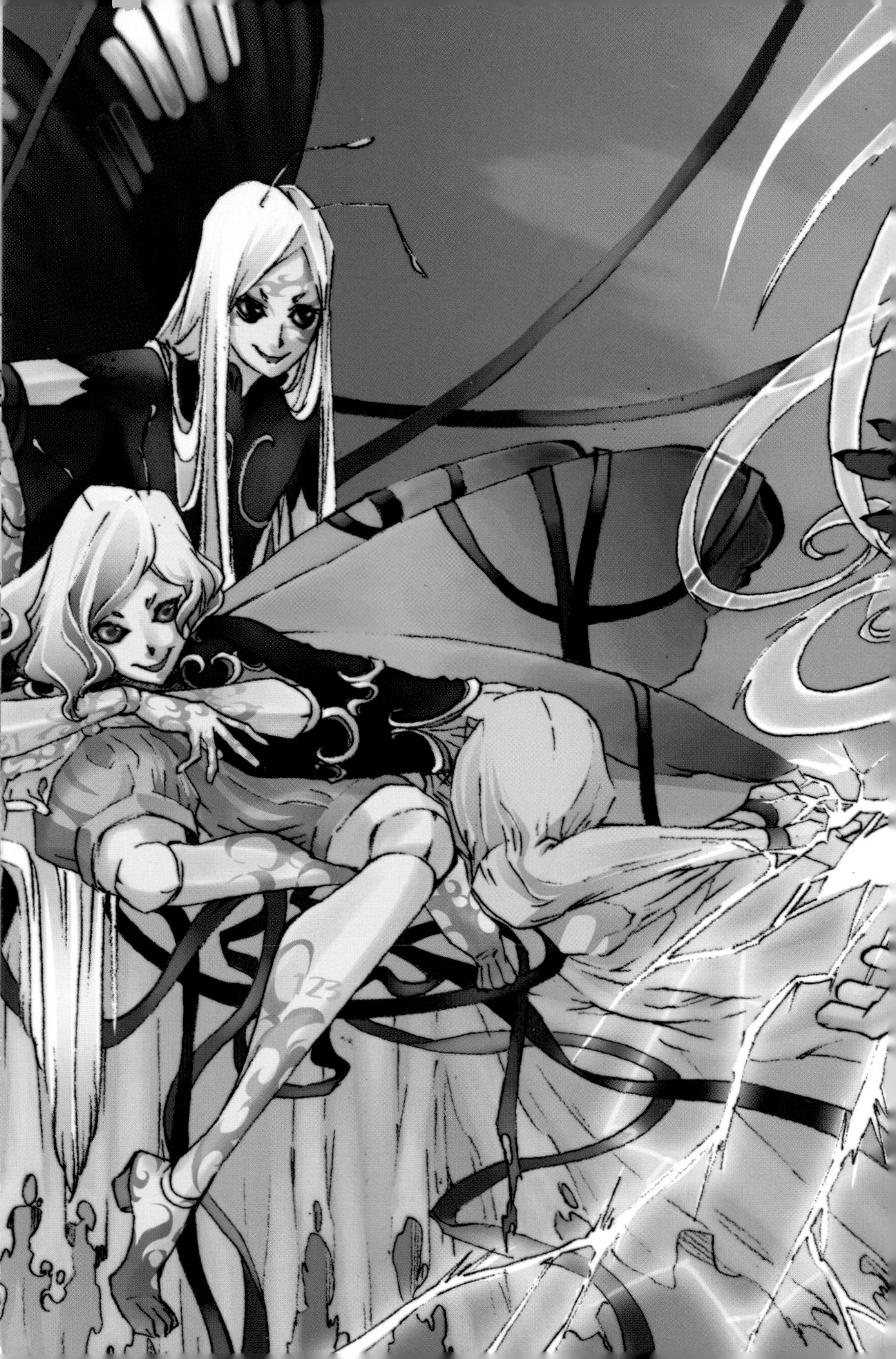
123

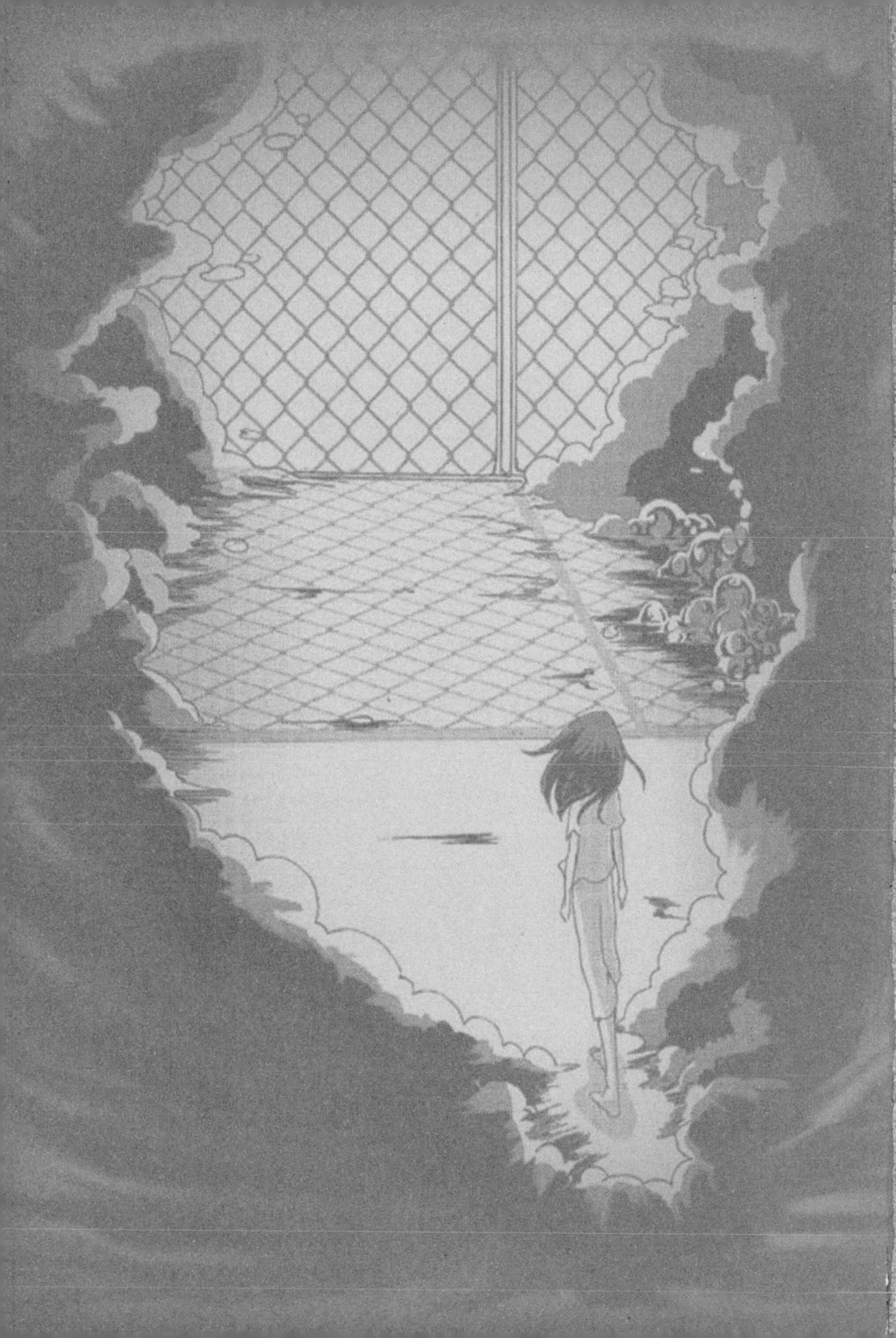

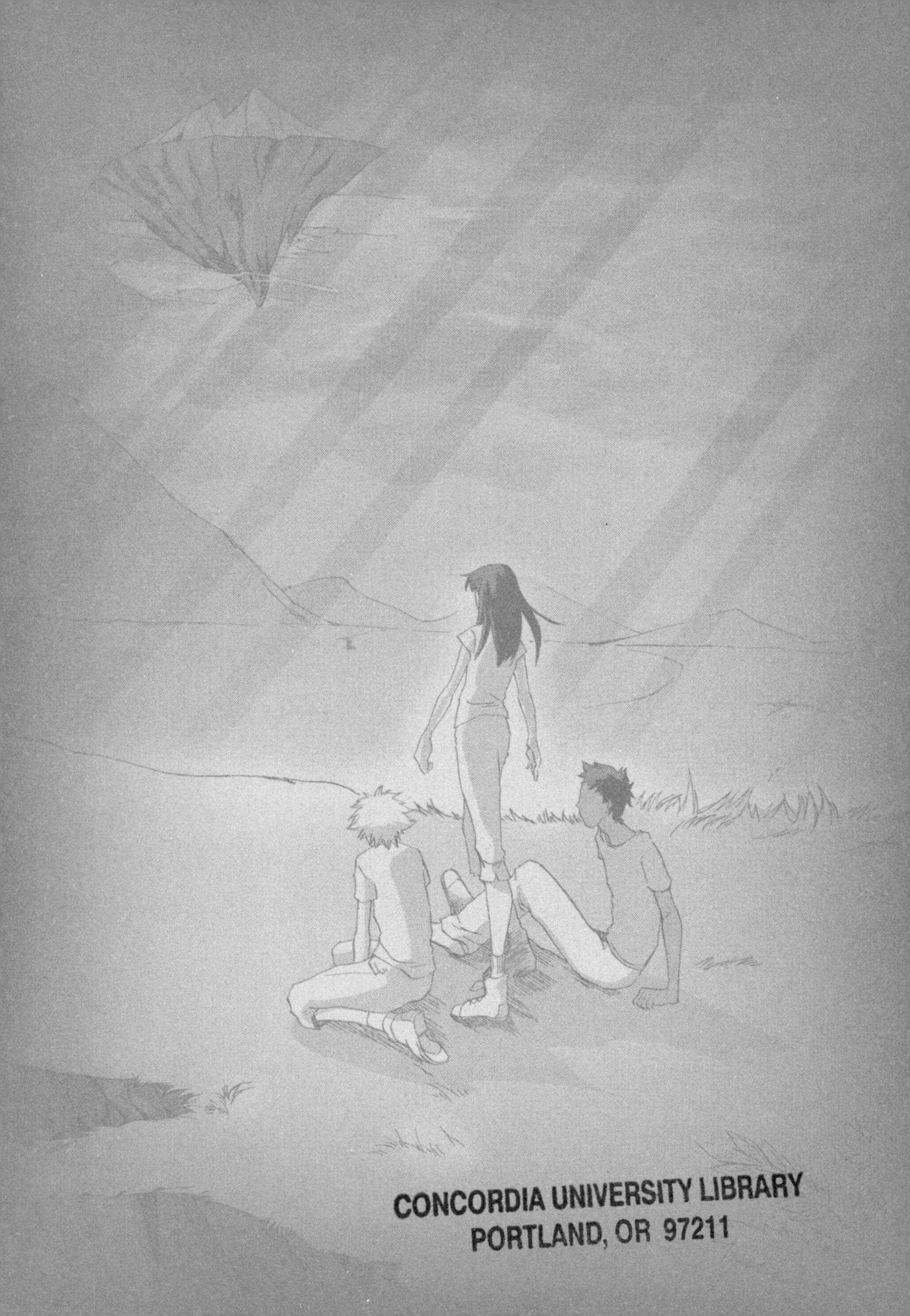